EVOlutioN

Created by   Joe Infurnari . Joseph Keatinge . Christopher Sebela . Joshua Williamson

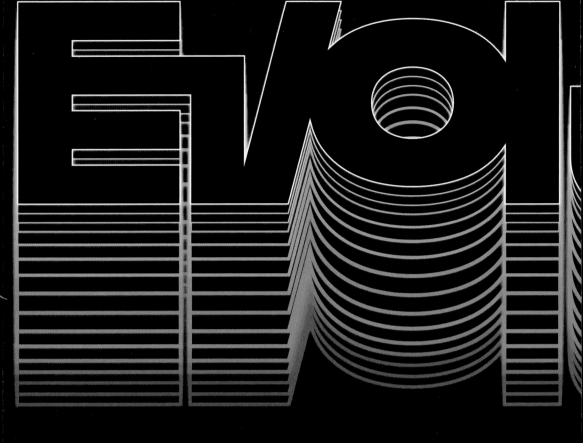

WRITERS

James Asmus

Joseph Keatinge

Christopher Sebela

Joshua Williamson

ARTIST

Joe Infurnari

COLORIST

Jordan Boyd

EVOLUTION VOLUME 1. FIRST PRINTING. MAY 2018. PUBLISHED BY IMAGE COMICS, INC. OFFICE OF PUBLICATION: 2701 NW VAUGHN ST., STE. 780, PORTLAND, OR 97210. ORIGINALLY PUBLISHED IN SINGLE MAGAZINE FORM AS EVOLUTION #1-6. EVOLUTION™ (INCLUDING ALL PROMINENT CHARACTERS FEATURED HEREIN), ITS LOGO AND ALL CHARACTER LIKENESSES ARE TRADEMARKS OF SKYBOUND, LLC. UNLESS OTHERWISE NOTED. IMAGE COMICS® AND ITS LOGOS ARE REGISTERED TRADEMARKS AND COPYRIGHTS OF IMAGE COMICS, INC. ALL RIGHTS RESERVED. NO PART OF THIS PUBLICATION MAY BE REPRODUCED OR TRANSMITTED IN ANY FORM OR BY ANY MEANS (EXCEPT FOR SHORT EXCERPTS FOR REVIEW PURPOSES) WITHOUT THE EXPRESS WRITTEN PERMISSION OF IMAGE COMICS, INC. ALL NAMES, CHARACTERS, EVENTS AND LOCALES IN THIS PUBLICATION ARE ENTIRELY FICTIONAL. ANY RESEMBLANCE TO ACTUAL PERSONS (LIVING OR DEAD), EVENTS OR PLACES, WITHOUT SATIRIC INTENT, IS COINCIDENTAL. PRINTED IN THE U.S.A. FOR INFORMATION REGARDING THE CPSIA ON THIS PRINTED MATERIAL CALL: 203-595-3636 AND PROVIDE REFERENCE # RICH – 787731. ISBN: 978-1-5343-0656-1

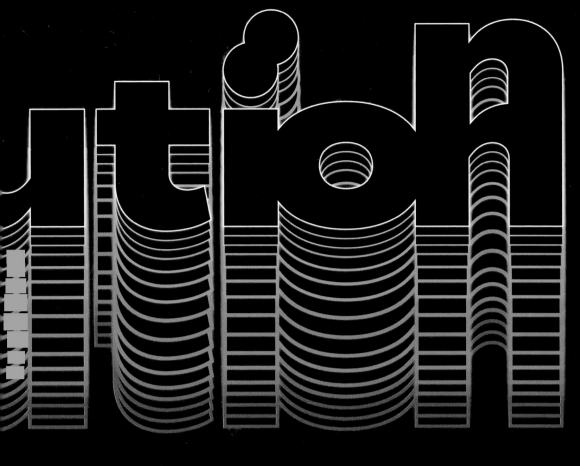

LETTERER
Pat Brosseau

EDITOR
Jon Moisan

ASSOCIATE EDITOR
Arielle Basich

COVER ART
Joe Infurnari
Jordan Boyd

SKYBOUND LLC. *ROBERT KIRKMAN* CHAIRMAN *DAVID ALPERT* CEO *SEAN MACKIEWICZ* SVP, EDITOR-IN-CHIEF *SHAWN KIRKHAM* SVP, BUSINESS DEVELOPMENT *BRIAN HUNTINGTON* ONLINE EDITORIAL DIRECTOR *JUNE ALIAN* PUBLICITY DIRECTOR *ANDRES JUAREZ* ART DIRECTOR *JON MOISAN* EDITOR *ARIELLE BASICH* ASSOCIATE EDITOR *CARINA TAYLOR* PRODUCTION ARTIST *PAUL SHIN* BUSINESS DEVELOPMENT ASSISTANT *JOHNNY O'DELL* SOCIAL MEDIA MANAGER *SALLY JACKA* SKYBOUND RETAILER REALATIONS *DAN PETERSEN* DIRECTOR OF OPERATIONS & EVENTS *NICK PALMER* OPERATIONS COORDINATOR INTERNATIONAL INQUIRIES: AG@SEQUENTIALRIGHTS.COM LICENSING INQUIRIES:CONTACT@SKYBOUND.COM WWW.SKYBOUND.COM

IMAGE COMICS, INC. *ROBERT KIRKMAN* CHIEF OPERATING OFFICER *ERIK LARSEN* CHIEF FINANCIAL OFFICER *TODD MCFARLANE* PRESIDENT *MARC SILVESTRI* CHIEF EXECUTIVE OFFICER *JIM VALENTINO* VICE PRESIDENT *ERIC STEPHENSON* PUBLISHER/CHIEF CREATIVE OFFICER *COREY HART* DIRECTOR OF SALES *JEFF BOISON* DIRECTOR OF PUBLISHING PLANNING & BOOK TRADE SALES *CHRIS ROSS* DIRECTOR OF DIGITAL SALES *JEFF STANG* DIRECTOR OF SPECIALTY SALES *KAT SALAZAR* DIRECTOR OF PR & MARKETING *DREW GILL* ART DIRECTOR *HEATHER DOORNINK* PRODUCTION DIRECTOR *NICOLE LAPALME* CONTROLLER WWW.IMAGECOMICS.COM

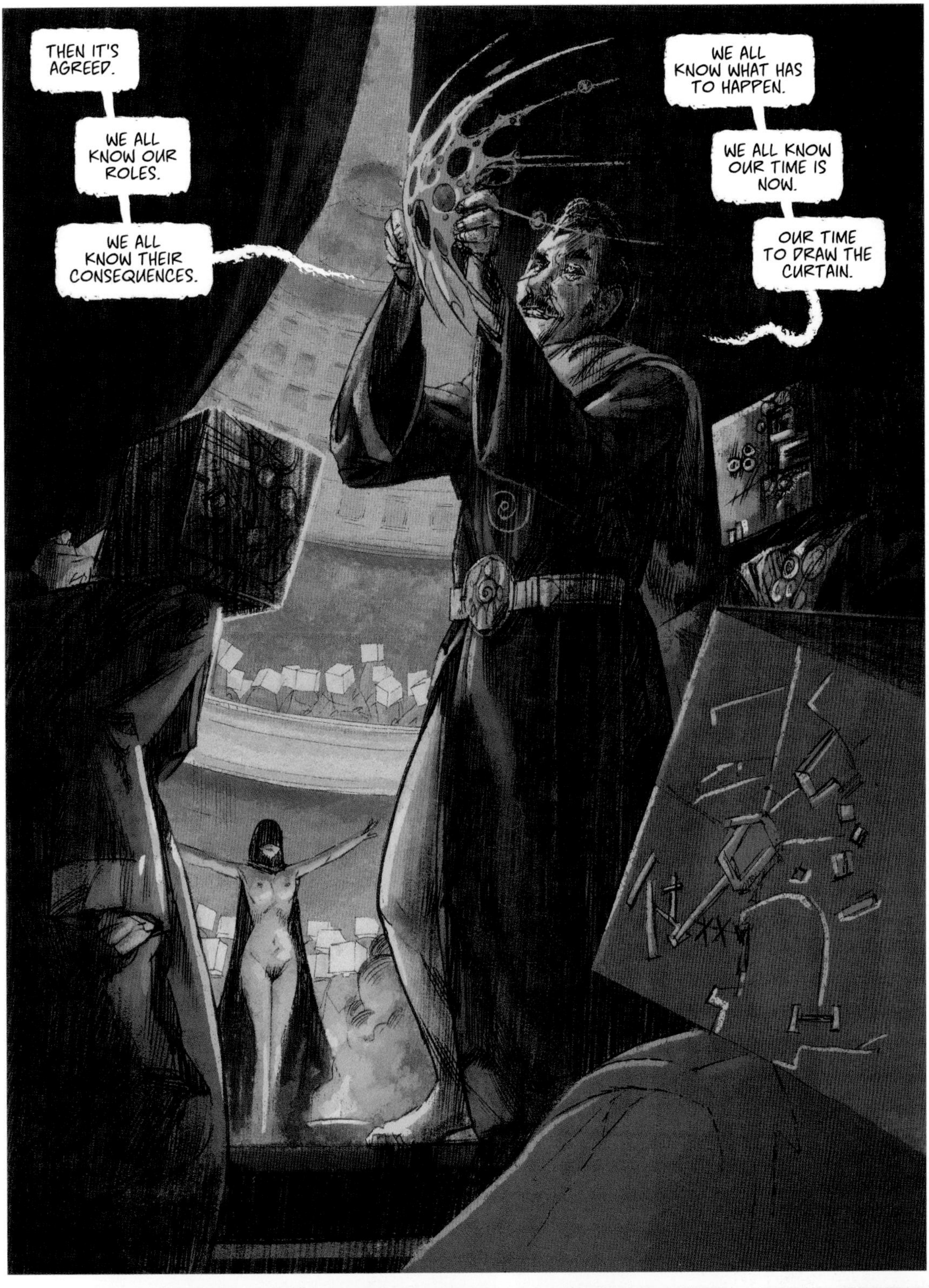
THEN IT'S AGREED.
WE ALL KNOW OUR ROLES.
WE ALL KNOW THEIR CONSEQUENCES.
WE ALL KNOW WHAT HAS TO HAPPEN.
WE ALL KNOW OUR TIME IS NOW.
OUR TIME TO DRAW THE CURTAIN.

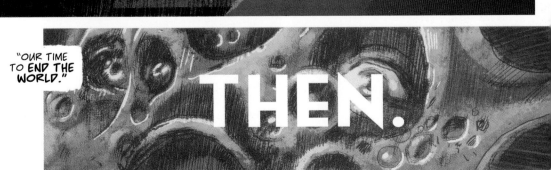

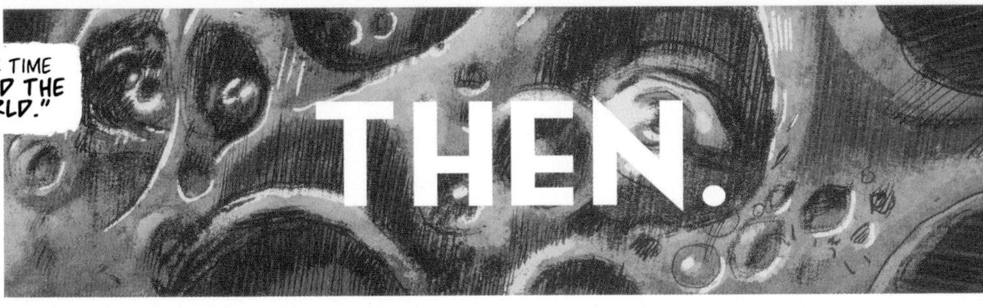
"OUR TIME TO END THE WORLD."
THEN.

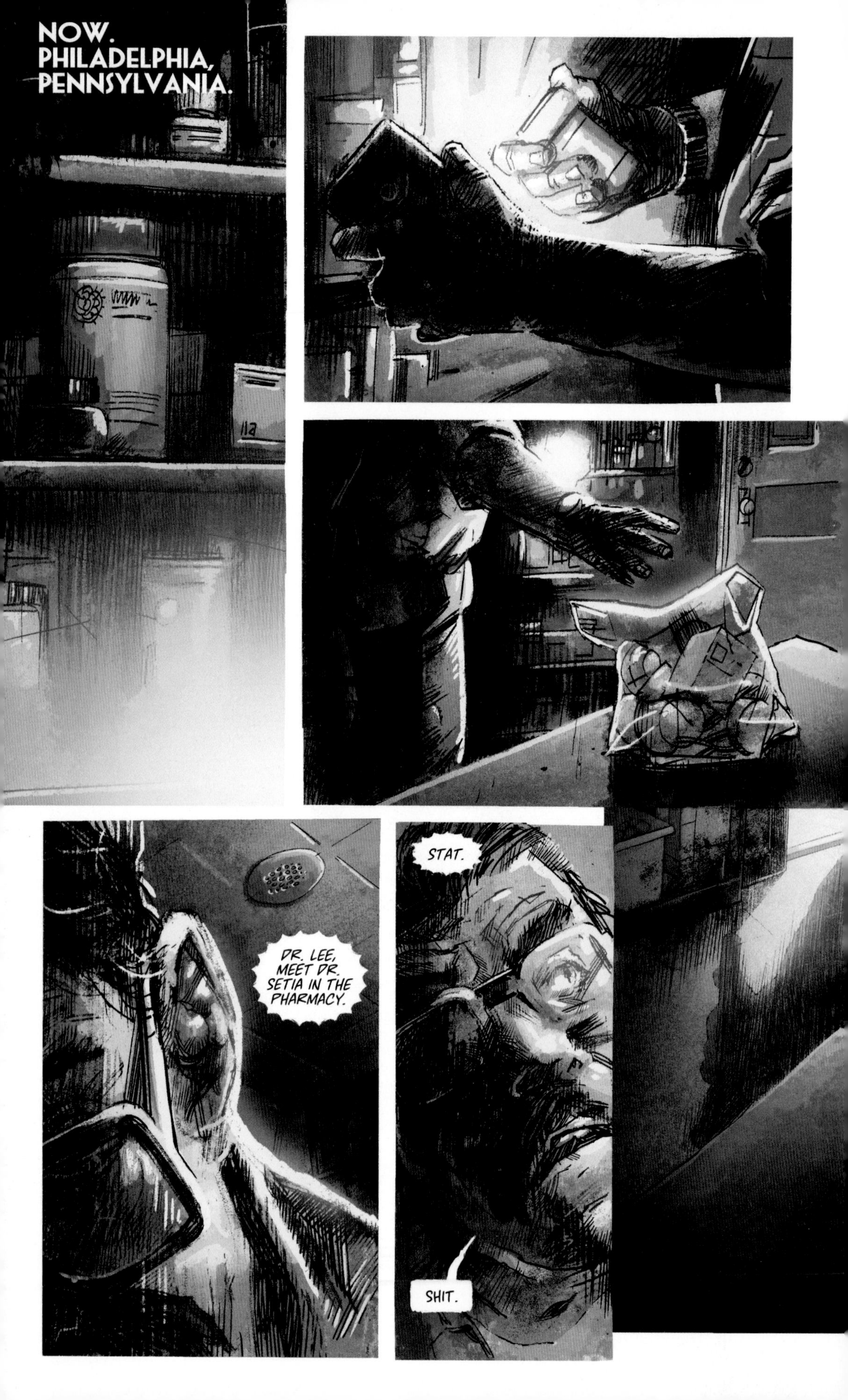
NOW.
PHILADELPHIA,
PENNSYLVANIA.
DR. LEE, MEET DR. SETIA IN THE PHARMACY.
STAT.
SHIT.

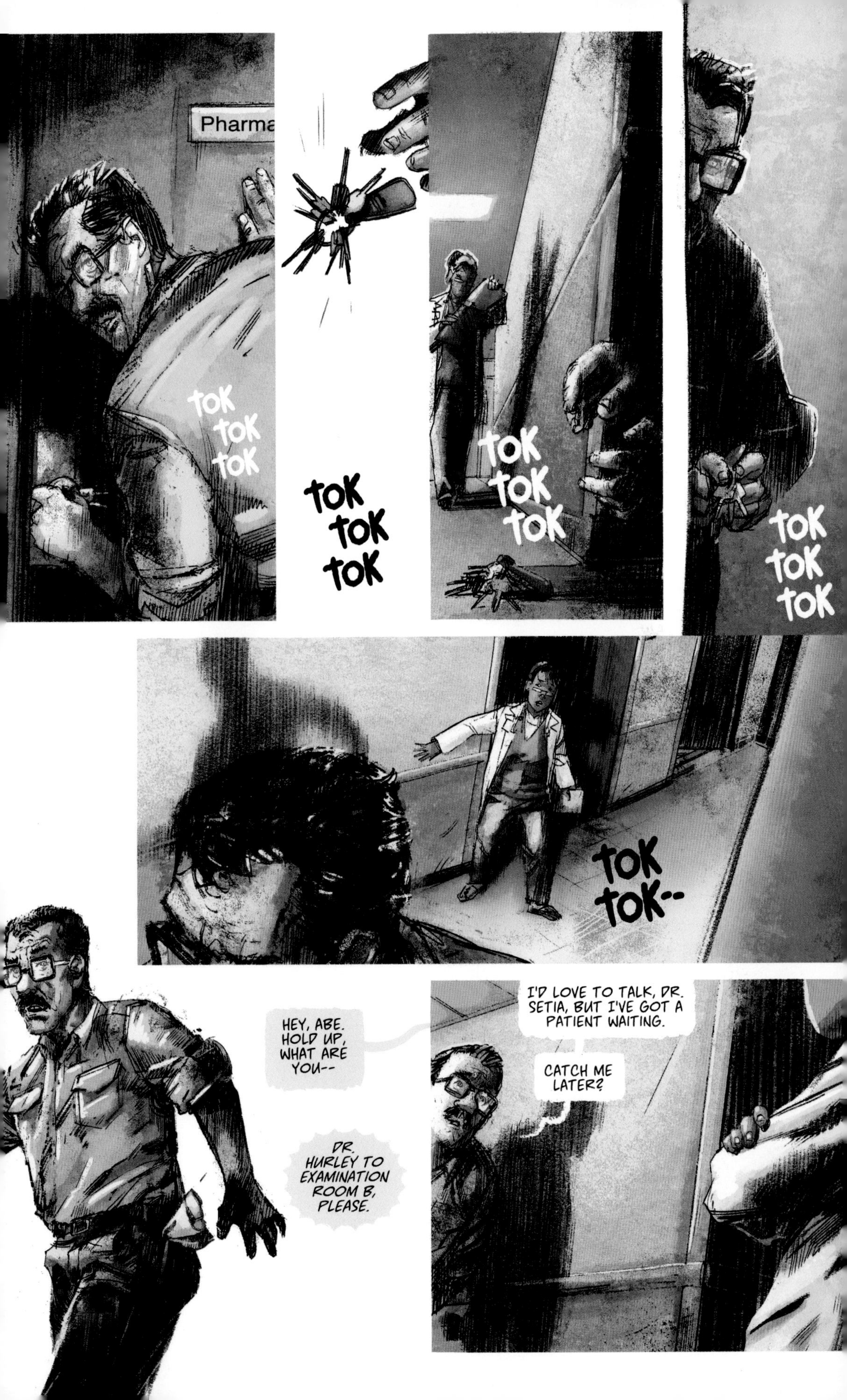
Pharma
TOK TOK TOK
TOK TOK TOK
TOK TOK TOK
TOK TOK TOK
TOK TOK--
HEY, ABE. HOLD UP, WHAT ARE YOU--
DR. HURLEY TO EXAMINATION ROOM B, PLEASE.
I'D LOVE TO TALK, DR. SETIA, BUT I'VE GOT A PATIENT WAITING.
CATCH ME LATER?

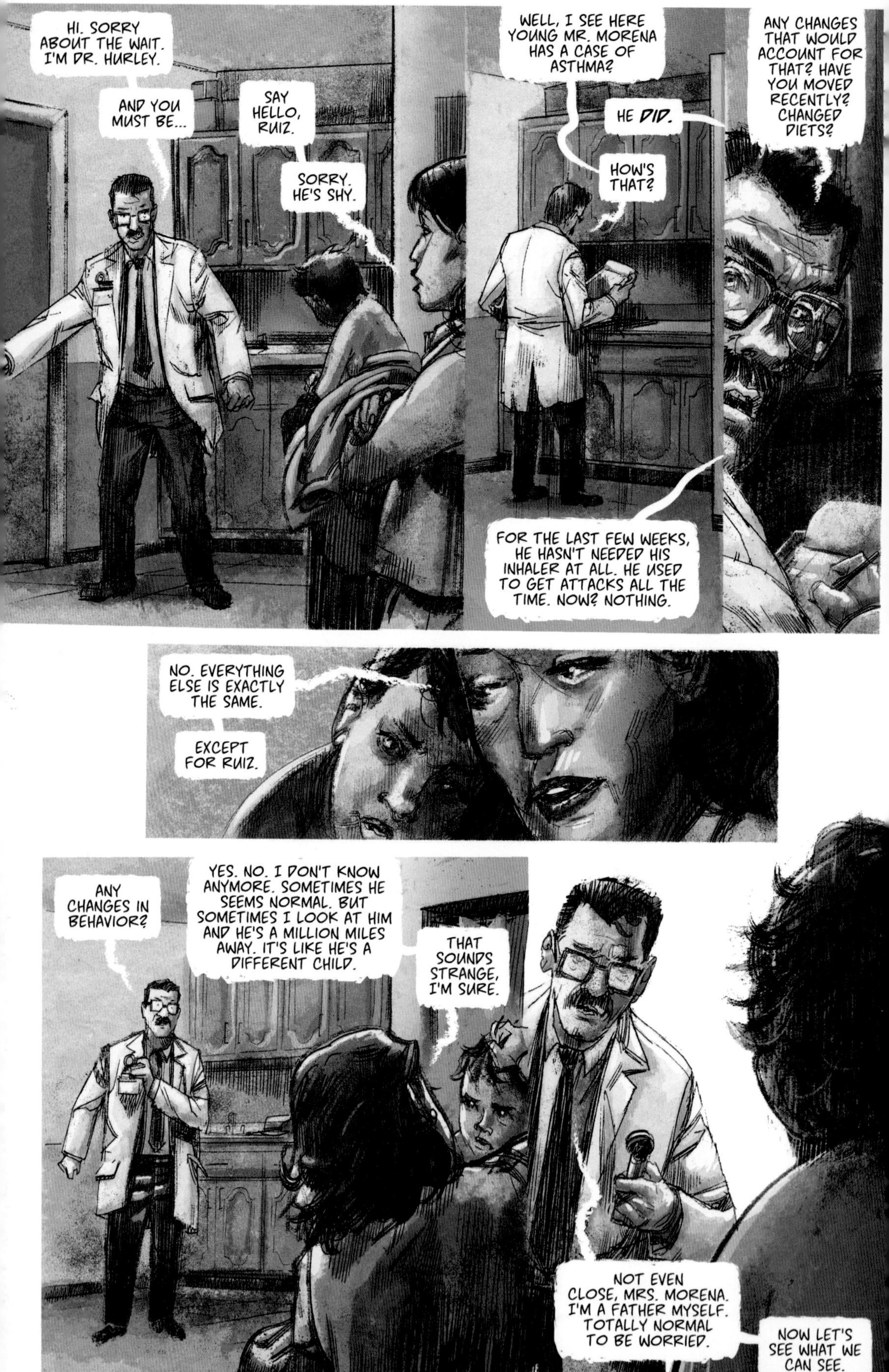
HI. SORRY ABOUT THE WAIT. I'M DR. HURLEY.
AND YOU MUST BE...
SAY HELLO, RUIZ.
SORRY. HE'S SHY.
WELL, I SEE HERE YOUNG MR. MORENA HAS A CASE OF ASTHMA?
HE DID.
HOW'S THAT?
FOR THE LAST FEW WEEKS, HE HASN'T NEEDED HIS INHALER AT ALL. HE USED TO GET ATTACKS ALL THE TIME. NOW? NOTHING.
ANY CHANGES THAT WOULD ACCOUNT FOR THAT? HAVE YOU MOVED RECENTLY? CHANGED DIETS?
NO. EVERYTHING ELSE IS EXACTLY THE SAME.
EXCEPT FOR RUIZ.
ANY CHANGES IN BEHAVIOR?
YES. NO. I DON'T KNOW ANYMORE. SOMETIMES HE SEEMS NORMAL. BUT SOMETIMES I LOOK AT HIM AND HE'S A MILLION MILES AWAY. IT'S LIKE HE'S A DIFFERENT CHILD.
THAT SOUNDS STRANGE, I'M SURE.
NOT EVEN CLOSE, MRS. MORENA. I'M A FATHER MYSELF. TOTALLY NORMAL TO BE WORRIED.
NOW LET'S SEE WHAT WE CAN SEE.

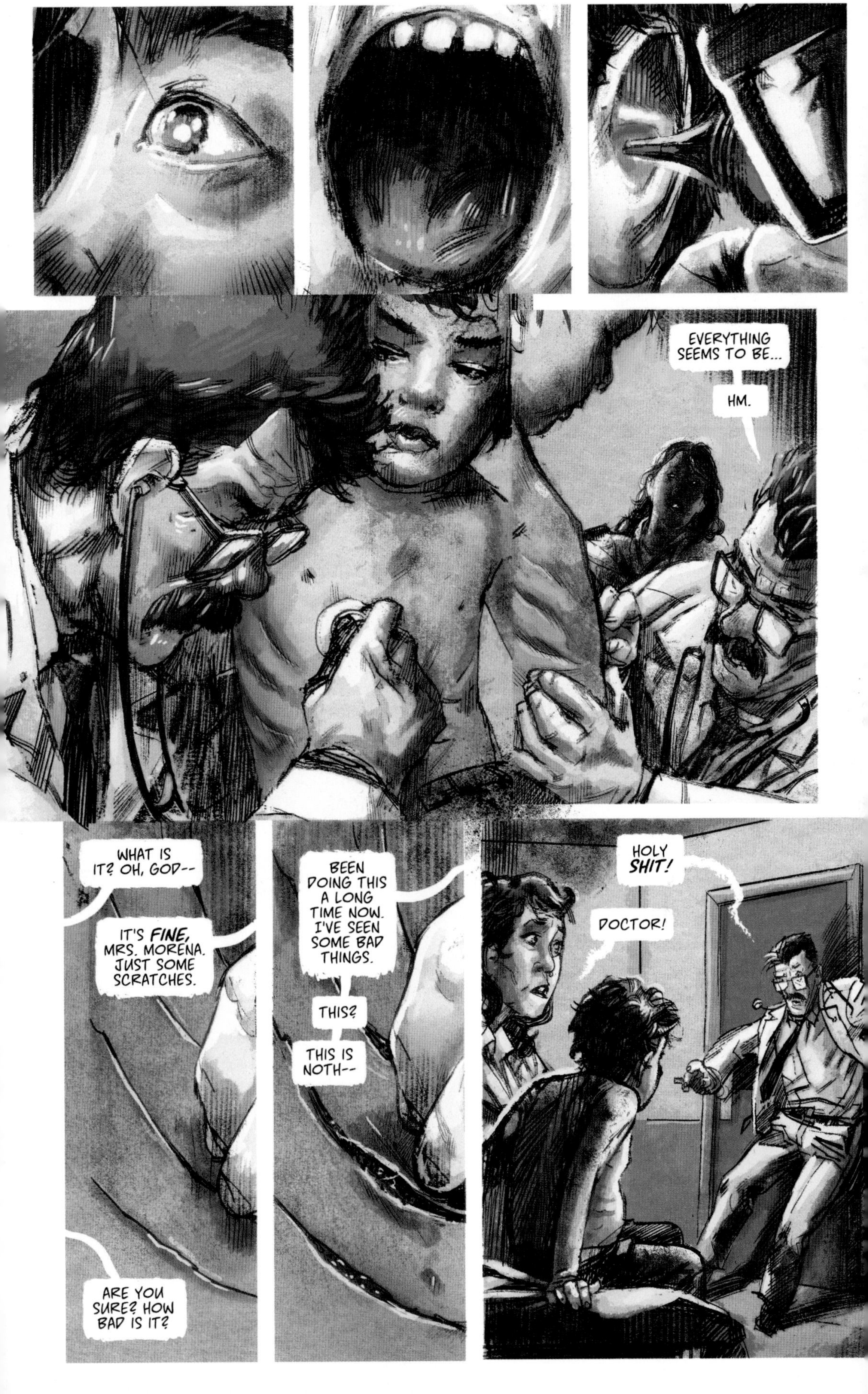
EVERYTHING SEEMS TO BE...
HM.
WHAT IS IT? OH, GOD--
IT'S **FINE,** MRS. MORENA. JUST SOME SCRATCHES.
ARE YOU SURE? HOW BAD IS IT?
BEEN DOING THIS A LONG TIME NOW. I'VE SEEN SOME BAD THINGS.
THIS?
THIS IS NOTH--
HOLY **SHIT!**
DOCTOR!

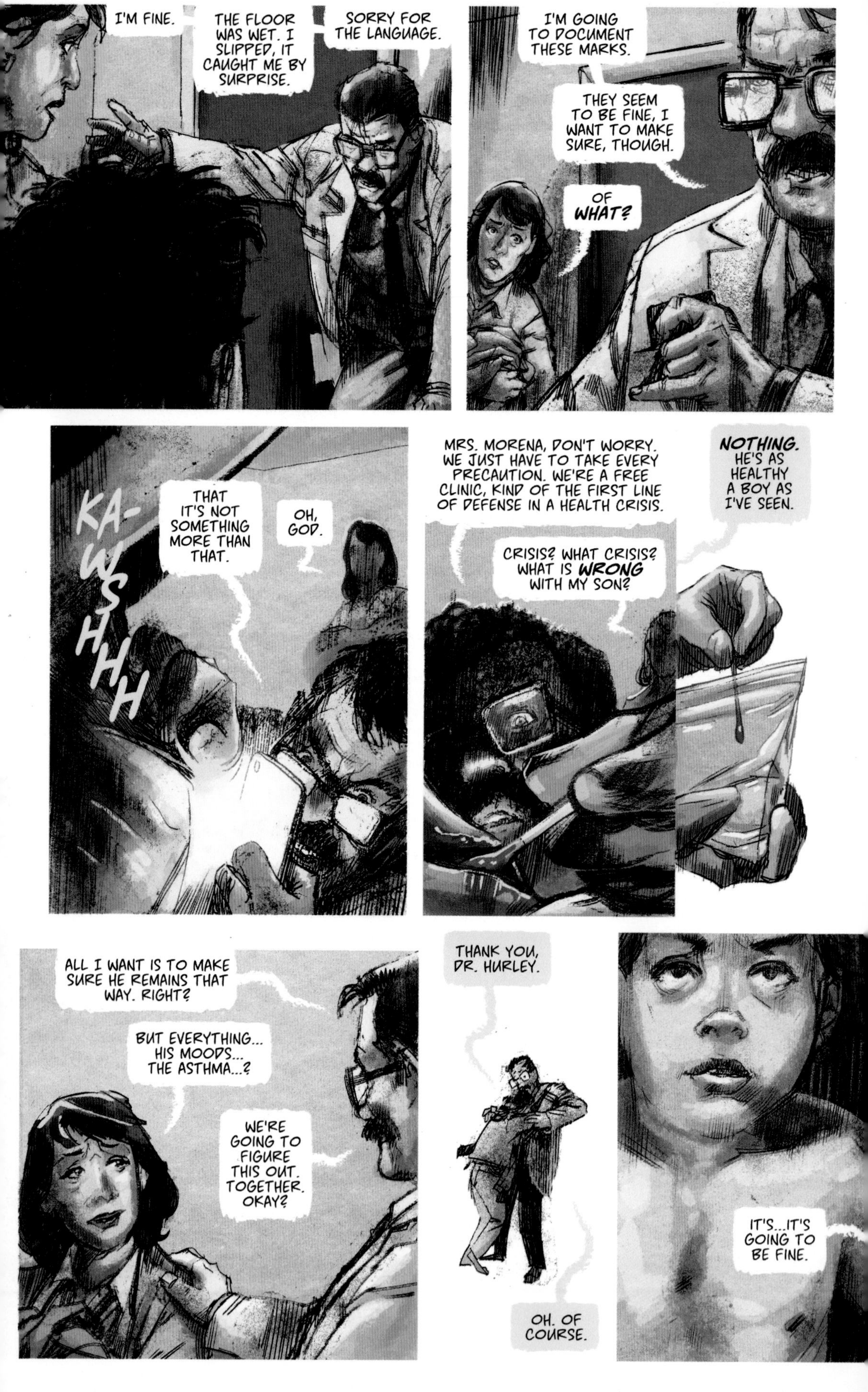
I'M FINE.
THE FLOOR WAS WET. I SLIPPED, IT CAUGHT ME BY SURPRISE.
SORRY FOR THE LANGUAGE.
I'M GOING TO DOCUMENT THESE MARKS.
THEY SEEM TO BE FINE, I WANT TO MAKE SURE, THOUGH.
OF **WHAT?**
KA-WSHHHH
THAT IT'S NOT SOMETHING MORE THAN THAT.
OH, GOD.
MRS. MORENA, DON'T WORRY. WE JUST HAVE TO TAKE EVERY PRECAUTION. WE'RE A FREE CLINIC, KIND OF THE FIRST LINE OF DEFENSE IN A HEALTH CRISIS.
CRISIS? WHAT CRISIS? WHAT IS **WRONG** WITH MY SON?
NOTHING. HE'S AS HEALTHY A BOY AS I'VE SEEN.
ALL I WANT IS TO MAKE SURE HE REMAINS THAT WAY. RIGHT?
BUT EVERYTHING... HIS MOODS... THE ASTHMA...?
WE'RE GOING TO FIGURE THIS OUT. TOGETHER. OKAY?
THANK YOU, DR. HURLEY.
OH. OF COURSE.
IT'S...IT'S GOING TO BE FINE.

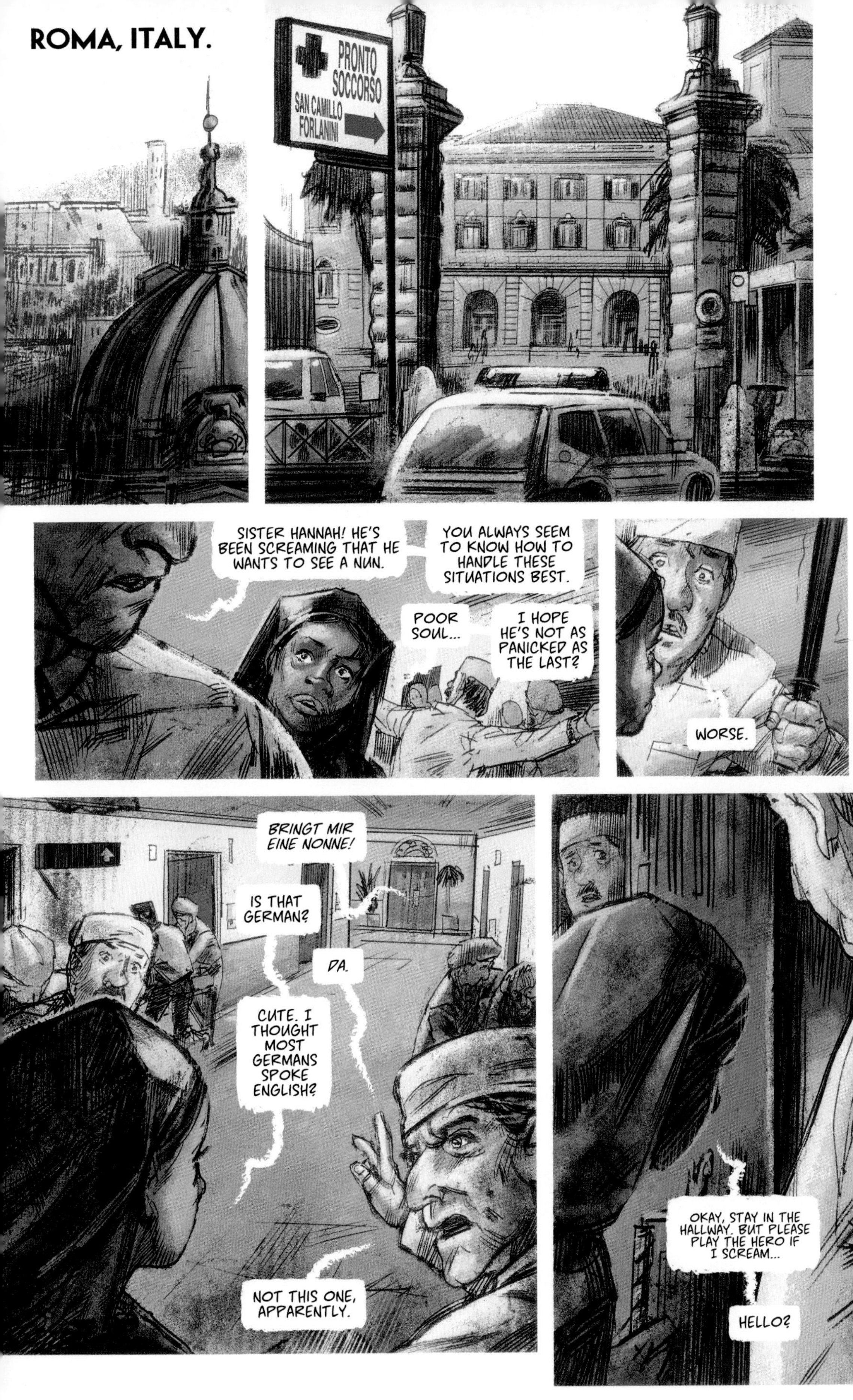
ROMA, ITALY.
PRONTO SOCCORSO
SAN CAMILLO FORLANINI
SISTER HANNAH! HE'S BEEN SCREAMING THAT HE WANTS TO SEE A NUN.
YOU ALWAYS SEEM TO KNOW HOW TO HANDLE THESE SITUATIONS BEST.
POOR SOUL...
I HOPE HE'S NOT AS PANICKED AS THE LAST?
WORSE.
BRINGT MIR EINE NONNE!
IS THAT GERMAN?
DA.
CUTE. I THOUGHT MOST GERMANS SPOKE ENGLISH?
NOT THIS ONE, APPARENTLY.
OKAY, STAY IN THE HALLWAY. BUT PLEASE PLAY THE HERO IF I SCREAM...
HELLO?

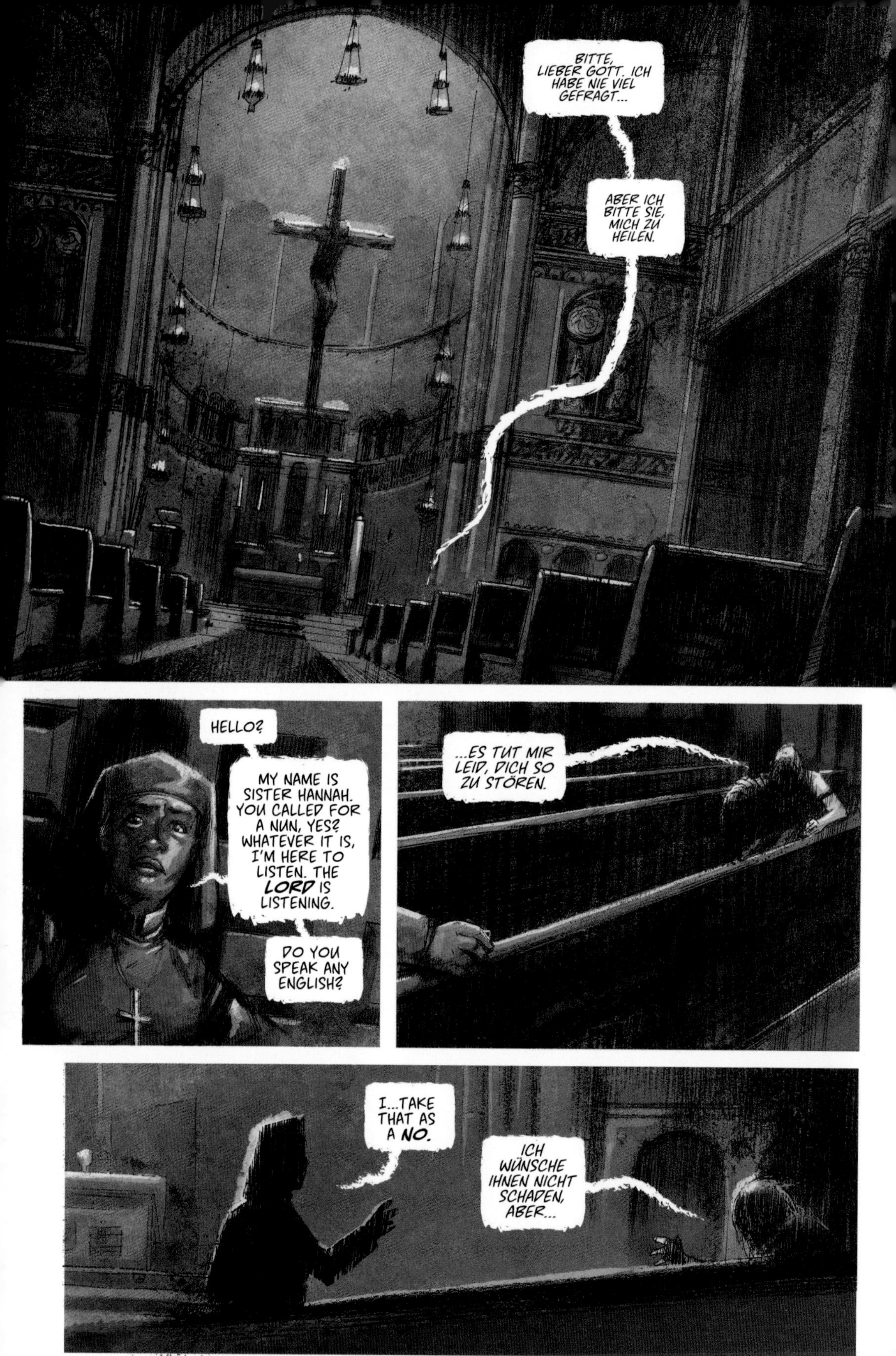
BITTE, LIEBER GOTT. ICH HABE NIE VIEL GEFRAGT...
ABER ICH BITTE SIE, MICH ZU HEILEN.
HELLO?
MY NAME IS SISTER HANNAH. YOU CALLED FOR A NUN, YES? WHATEVER IT IS, I'M HERE TO LISTEN. THE LORD IS LISTENING.
DO YOU SPEAK ANY ENGLISH?
...ES TUT MIR LEID, DICH SO ZU STÖREN.
I...TAKE THAT AS A NO.
ICH WÜNSCHE IHNEN NICHT SCHADEN, ABER...

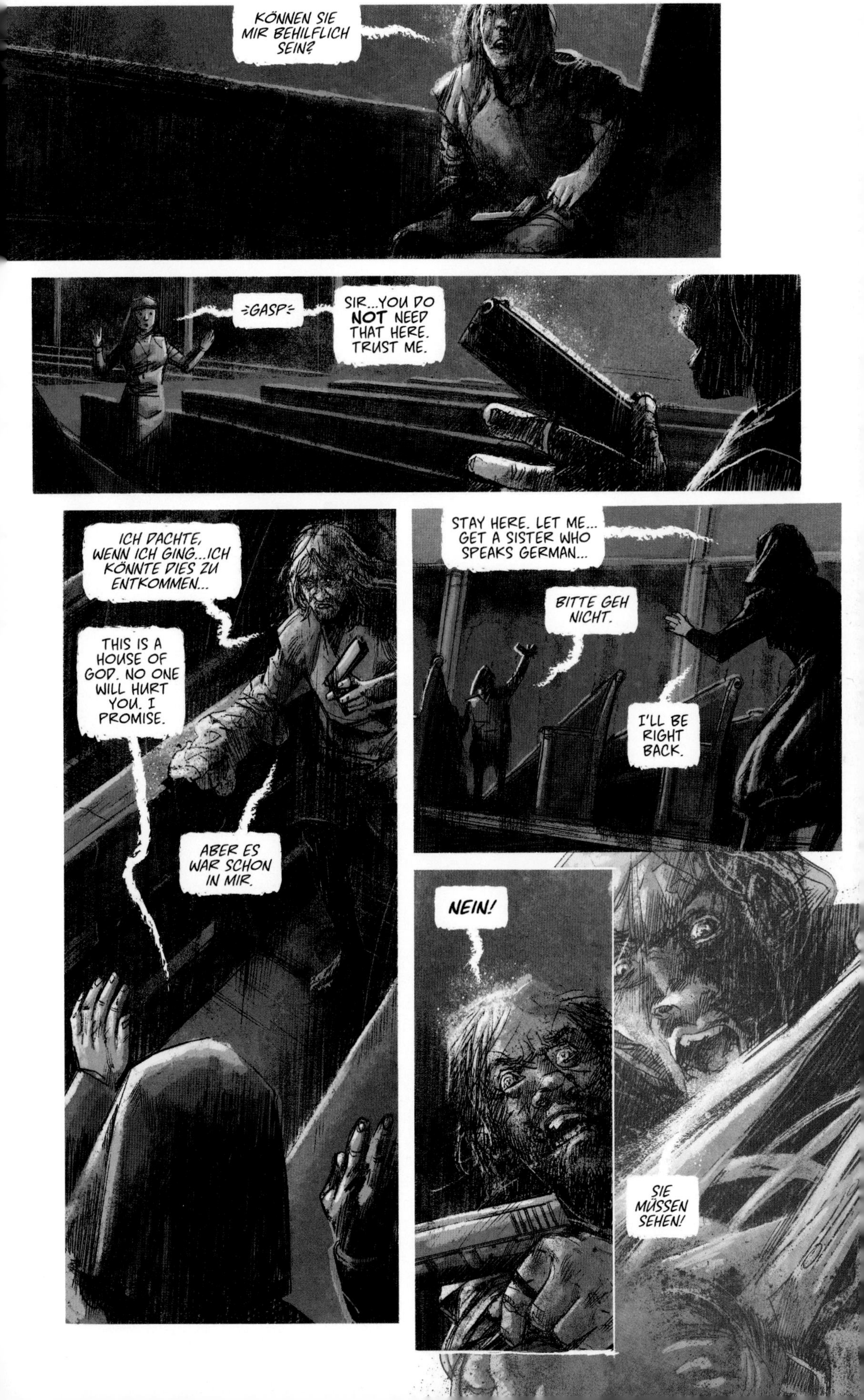
KÖNNEN SIE MIR BEHILFLICH SEIN?
GASP
SIR...YOU DO NOT NEED THAT HERE. TRUST ME.
ICH DACHTE, WENN ICH GING...ICH KÖNNTE DIES ZU ENTKOMMEN...
THIS IS A HOUSE OF GOD. NO ONE WILL HURT YOU. I PROMISE.
ABER ES WAR SCHON IN MIR.
STAY HERE. LET ME... GET A SISTER WHO SPEAKS GERMAN...
BITTE GEH NICHT.
I'LL BE RIGHT BACK.
NEIN!
SIE MÜSSEN SEHEN!

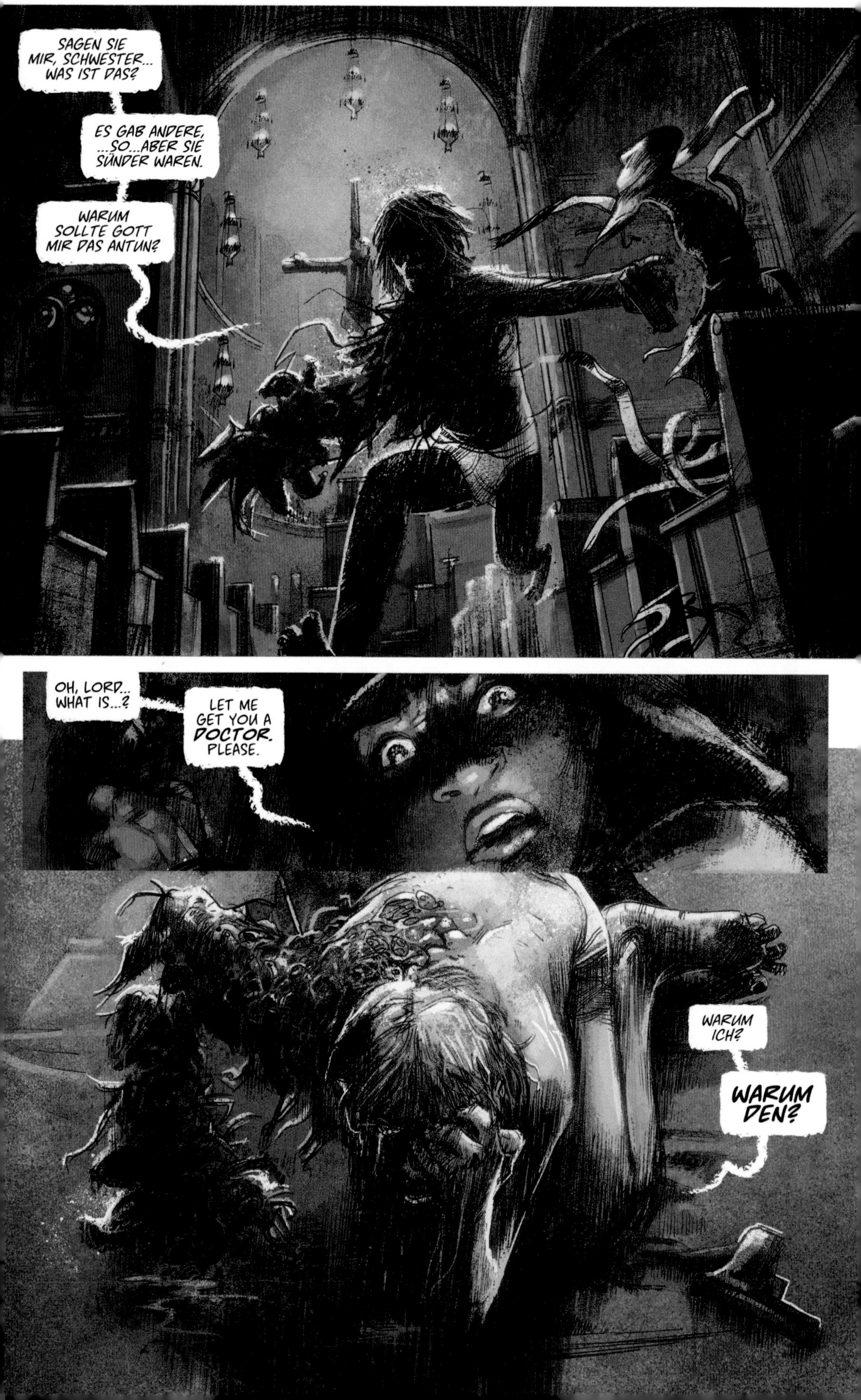
SAGEN SIE MIR, SCHWESTER... WAS IST DAS?
ES GAB ANDERE, ...SO...ABER SIE SÜNDER WAREN.
WARUM SOLLTE GOTT MIR DAS ANTUN?
OH, LORD... WHAT IS...?
LET ME GET YOU A DOCTOR. PLEASE.
WARUM ICH?
WARUM DEN?

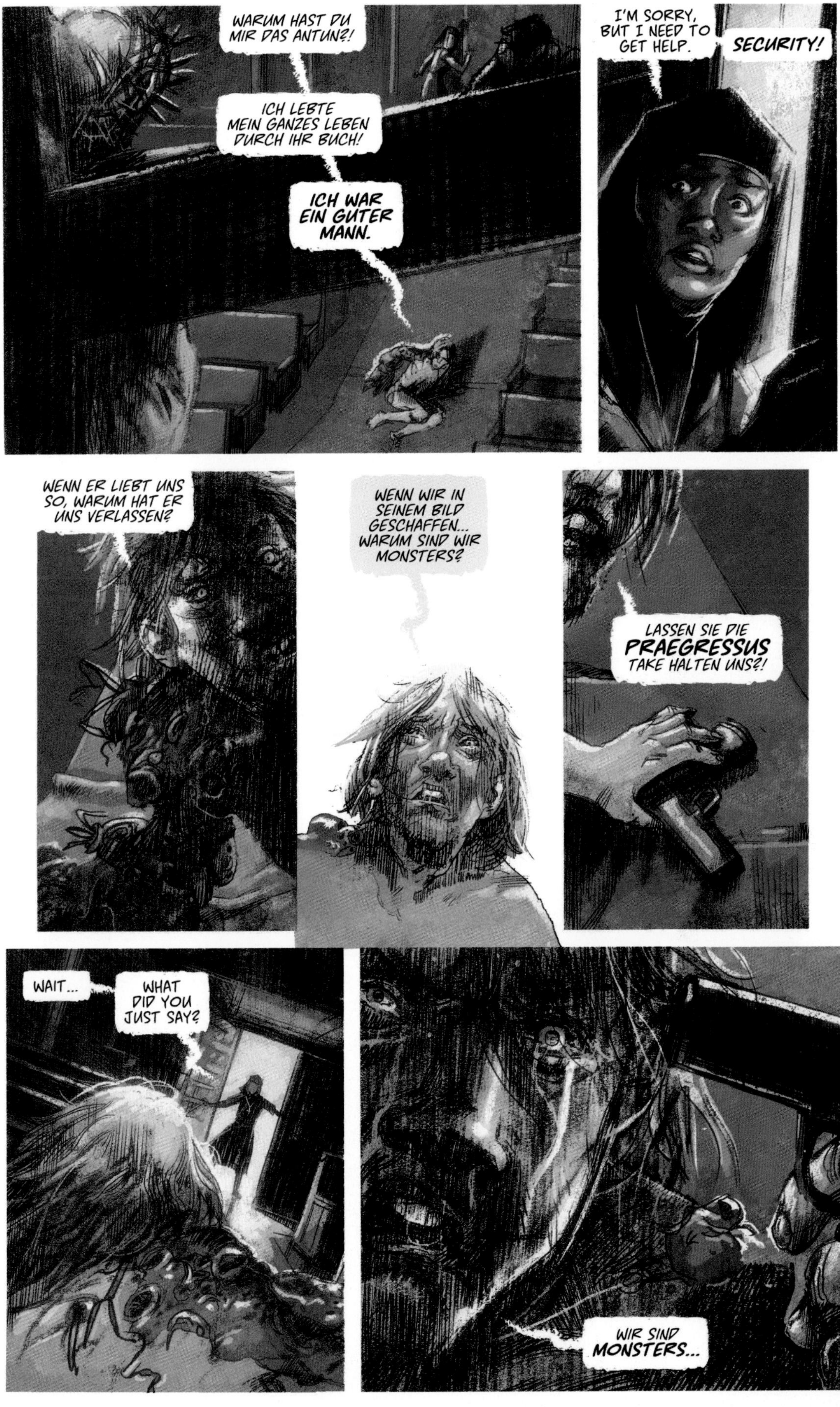
WARUM HAST DU MIR DAS ANTUN?!
ICH LEBTE MEIN GANZES LEBEN DURCH IHR BUCH!
ICH WAR EIN GUTER MANN.
I'M SORRY, BUT I NEED TO GET HELP.
SECURITY!
WENN ER LIEBT UNS SO, WARUM HAT ER UNS VERLASSEN?
WENN WIR IN SEINEM BILD GESCHAFFEN... WARUM SIND WIR MONSTERS?
LASSEN SIE DIE PRAEGRESSUS TAKE HALTEN UNS?!
WAIT...
WHAT DID YOU JUST SAY?
WIR SIND MONSTERS...

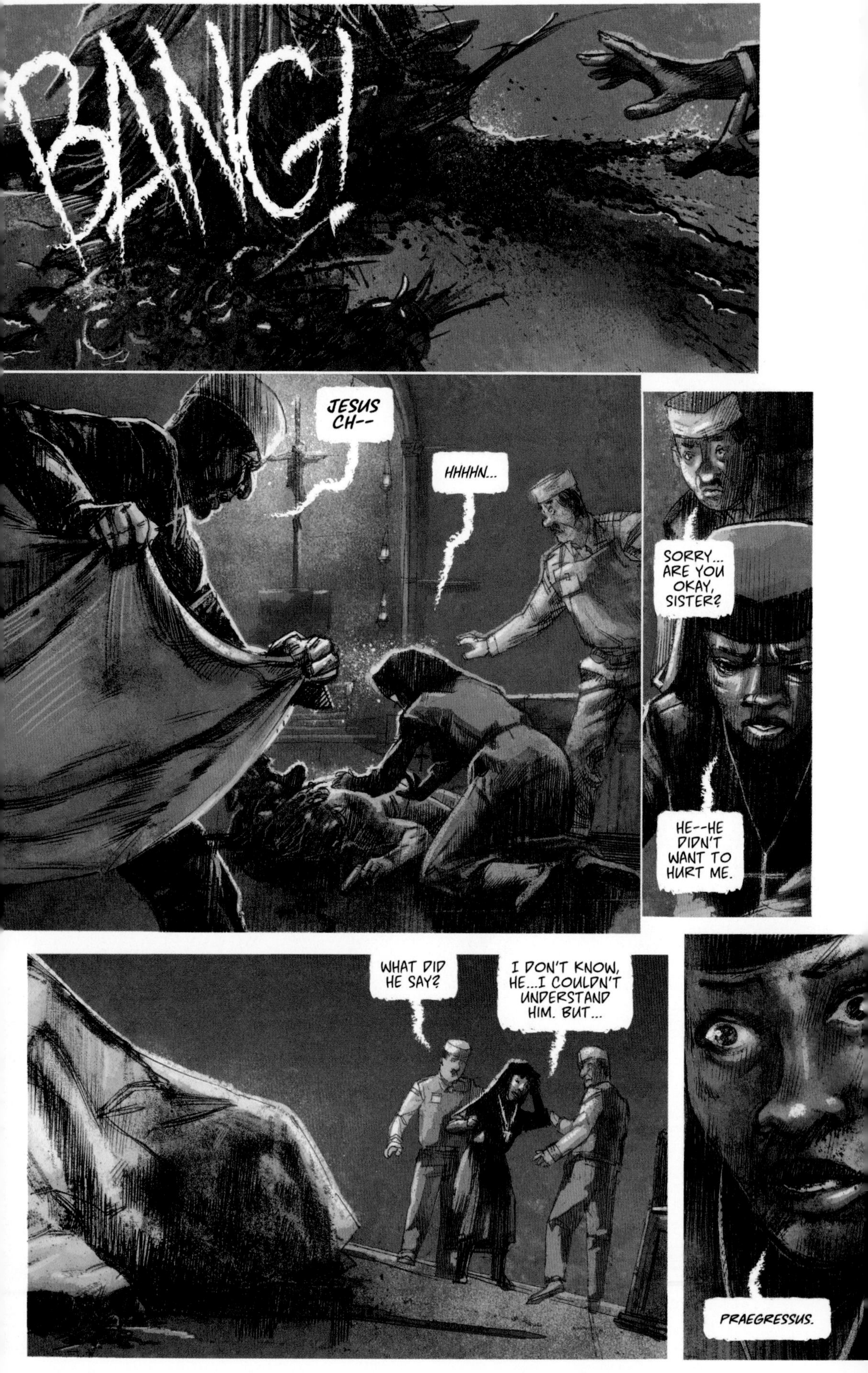
BANG!
JESUS CH--
HHHHN...
SORRY... ARE YOU OKAY, SISTER?
HE--HE DIDN'T WANT TO HURT ME.
WHAT DID HE SAY?
I DON'T KNOW, HE...I COULDN'T UNDERSTAND HIM. BUT...
PRAEGRESSUS.

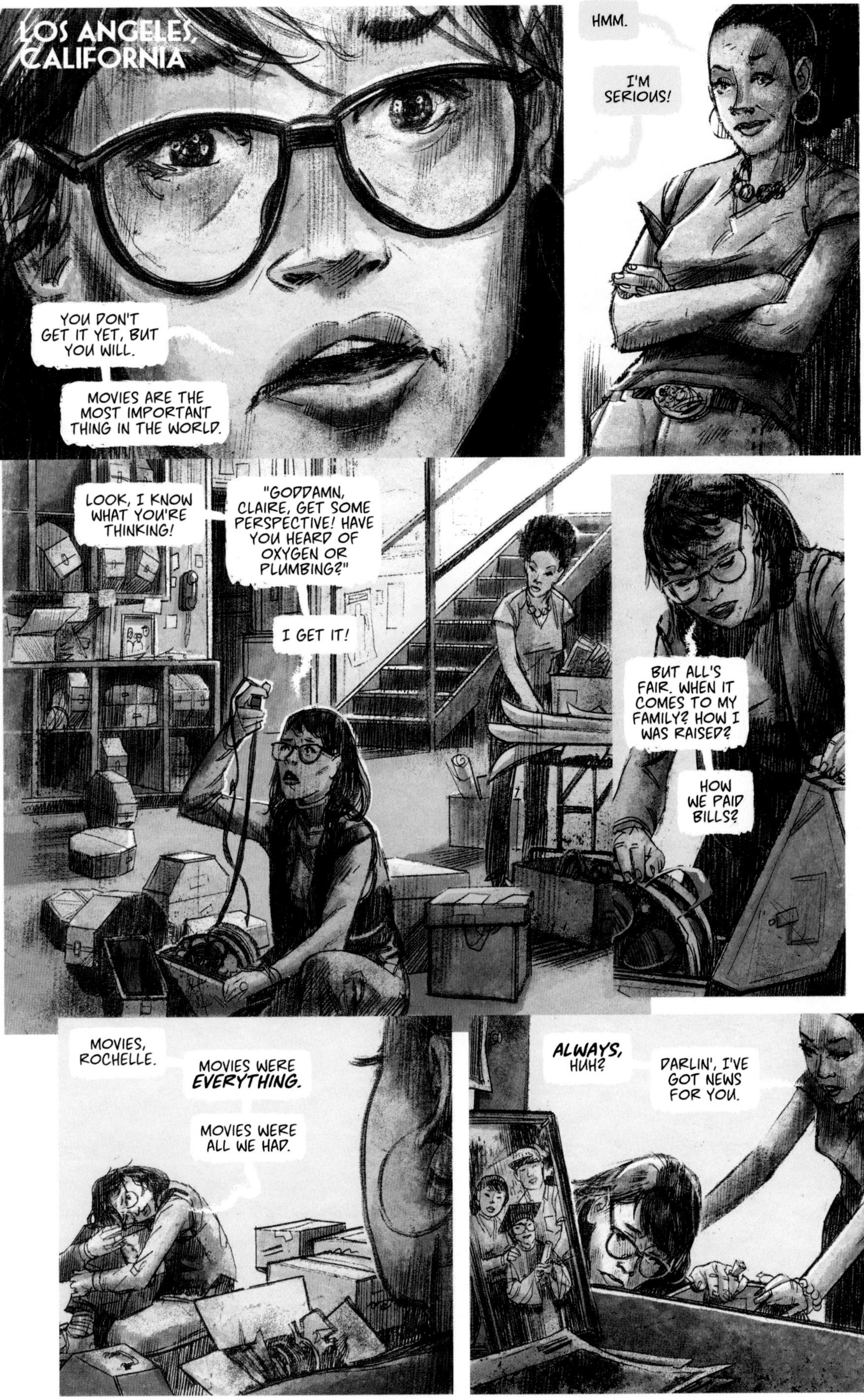
LOS ANGELES, CALIFORNIA
YOU DON'T GET IT YET, BUT YOU WILL.
MOVIES ARE THE MOST IMPORTANT THING IN THE WORLD.
HMM.
I'M SERIOUS!
LOOK, I KNOW WHAT YOU'RE THINKING!
"GODDAMN, CLAIRE, GET SOME PERSPECTIVE! HAVE YOU HEARD OF OXYGEN OR PLUMBING?"
I GET IT!
BUT ALL'S FAIR. WHEN IT COMES TO MY FAMILY? HOW I WAS RAISED?
HOW WE PAID BILLS?
MOVIES, ROCHELLE.
MOVIES WERE EVERYTHING.
MOVIES WERE ALL WE HAD.
ALWAYS, HUH?
DARLIN', I'VE GOT NEWS FOR YOU.

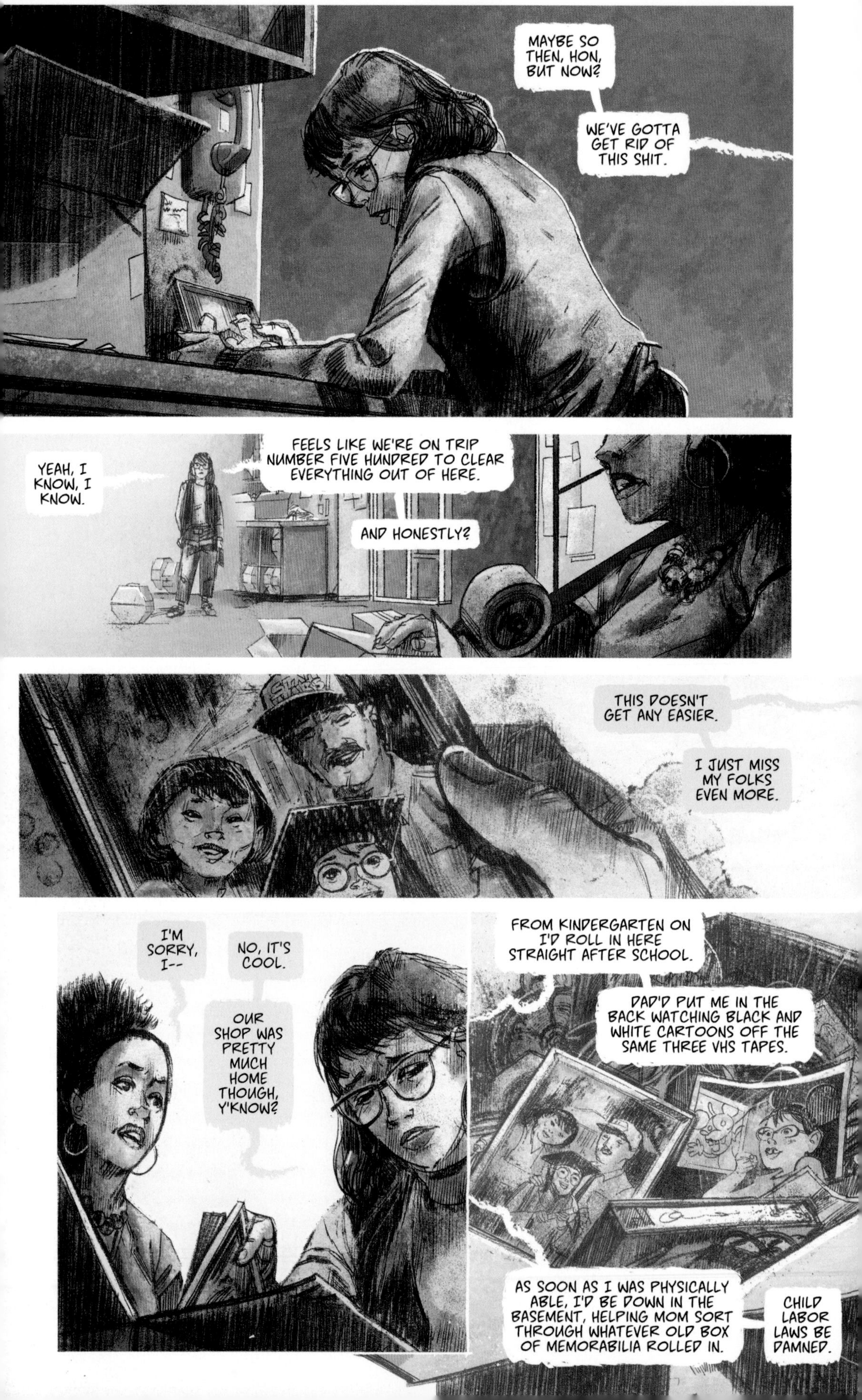
MAYBE SO THEN, HON, BUT NOW?
WE'VE GOTTA GET RID OF THIS SHIT.
YEAH, I KNOW, I KNOW.
FEELS LIKE WE'RE ON TRIP NUMBER FIVE HUNDRED TO CLEAR EVERYTHING OUT OF HERE.
AND HONESTLY?
THIS DOESN'T GET ANY EASIER.
I JUST MISS MY FOLKS EVEN MORE.
I'M SORRY, I--
NO, IT'S COOL.
OUR SHOP WAS PRETTY MUCH HOME THOUGH, Y'KNOW?
FROM KINDERGARTEN ON I'D ROLL IN HERE STRAIGHT AFTER SCHOOL.
DAD'D PUT ME IN THE BACK WATCHING BLACK AND WHITE CARTOONS OFF THE SAME THREE VHS TAPES.
AS SOON AS I WAS PHYSICALLY ABLE, I'D BE DOWN IN THE BASEMENT, HELPING MOM SORT THROUGH WHATEVER OLD BOX OF MEMORABILIA ROLLED IN.
CHILD LABOR LAWS BE DAMNED.

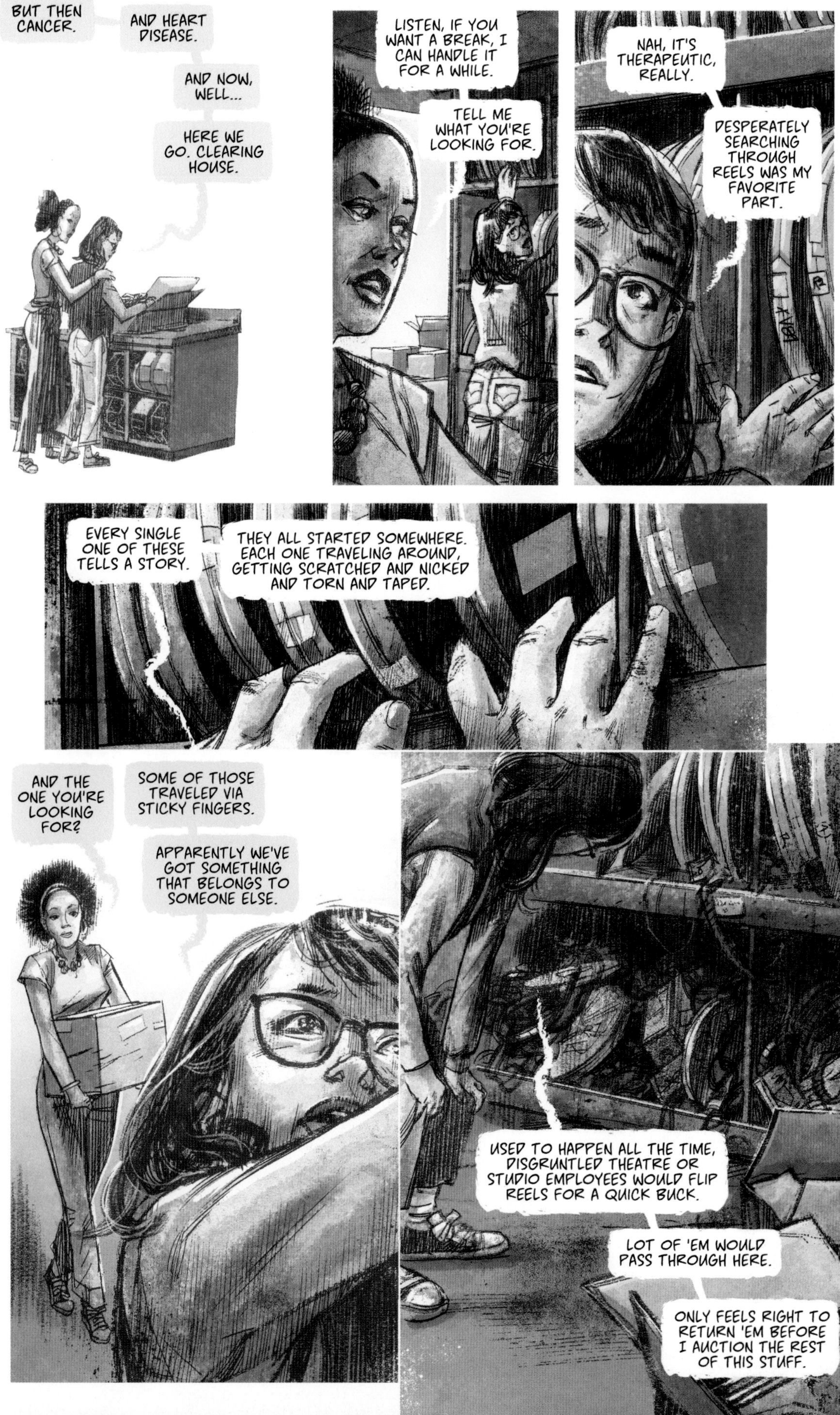
BUT THEN CANCER.
AND HEART DISEASE.
AND NOW, WELL...
HERE WE GO. CLEARING HOUSE.
LISTEN, IF YOU WANT A BREAK, I CAN HANDLE IT FOR A WHILE.
TELL ME WHAT YOU'RE LOOKING FOR.
NAH, IT'S THERAPEUTIC, REALLY.
DESPERATELY SEARCHING THROUGH REELS WAS MY FAVORITE PART.
EVERY SINGLE ONE OF THESE TELLS A STORY.
THEY ALL STARTED SOMEWHERE. EACH ONE TRAVELING AROUND, GETTING SCRATCHED AND NICKED AND TORN AND TAPED.
AND THE ONE YOU'RE LOOKING FOR?
SOME OF THOSE TRAVELED VIA STICKY FINGERS.
APPARENTLY WE'VE GOT SOMETHING THAT BELONGS TO SOMEONE ELSE.
USED TO HAPPEN ALL THE TIME, DISGRUNTLED THEATRE OR STUDIO EMPLOYEES WOULD FLIP REELS FOR A QUICK BUCK.
LOT OF 'EM WOULD PASS THROUGH HERE.
ONLY FEELS RIGHT TO RETURN 'EM BEFORE I AUCTION THE REST OF THIS STUFF.

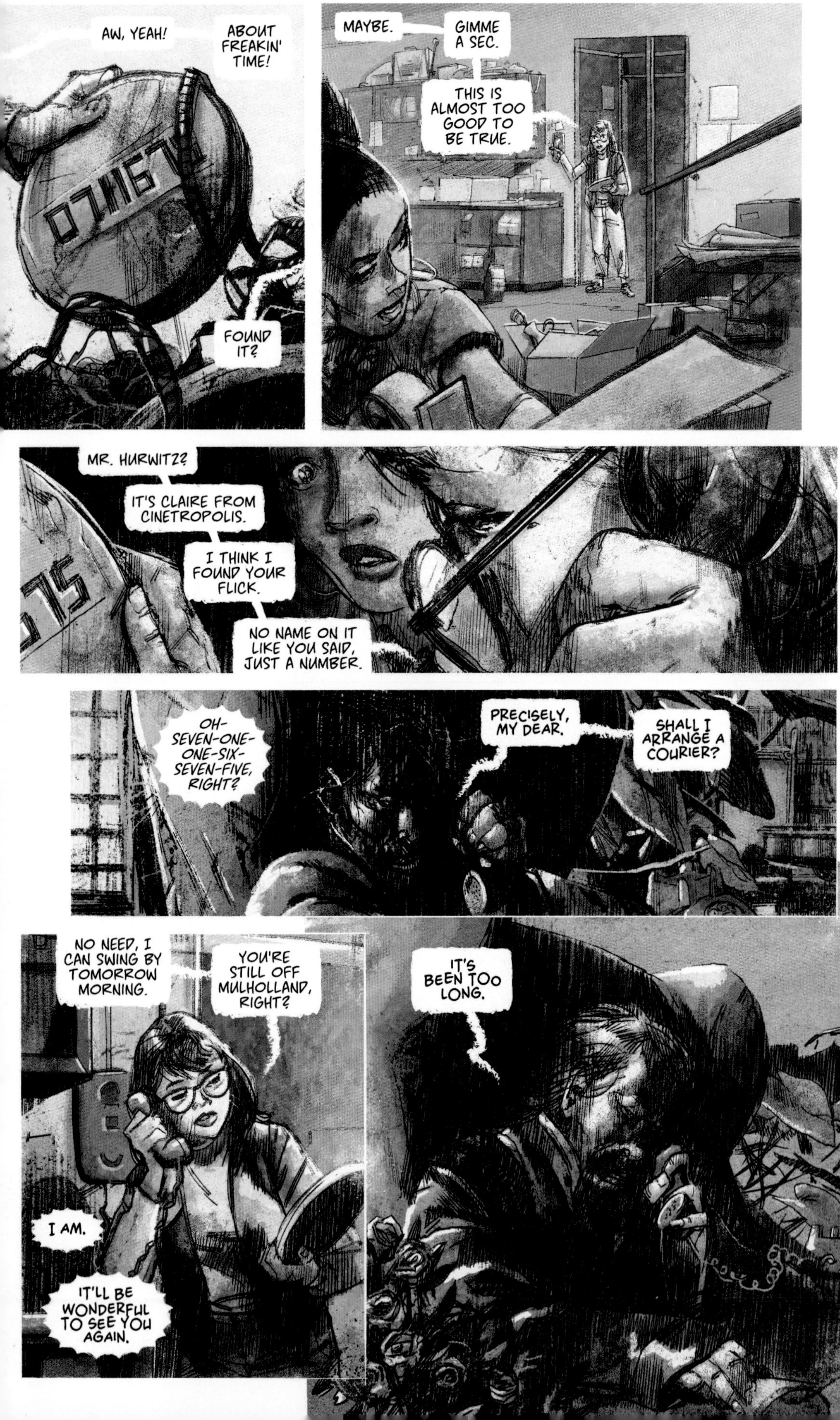
AW, YEAH!
ABOUT FREAKIN' TIME!
FOUND IT?
MAYBE.
GIMME A SEC.
THIS IS ALMOST TOO GOOD TO BE TRUE.
MR. HURWITZ?
IT'S CLAIRE FROM CINETROPOLIS.
I THINK I FOUND YOUR FLICK.
NO NAME ON IT LIKE YOU SAID, JUST A NUMBER.
OH-SEVEN-ONE-ONE-SIX-SEVEN-FIVE, RIGHT?
PRECISELY, MY DEAR.
SHALL I ARRANGE A COURIER?
NO NEED, I CAN SWING BY TOMORROW MORNING.
YOU'RE STILL OFF MULHOLLAND, RIGHT?
I AM.
IT'LL BE WONDERFUL TO SEE YOU AGAIN.
IT'S BEEN TOO LONG.

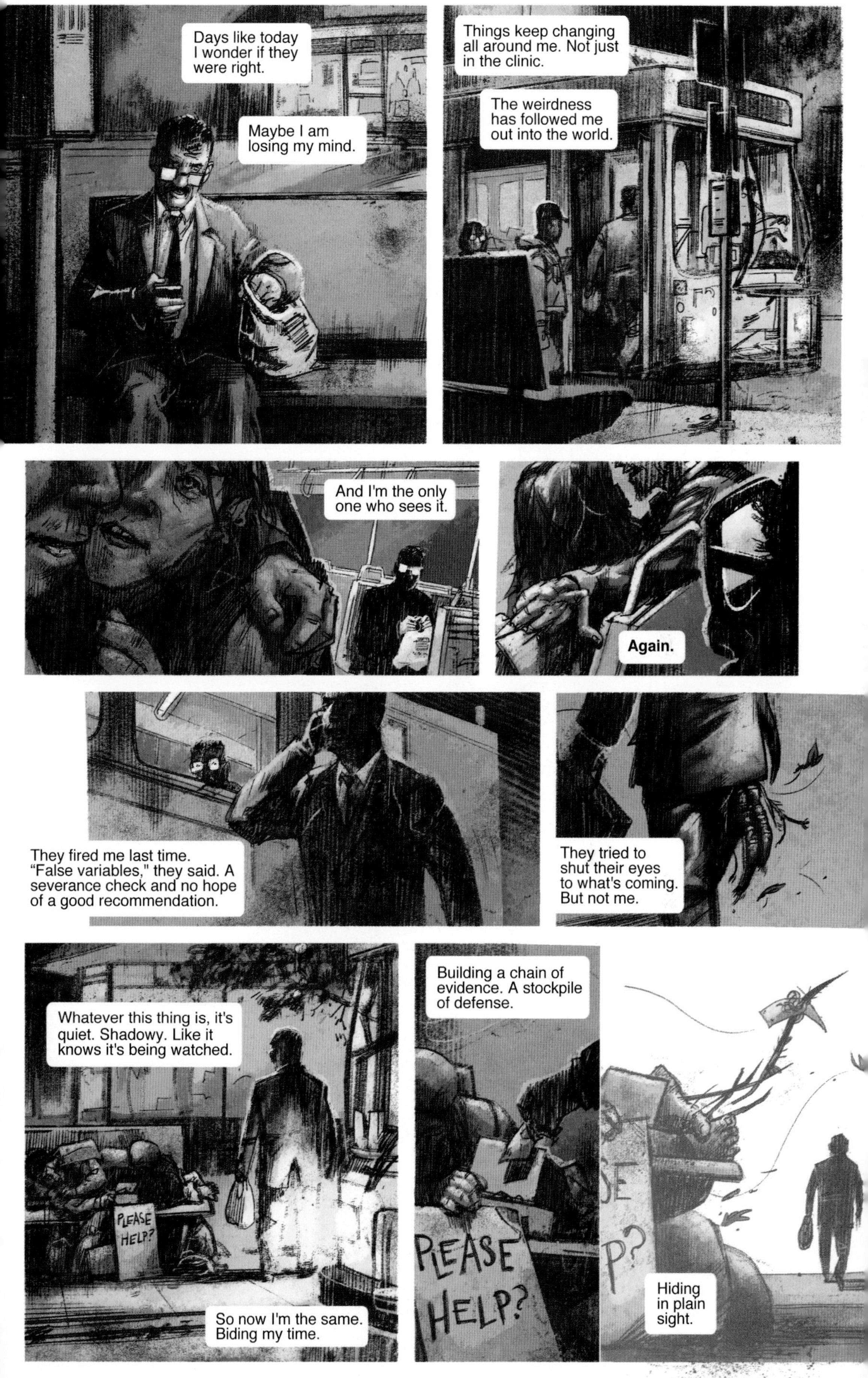
Days like today I wonder if they were right.
Maybe I am losing my mind.
Things keep changing all around me. Not just in the clinic.
The weirdness has followed me out into the world.
And I'm the only one who sees it.
Again.
They fired me last time. "False variables," they said. A severance check and no hope of a good recommendation.
They tried to shut their eyes to what's coming. But not me.
Whatever this thing is, it's quiet. Shadowy. Like it knows it's being watched.
PLEASE HELP?
So now I'm the same. Biding my time.
Building a chain of evidence. A stockpile of defense.
PLEASE HELP?
Hiding in plain sight.

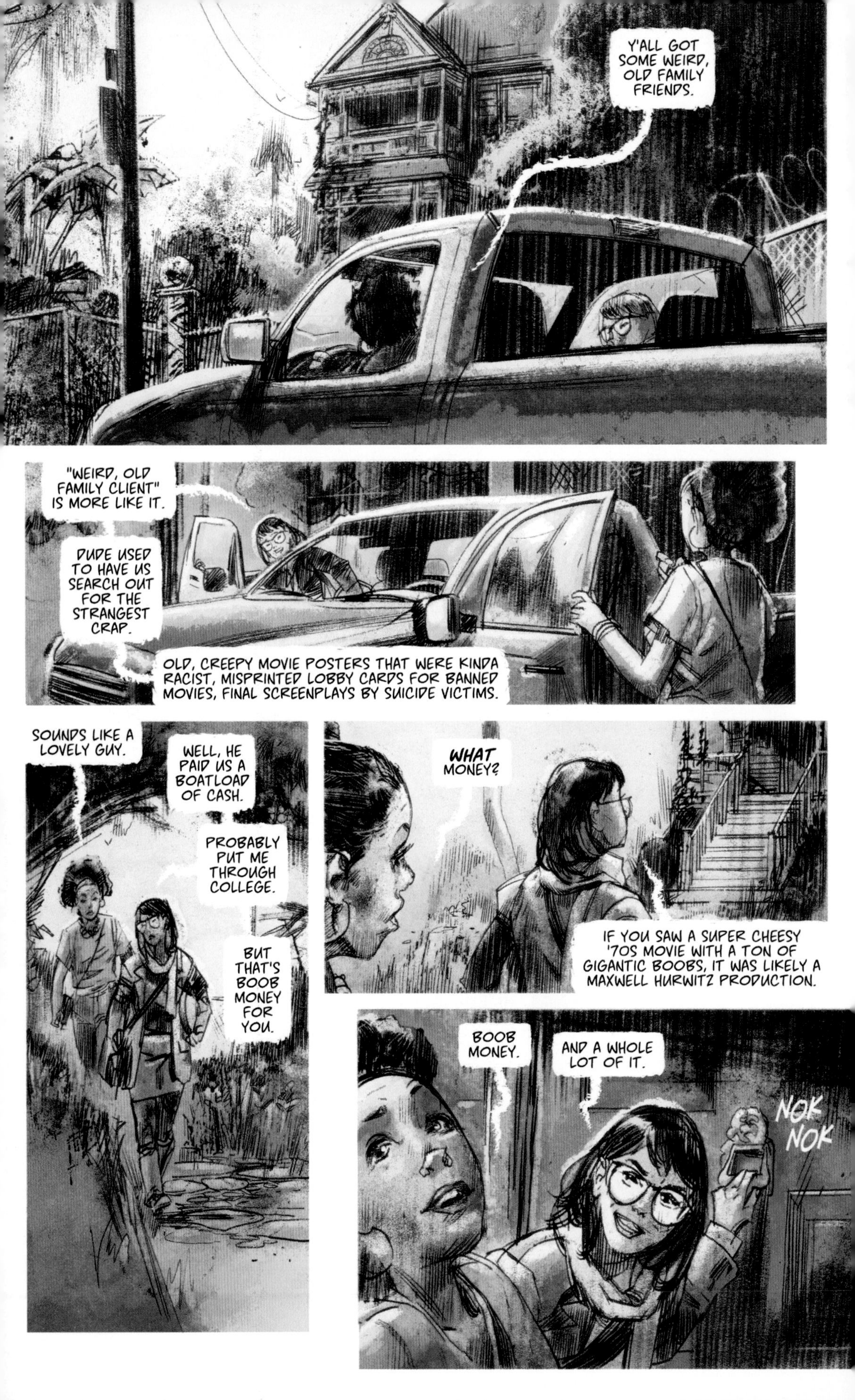
Y'ALL GOT SOME WEIRD, OLD FAMILY FRIENDS.
"WEIRD, OLD FAMILY CLIENT" IS MORE LIKE IT.
DUDE USED TO HAVE US SEARCH OUT FOR THE STRANGEST CRAP.
OLD, CREEPY MOVIE POSTERS THAT WERE KINDA RACIST, MISPRINTED LOBBY CARDS FOR BANNED MOVIES, FINAL SCREENPLAYS BY SUICIDE VICTIMS.
SOUNDS LIKE A LOVELY GUY.
WELL, HE PAID US A BOATLOAD OF CASH.
PROBABLY PUT ME THROUGH COLLEGE.
BUT THAT'S BOOB MONEY FOR YOU.
WHAT MONEY?
IF YOU SAW A SUPER CHEESY '70S MOVIE WITH A TON OF GIGANTIC BOOBS, IT WAS LIKELY A MAXWELL HURWITZ PRODUCTION.
BOOB MONEY.
AND A WHOLE LOT OF IT.
NOK NOK

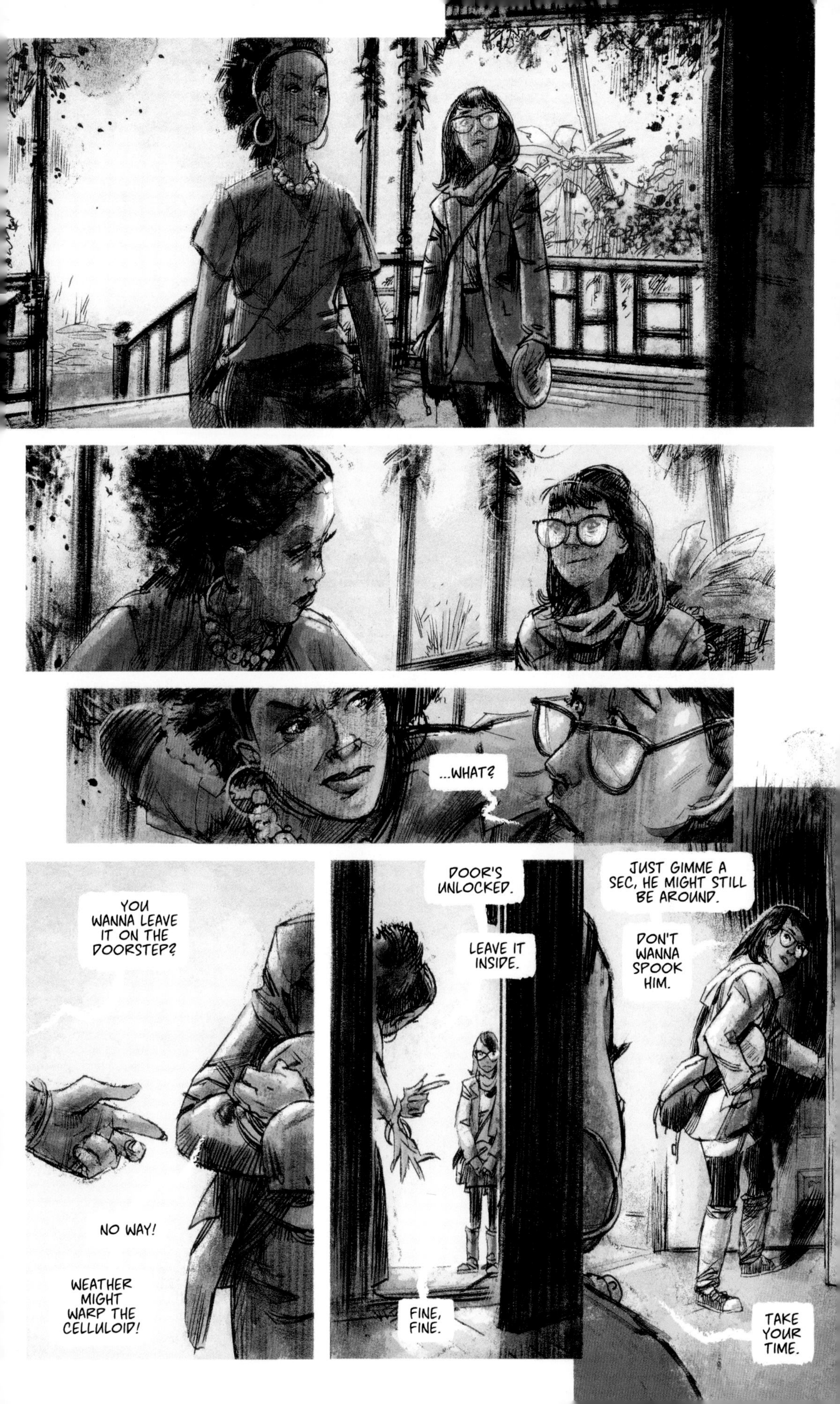
...WHAT?
YOU WANNA LEAVE IT ON THE DOORSTEP?
NO WAY!
WEATHER MIGHT WARP THE CELLULOID!
DOOR'S UNLOCKED.
LEAVE IT INSIDE.
FINE, FINE.
JUST GIMME A SEC, HE MIGHT STILL BE AROUND.
DON'T WANNA SPOOK HIM.
TAKE YOUR TIME.

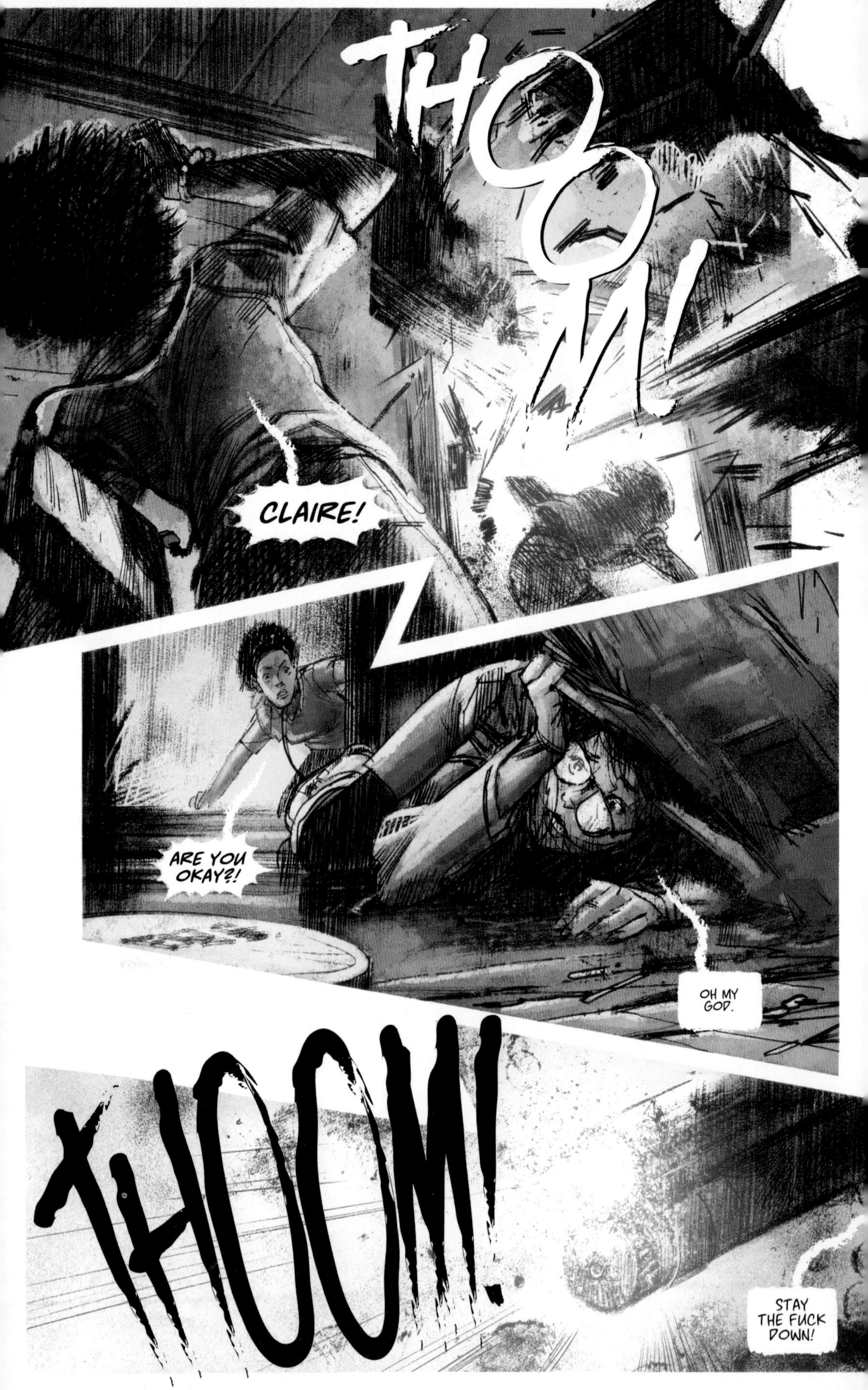
THOOM!
CLAIRE!
ARE YOU OKAY?!
OH MY GOD.
THOOM!
STAY THE FUCK DOWN!

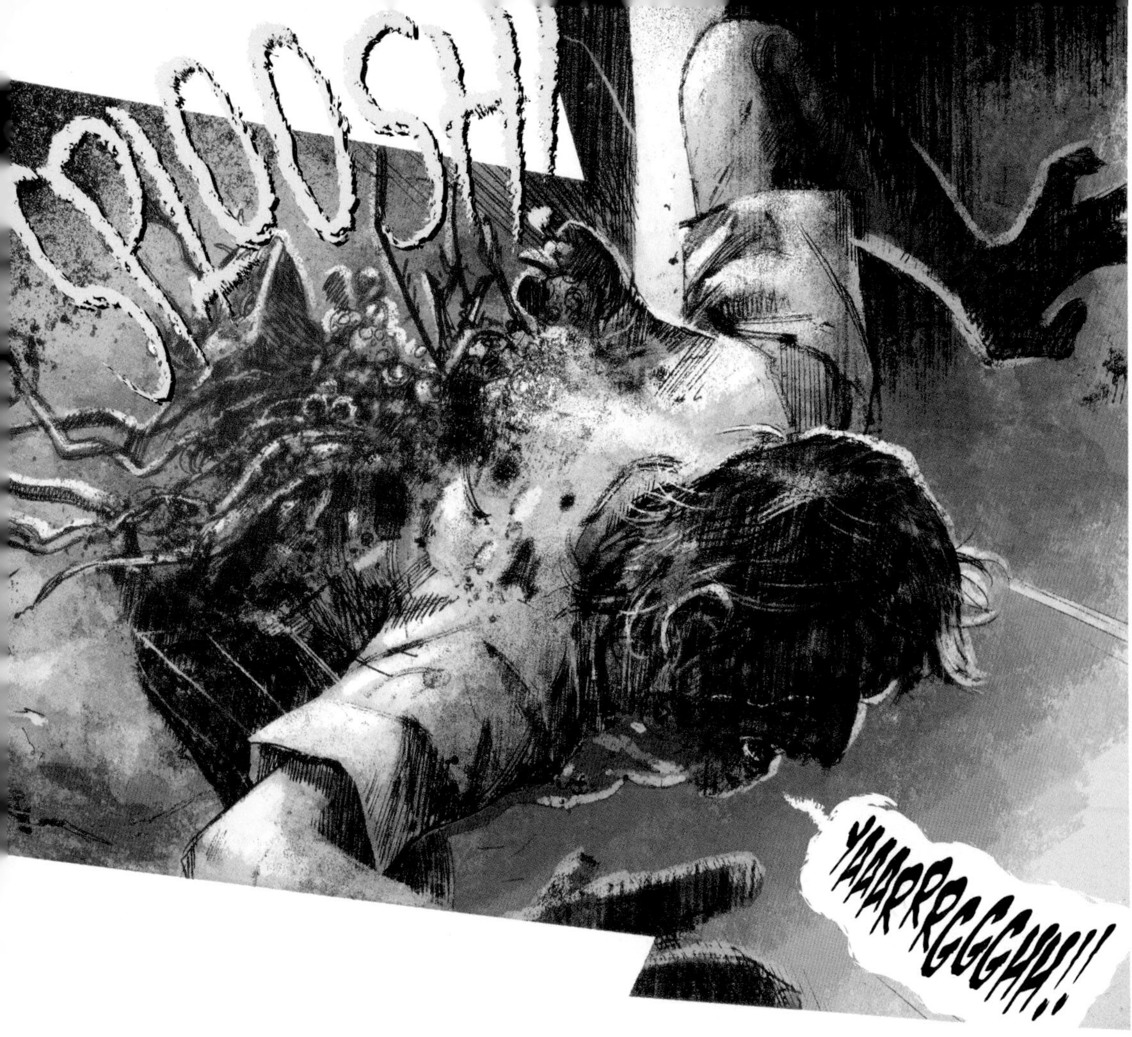
SPLOOSH!
YAAARRRGGGHH!!
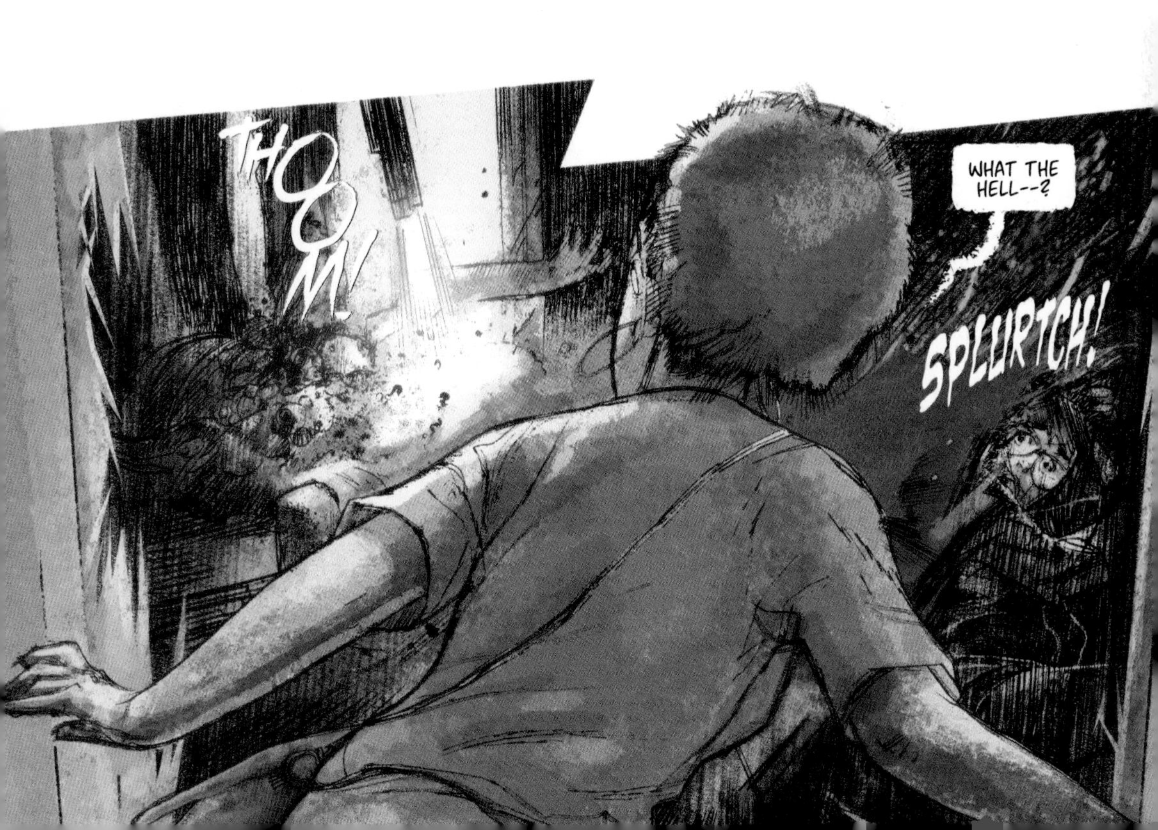
THOOM!
WHAT THE HELL--?
SPLURTCH!

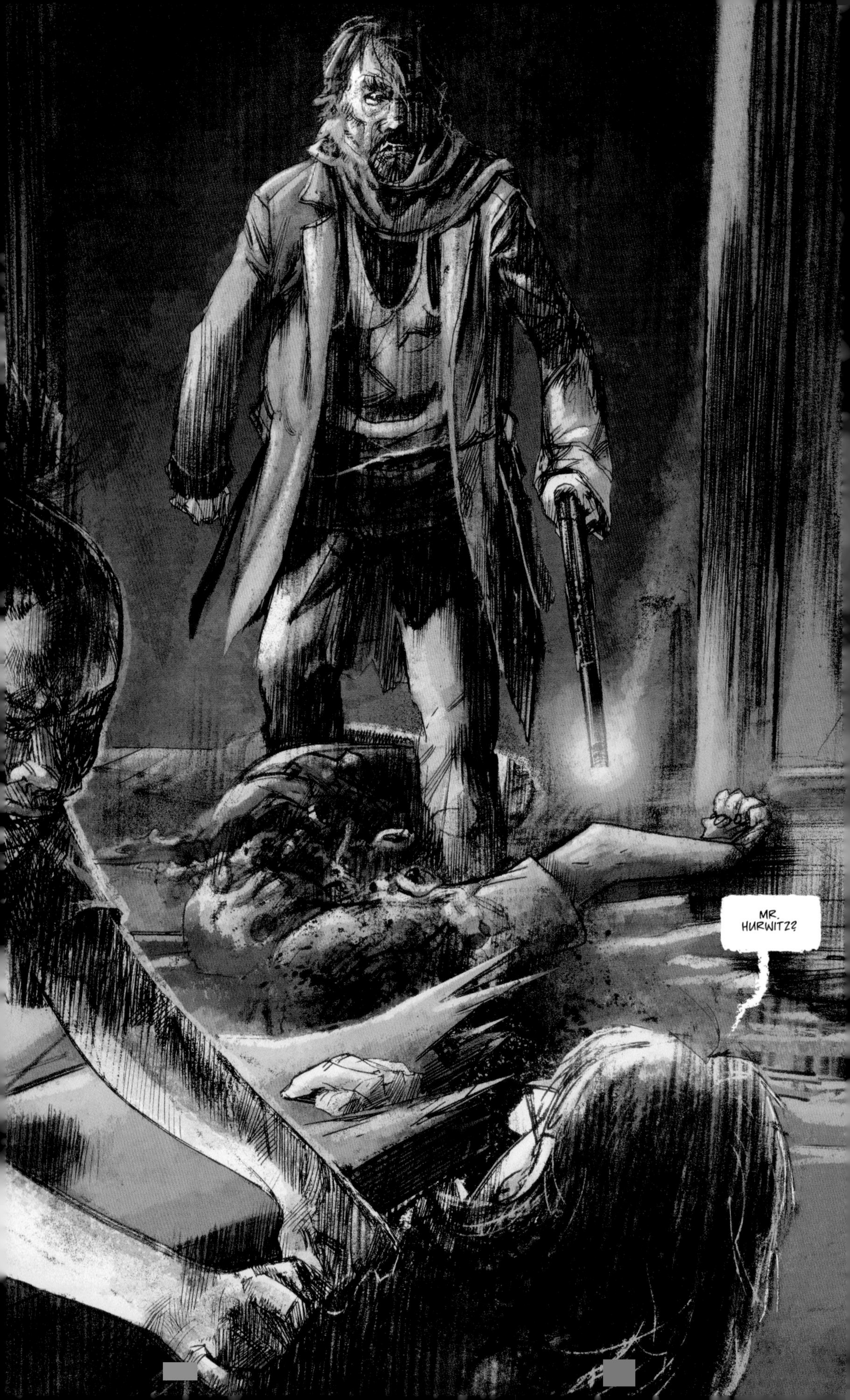
MR. HURWITZ?

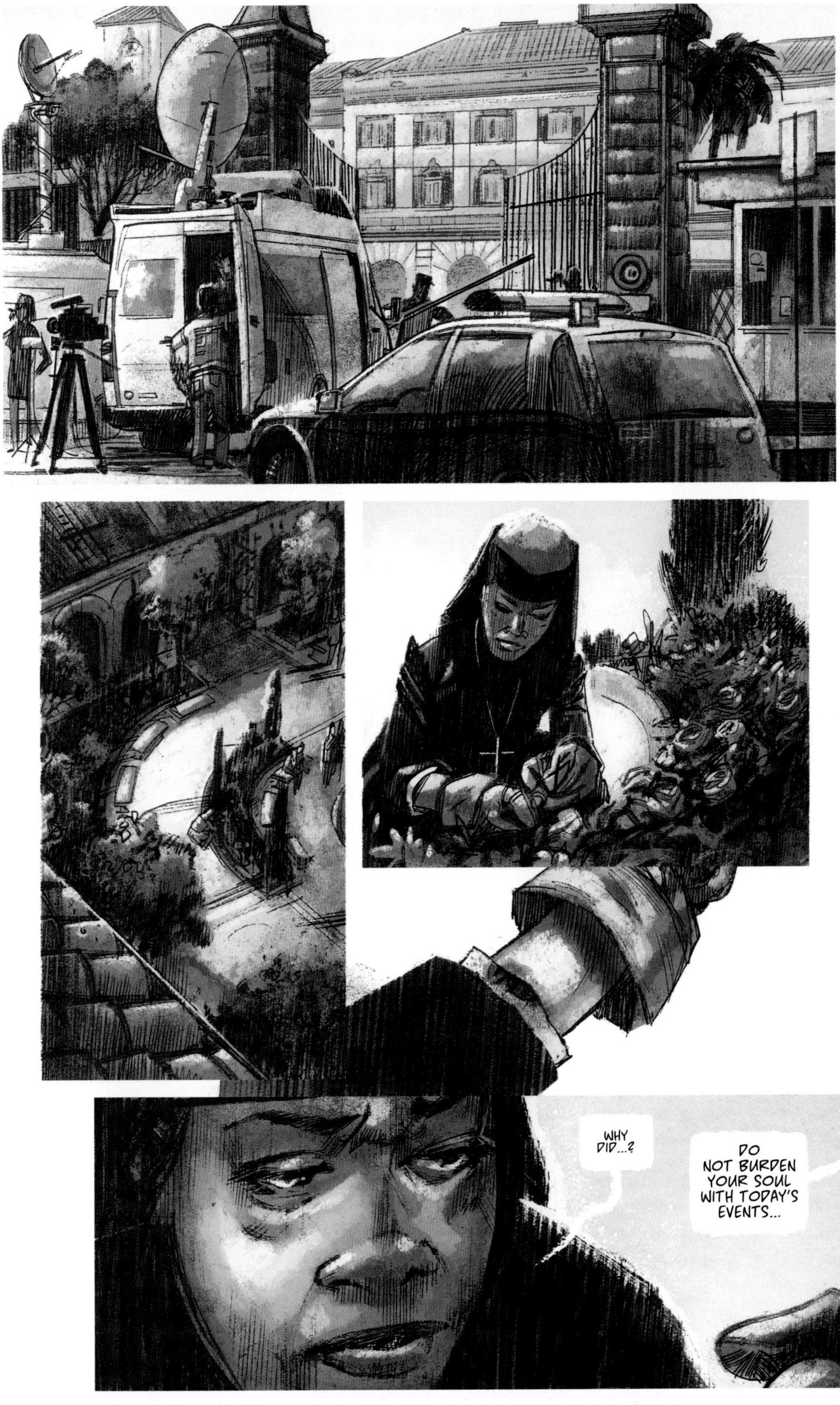
WHY DID...?
DO NOT BURDEN YOUR SOUL WITH TODAY'S EVENTS...

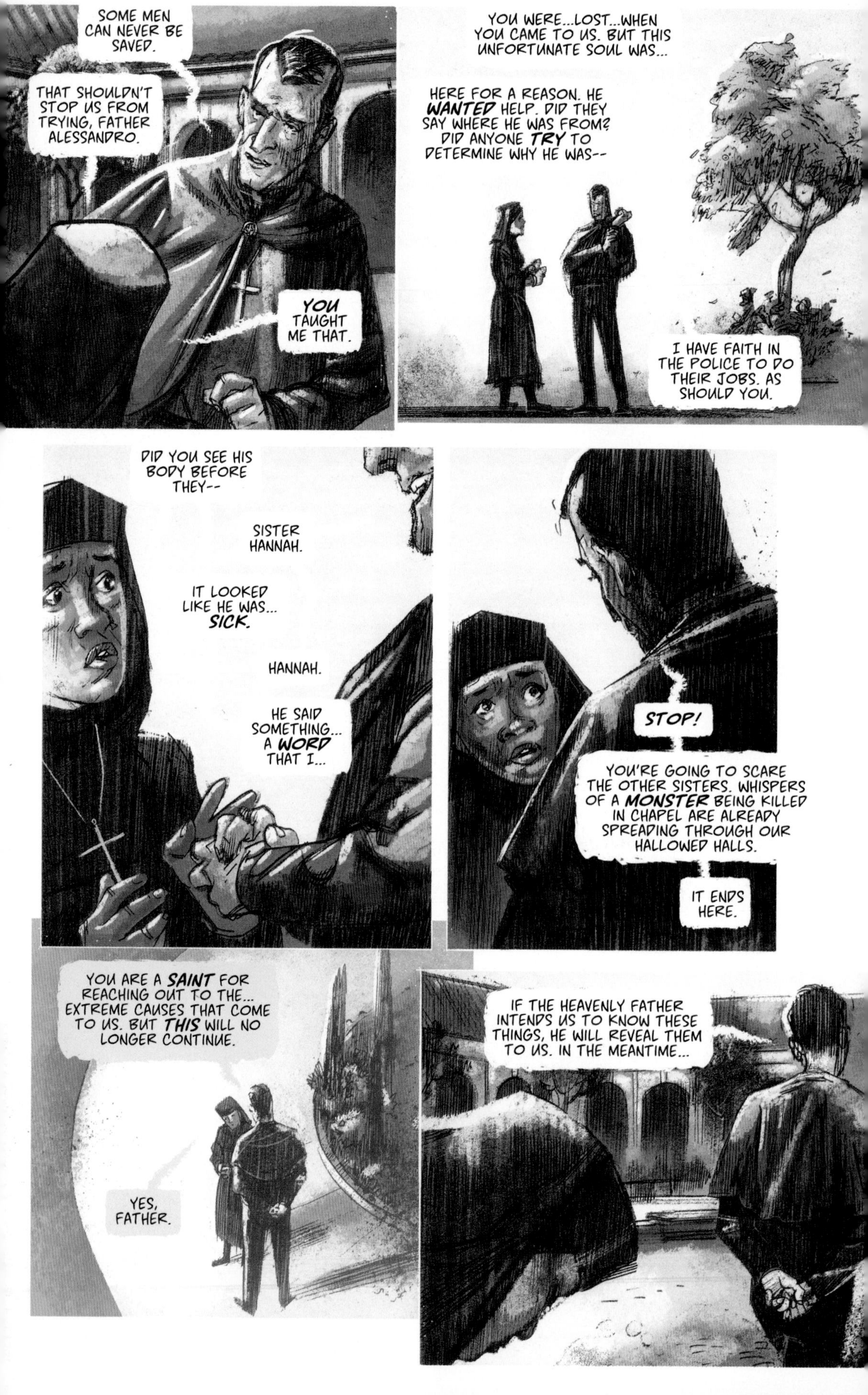
SOME MEN CAN NEVER BE SAVED.
THAT SHOULDN'T STOP US FROM TRYING, FATHER ALESSANDRO.
YOU TAUGHT ME THAT.
YOU WERE...LOST...WHEN YOU CAME TO US. BUT THIS UNFORTUNATE SOUL WAS...
HERE FOR A REASON. HE WANTED HELP. DID THEY SAY WHERE HE WAS FROM? DID ANYONE TRY TO DETERMINE WHY HE WAS--
I HAVE FAITH IN THE POLICE TO DO THEIR JOBS. AS SHOULD YOU.
DID YOU SEE HIS BODY BEFORE THEY--
SISTER HANNAH.
IT LOOKED LIKE HE WAS... SICK.
HANNAH.
HE SAID SOMETHING... A WORD THAT I...
STOP!
YOU'RE GOING TO SCARE THE OTHER SISTERS. WHISPERS OF A MONSTER BEING KILLED IN CHAPEL ARE ALREADY SPREADING THROUGH OUR HALLOWED HALLS.
IT ENDS HERE.
YOU ARE A SAINT FOR REACHING OUT TO THE... EXTREME CAUSES THAT COME TO US. BUT THIS WILL NO LONGER CONTINUE.
YES, FATHER.
IF THE HEAVENLY FATHER INTENDS US TO KNOW THESE THINGS, HE WILL REVEAL THEM TO US. IN THE MEANTIME...

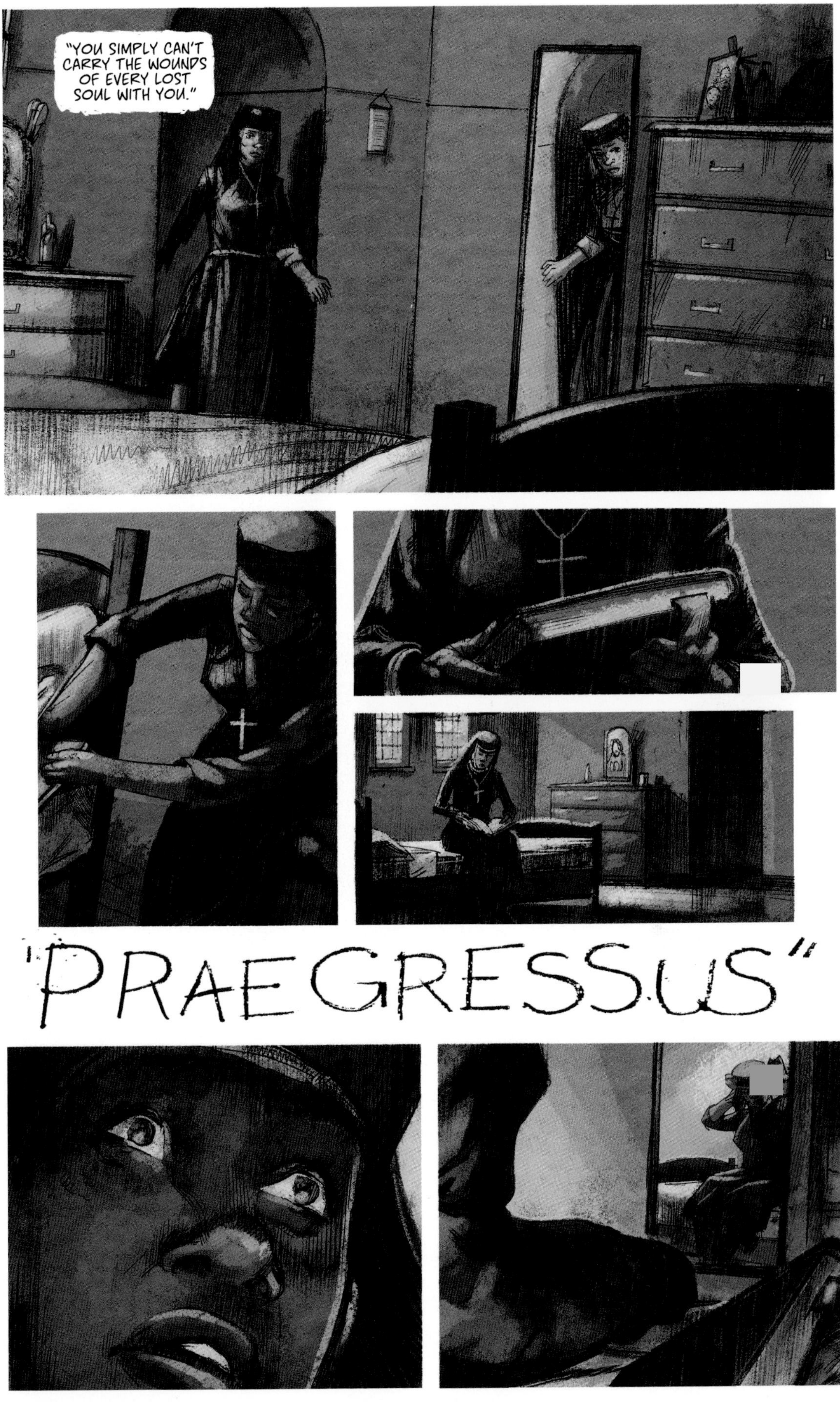
"YOU SIMPLY CAN'T CARRY THE WOUNDS OF EVERY LOST SOUL WITH YOU."
"PRAEGRESSUS"

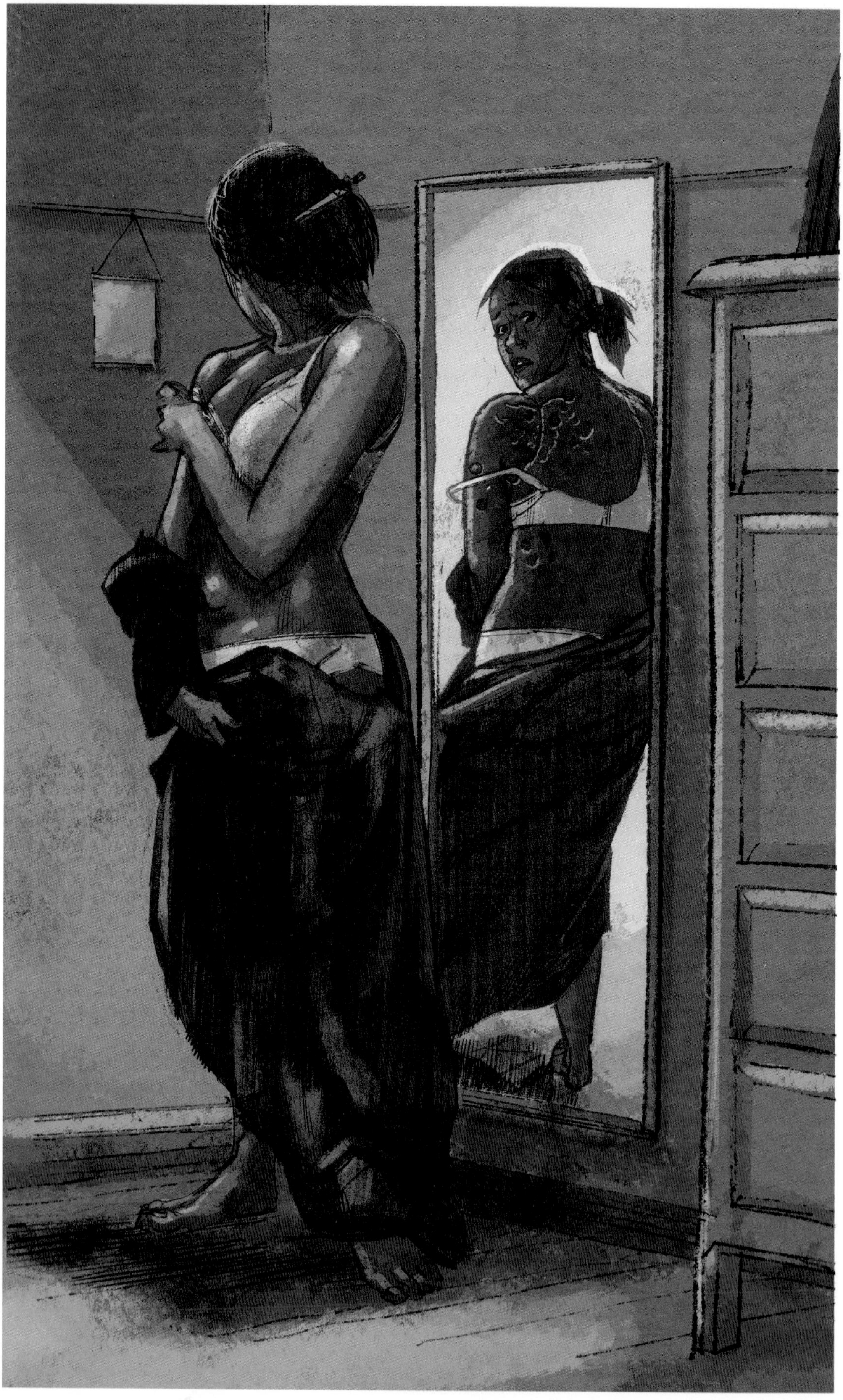

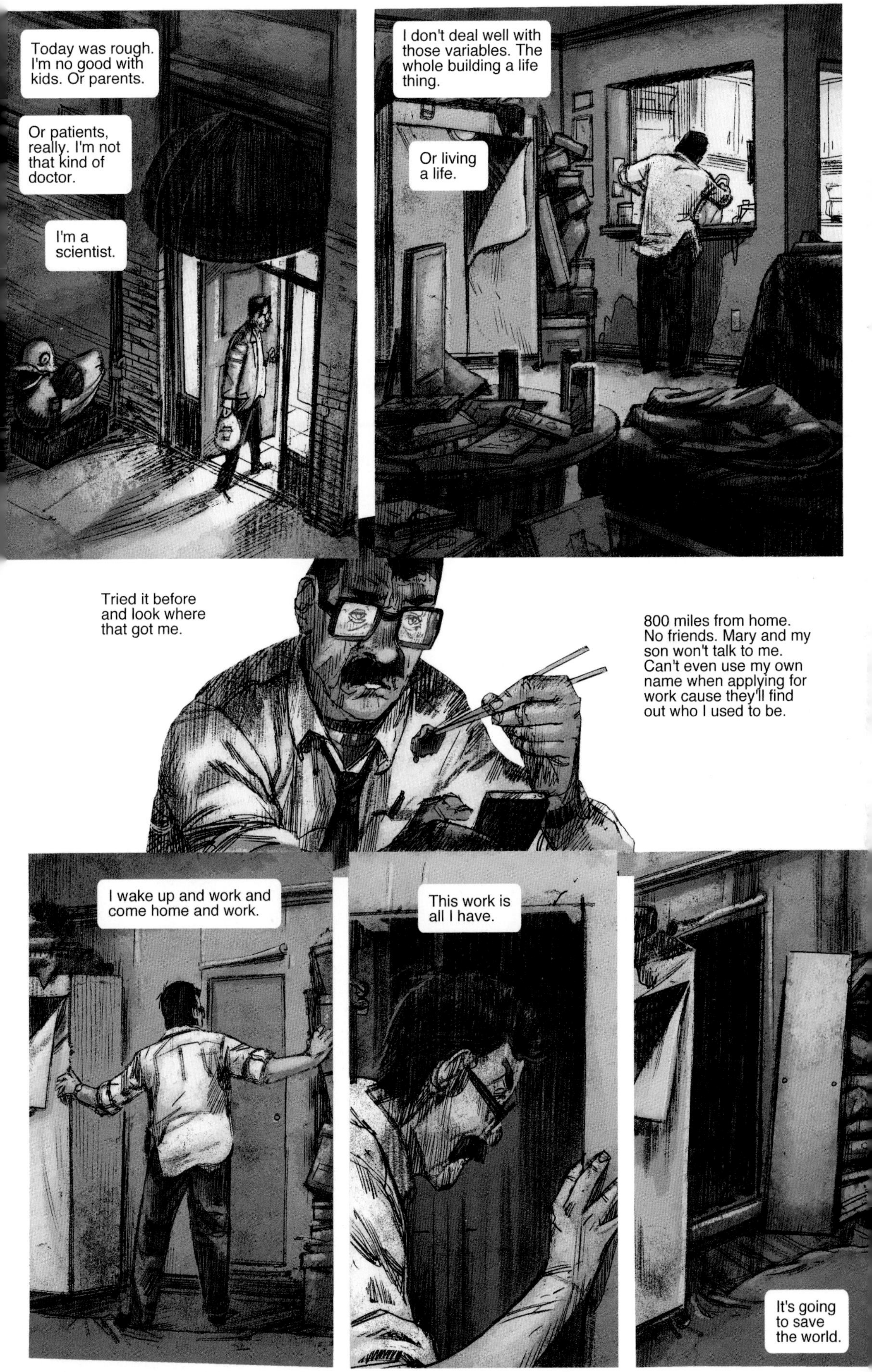
Today was rough. I'm no good with kids. Or parents.
Or patients, really. I'm not that kind of doctor.
I'm a scientist.
I don't deal well with those variables. The whole building a life thing.
Or living a life.
Tried it before and look where that got me.
800 miles from home. No friends. Mary and my son won't talk to me. Can't even use my own name when applying for work cause they'll find out who I used to be.
I wake up and work and come home and work.
This work is all I have.
It's going to save the world.

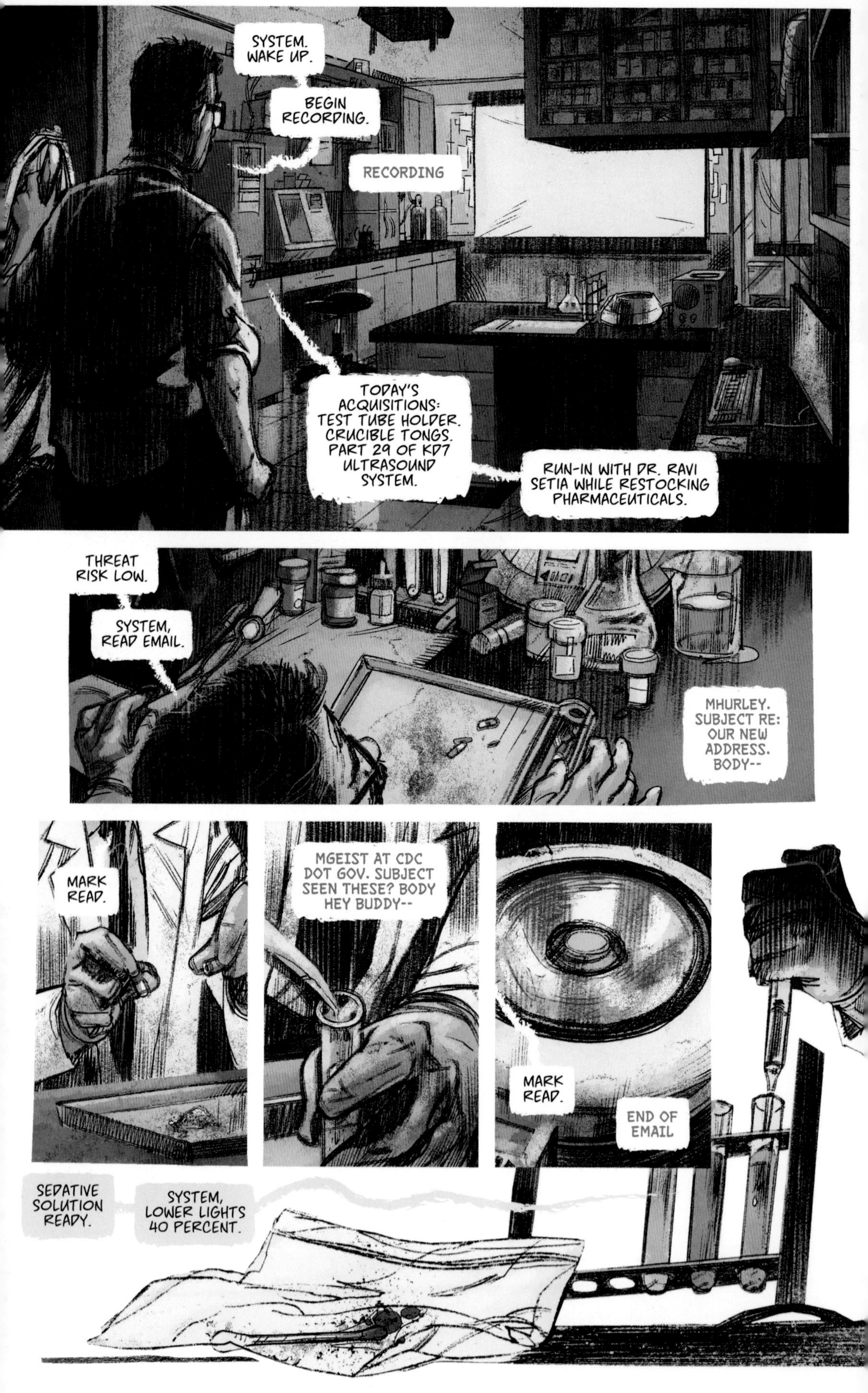
SYSTEM. WAKE UP.
BEGIN RECORDING.
RECORDING
TODAY'S ACQUISITIONS: TEST TUBE HOLDER. CRUCIBLE TONGS. PART 29 OF KD7 ULTRASOUND SYSTEM.
RUN-IN WITH DR. RAVI SETIA WHILE RESTOCKING PHARMACEUTICALS.
THREAT RISK LOW.
SYSTEM, READ EMAIL.
MHURLEY. SUBJECT RE: OUR NEW ADDRESS. BODY--
MARK READ.
MGEIST AT CDC DOT GOV. SUBJECT SEEN THESE? BODY HEY BUDDY--
MARK READ.
END OF EMAIL
SEDATIVE SOLUTION READY.
SYSTEM, LOWER LIGHTS 40 PERCENT.

SUBJECT: SEVEN-YEAR-OLD. HISPANIC. DIAGNOSED WITH ASTHMA.

SYMPTOMS HAVE ALLEGEDLY VANISHED. FURTHER EXPLORATION INTERRUPTED BY...

GILLS. THE KID HAD GILLS.

IF THEIR ARRIVAL COINCIDES WITH THE ERASURE OF SYMPTOMS, THIS FOLLOWS MY HYPOTHESIS.

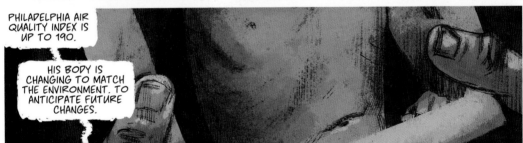

PHILADELPHIA AIR QUALITY INDEX IS UP TO 190.

HIS BODY IS CHANGING TO MATCH THE ENVIRONMENT. TO ANTICIPATE FUTURE CHANGES.

IT'S AN *EVOLUTION.*

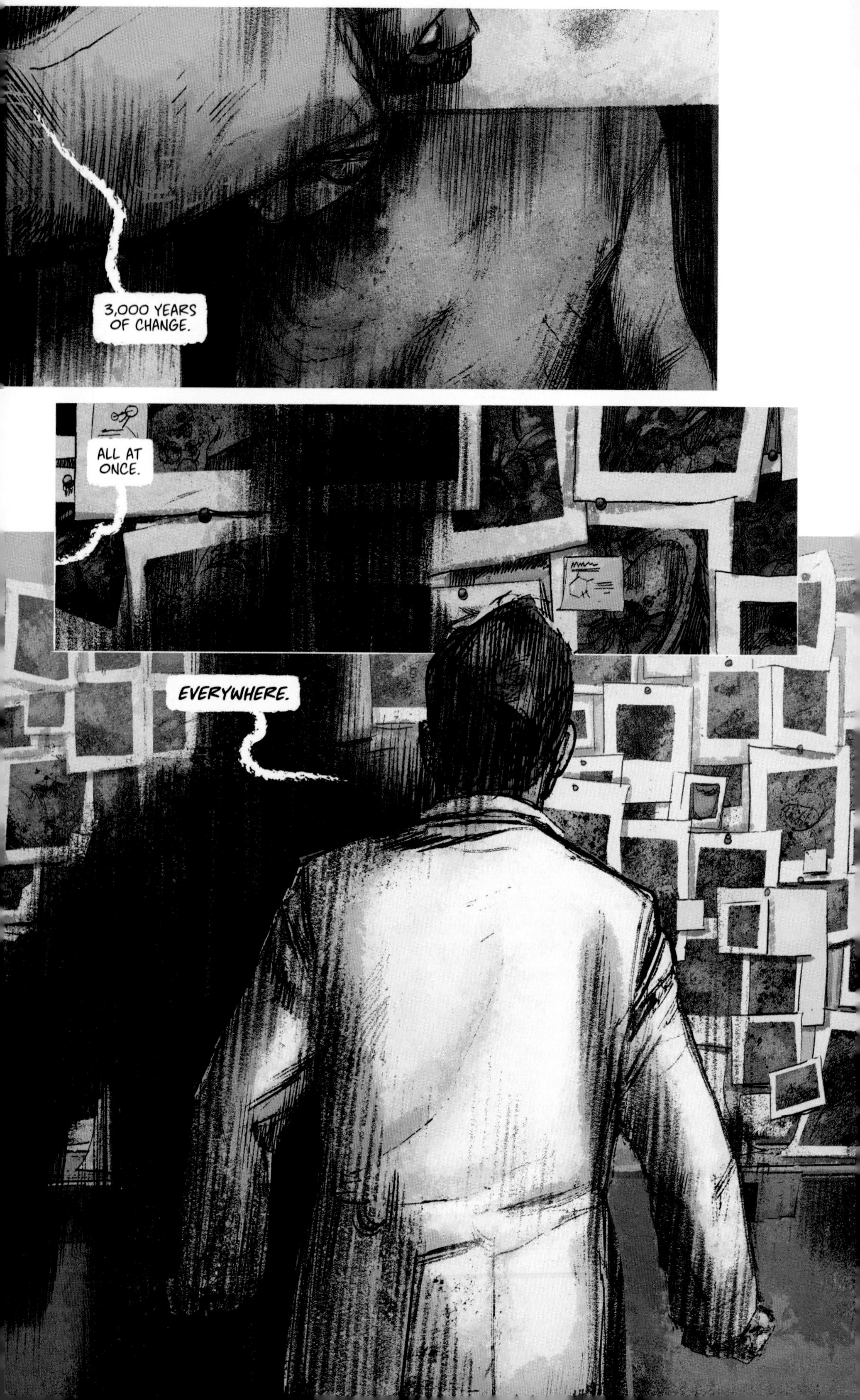
3,000 YEARS OF CHANGE.
ALL AT ONCE.
EVERYWHERE.

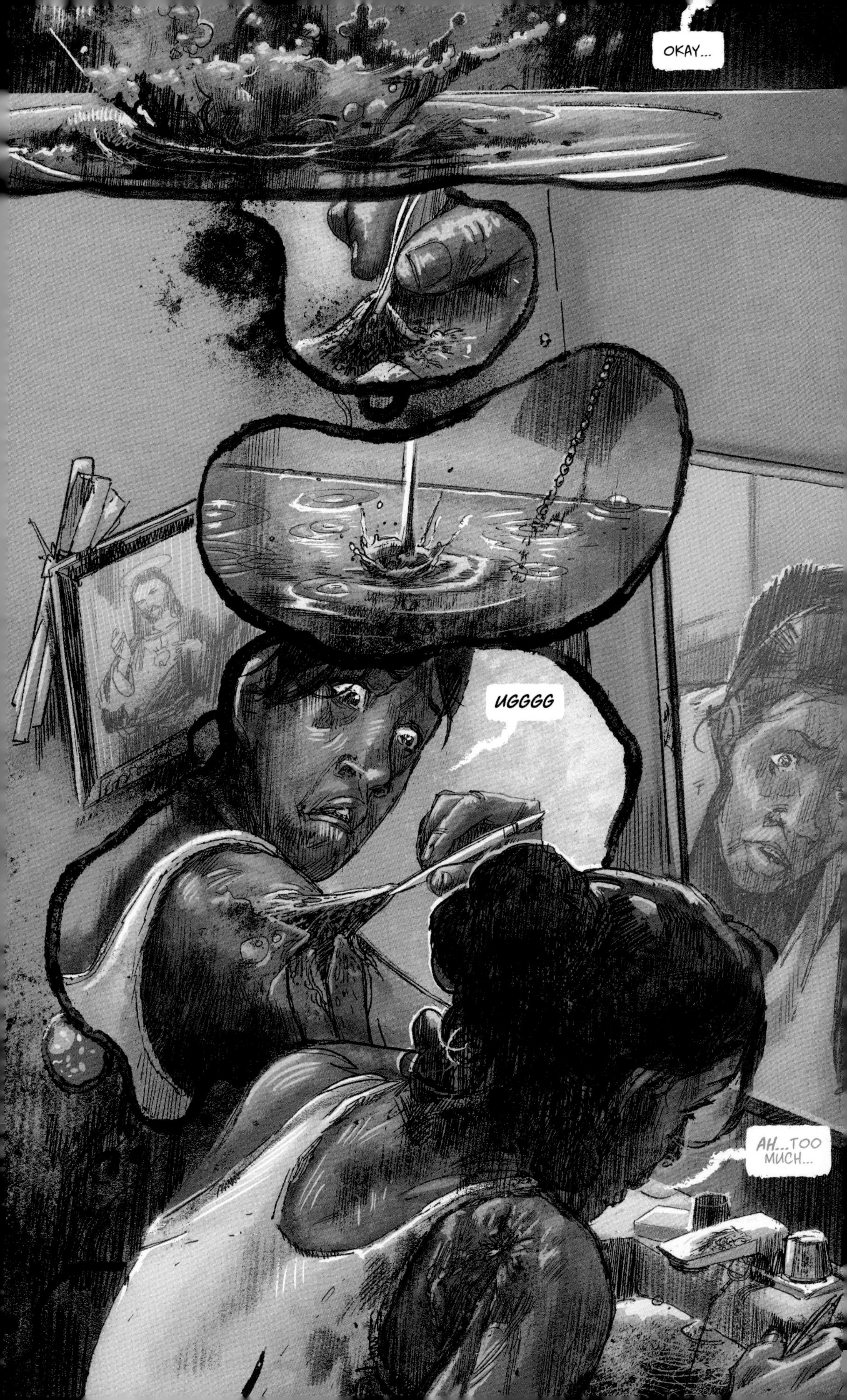
OKAY...
UGGGG
AH...TOO MUCH...

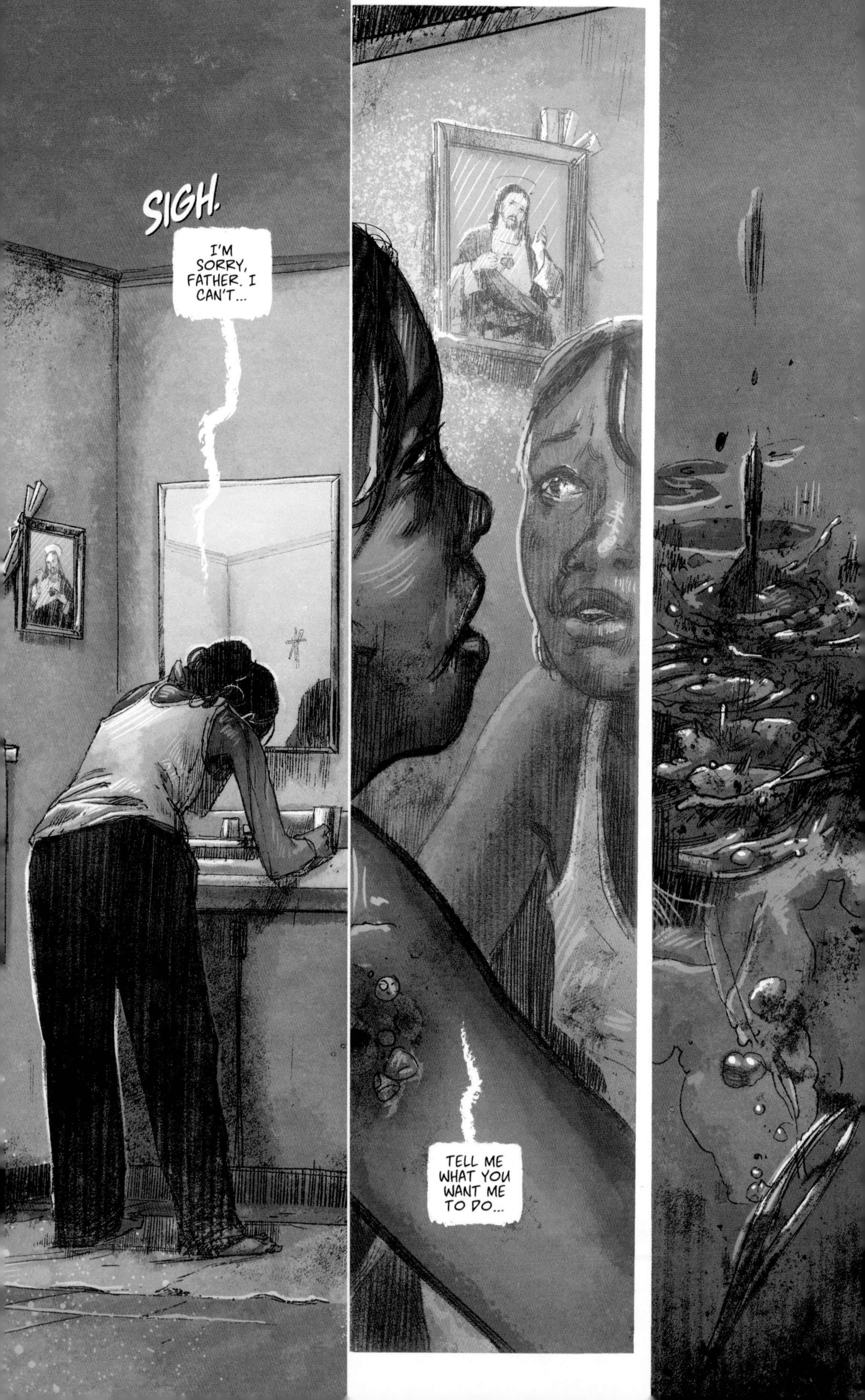
SIGH.
I'M SORRY, FATHER. I CAN'T...
TELL ME WHAT YOU WANT ME TO DO...

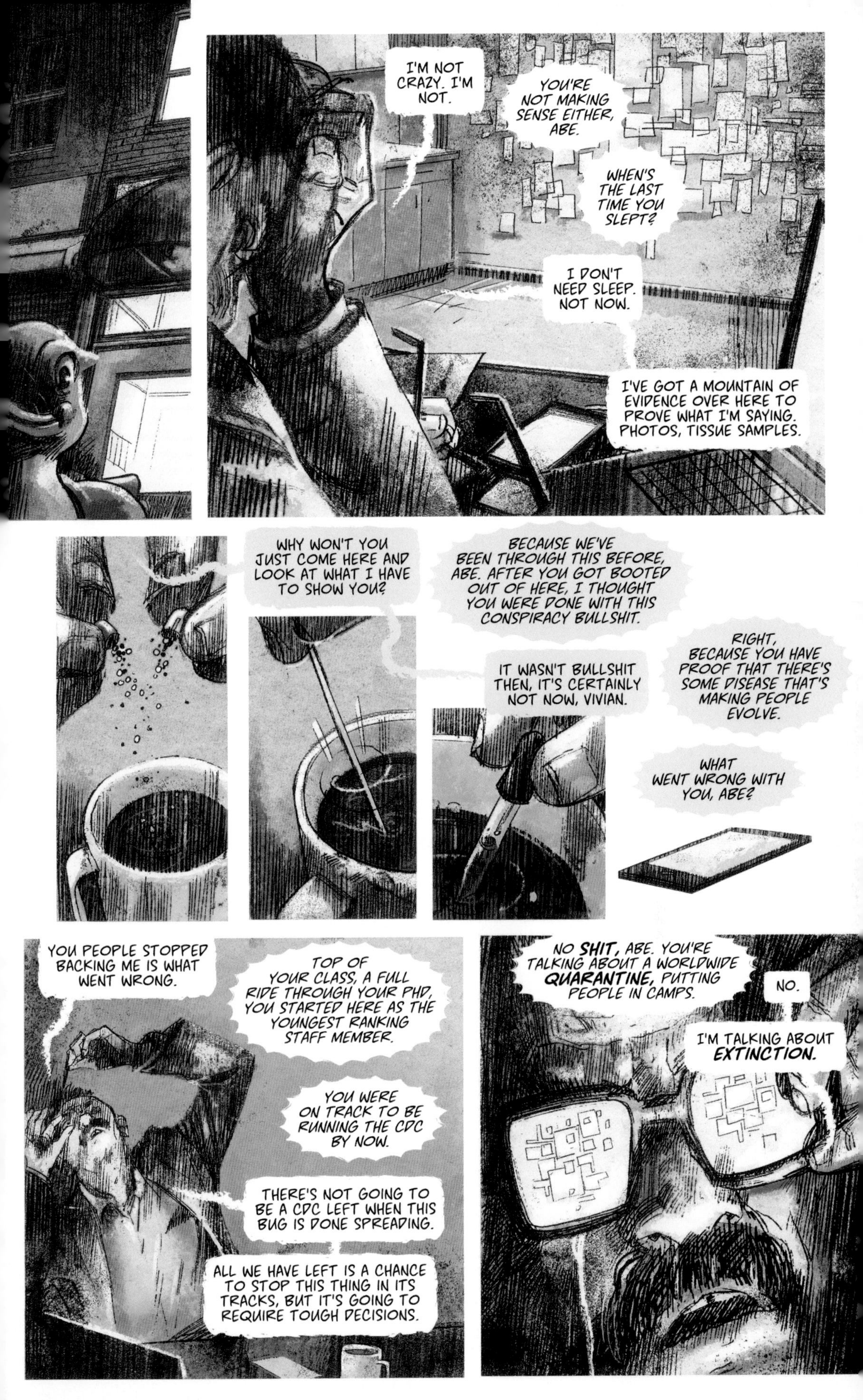
I'M NOT CRAZY. I'M NOT.
YOU'RE NOT MAKING SENSE EITHER, ABE.
WHEN'S THE LAST TIME YOU SLEPT?
I DON'T NEED SLEEP. NOT NOW.
I'VE GOT A MOUNTAIN OF EVIDENCE OVER HERE TO PROVE WHAT I'M SAYING. PHOTOS, TISSUE SAMPLES.
WHY WON'T YOU JUST COME HERE AND LOOK AT WHAT I HAVE TO SHOW YOU?
BECAUSE WE'VE BEEN THROUGH THIS BEFORE, ABE. AFTER YOU GOT BOOTED OUT OF HERE, I THOUGHT YOU WERE DONE WITH THIS CONSPIRACY BULLSHIT.
IT WASN'T BULLSHIT THEN, IT'S CERTAINLY NOT NOW, VIVIAN.
RIGHT, BECAUSE YOU HAVE PROOF THAT THERE'S SOME DISEASE THAT'S MAKING PEOPLE EVOLVE.
WHAT WENT WRONG WITH YOU, ABE?
YOU PEOPLE STOPPED BACKING ME IS WHAT WENT WRONG.
TOP OF YOUR CLASS, A FULL RIDE THROUGH YOUR PHD, YOU STARTED HERE AS THE YOUNGEST RANKING STAFF MEMBER.
YOU WERE ON TRACK TO BE RUNNING THE CDC BY NOW.
THERE'S NOT GOING TO BE A CDC LEFT WHEN THIS BUG IS DONE SPREADING.
ALL WE HAVE LEFT IS A CHANCE TO STOP THIS THING IN ITS TRACKS, BUT IT'S GOING TO REQUIRE TOUGH DECISIONS.
NO SHIT, ABE. YOU'RE TALKING ABOUT A WORLDWIDE QUARANTINE, PUTTING PEOPLE IN CAMPS.
NO.
I'M TALKING ABOUT EXTINCTION.

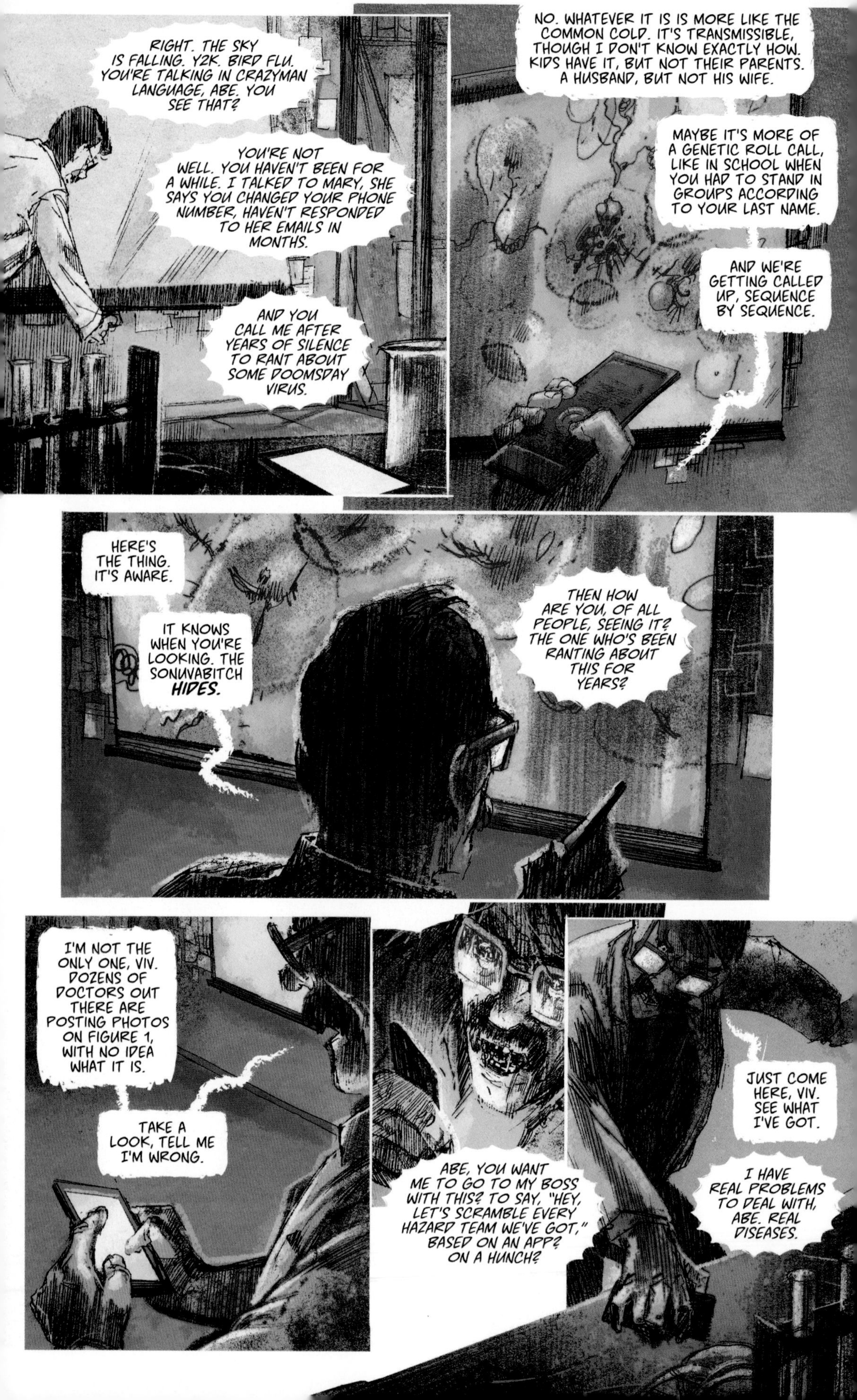
RIGHT. THE SKY IS FALLING. Y2K. BIRD FLU. YOU'RE TALKING IN CRAZYMAN LANGUAGE, ABE. YOU SEE THAT?
YOU'RE NOT WELL. YOU HAVEN'T BEEN FOR A WHILE. I TALKED TO MARY, SHE SAYS YOU CHANGED YOUR PHONE NUMBER, HAVEN'T RESPONDED TO HER EMAILS IN MONTHS.
AND YOU CALL ME AFTER YEARS OF SILENCE TO RANT ABOUT SOME DOOMSDAY VIRUS.
NO. WHATEVER IT IS IS MORE LIKE THE COMMON COLD. IT'S TRANSMISSIBLE, THOUGH I DON'T KNOW EXACTLY HOW. KIDS HAVE IT, BUT NOT THEIR PARENTS. A HUSBAND, BUT NOT HIS WIFE.
MAYBE IT'S MORE OF A GENETIC ROLL CALL, LIKE IN SCHOOL WHEN YOU HAD TO STAND IN GROUPS ACCORDING TO YOUR LAST NAME.
AND WE'RE GETTING CALLED UP, SEQUENCE BY SEQUENCE.
HERE'S THE THING. IT'S AWARE.
IT KNOWS WHEN YOU'RE LOOKING. THE SONUVABITCH **HIDES.**
THEN HOW ARE YOU, OF ALL PEOPLE, SEEING IT? THE ONE WHO'S BEEN RANTING ABOUT THIS FOR YEARS?
I'M NOT THE ONLY ONE, VIV. DOZENS OF DOCTORS OUT THERE ARE POSTING PHOTOS ON FIGURE 1, WITH NO IDEA WHAT IT IS.
TAKE A LOOK, TELL ME I'M WRONG.
ABE, YOU WANT ME TO GO TO MY BOSS WITH THIS? TO SAY, "HEY, LET'S SCRAMBLE EVERY HAZARD TEAM WE'VE GOT," BASED ON AN APP? ON A HUNCH?
JUST COME HERE, VIV. SEE WHAT I'VE GOT.
I HAVE REAL PROBLEMS TO DEAL WITH, ABE. REAL DISEASES.

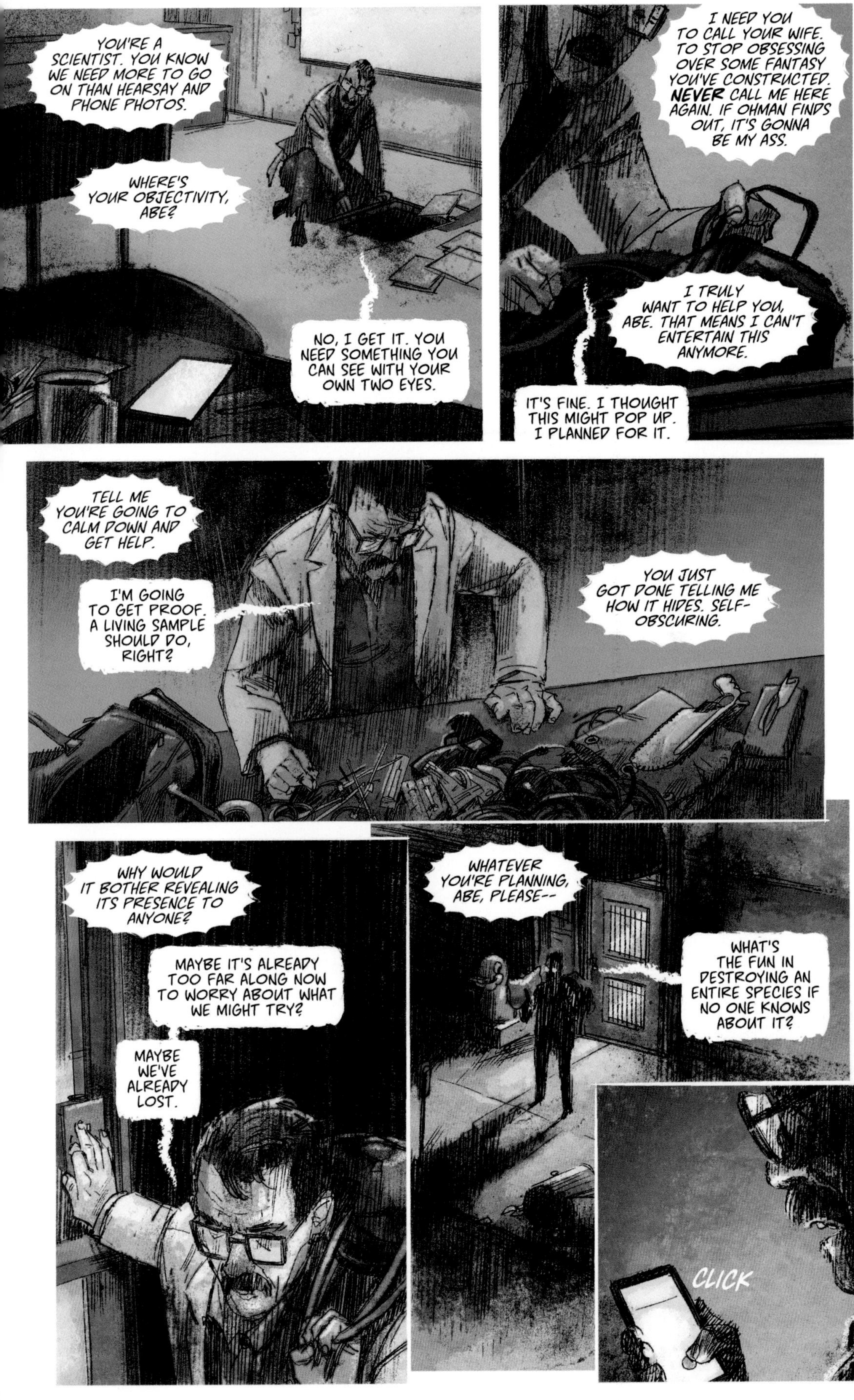
YOU'RE A SCIENTIST. YOU KNOW WE NEED MORE TO GO ON THAN HEARSAY AND PHONE PHOTOS.
WHERE'S YOUR OBJECTIVITY, ABE?
NO, I GET IT. YOU NEED SOMETHING YOU CAN SEE WITH YOUR OWN TWO EYES.
I NEED YOU TO CALL YOUR WIFE. TO STOP OBSESSING OVER SOME FANTASY YOU'VE CONSTRUCTED. **NEVER** CALL ME HERE AGAIN. IF OHMAN FINDS OUT, IT'S GONNA BE MY ASS.
I TRULY WANT TO HELP YOU, ABE. THAT MEANS I CAN'T ENTERTAIN THIS ANYMORE.
IT'S FINE. I THOUGHT THIS MIGHT POP UP. I PLANNED FOR IT.
TELL ME YOU'RE GOING TO CALM DOWN AND GET HELP.
I'M GOING TO GET PROOF. A LIVING SAMPLE SHOULD DO, RIGHT?
YOU JUST GOT DONE TELLING ME HOW IT HIDES. SELF-OBSCURING.
WHY WOULD IT BOTHER REVEALING ITS PRESENCE TO ANYONE?
MAYBE IT'S ALREADY TOO FAR ALONG NOW TO WORRY ABOUT WHAT WE MIGHT TRY?
MAYBE WE'VE ALREADY LOST.
WHATEVER YOU'RE PLANNING, ABE, PLEASE--
WHAT'S THE FUN IN DESTROYING AN ENTIRE SPECIES IF NO ONE KNOWS ABOUT IT?
CLICK

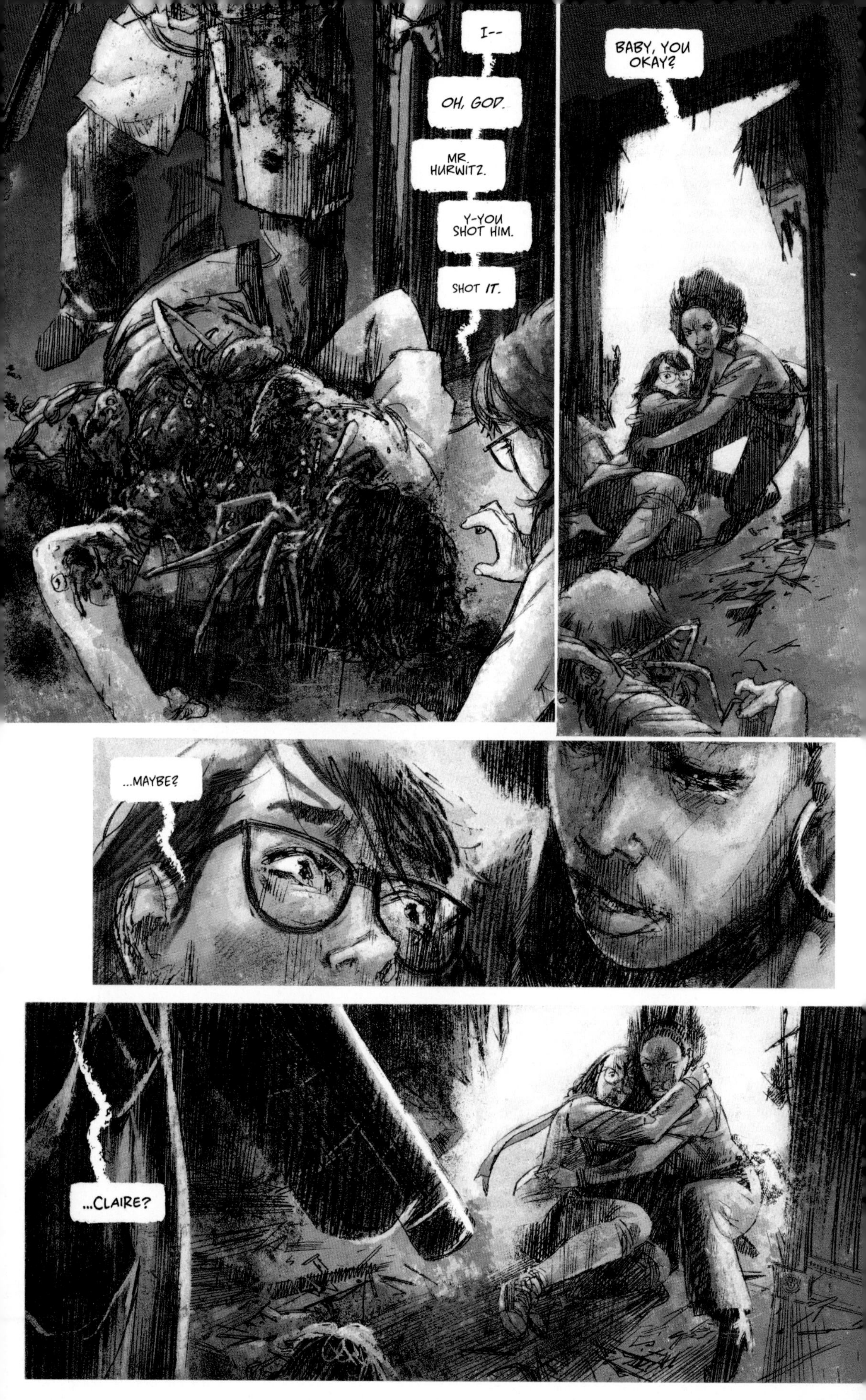
I--
OH, GOD.
MR. HURWITZ.
Y-YOU SHOT HIM.
SHOT IT.
BABY, YOU OKAY?
...MAYBE?
...CLAIRE?

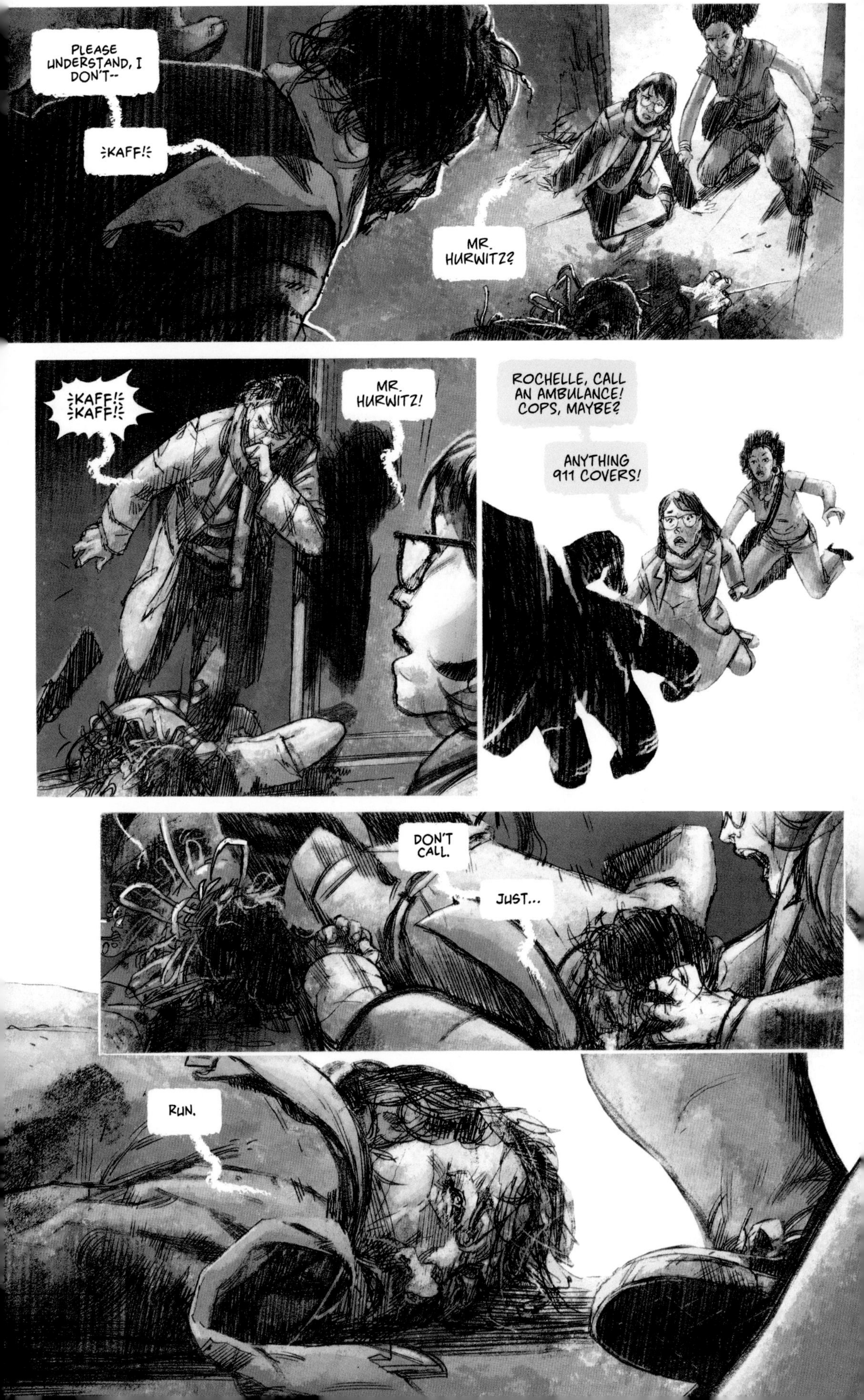
PLEASE UNDERSTAND, I DON'T--
¦KAFF!¦
MR. HURWITZ?
KAFF! KAFF!
MR. HURWITZ!
ROCHELLE, CALL AN AMBULANCE! COPS, MAYBE?
ANYTHING 911 COVERS!
DON'T CALL.
JUST...
RUN.

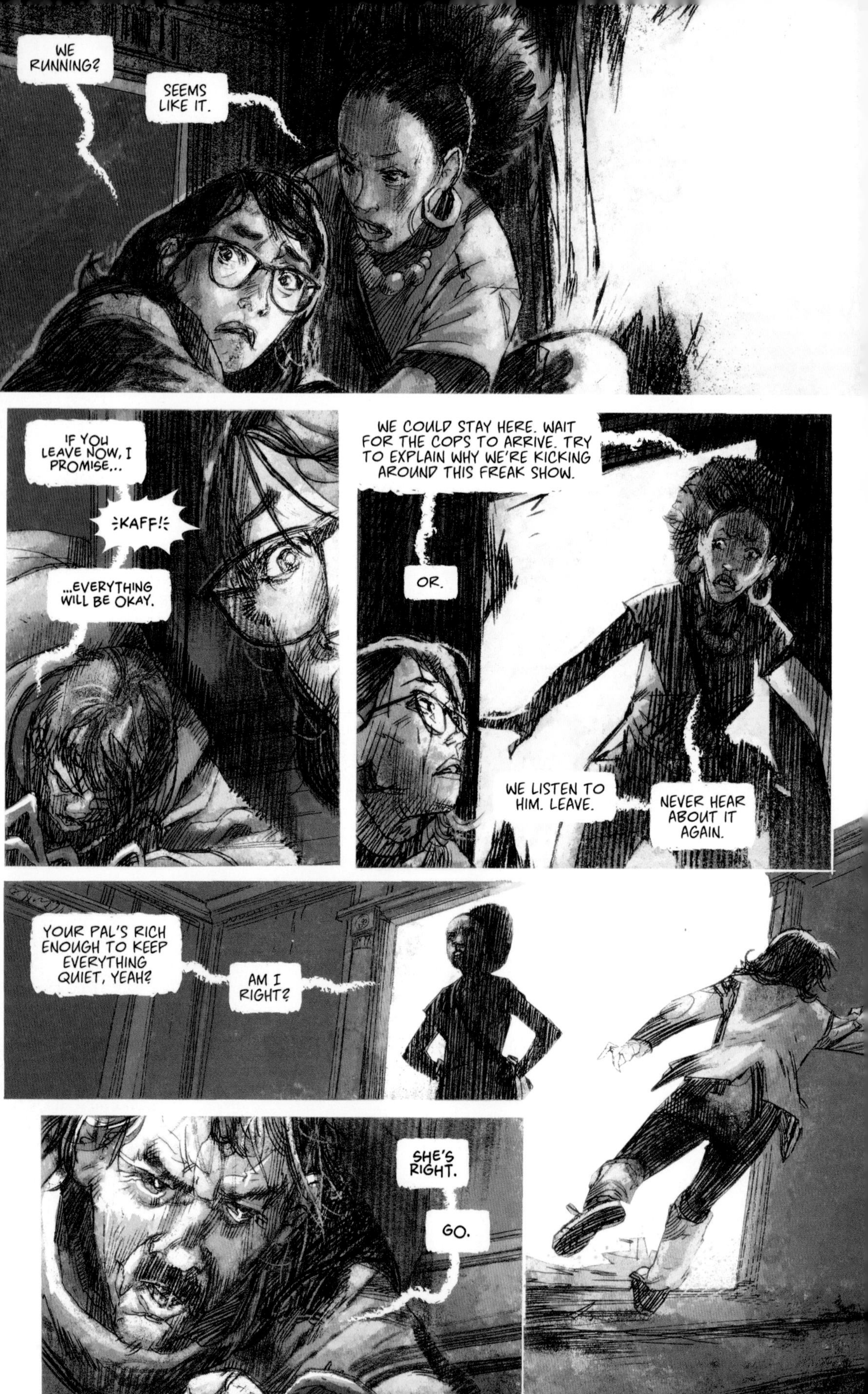
WE RUNNING?
SEEMS LIKE IT.
IF YOU LEAVE NOW, I PROMISE...
KAFF!
...EVERYTHING WILL BE OKAY.
WE COULD STAY HERE. WAIT FOR THE COPS TO ARRIVE. TRY TO EXPLAIN WHY WE'RE KICKING AROUND THIS FREAK SHOW.
OR.
WE LISTEN TO HIM. LEAVE.
NEVER HEAR ABOUT IT AGAIN.
YOUR PAL'S RICH ENOUGH TO KEEP EVERYTHING QUIET, YEAH?
AM I RIGHT?
SHE'S RIGHT.
GO.

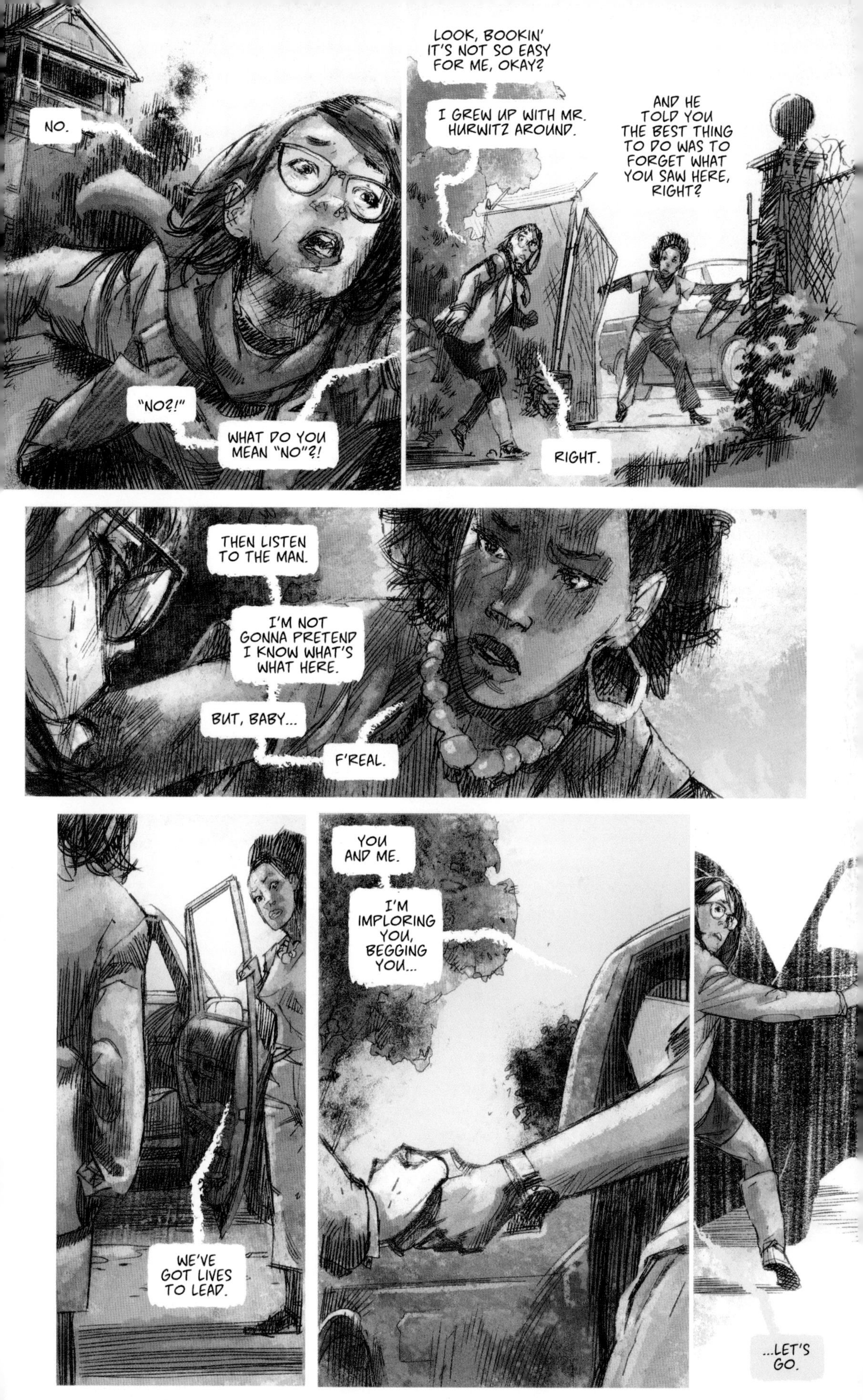
NO.
"NO?!"
WHAT DO YOU MEAN "NO"?!
LOOK, BOOKIN' IT'S NOT SO EASY FOR ME, OKAY?
I GREW UP WITH MR. HURWITZ AROUND.
AND HE TOLD YOU THE BEST THING TO DO WAS TO FORGET WHAT YOU SAW HERE, RIGHT?
RIGHT.
THEN LISTEN TO THE MAN.
I'M NOT GONNA PRETEND I KNOW WHAT'S WHAT HERE.
BUT, BABY...
F'REAL.
WE'VE GOT LIVES TO LEAD.
YOU AND ME.
I'M IMPLORING YOU, BEGGING YOU...
...LET'S GO.

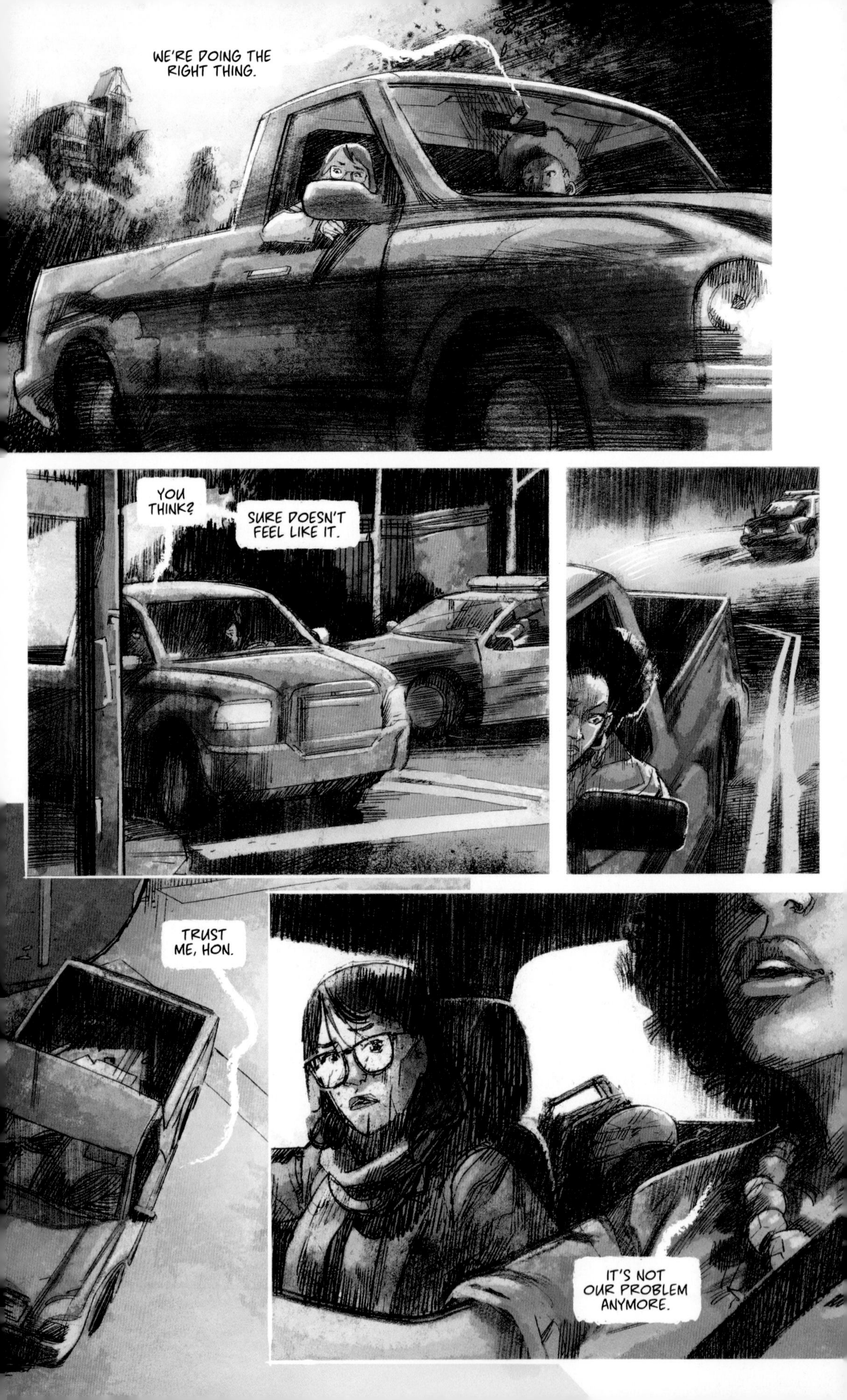
WE'RE DOING THE RIGHT THING.
YOU THINK?
SURE DOESN'T FEEL LIKE IT.
TRUST ME, HON.
IT'S NOT OUR PROBLEM ANYMORE.

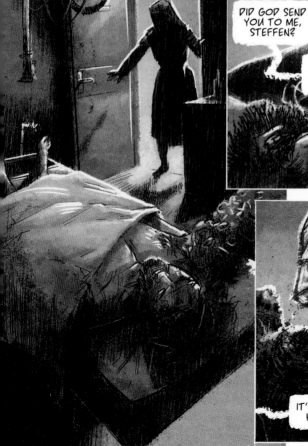

DID GOD SEND YOU TO ME, STEFFEN?

DID YOU WITNESS THE SAME SIN?

IT'S OVER HERE.

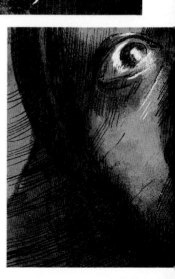

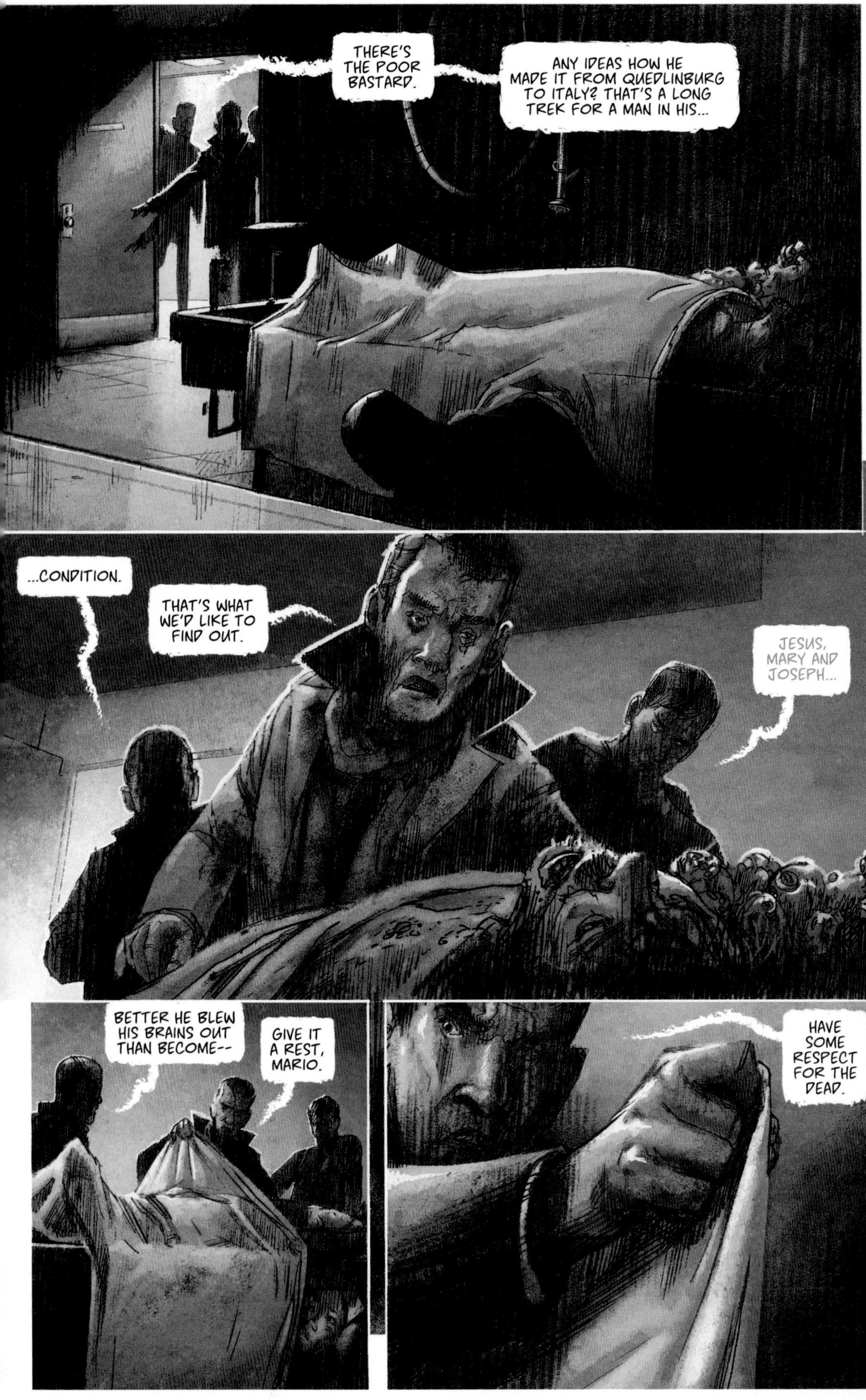
THERE'S THE POOR BASTARD.
ANY IDEAS HOW HE MADE IT FROM QUEDLINBURG TO ITALY? THAT'S A LONG TREK FOR A MAN IN HIS...
...CONDITION.
THAT'S WHAT WE'D LIKE TO FIND OUT.
JESUS, MARY AND JOSEPH...
BETTER HE BLEW HIS BRAINS OUT THAN BECOME--
GIVE IT A REST, MARIO.
HAVE SOME RESPECT FOR THE DEAD.

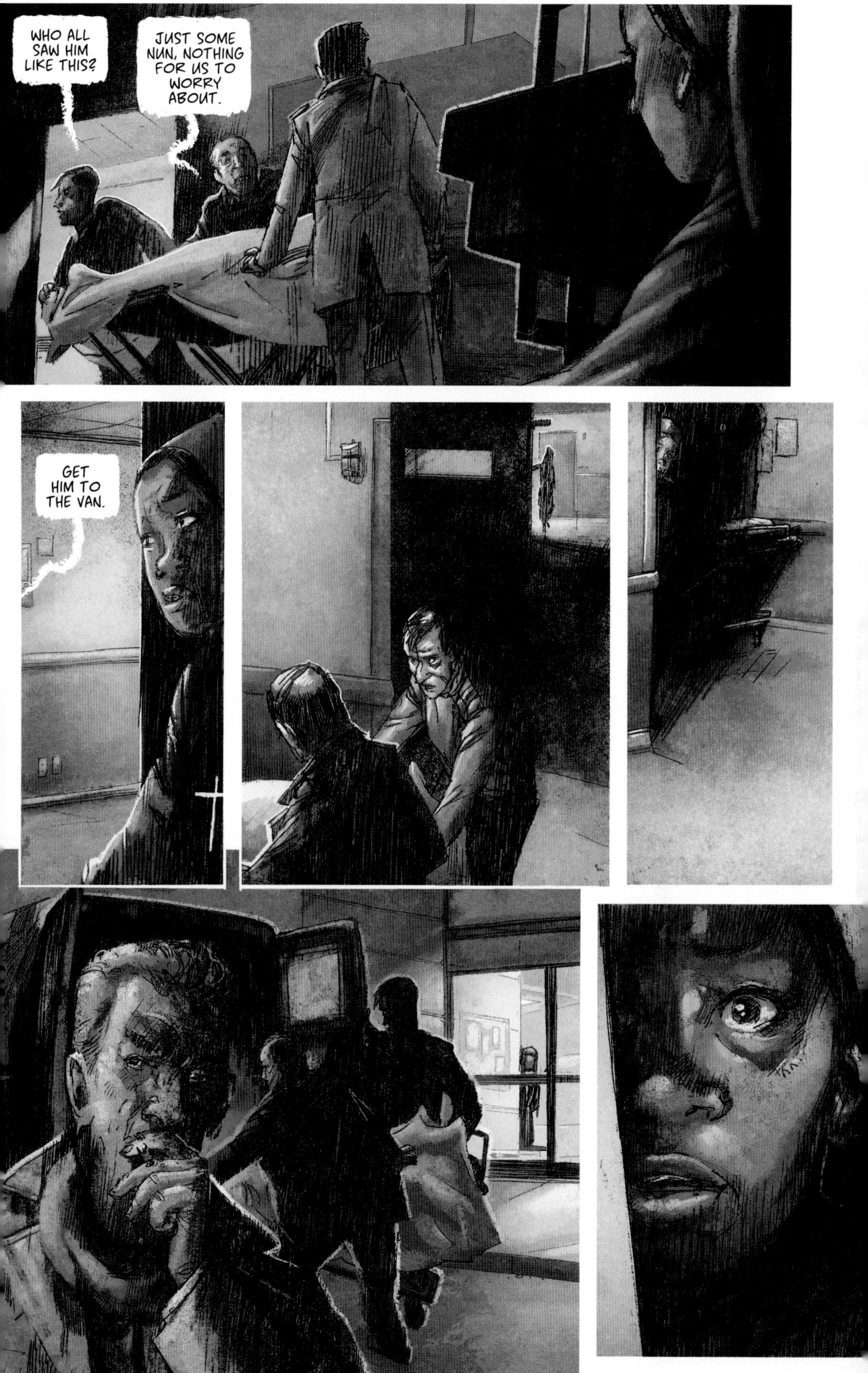
WHO ALL SAW HIM LIKE THIS?
JUST SOME NUN, NOTHING FOR US TO WORRY ABOUT.
GET HIM TO THE VAN.

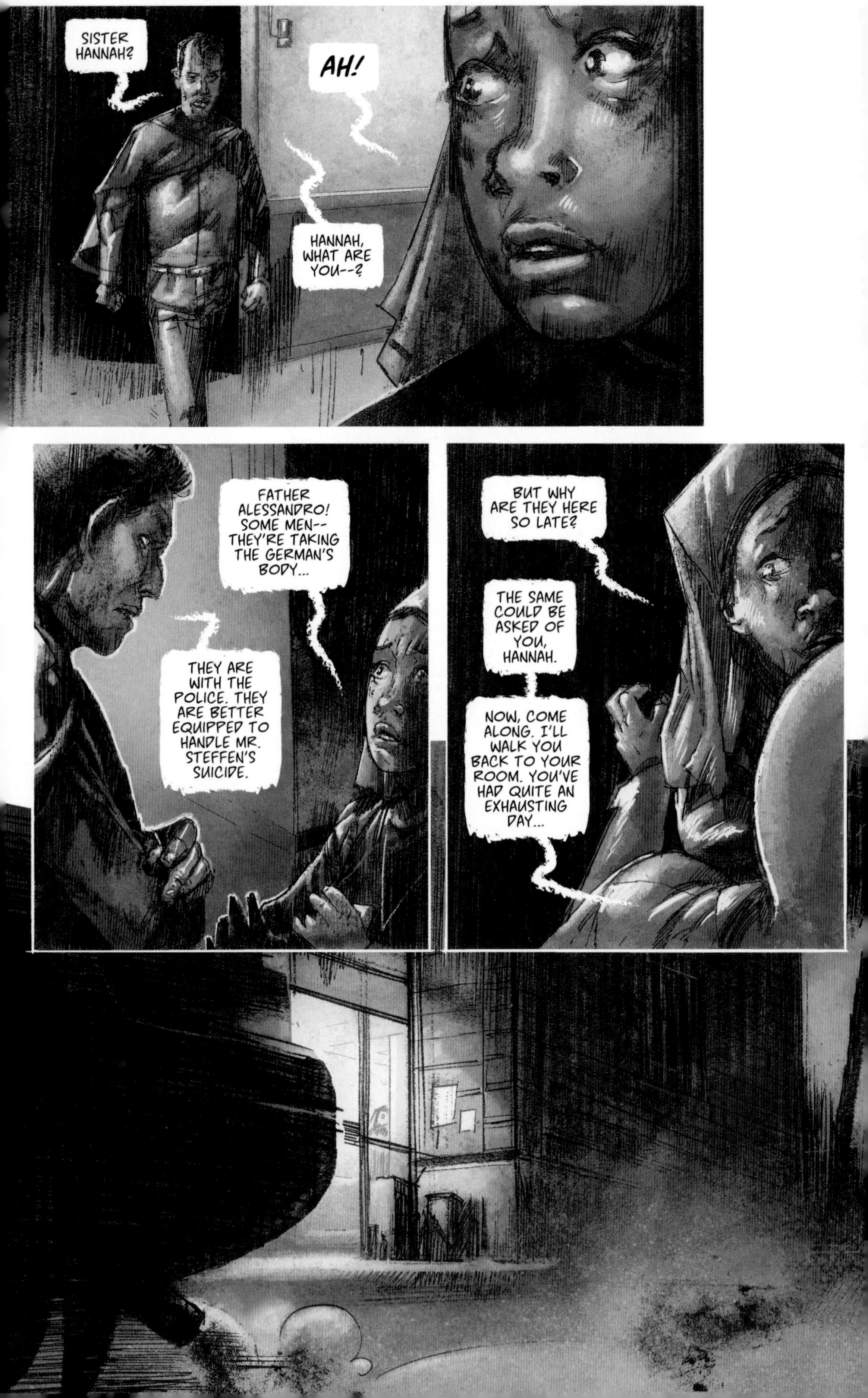
SISTER HANNAH?
AH!
HANNAH, WHAT ARE YOU--?
FATHER ALESSANDRO! SOME MEN--THEY'RE TAKING THE GERMAN'S BODY...
THEY ARE WITH THE POLICE. THEY ARE BETTER EQUIPPED TO HANDLE MR. STEFFEN'S SUICIDE.
BUT WHY ARE THEY HERE SO LATE?
THE SAME COULD BE ASKED OF YOU, HANNAH.
NOW, COME ALONG. I'LL WALK YOU BACK TO YOUR ROOM. YOU'VE HAD QUITE AN EXHAUSTING DAY...

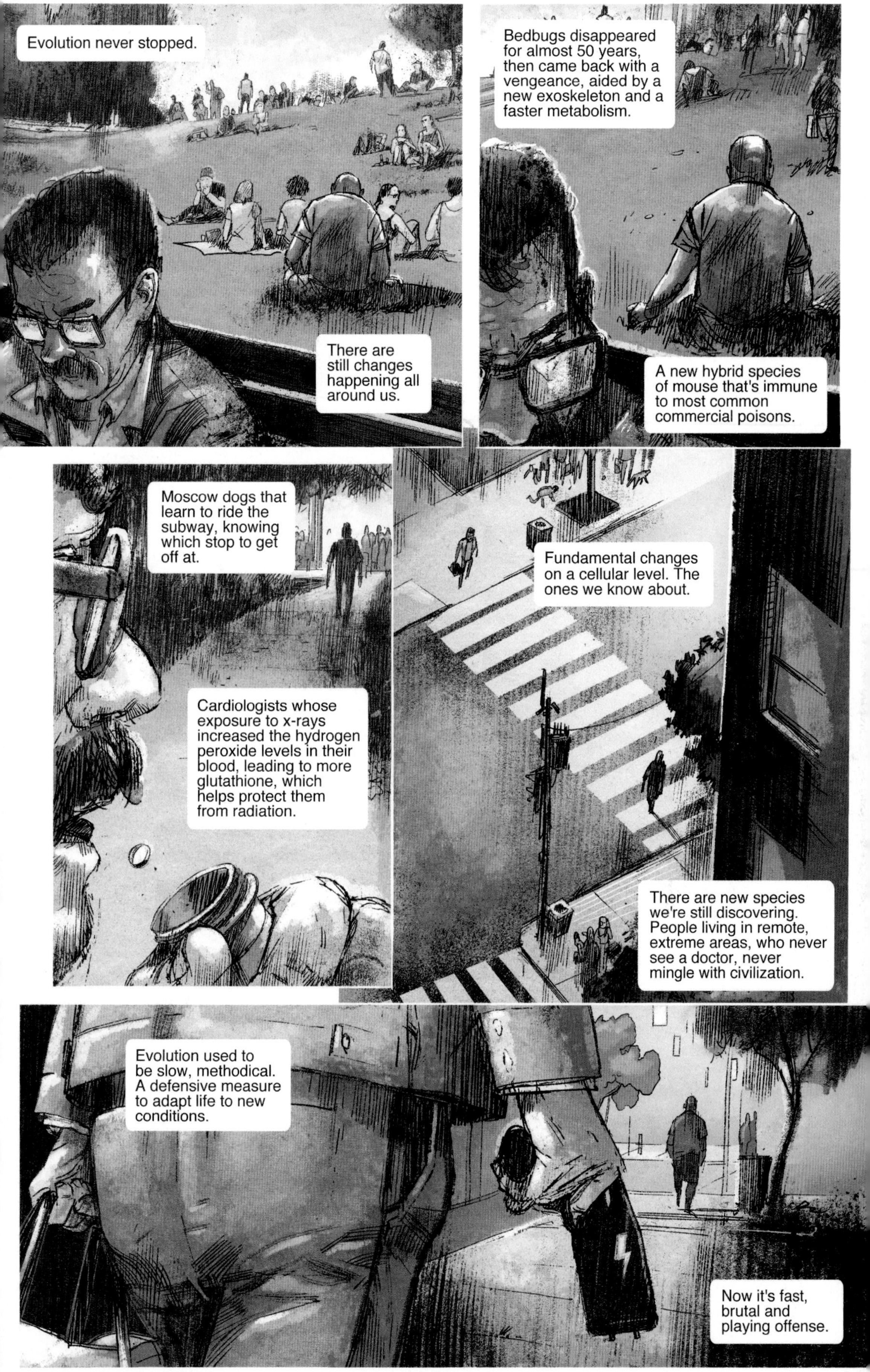
Evolution never stopped.
There are still changes happening all around us.
Bedbugs disappeared for almost 50 years, then came back with a vengeance, aided by a new exoskeleton and a faster metabolism.
A new hybrid species of mouse that's immune to most common commercial poisons.
Moscow dogs that learn to ride the subway, knowing which stop to get off at.
Cardiologists whose exposure to x-rays increased the hydrogen peroxide levels in their blood, leading to more glutathione, which helps protect them from radiation.
Fundamental changes on a cellular level. The ones we know about.
There are new species we're still discovering. People living in remote, extreme areas, who never see a doctor, never mingle with civilization.
Evolution used to be slow, methodical. A defensive measure to adapt life to new conditions.
Now it's fast, brutal and playing offense.

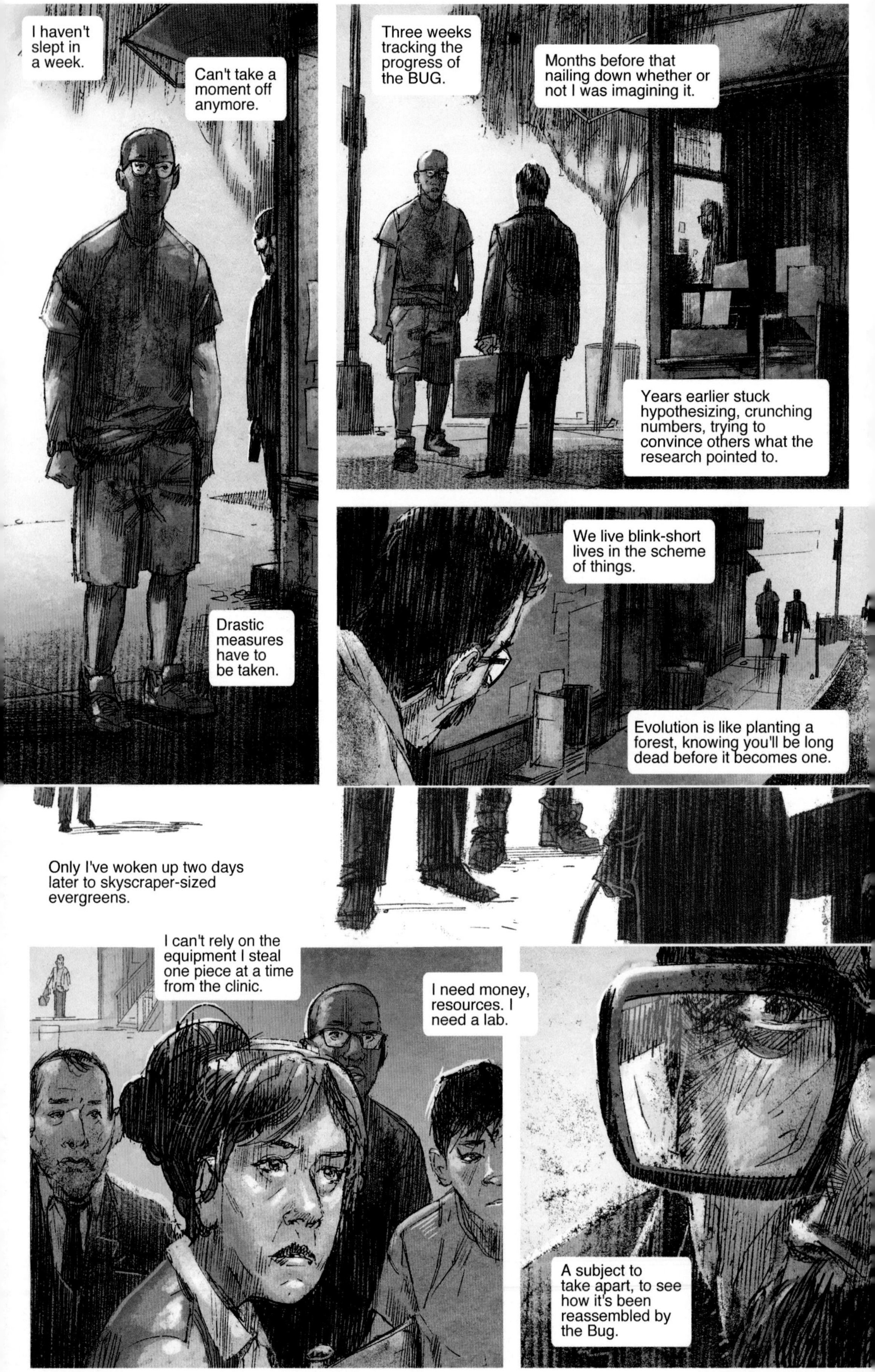

I haven't slept in a week.
Can't take a moment off anymore.
Drastic measures have to be taken.
Three weeks tracking the progress of the BUG.
Months before that nailing down whether or not I was imagining it.
Years earlier stuck hypothesizing, crunching numbers, trying to convince others what the research pointed to.
We live blink-short lives in the scheme of things.
Evolution is like planting a forest, knowing you'll be long dead before it becomes one.
Only I've woken up two days later to skyscraper-sized evergreens.
I can't rely on the equipment I steal one piece at a time from the clinic.
I need money, resources. I need a lab.
A subject to take apart, to see how it's been reassembled by the Bug.

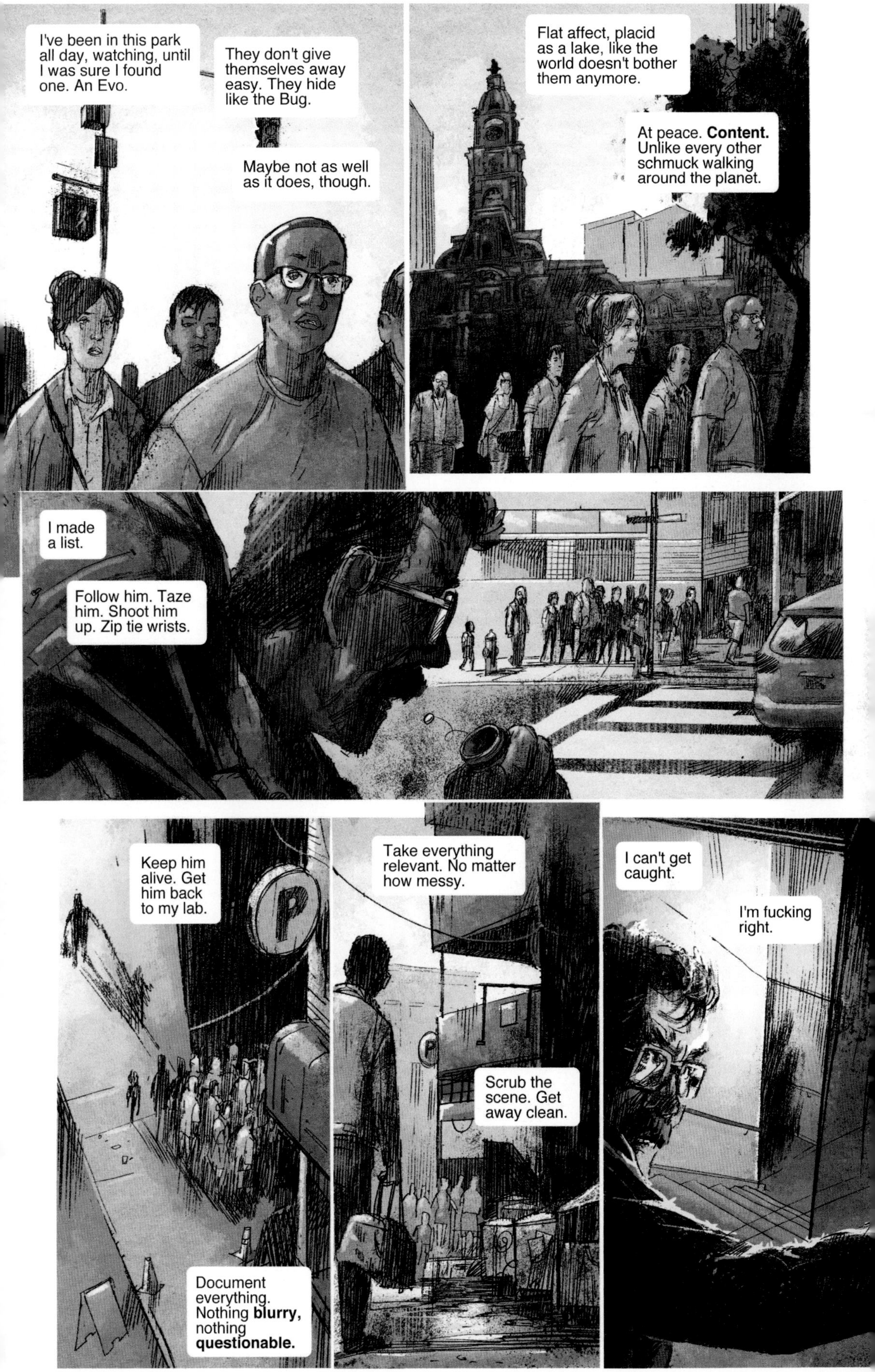
I've been in this park all day, watching, until I was sure I found one. An Evo.
They don't give themselves away easy. They hide like the Bug.
Maybe not as well as it does, though.
Flat affect, placid as a lake, like the world doesn't bother them anymore.
At peace. **Content.** Unlike every other schmuck walking around the planet.
I made a list.
Follow him. Taze him. Shoot him up. Zip tie wrists.
Keep him alive. Get him back to my lab.
Document everything. Nothing **blurry,** nothing **questionable.**
Take everything relevant. No matter how messy.
Scrub the scene. Get away clean.
I can't get caught.
I'm fucking right.

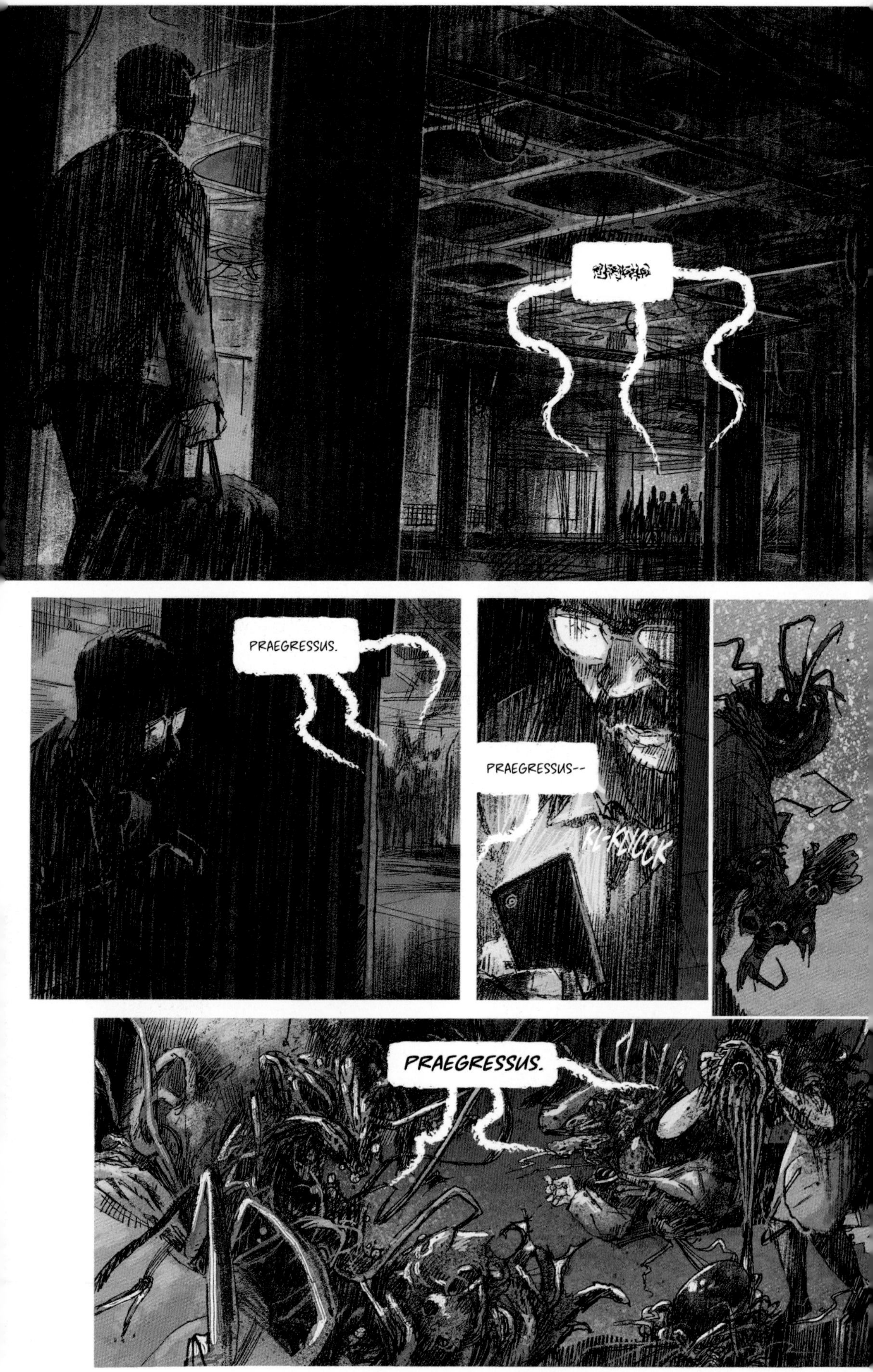
PRAEGRESSUS.
PRAEGRESSUS--
PRAEGRESSUS.

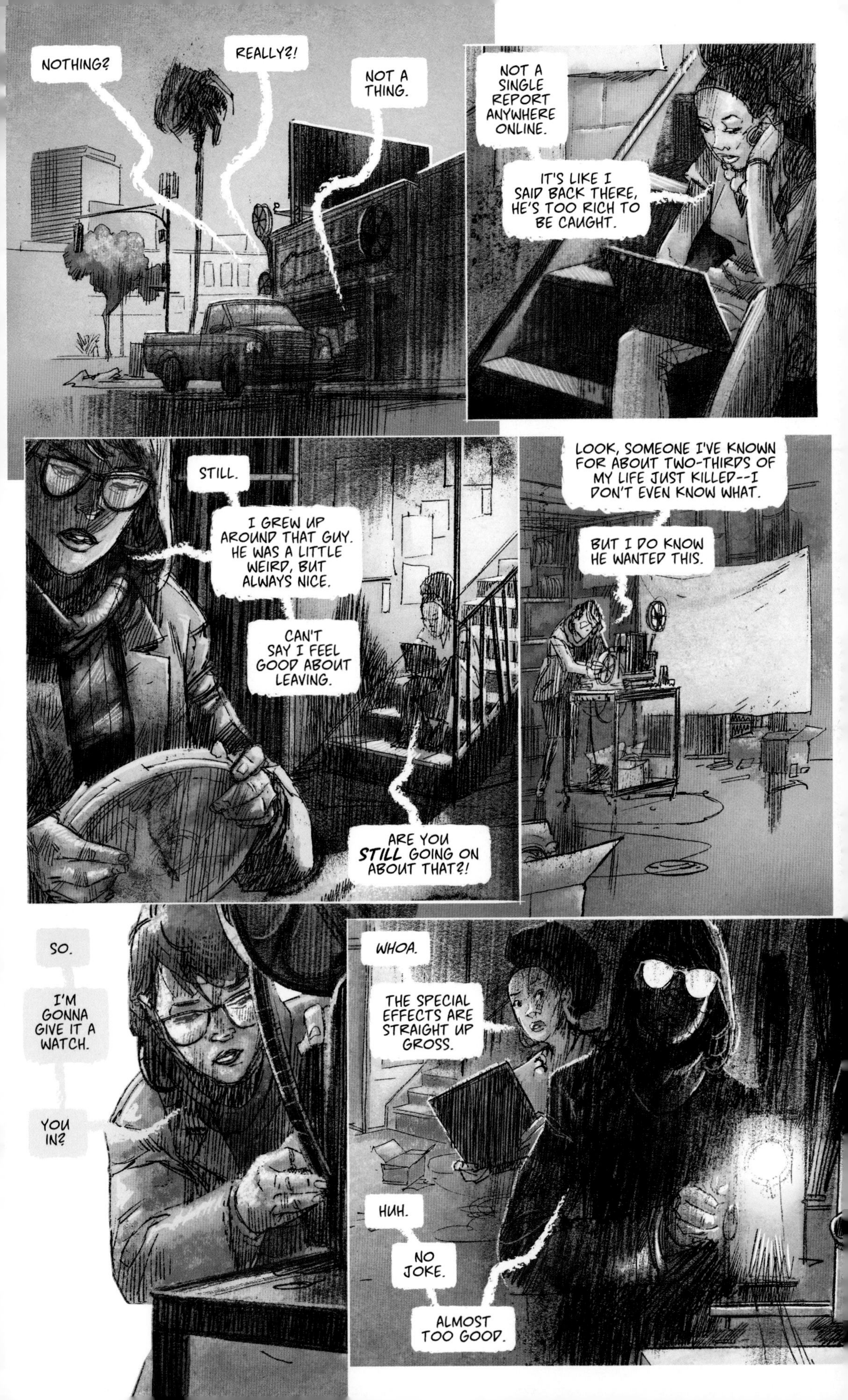
NOTHING?
REALLY?!
NOT A THING.
NOT A SINGLE REPORT ANYWHERE ONLINE.
IT'S LIKE I SAID BACK THERE, HE'S TOO RICH TO BE CAUGHT.
STILL.
I GREW UP AROUND THAT GUY. HE WAS A LITTLE WEIRD, BUT ALWAYS NICE.
CAN'T SAY I FEEL GOOD ABOUT LEAVING.
ARE YOU **STILL** GOING ON ABOUT THAT?!
LOOK, SOMEONE I'VE KNOWN FOR ABOUT TWO-THIRDS OF MY LIFE JUST KILLED--I DON'T EVEN KNOW WHAT.
BUT I DO KNOW HE WANTED THIS.
SO.
I'M GONNA GIVE IT A WATCH.
YOU IN?
WHOA.
THE SPECIAL EFFECTS ARE STRAIGHT UP GROSS.
HUH.
NO JOKE.
ALMOST TOO GOOD.

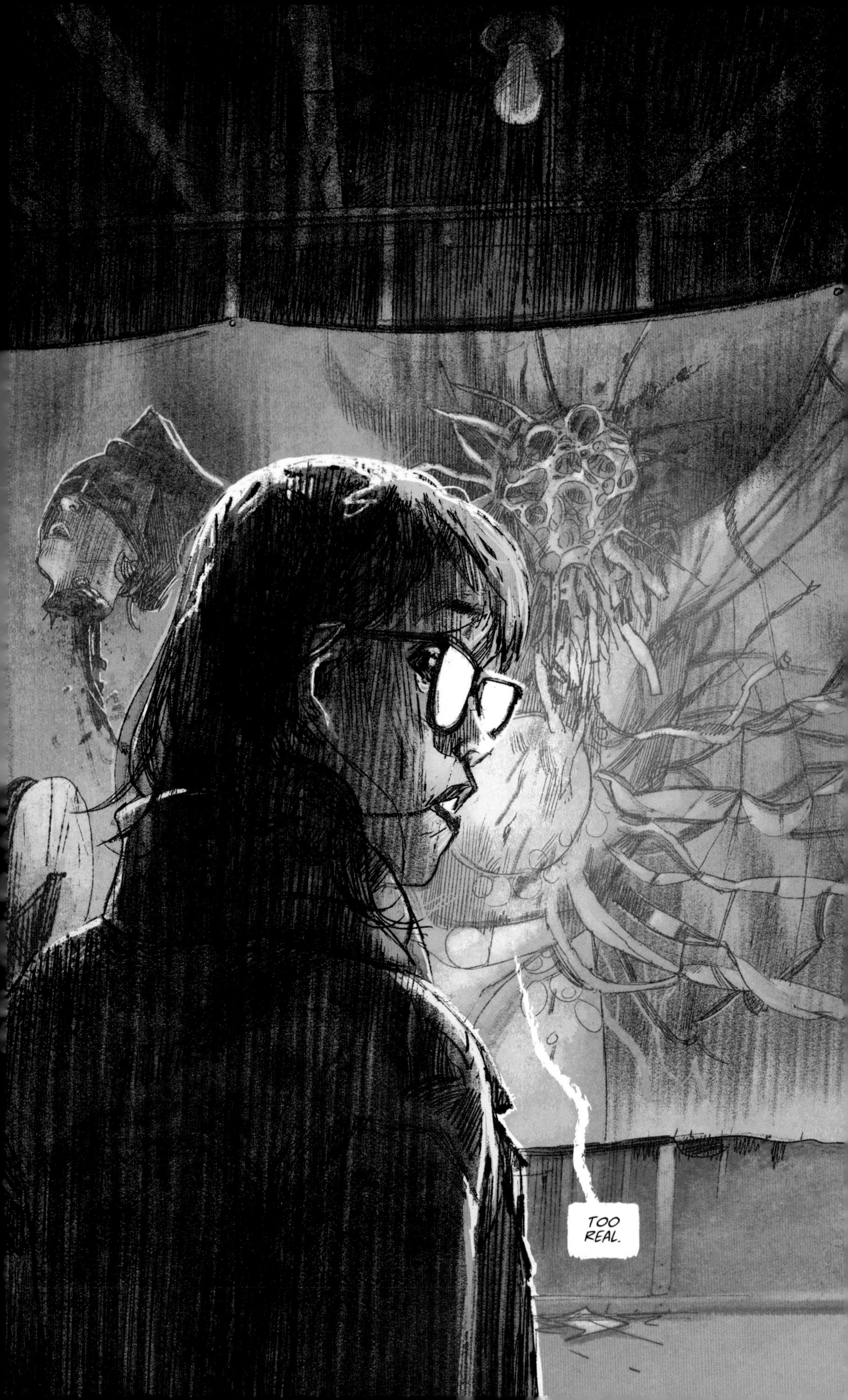
TOO REAL.

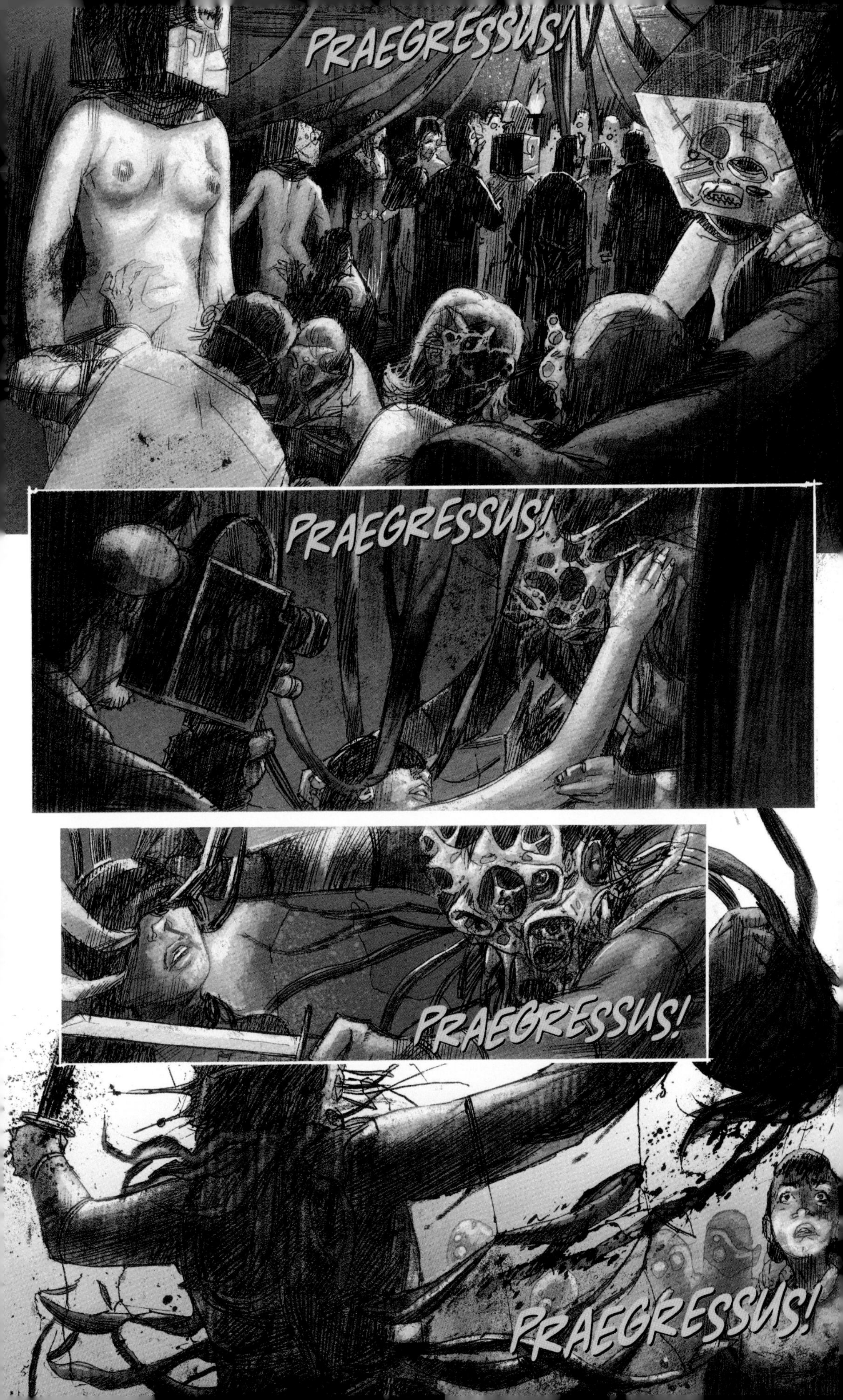
PRAEGRESSUS!
PRAEGRESSUS!
PRAEGRESSUS!
PRAEGRESSUS!

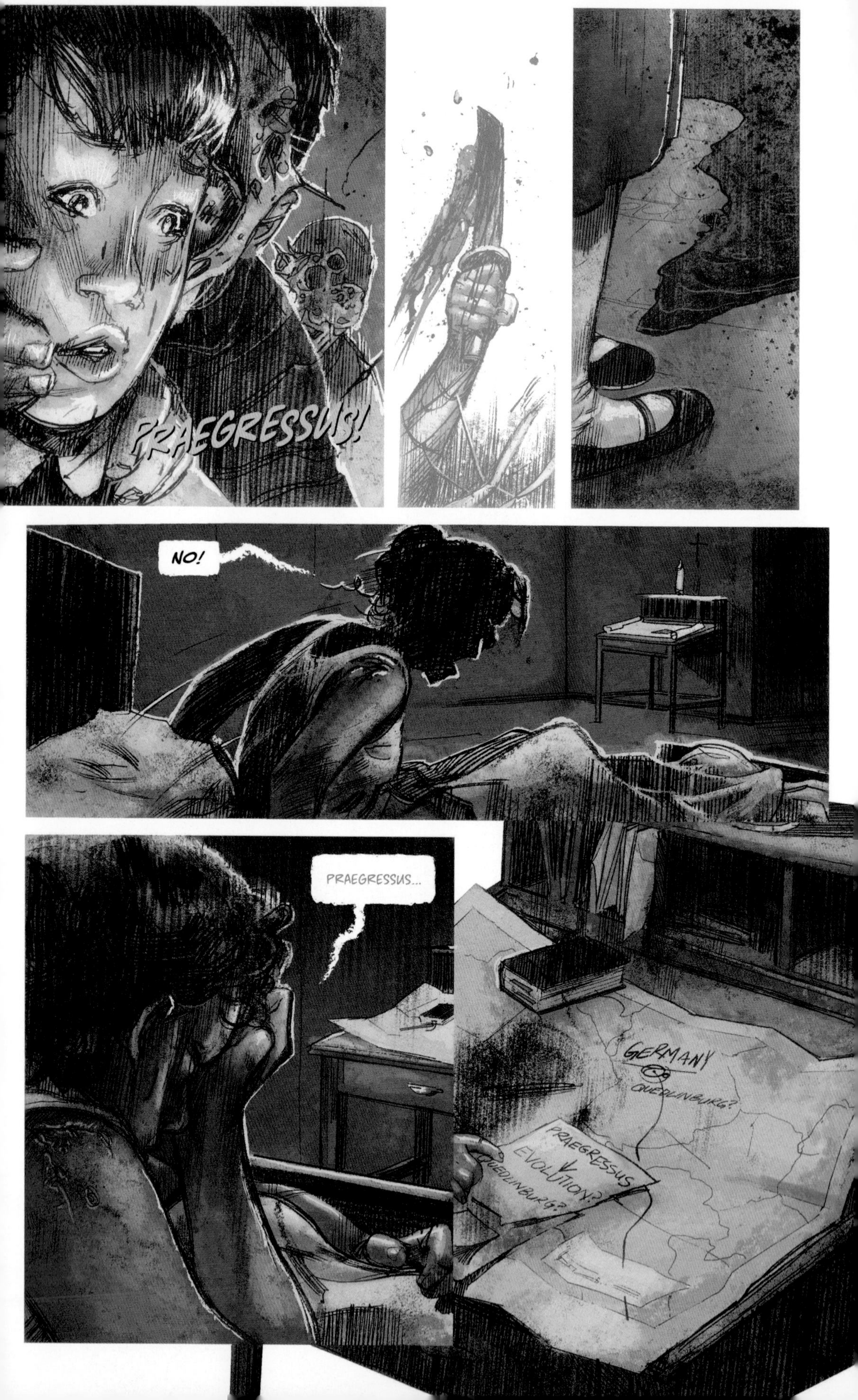
PRAEGRESSUS!
NO!
PRAEGRESSUS...
GERMANY
QUEDLINBURG?
PRAEGRESSUS
EVOLUTION?
QUEDLINBURG?

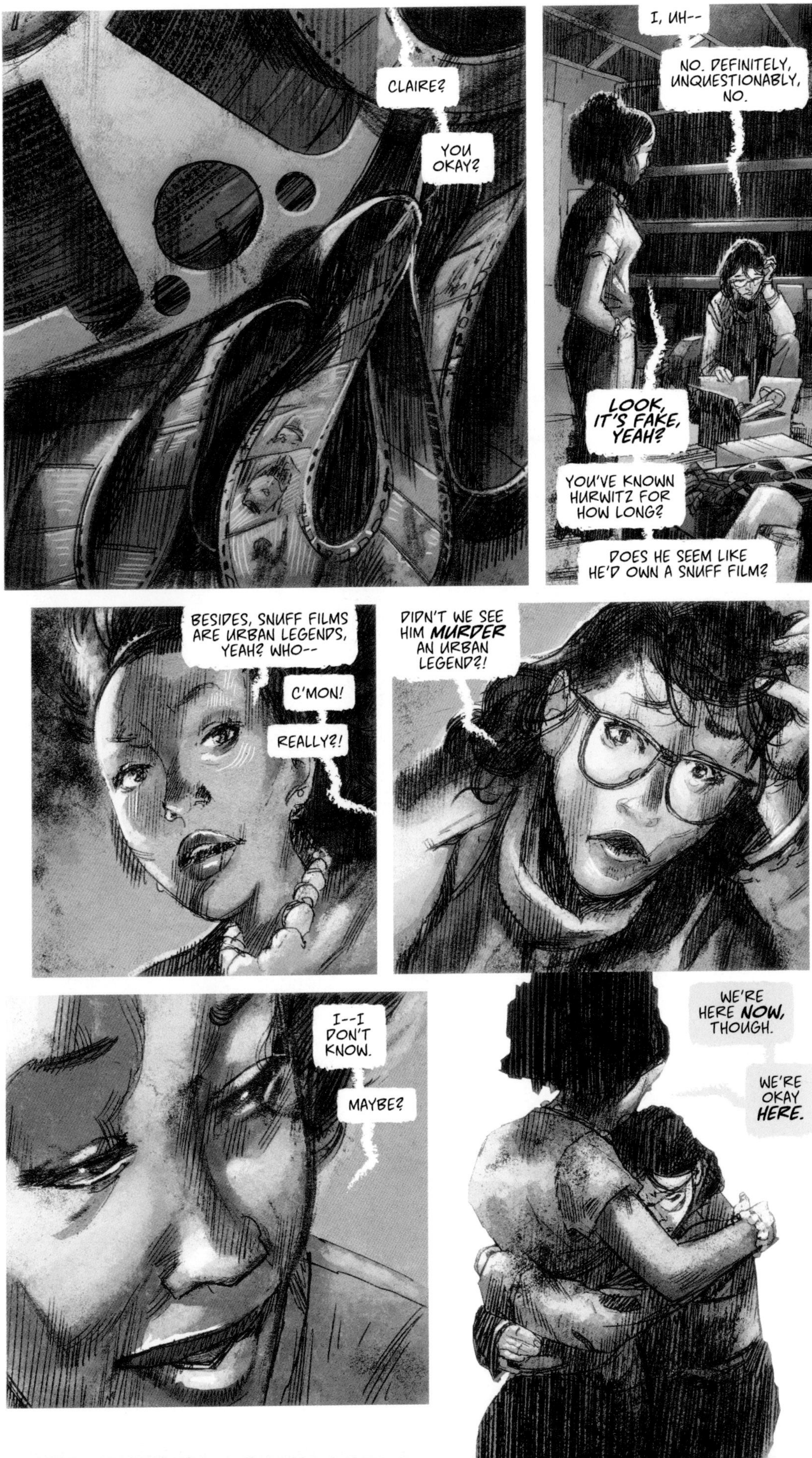
CLAIRE?
YOU OKAY?
I, UH--
NO. DEFINITELY, UNQUESTIONABLY, NO.
LOOK, IT'S FAKE, YEAH?
YOU'VE KNOWN HURWITZ FOR HOW LONG?
DOES HE SEEM LIKE HE'D OWN A SNUFF FILM?
BESIDES, SNUFF FILMS ARE URBAN LEGENDS, YEAH? WHO--
C'MON!
REALLY?!
DIDN'T WE SEE HIM MURDER AN URBAN LEGEND?!
I--I DON'T KNOW.
MAYBE?
WE'RE HERE NOW, THOUGH.
WE'RE OKAY HERE.

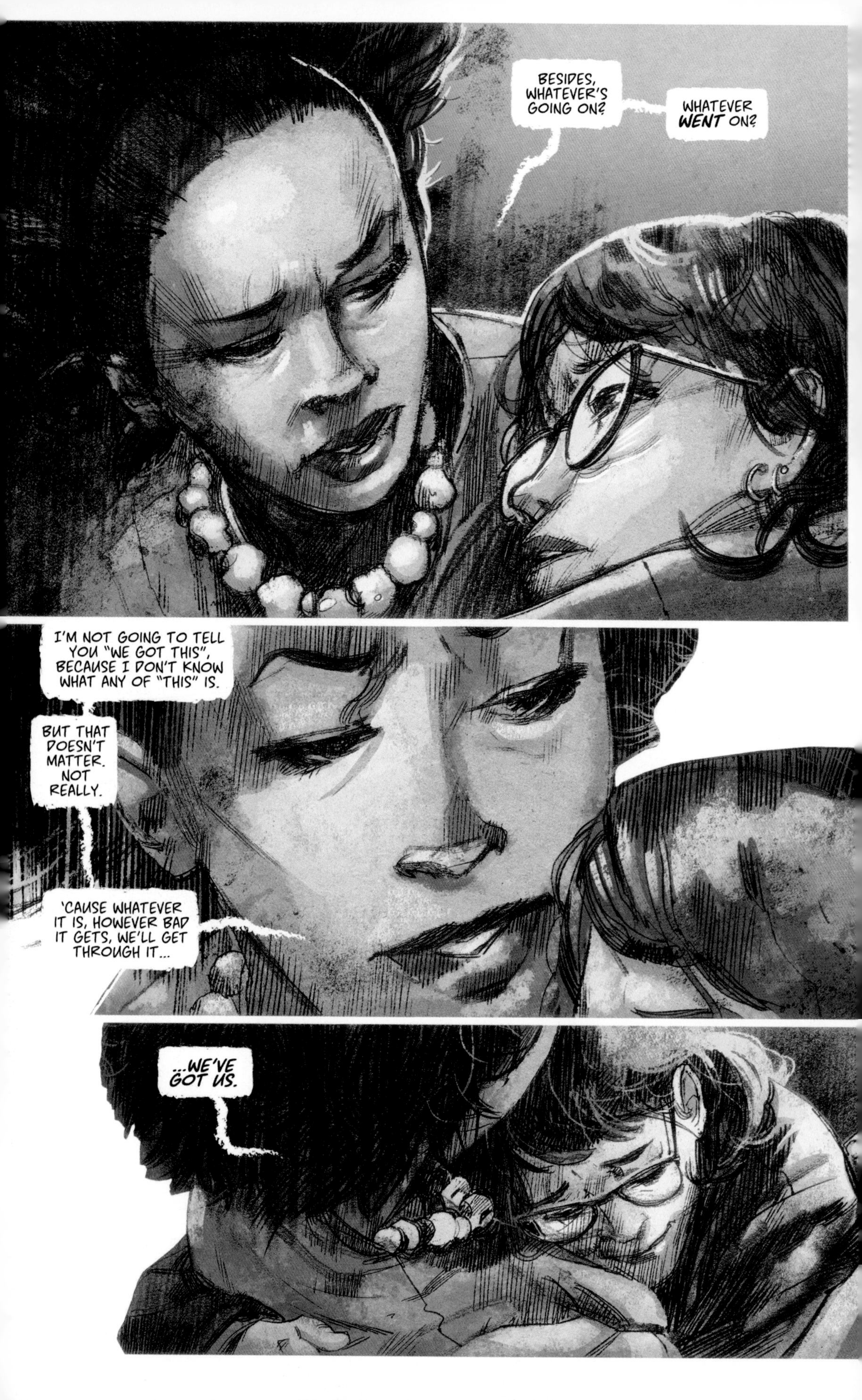
BESIDES, WHATEVER'S GOING ON?
WHATEVER WENT ON?
I'M NOT GOING TO TELL YOU "WE GOT THIS", BECAUSE I DON'T KNOW WHAT ANY OF "THIS" IS.
BUT THAT DOESN'T MATTER. NOT REALLY.
'CAUSE WHATEVER IT IS, HOWEVER BAD IT GETS, WE'LL GET THROUGH IT...
...WE'VE GOT US.

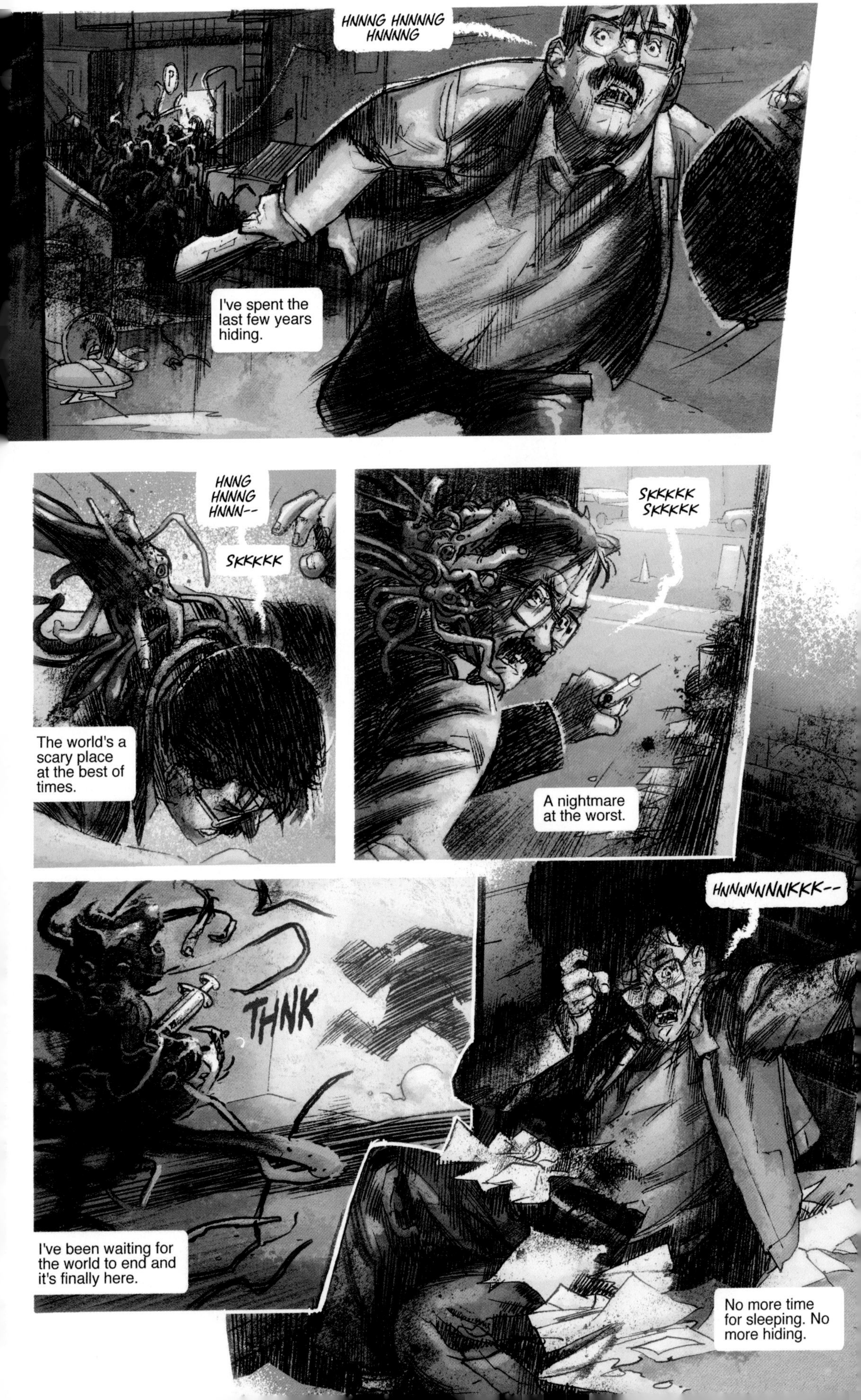
HNNNG HNNNNG HNNNNG
I've spent the last few years hiding.
HNNG HNNNG HNNN--
SKKKKK
The world's a scary place at the best of times.
SKKKKK SKKKKK
A nightmare at the worst.
THNK
I've been waiting for the world to end and it's finally here.
HNNNNNNNKKK--
No more time for sleeping. No more hiding.

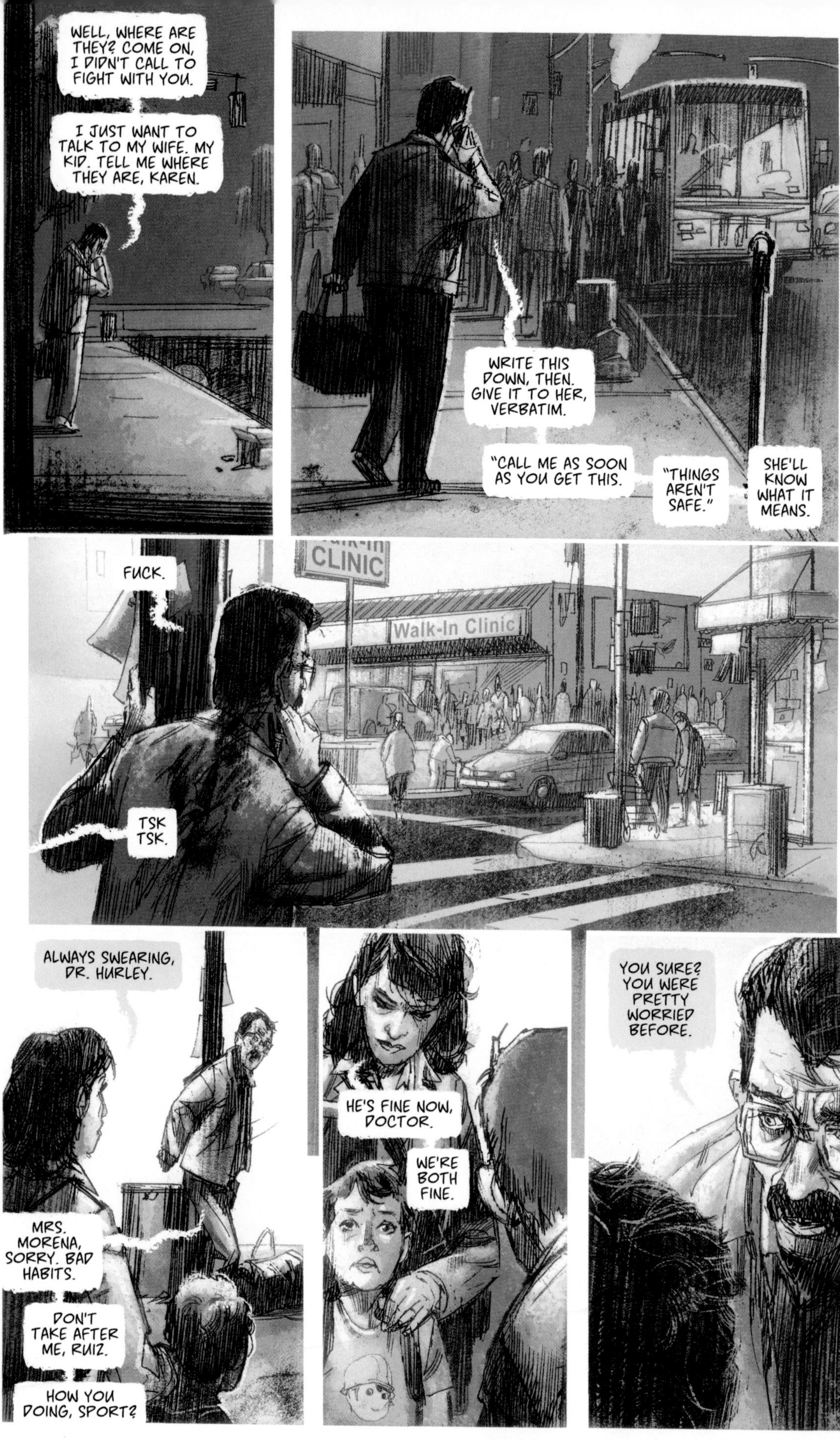
WELL, WHERE ARE THEY? COME ON, I DIDN'T CALL TO FIGHT WITH YOU.
I JUST WANT TO TALK TO MY WIFE. MY KID. TELL ME WHERE THEY ARE, KAREN.
WRITE THIS DOWN, THEN. GIVE IT TO HER, VERBATIM.
"CALL ME AS SOON AS YOU GET THIS.
"THINGS AREN'T SAFE."
SHE'LL KNOW WHAT IT MEANS.
CLINIC
Walk-In Clinic
FUCK.
TSK TSK.
ALWAYS SWEARING, DR. HURLEY.
MRS. MORENA, SORRY. BAD HABITS.
DON'T TAKE AFTER ME, RUIZ.
HOW YOU DOING, SPORT?
HE'S FINE NOW, DOCTOR.
WE'RE BOTH FINE.
YOU SURE? YOU WERE PRETTY WORRIED BEFORE.

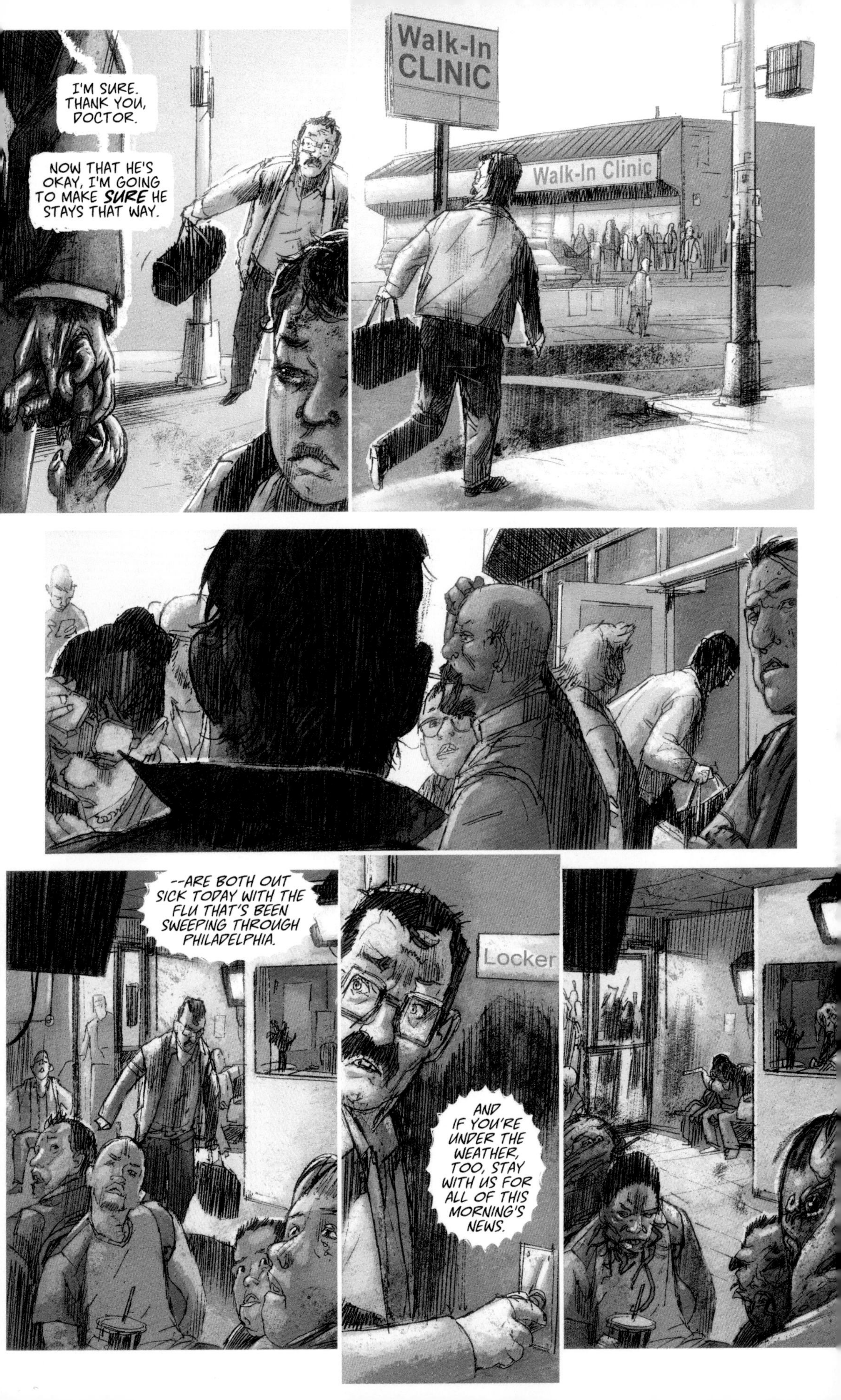
I'M SURE. THANK YOU, DOCTOR.
NOW THAT HE'S OKAY, I'M GOING TO MAKE *SURE* HE STAYS THAT WAY.
Walk-In CLINIC
Walk-In Clinic
--ARE BOTH OUT SICK TODAY WITH THE FLU THAT'S BEEN SWEEPING THROUGH PHILADELPHIA.
Locker
AND IF YOU'RE UNDER THE WEATHER, TOO, STAY WITH US FOR ALL OF THIS MORNING'S NEWS.

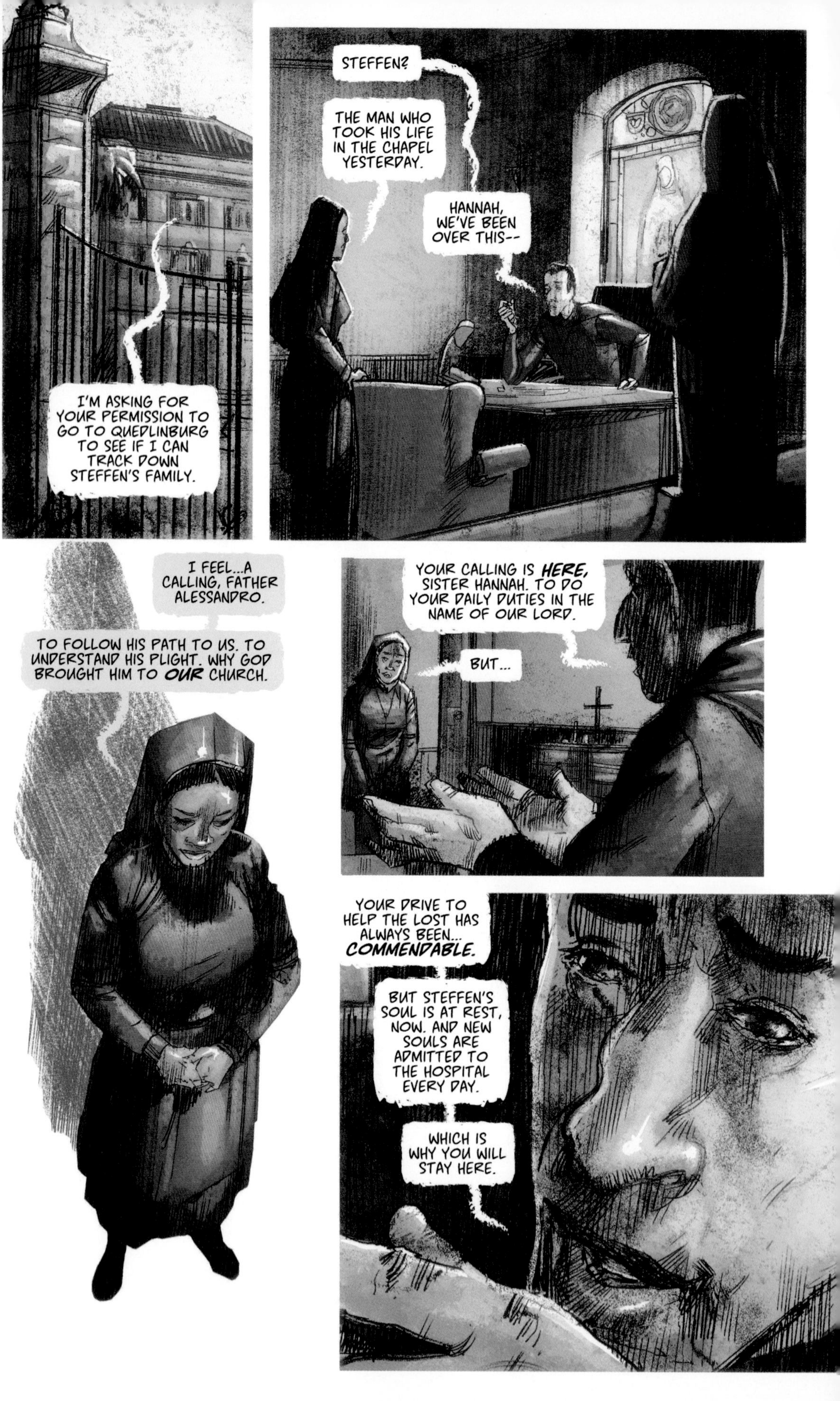
I'M ASKING FOR YOUR PERMISSION TO GO TO QUEDLINBURG TO SEE IF I CAN TRACK DOWN STEFFEN'S FAMILY.
STEFFEN?
THE MAN WHO TOOK HIS LIFE IN THE CHAPEL YESTERDAY.
HANNAH, WE'VE BEEN OVER THIS--
I FEEL...A CALLING, FATHER ALESSANDRO.
TO FOLLOW HIS PATH TO US. TO UNDERSTAND HIS PLIGHT. WHY GOD BROUGHT HIM TO ***OUR*** CHURCH.
YOUR CALLING IS ***HERE,*** SISTER HANNAH. TO DO YOUR DAILY DUTIES IN THE NAME OF OUR LORD.
BUT...
YOUR DRIVE TO HELP THE LOST HAS ALWAYS BEEN... ***COMMENDABLE.***
BUT STEFFEN'S SOUL IS AT REST, NOW. AND NEW SOULS ARE ADMITTED TO THE HOSPITAL EVERY DAY.
WHICH IS WHY YOU WILL STAY HERE.

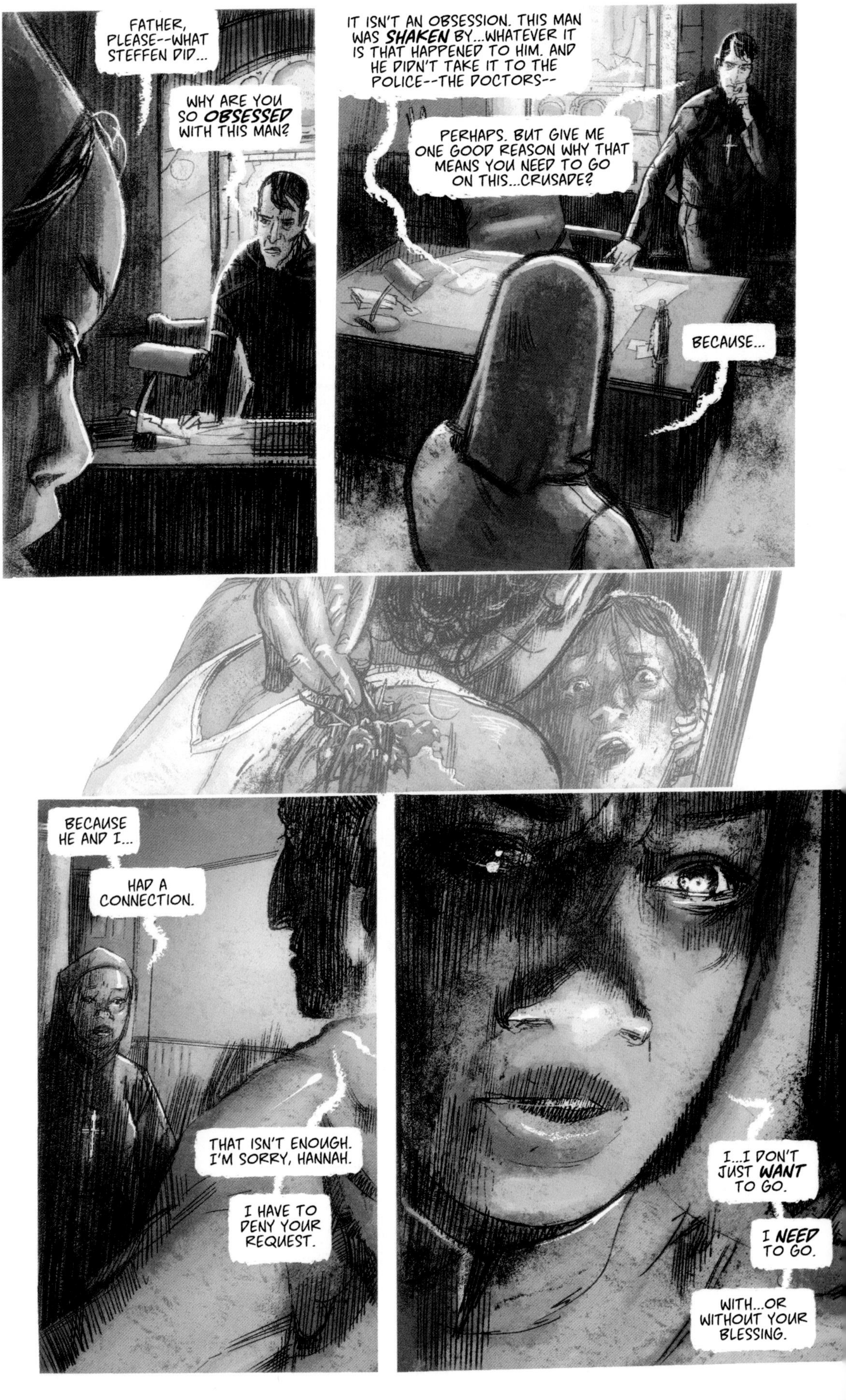
FATHER, PLEASE--WHAT STEFFEN DID...
WHY ARE YOU SO OBSESSED WITH THIS MAN?
IT ISN'T AN OBSESSION. THIS MAN WAS SHAKEN BY...WHATEVER IT IS THAT HAPPENED TO HIM. AND HE DIDN'T TAKE IT TO THE POLICE--THE DOCTORS--
PERHAPS. BUT GIVE ME ONE GOOD REASON WHY THAT MEANS YOU NEED TO GO ON THIS...CRUSADE?
BECAUSE...
BECAUSE HE AND I...
HAD A CONNECTION.
THAT ISN'T ENOUGH. I'M SORRY, HANNAH.
I HAVE TO DENY YOUR REQUEST.
I...I DON'T JUST WANT TO GO.
I NEED TO GO.
WITH...OR WITHOUT YOUR BLESSING.

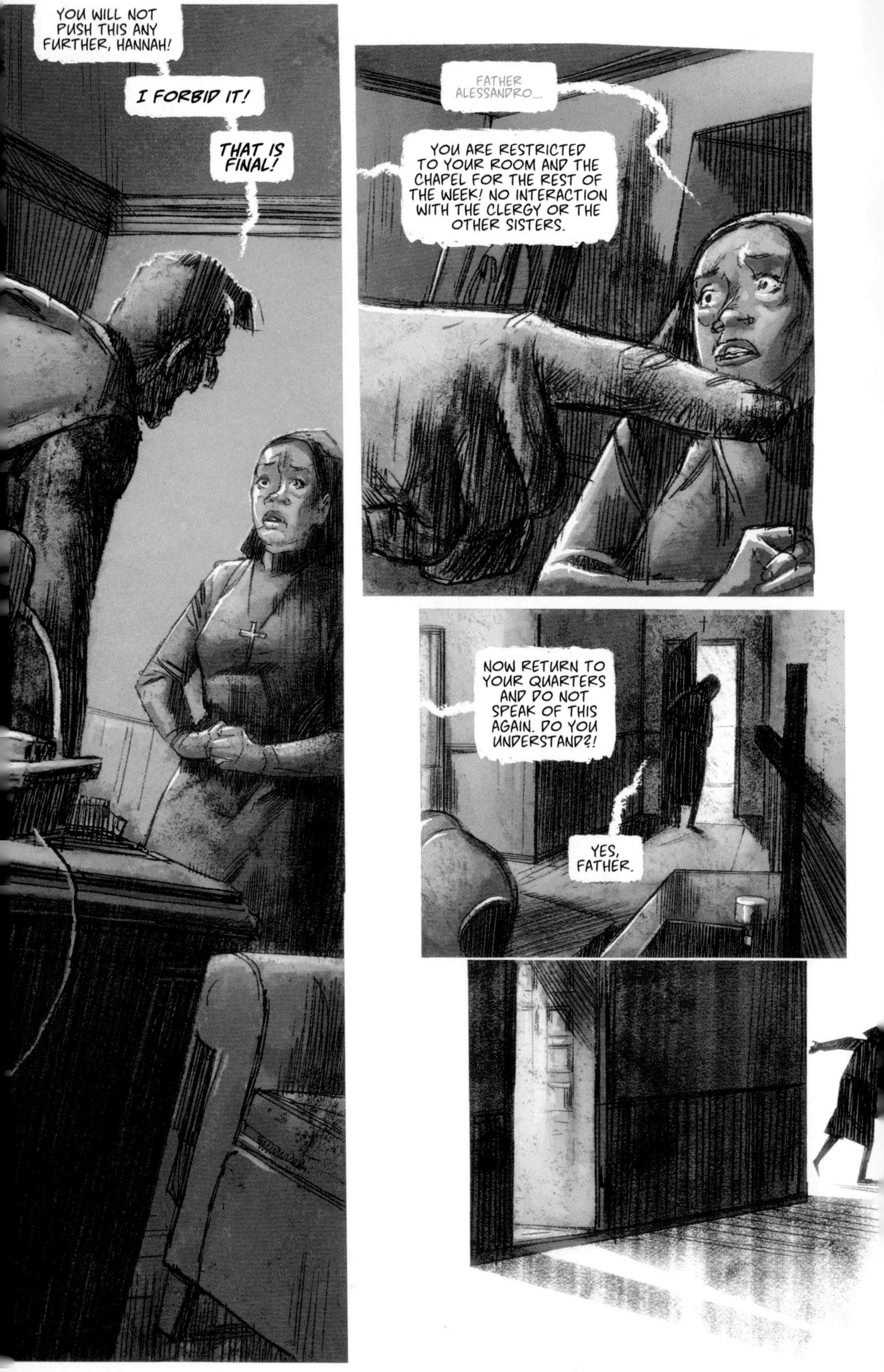
YOU WILL NOT PUSH THIS ANY FURTHER, HANNAH!
I FORBID IT!
THAT IS FINAL!
FATHER ALESSANDRO...
YOU ARE RESTRICTED TO YOUR ROOM AND THE CHAPEL FOR THE REST OF THE WEEK! NO INTERACTION WITH THE CLERGY OR THE OTHER SISTERS.
NOW RETURN TO YOUR QUARTERS AND DO NOT SPEAK OF THIS AGAIN. DO YOU UNDERSTAND?!
YES, FATHER.

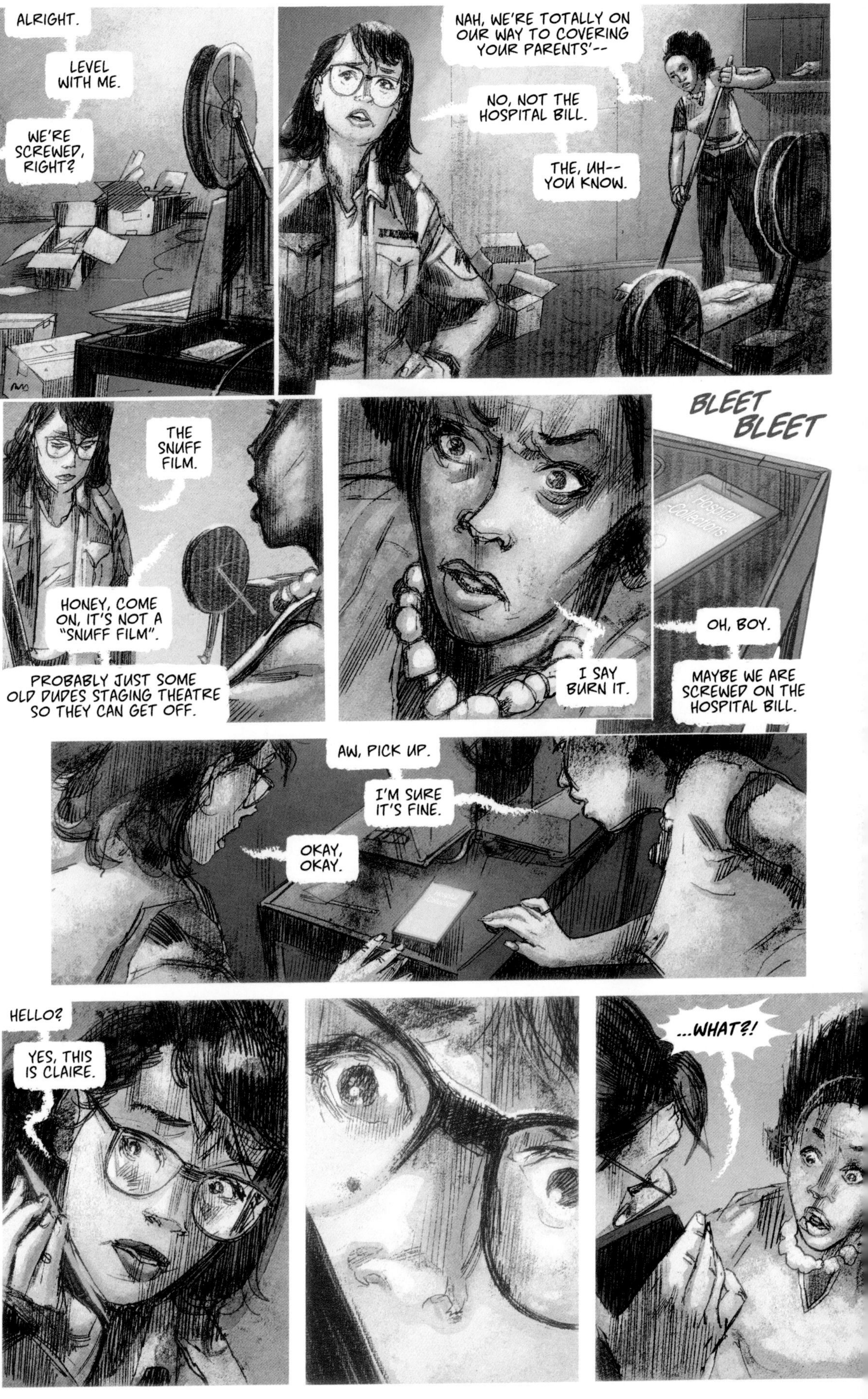
ALRIGHT.
LEVEL WITH ME.
WE'RE SCREWED, RIGHT?
NAH, WE'RE TOTALLY ON OUR WAY TO COVERING YOUR PARENTS'--
NO, NOT THE HOSPITAL BILL.
THE, UH-- YOU KNOW.
THE SNUFF FILM.
HONEY, COME ON, IT'S NOT A "SNUFF FILM".
PROBABLY JUST SOME OLD DUDES STAGING THEATRE SO THEY CAN GET OFF.
I SAY BURN IT.
BLEET BLEET
Hospital Collections
OH, BOY.
MAYBE WE ARE SCREWED ON THE HOSPITAL BILL.
AW, PICK UP.
I'M SURE IT'S FINE.
OKAY, OKAY.
HELLO?
YES, THIS IS CLAIRE.
...WHAT?!

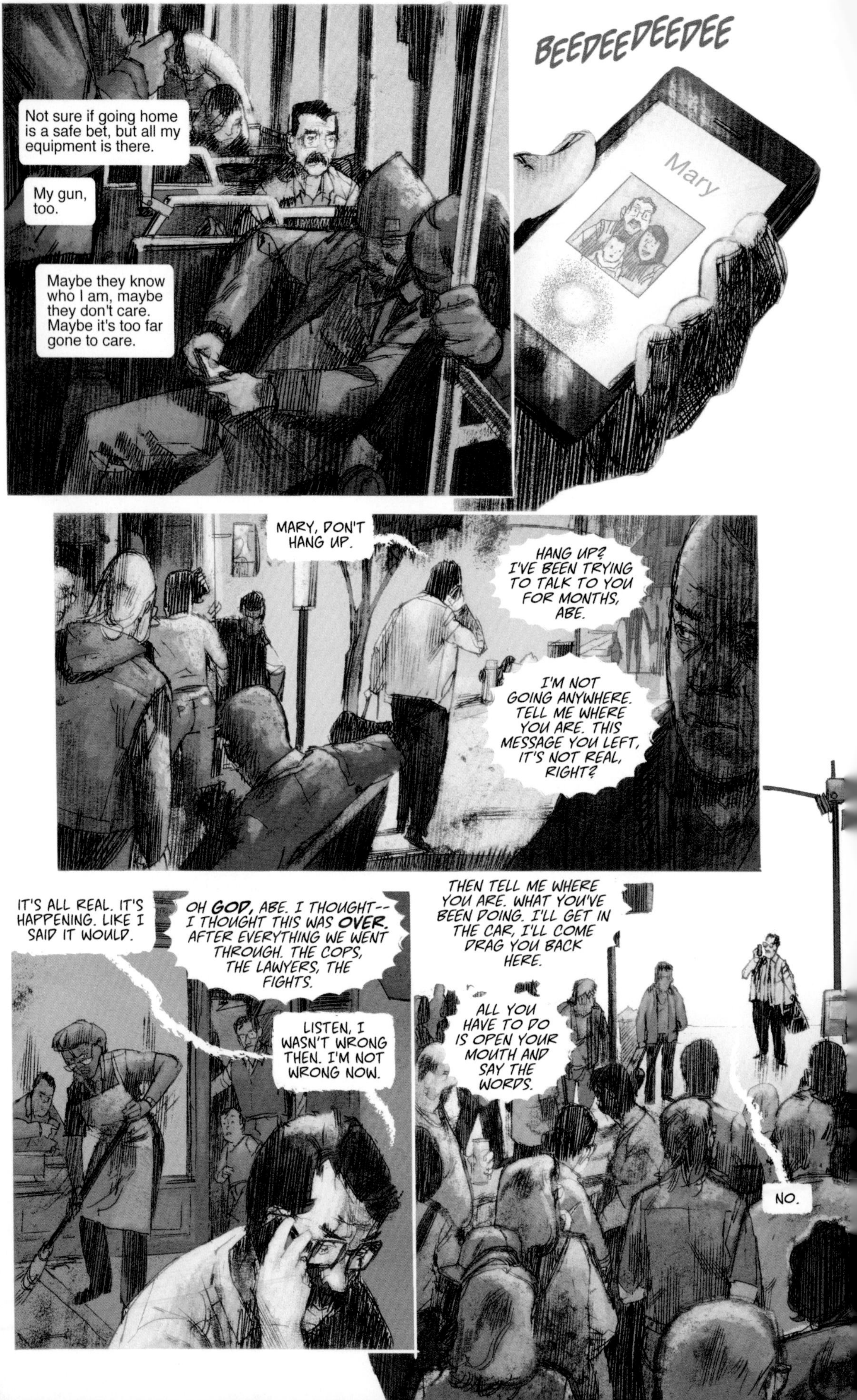
Not sure if going home is a safe bet, but all my equipment is there.
My gun, too.
Maybe they know who I am, maybe they don't care. Maybe it's too far gone to care.
BEEDEEDEEDEE
Mary
MARY, DON'T HANG UP.
HANG UP? I'VE BEEN TRYING TO TALK TO YOU FOR MONTHS, ABE.
I'M NOT GOING ANYWHERE. TELL ME WHERE YOU ARE. THIS MESSAGE YOU LEFT, IT'S NOT REAL, RIGHT?
IT'S ALL REAL. IT'S HAPPENING. LIKE I SAID IT WOULD.
OH GOD, ABE. I THOUGHT-- I THOUGHT THIS WAS OVER. AFTER EVERYTHING WE WENT THROUGH. THE COPS, THE LAWYERS, THE FIGHTS.
LISTEN, I WASN'T WRONG THEN. I'M NOT WRONG NOW.
THEN TELL ME WHERE YOU ARE. WHAT YOU'VE BEEN DOING. I'LL GET IN THE CAR, I'LL COME DRAG YOU BACK HERE.
ALL YOU HAVE TO DO IS OPEN YOUR MOUTH AND SAY THE WORDS.
NO.

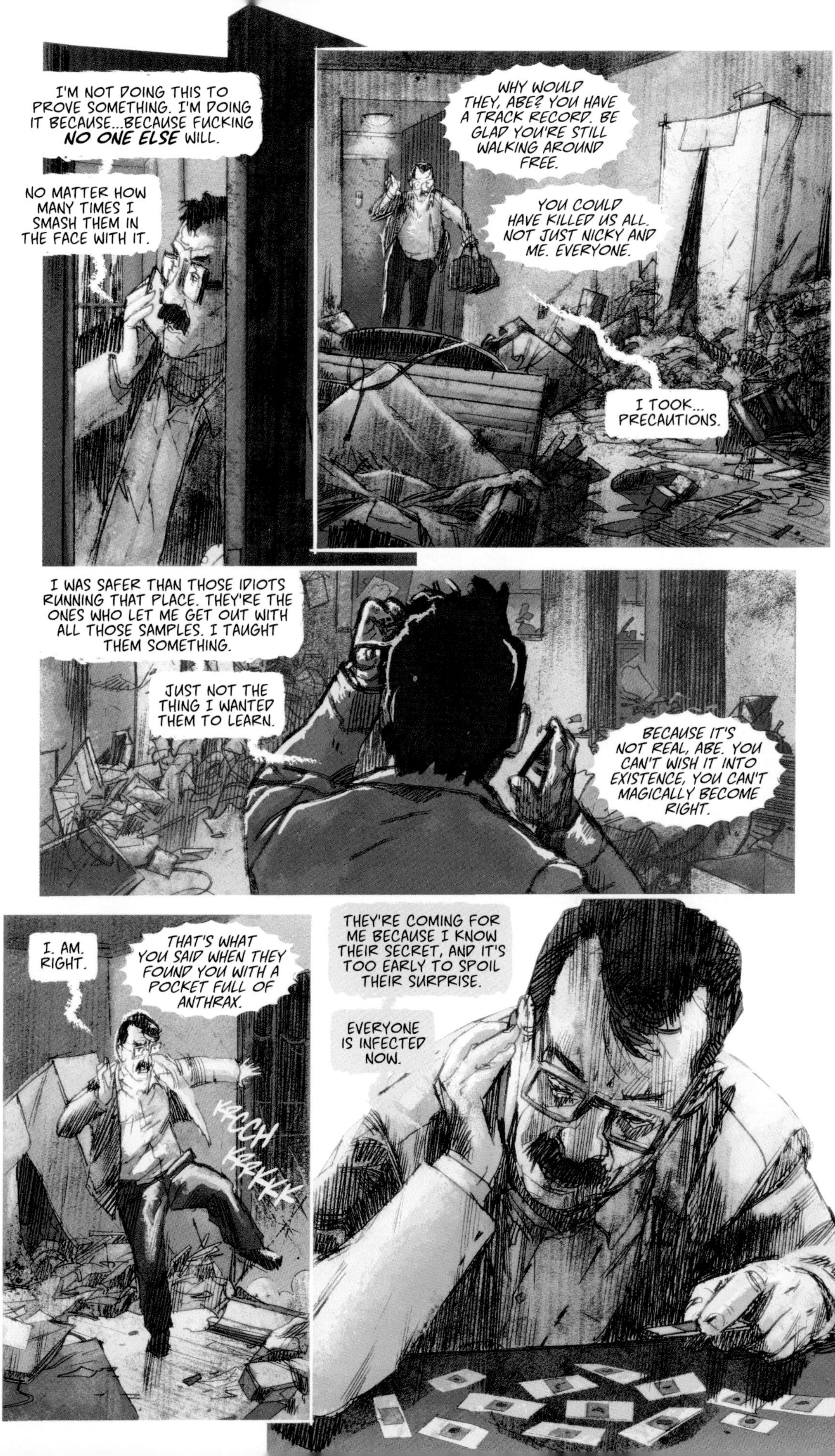
I'M NOT DOING THIS TO PROVE SOMETHING. I'M DOING IT BECAUSE...BECAUSE FUCKING NO ONE ELSE WILL.
NO MATTER HOW MANY TIMES I SMASH THEM IN THE FACE WITH IT.
WHY WOULD THEY, ABE? YOU HAVE A TRACK RECORD. BE GLAD YOU'RE STILL WALKING AROUND FREE.
YOU COULD HAVE KILLED US ALL. NOT JUST NICKY AND ME. EVERYONE.
I TOOK... PRECAUTIONS.
I WAS SAFER THAN THOSE IDIOTS RUNNING THAT PLACE. THEY'RE THE ONES WHO LET ME GET OUT WITH ALL THOSE SAMPLES. I TAUGHT THEM SOMETHING.
JUST NOT THE THING I WANTED THEM TO LEARN.
BECAUSE IT'S NOT REAL, ABE. YOU CAN'T WISH IT INTO EXISTENCE, YOU CAN'T MAGICALLY BECOME RIGHT.
I. AM. RIGHT.
THAT'S WHAT YOU SAID WHEN THEY FOUND YOU WITH A POCKET FULL OF ANTHRAX.
KRCCH
KRKKK
THEY'RE COMING FOR ME BECAUSE I KNOW THEIR SECRET, AND IT'S TOO EARLY TO SPOIL THEIR SURPRISE.
EVERYONE IS INFECTED NOW.

EVERYONE I SAW TODAY. HALF DIDN'T EVEN SHOW SYMPTOMS, BUT I JUST KNEW THEY HAD IT. AND THEY DO.

ABE...

THIS ISN'T A DISEASE ANYMORE. IT'S A PANDEMIC.

SOMETHING HAS ITS HAND ON THE SWITCH. WAITING. FOR WHAT?

ABE.

LAST NIGHT, I SAW WHAT THEY'RE BECOMING. I KNOW HOW TO SHOW EVERYONE.

I'M HANGING UP.

GOOD. GO, MARY. TAKE NICKY, GET SOMEWHERE SAFE.

SOMEWHERE *CLEAN.* BEFORE IT GETS TO YOU, TOO.

I'M GOING BACK TO THE REAL WORLD, ABE.

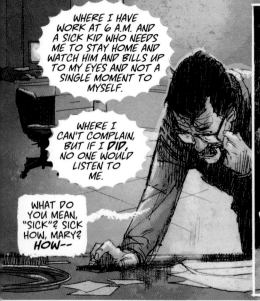

WHERE I HAVE WORK AT 6 A.M. AND A SICK KID WHO NEEDS ME TO STAY HOME AND WATCH HIM AND BILLS UP TO MY EYES AND NOT A SINGLE MOMENT TO MYSELF.

WHERE I CAN'T COMPLAIN, BUT IF I *DID,* NO ONE WOULD LISTEN TO ME.

WHAT DO YOU MEAN, "SICK"? SICK HOW, MARY? *HOW--*

KLIK

HE'S NOT SICK.

NOT SICK.

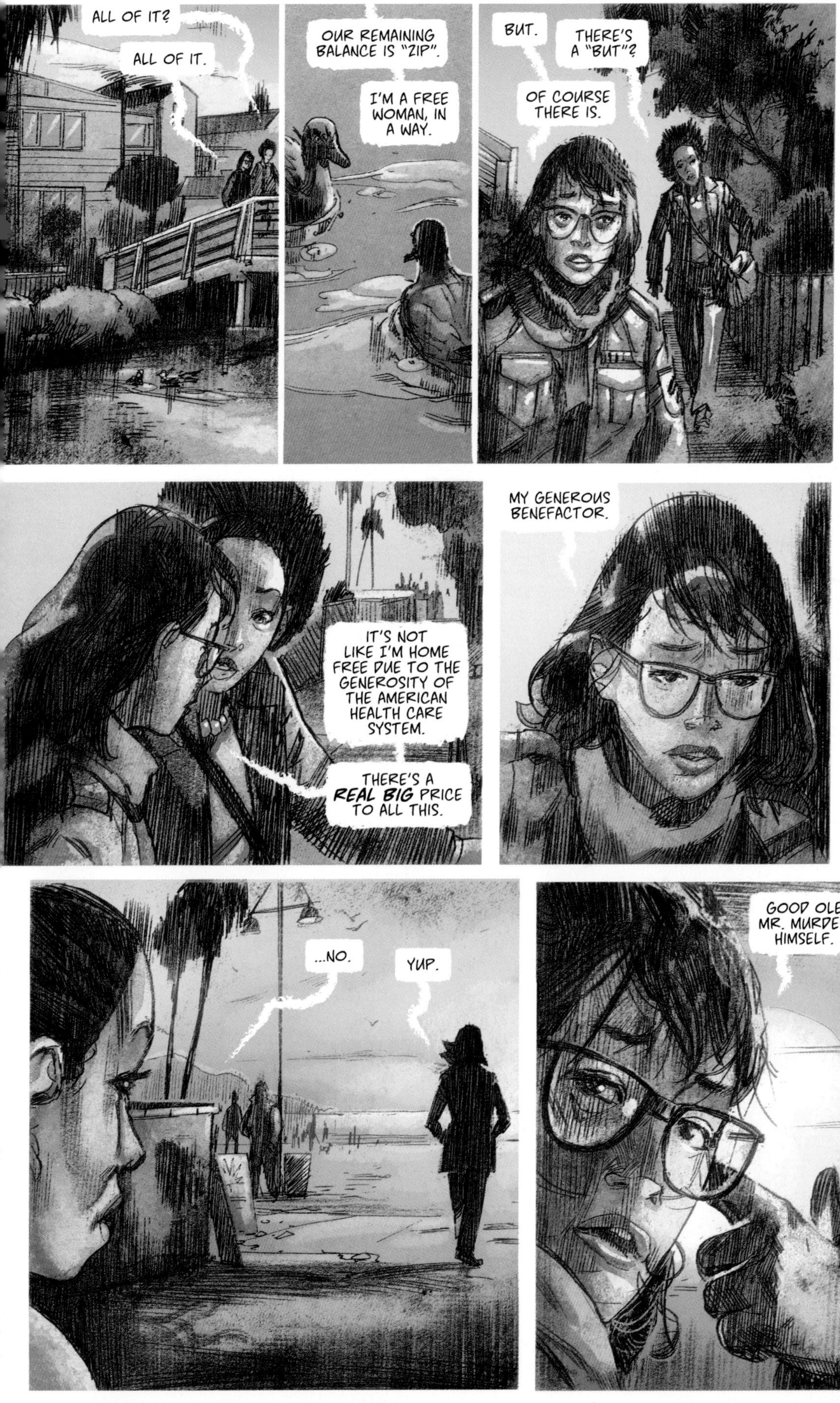
ALL OF IT?
ALL OF IT.
OUR REMAINING BALANCE IS "ZIP".
I'M A FREE WOMAN, IN A WAY.
BUT.
THERE'S A "BUT"?
OF COURSE THERE IS.
IT'S NOT LIKE I'M HOME FREE DUE TO THE GENEROSITY OF THE AMERICAN HEALTH CARE SYSTEM.
THERE'S A **REAL BIG** PRICE TO ALL THIS.
MY GENEROUS BENEFACTOR.
...NO.
YUP.
GOOD OLE MR. MURDER HIMSELF.

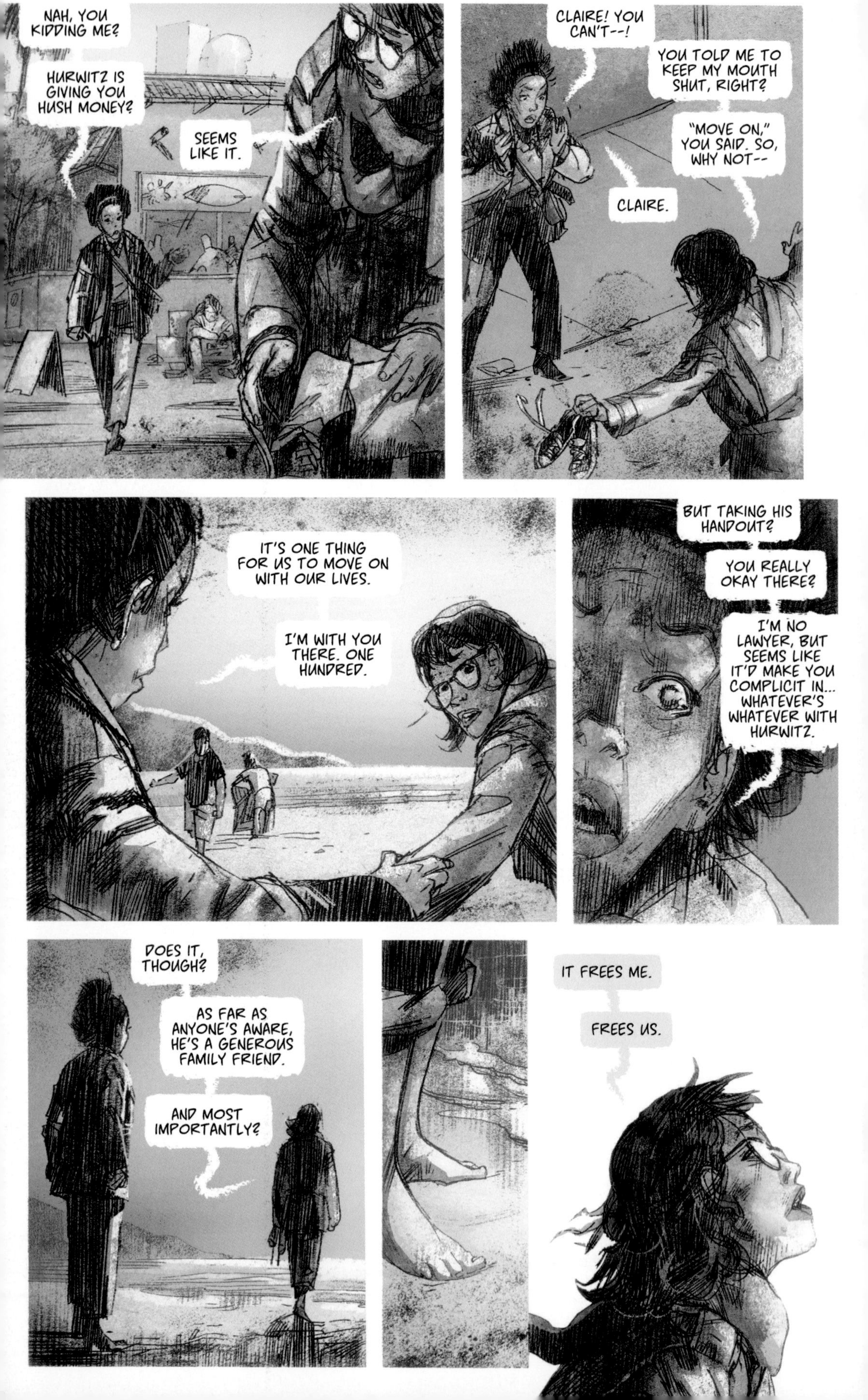

NAH, YOU KIDDING ME?
HURWITZ IS GIVING YOU HUSH MONEY?
SEEMS LIKE IT.
CLAIRE! YOU CAN'T--!
YOU TOLD ME TO KEEP MY MOUTH SHUT, RIGHT?
"MOVE ON," YOU SAID. SO, WHY NOT--
CLAIRE.
IT'S ONE THING FOR US TO MOVE ON WITH OUR LIVES.
I'M WITH YOU THERE. ONE HUNDRED.
BUT TAKING HIS HANDOUT?
YOU REALLY OKAY THERE?
I'M NO LAWYER, BUT SEEMS LIKE IT'D MAKE YOU COMPLICIT IN... WHATEVER'S WHATEVER WITH HURWITZ.
DOES IT, THOUGH?
AS FAR AS ANYONE'S AWARE, HE'S A GENEROUS FAMILY FRIEND.
AND MOST IMPORTANTLY?
IT FREES ME.
FREES US.

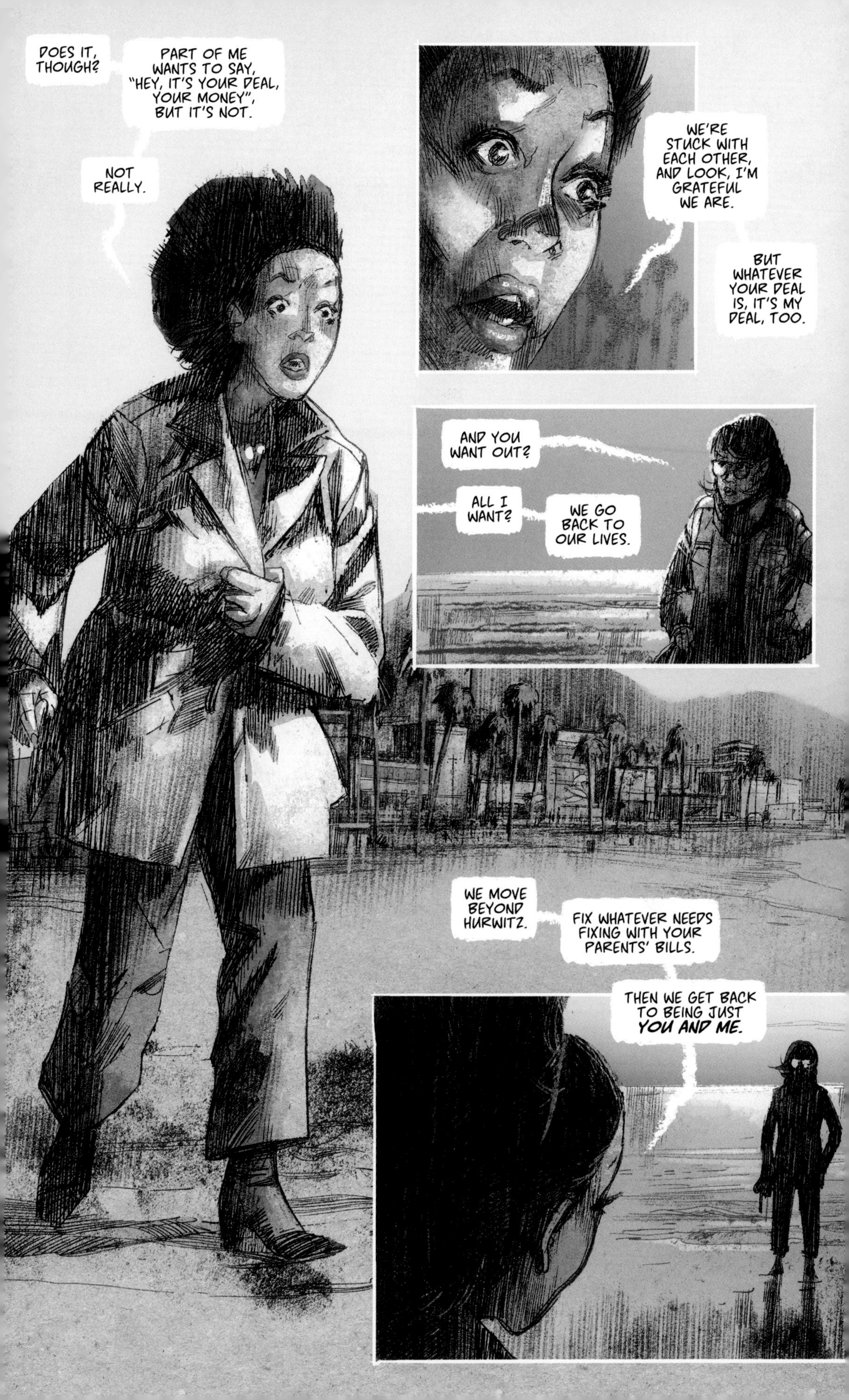
DOES IT, THOUGH?
PART OF ME WANTS TO SAY, "HEY, IT'S YOUR DEAL, YOUR MONEY", BUT IT'S NOT.
NOT REALLY.
WE'RE STUCK WITH EACH OTHER, AND LOOK, I'M GRATEFUL WE ARE.
BUT WHATEVER YOUR DEAL IS, IT'S MY DEAL, TOO.
AND YOU WANT OUT?
ALL I WANT?
WE GO BACK TO OUR LIVES.
WE MOVE BEYOND HURWITZ.
FIX WHATEVER NEEDS FIXING WITH YOUR PARENTS' BILLS.
THEN WE GET BACK TO BEING JUST ***YOU AND ME.***

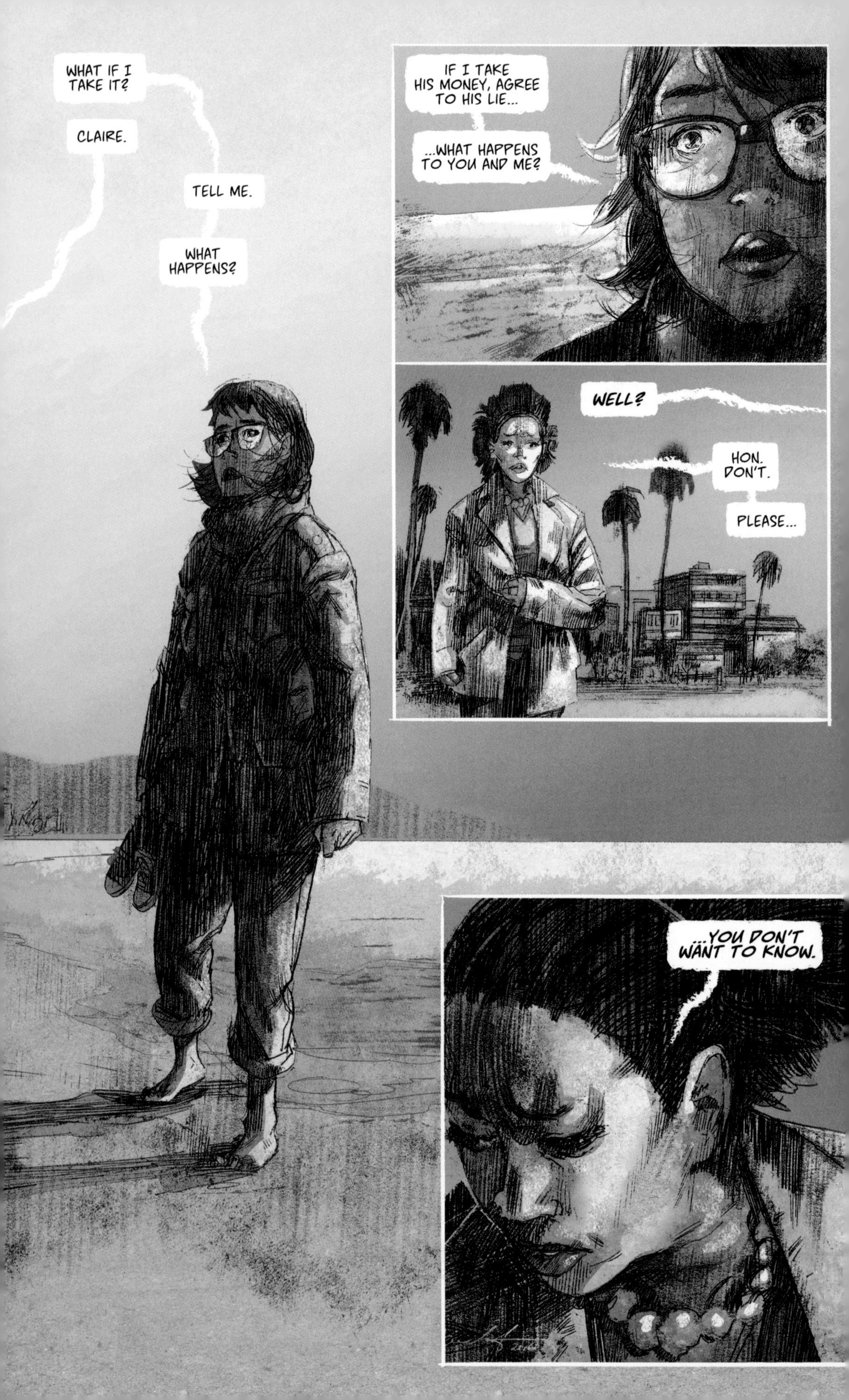
WHAT IF I TAKE IT?
CLAIRE.
TELL ME.
WHAT HAPPENS?
IF I TAKE HIS MONEY, AGREE TO HIS LIE...
...WHAT HAPPENS TO YOU AND ME?
WELL?
HON. DON'T.
PLEASE...
...YOU DON'T WANT TO KNOW.

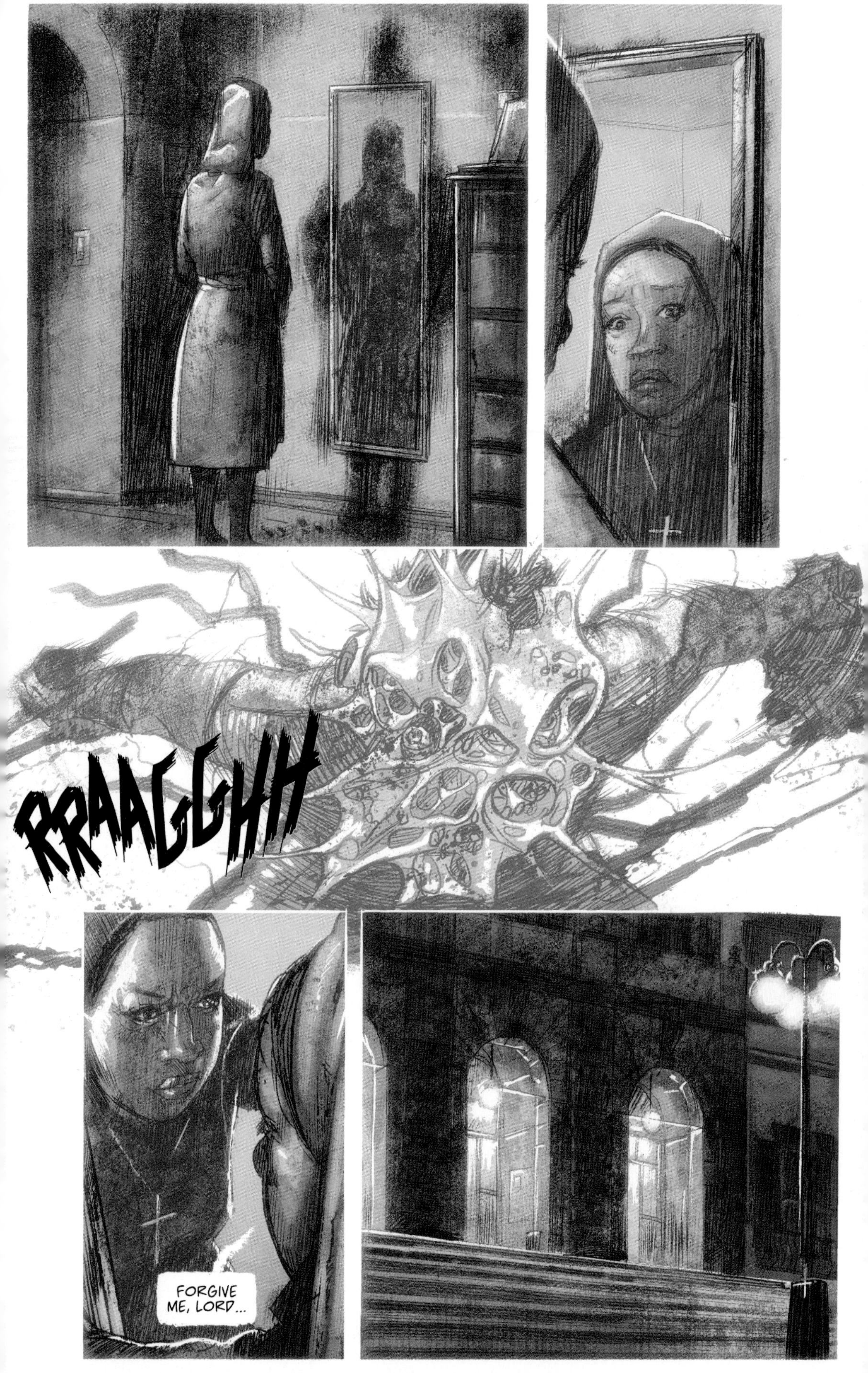
RRAAGGHH
FORGIVE ME, LORD...

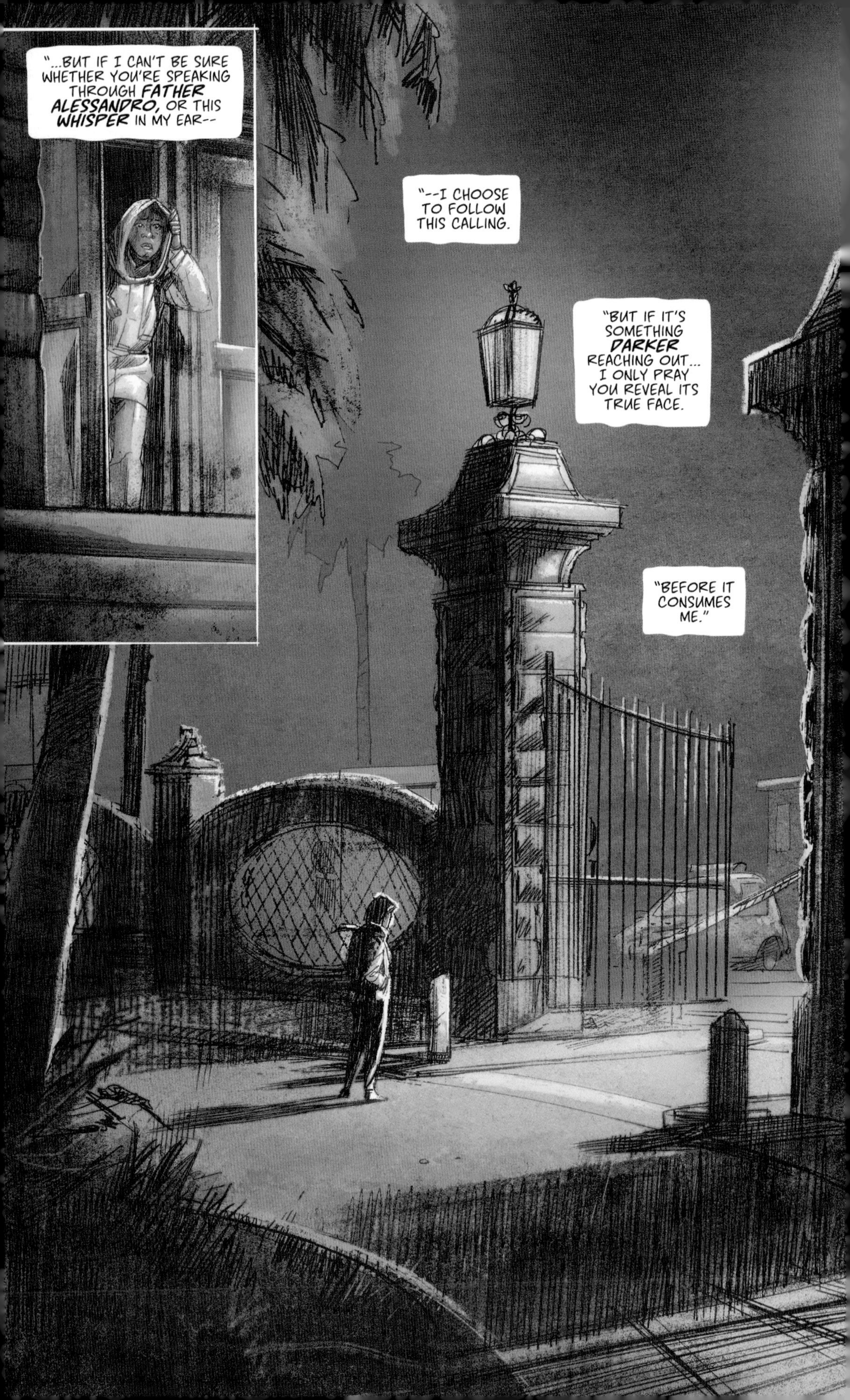
"...BUT IF I CAN'T BE SURE WHETHER YOU'RE SPEAKING THROUGH FATHER ALESSANDRO, OR THIS WHISPER IN MY EAR--
"--I CHOOSE TO FOLLOW THIS CALLING.
"BUT IF IT'S SOMETHING DARKER REACHING OUT... I ONLY PRAY YOU REVEAL ITS TRUE FACE.
"BEFORE IT CONSUMES ME."

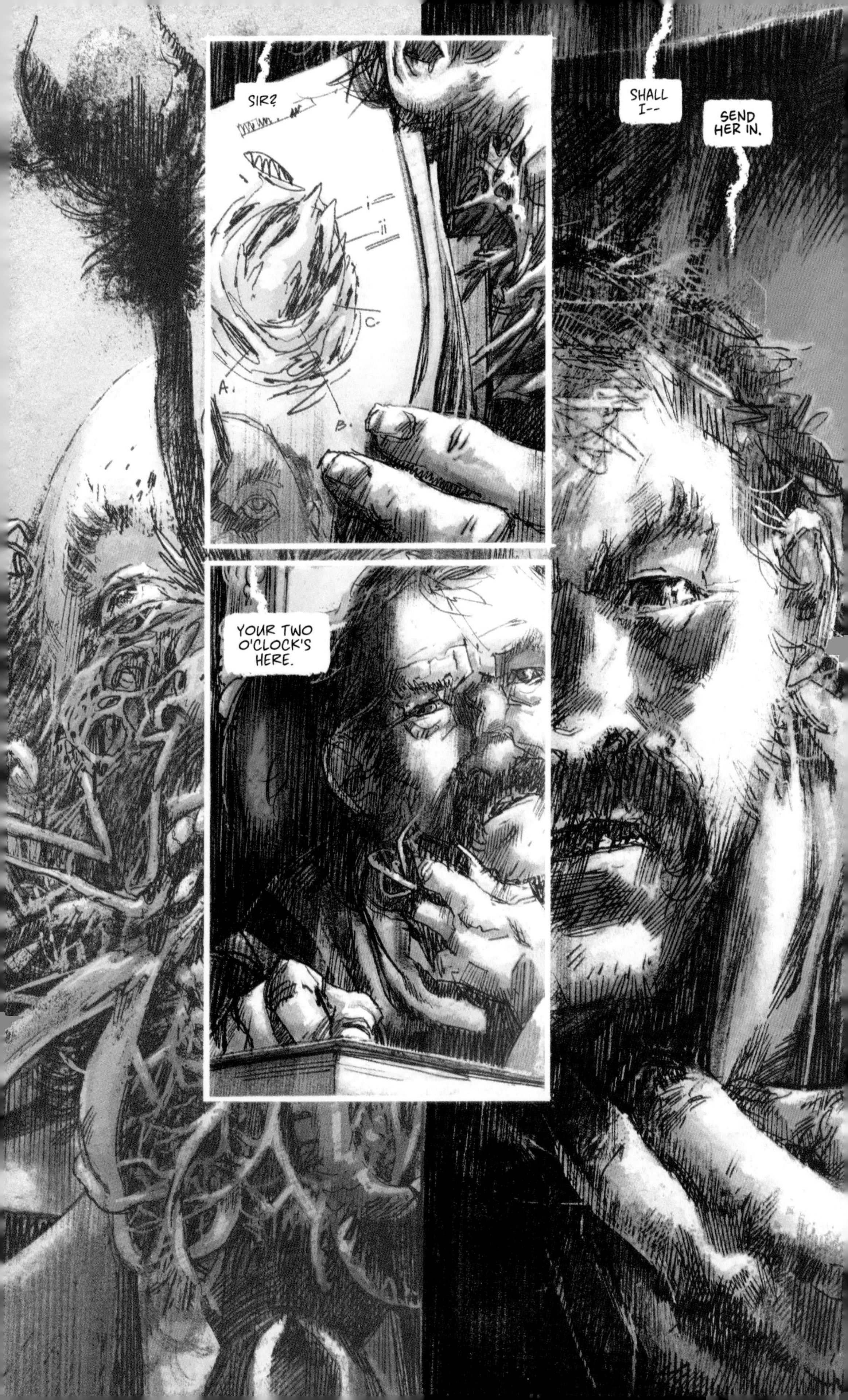
SIR?
YOUR TWO O'CLOCK'S HERE.
SHALL I--
SEND HER IN.

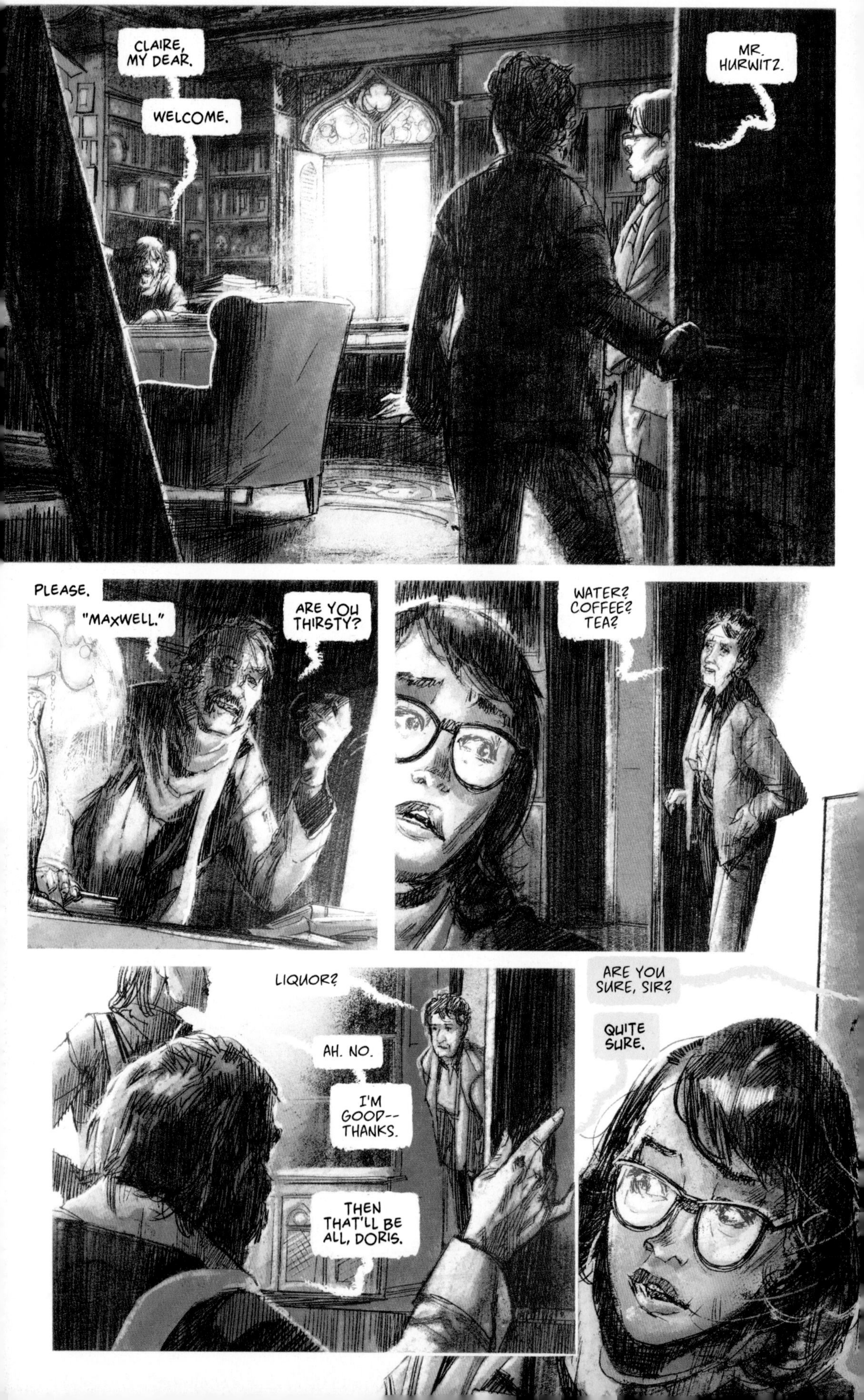
CLAIRE, MY DEAR.
WELCOME.
MR. HURWITZ.
PLEASE.
"MAXWELL."
ARE YOU THIRSTY?
WATER? COFFEE? TEA?
LIQUOR?
AH. NO.
I'M GOOD-- THANKS.
ARE YOU SURE, SIR?
QUITE SURE.
THEN THAT'LL BE ALL, DORIS.

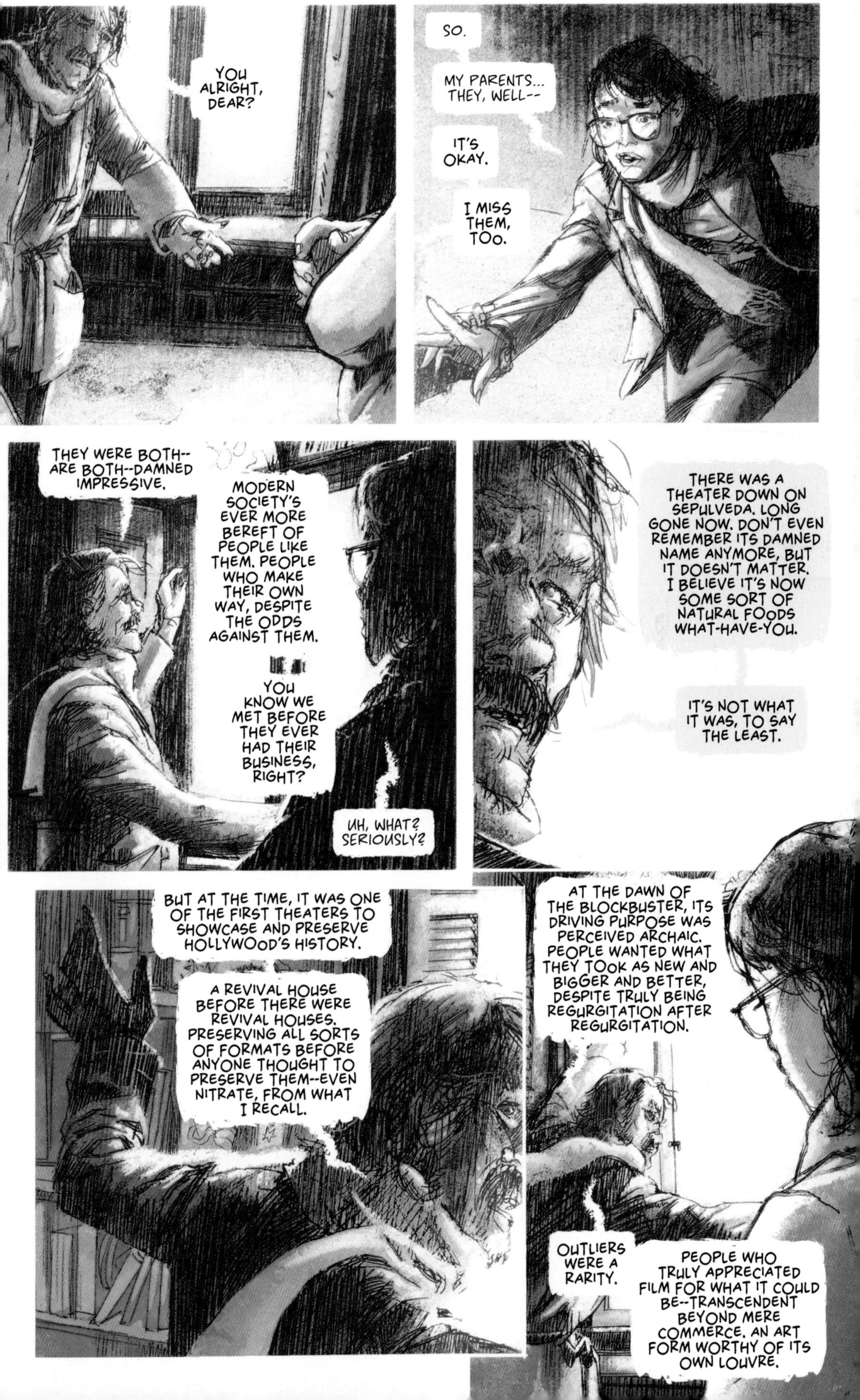
YOU ALRIGHT, DEAR?
SO.
MY PARENTS... THEY, WELL--
IT'S OKAY.
I MISS THEM, TOO.
THEY WERE BOTH--ARE BOTH--DAMNED IMPRESSIVE.
MODERN SOCIETY'S EVER MORE BEREFT OF PEOPLE LIKE THEM. PEOPLE WHO MAKE THEIR OWN WAY, DESPITE THE ODDS AGAINST THEM.
YOU KNOW WE MET BEFORE THEY EVER HAD THEIR BUSINESS, RIGHT?
UH, WHAT? SERIOUSLY?
THERE WAS A THEATER DOWN ON SEPULVEDA. LONG GONE NOW. DON'T EVEN REMEMBER ITS DAMNED NAME ANYMORE, BUT IT DOESN'T MATTER. I BELIEVE IT'S NOW SOME SORT OF NATURAL FOODS WHAT-HAVE-YOU.
IT'S NOT WHAT IT WAS, TO SAY THE LEAST.
BUT AT THE TIME, IT WAS ONE OF THE FIRST THEATERS TO SHOWCASE AND PRESERVE HOLLYWOOD'S HISTORY.
A REVIVAL HOUSE BEFORE THERE WERE REVIVAL HOUSES. PRESERVING ALL SORTS OF FORMATS BEFORE ANYONE THOUGHT TO PRESERVE THEM--EVEN NITRATE, FROM WHAT I RECALL.
AT THE DAWN OF THE BLOCKBUSTER, ITS DRIVING PURPOSE WAS PERCEIVED ARCHAIC. PEOPLE WANTED WHAT THEY TOOK AS NEW AND BIGGER AND BETTER, DESPITE TRULY BEING REGURGITATION AFTER REGURGITATION.
OUTLIERS WERE A RARITY.
PEOPLE WHO TRULY APPRECIATED FILM FOR WHAT IT COULD BE--TRANSCENDENT BEYOND MERE COMMERCE. AN ART FORM WORTHY OF ITS OWN LOUVRE.

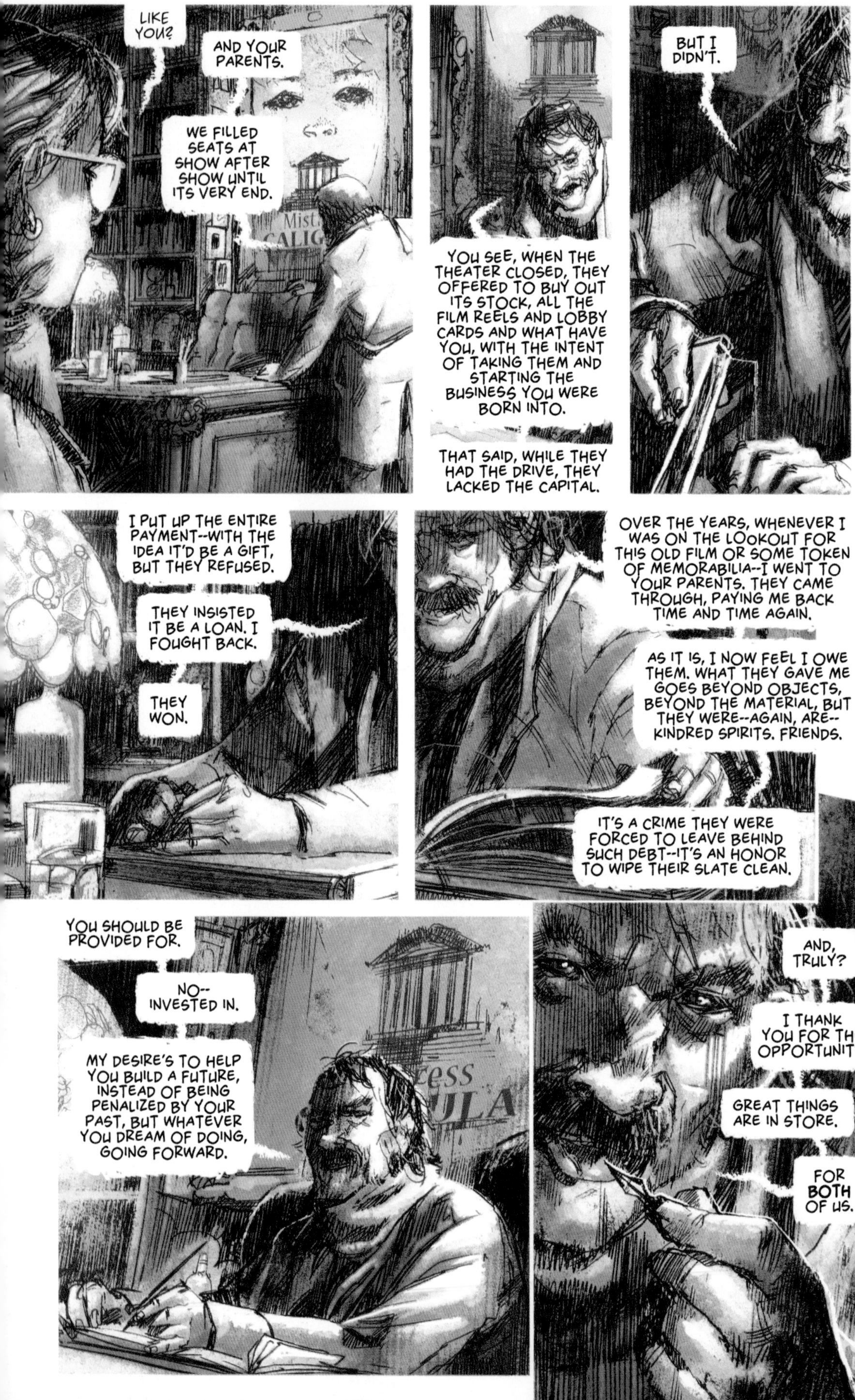
LIKE YOU?
AND YOUR PARENTS.
WE FILLED SEATS AT SHOW AFTER SHOW UNTIL ITS VERY END.
YOU SEE, WHEN THE THEATER CLOSED, THEY OFFERED TO BUY OUT ITS STOCK, ALL THE FILM REELS AND LOBBY CARDS AND WHAT HAVE YOU, WITH THE INTENT OF TAKING THEM AND STARTING THE BUSINESS YOU WERE BORN INTO.
THAT SAID, WHILE THEY HAD THE DRIVE, THEY LACKED THE CAPITAL.
BUT I DIDN'T.
I PUT UP THE ENTIRE PAYMENT--WITH THE IDEA IT'D BE A GIFT, BUT THEY REFUSED.
THEY INSISTED IT BE A LOAN. I FOUGHT BACK.
THEY WON.
OVER THE YEARS, WHENEVER I WAS ON THE LOOKOUT FOR THIS OLD FILM OR SOME TOKEN OF MEMORABILIA--I WENT TO YOUR PARENTS. THEY CAME THROUGH, PAYING ME BACK TIME AND TIME AGAIN.
AS IT IS, I NOW FEEL I OWE THEM. WHAT THEY GAVE ME GOES BEYOND OBJECTS, BEYOND THE MATERIAL, BUT THEY WERE--AGAIN, ARE--KINDRED SPIRITS. FRIENDS.
IT'S A CRIME THEY WERE FORCED TO LEAVE BEHIND SUCH DEBT--IT'S AN HONOR TO WIPE THEIR SLATE CLEAN.
YOU SHOULD BE PROVIDED FOR.
NO-- INVESTED IN.
MY DESIRE'S TO HELP YOU BUILD A FUTURE, INSTEAD OF BEING PENALIZED BY YOUR PAST, BUT WHATEVER YOU DREAM OF DOING, GOING FORWARD.
AND, TRULY?
I THANK YOU FOR THE OPPORTUNITY.
GREAT THINGS ARE IN STORE.
FOR **BOTH** OF US.

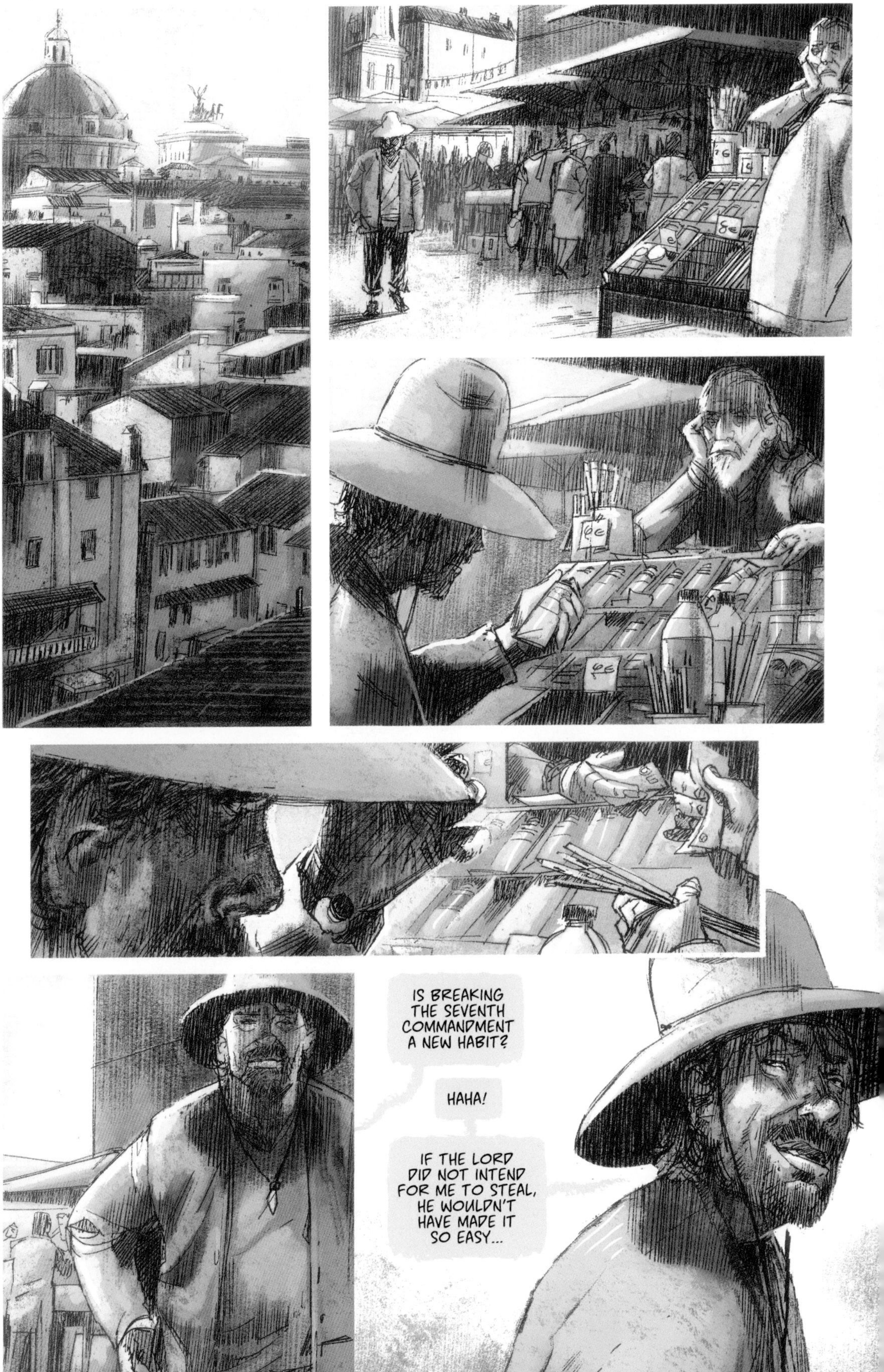
IS BREAKING THE SEVENTH COMMANDMENT A NEW HABIT?
HAHA!
IF THE LORD DID NOT INTEND FOR ME TO STEAL, HE WOULDN'T HAVE MADE IT SO EASY...

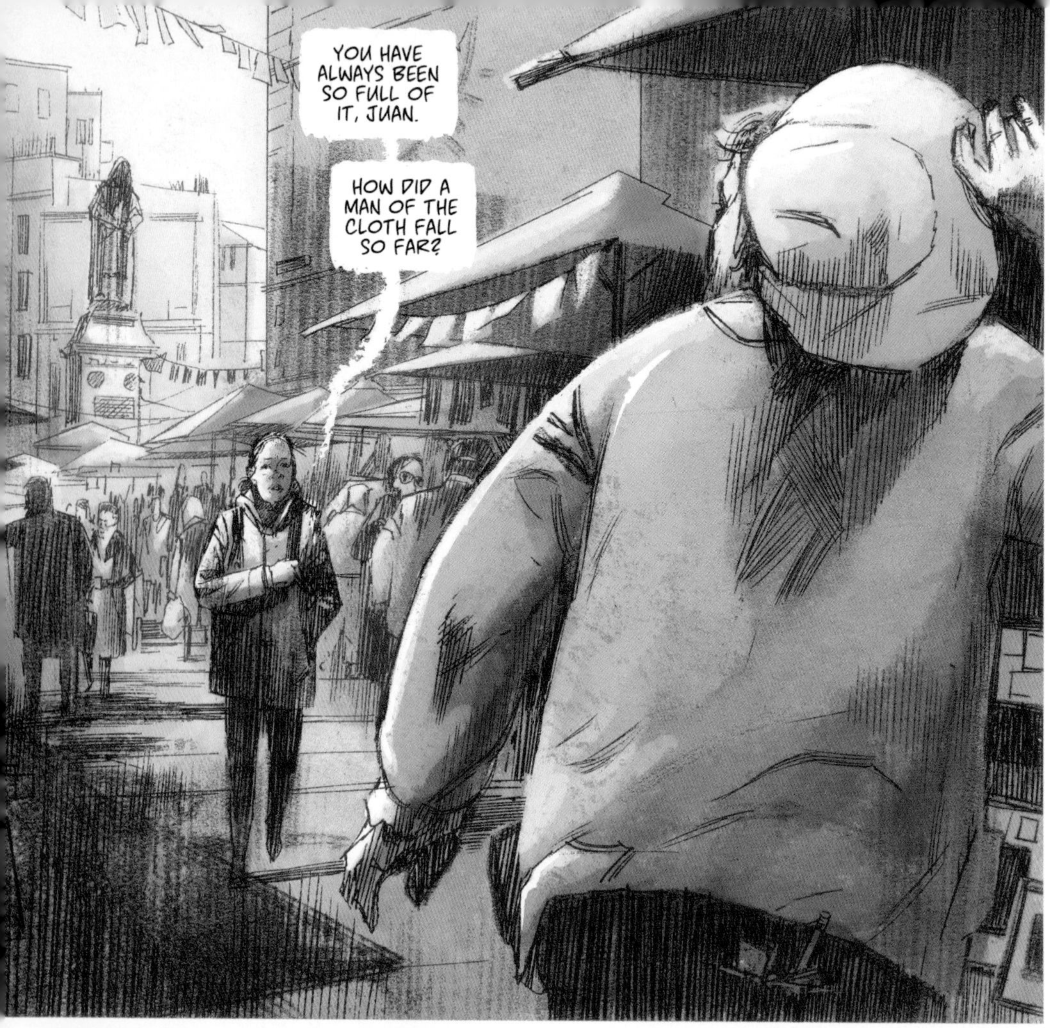
YOU HAVE ALWAYS BEEN SO FULL OF IT, JUAN.
HOW DID A MAN OF THE CLOTH FALL SO FAR?
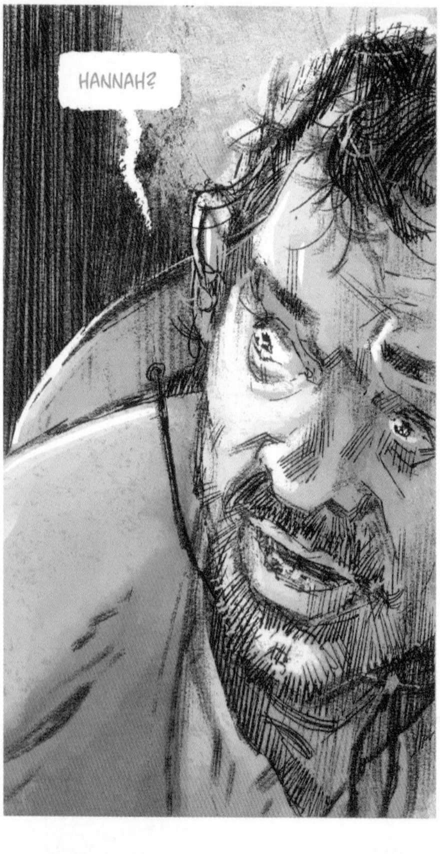
HANNAH?
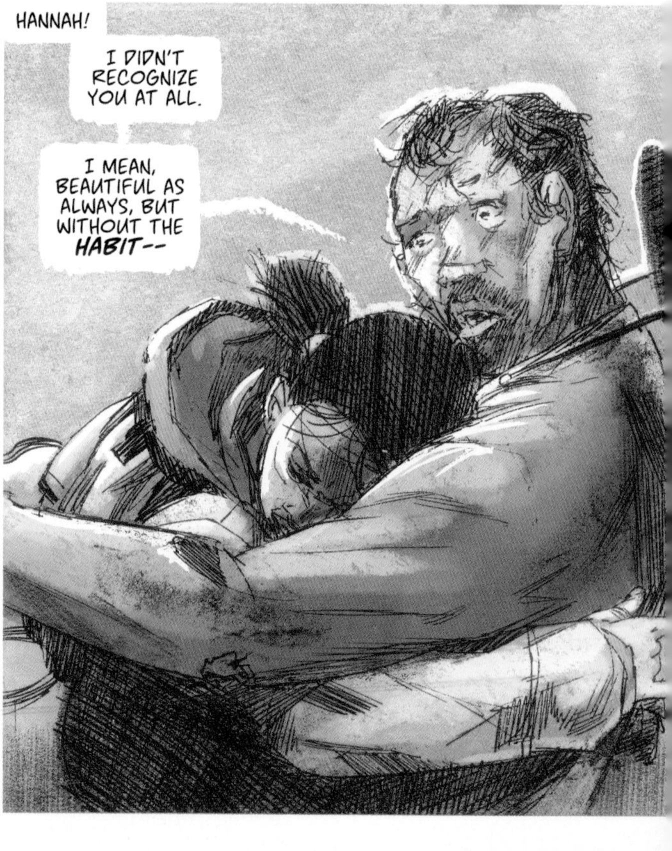
HANNAH!
I DIDN'T RECOGNIZE YOU AT ALL.
I MEAN, BEAUTIFUL AS ALWAYS, BUT WITHOUT THE *HABIT*--

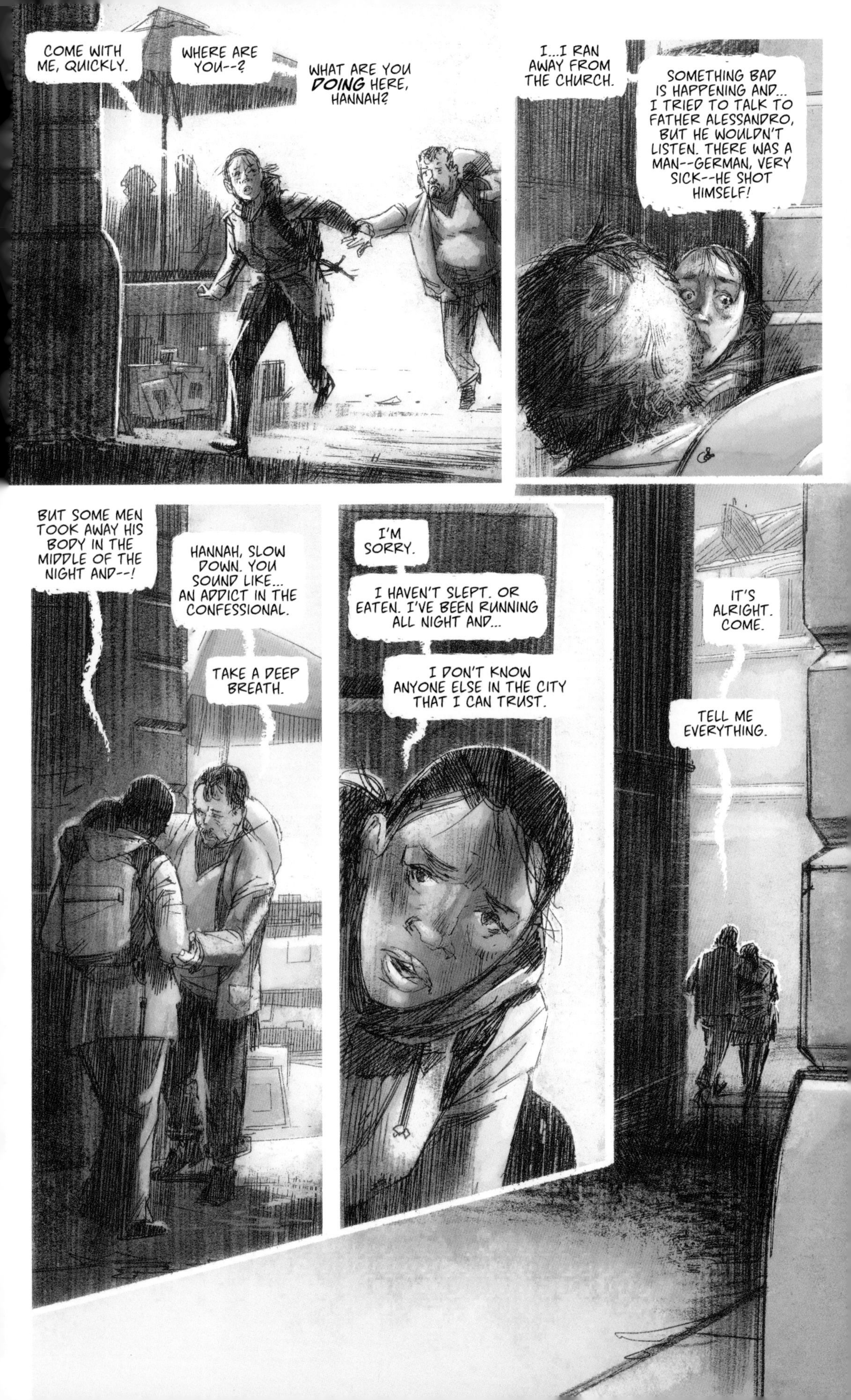
COME WITH ME, QUICKLY.
WHERE ARE YOU--?
WHAT ARE YOU **DOING** HERE, HANNAH?
I...I RAN AWAY FROM THE CHURCH.
SOMETHING BAD IS HAPPENING AND... I TRIED TO TALK TO FATHER ALESSANDRO, BUT HE WOULDN'T LISTEN. THERE WAS A MAN--GERMAN, VERY SICK--HE SHOT HIMSELF!
BUT SOME MEN TOOK AWAY HIS BODY IN THE MIDDLE OF THE NIGHT AND--!
HANNAH, SLOW DOWN. YOU SOUND LIKE... AN ADDICT IN THE CONFESSIONAL.
TAKE A DEEP BREATH.
I'M SORRY.
I HAVEN'T SLEPT. OR EATEN. I'VE BEEN RUNNING ALL NIGHT AND...
I DON'T KNOW ANYONE ELSE IN THE CITY THAT I CAN TRUST.
IT'S ALRIGHT. COME.
TELL ME EVERYTHING.

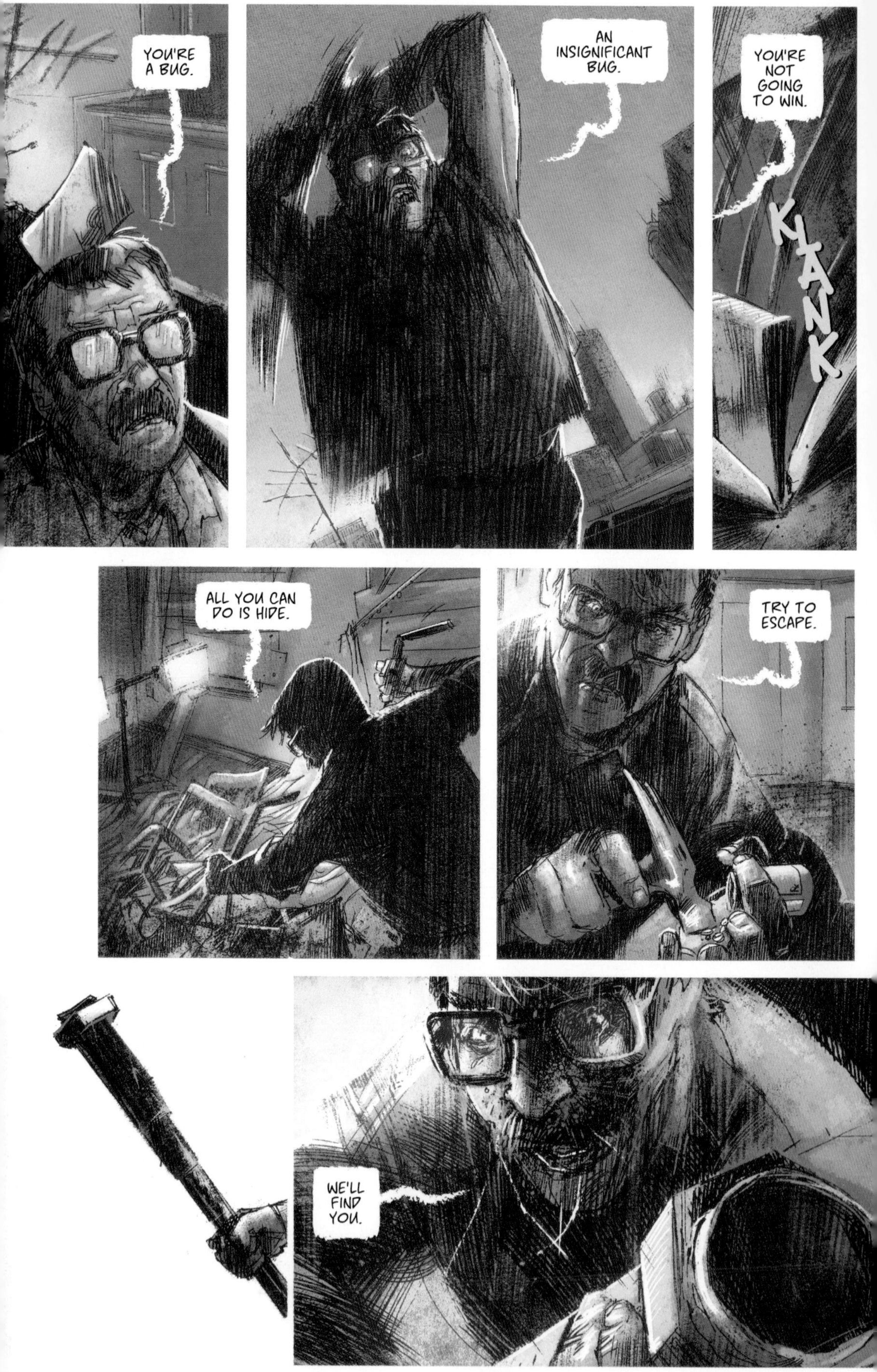
YOU'RE A BUG.
AN INSIGNIFICANT BUG.
YOU'RE NOT GOING TO WIN.
KLANK
ALL YOU CAN DO IS HIDE.
TRY TO ESCAPE.
WE'LL FIND YOU.

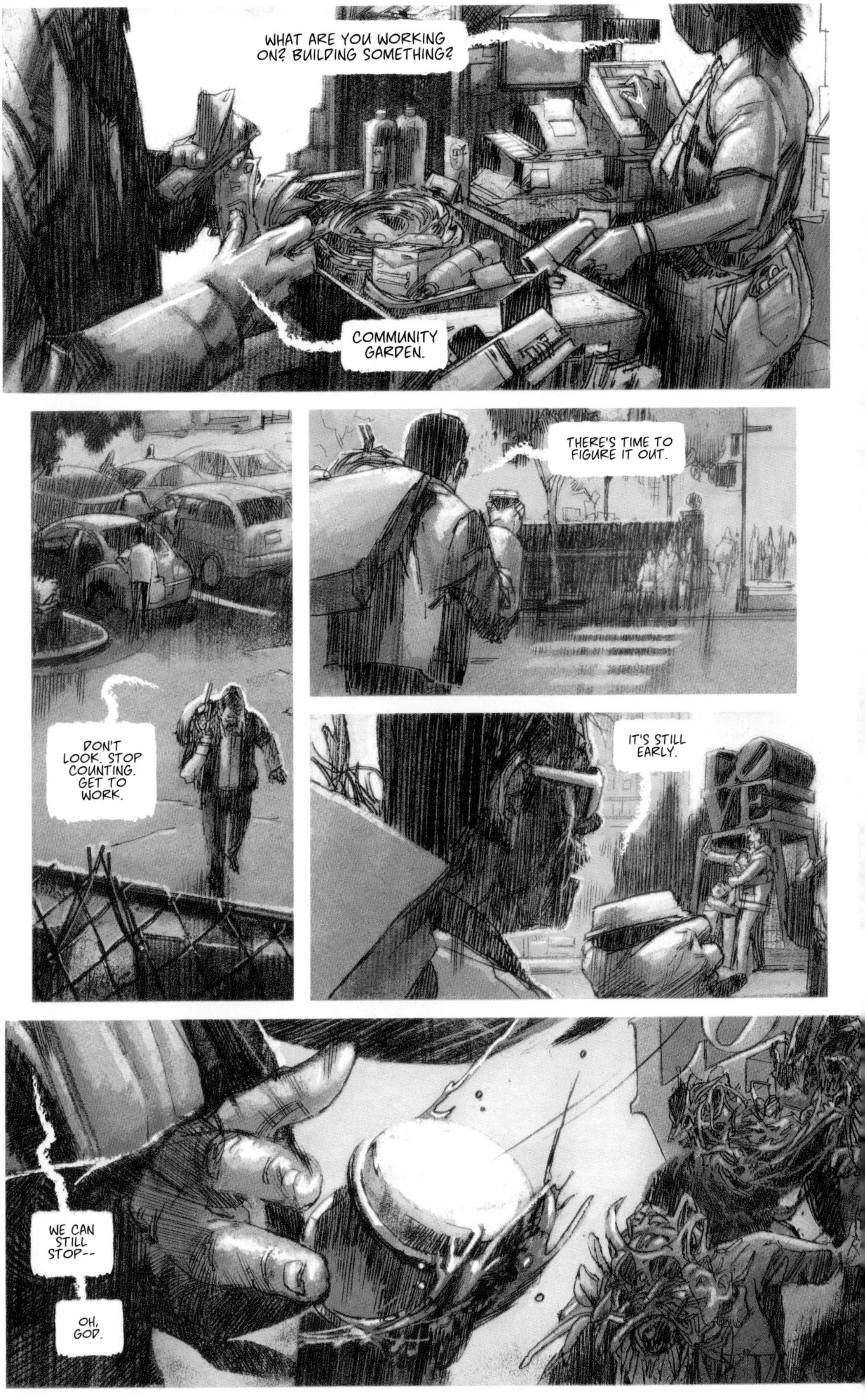
WHAT ARE YOU WORKING ON? BUILDING SOMETHING?
COMMUNITY GARDEN.
THERE'S TIME TO FIGURE IT OUT.
DON'T LOOK. STOP COUNTING. GET TO WORK.
IT'S STILL EARLY.
WE CAN STILL STOP--
OH, GOD.

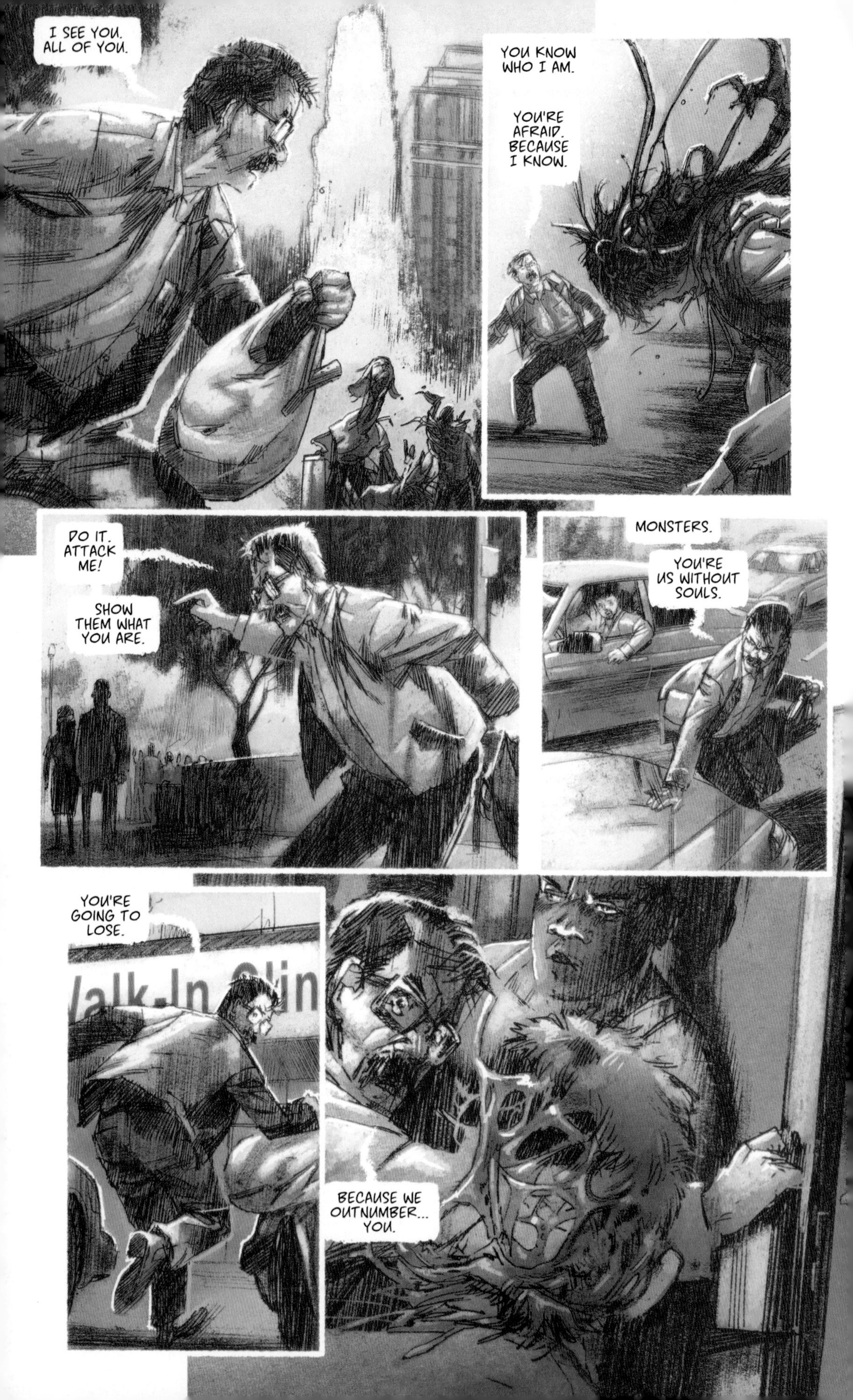
I SEE YOU. ALL OF YOU.
YOU KNOW WHO I AM.
YOU'RE AFRAID. BECAUSE I KNOW.
DO IT. ATTACK ME!
SHOW THEM WHAT YOU ARE.
MONSTERS.
YOU'RE US WITHOUT SOULS.
YOU'RE GOING TO LOSE.
BECAUSE WE OUTNUMBER... YOU.

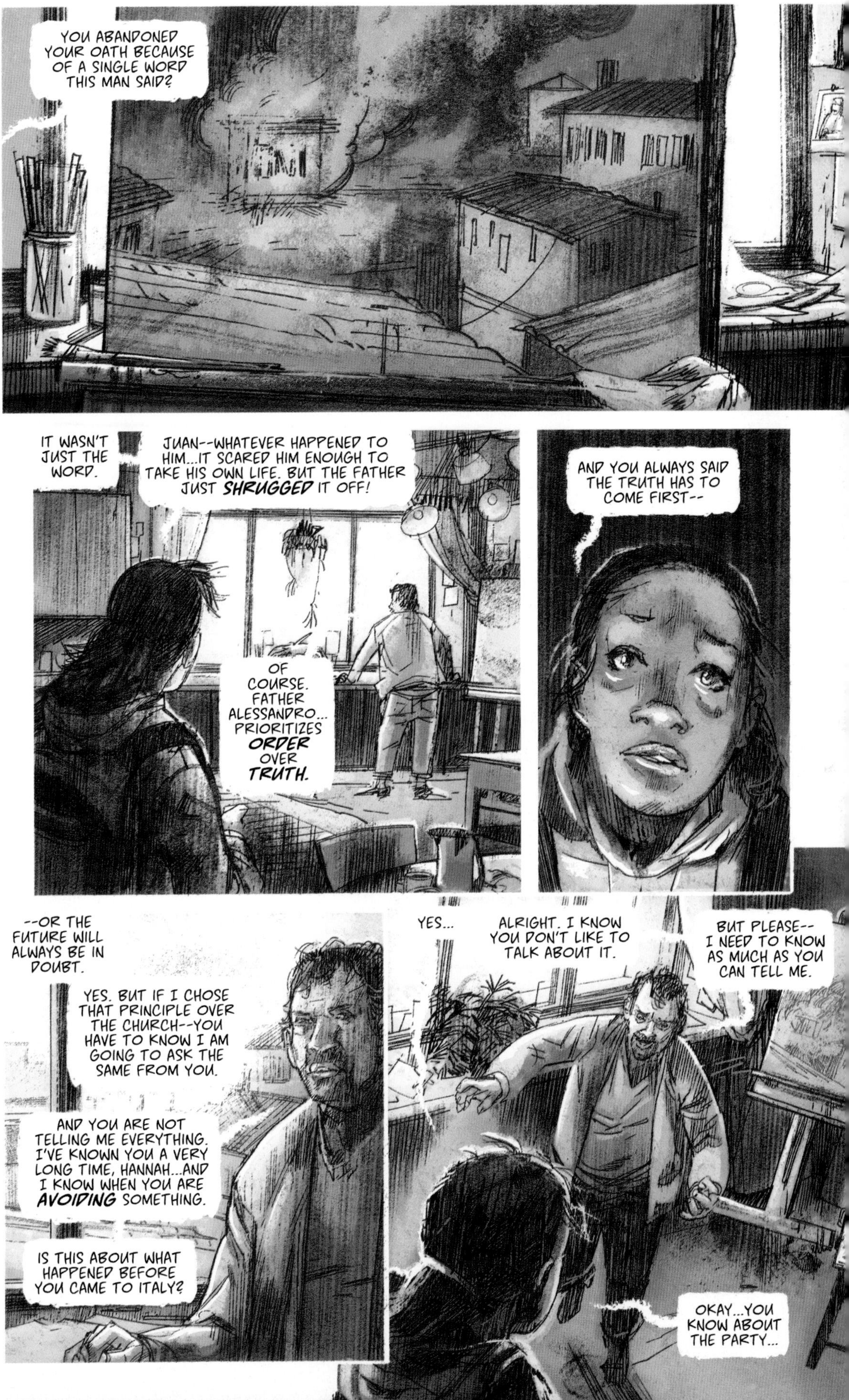
YOU ABANDONED YOUR OATH BECAUSE OF A SINGLE WORD THIS MAN SAID?
IT WASN'T JUST THE WORD.
JUAN--WHATEVER HAPPENED TO HIM...IT SCARED HIM ENOUGH TO TAKE HIS OWN LIFE. BUT THE FATHER JUST SHRUGGED IT OFF!
OF COURSE. FATHER ALESSANDRO... PRIORITIZES ORDER OVER TRUTH.
AND YOU ALWAYS SAID THE TRUTH HAS TO COME FIRST--
--OR THE FUTURE WILL ALWAYS BE IN DOUBT.
YES. BUT IF I CHOSE THAT PRINCIPLE OVER THE CHURCH--YOU HAVE TO KNOW I AM GOING TO ASK THE SAME FROM YOU.
AND YOU ARE NOT TELLING ME EVERYTHING. I'VE KNOWN YOU A VERY LONG TIME, HANNAH...AND I KNOW WHEN YOU ARE AVOIDING SOMETHING.
IS THIS ABOUT WHAT HAPPENED BEFORE YOU CAME TO ITALY?
YES...
ALRIGHT. I KNOW YOU DON'T LIKE TO TALK ABOUT IT.
BUT PLEASE--I NEED TO KNOW AS MUCH AS YOU CAN TELL ME.
OKAY...YOU KNOW ABOUT THE PARTY...

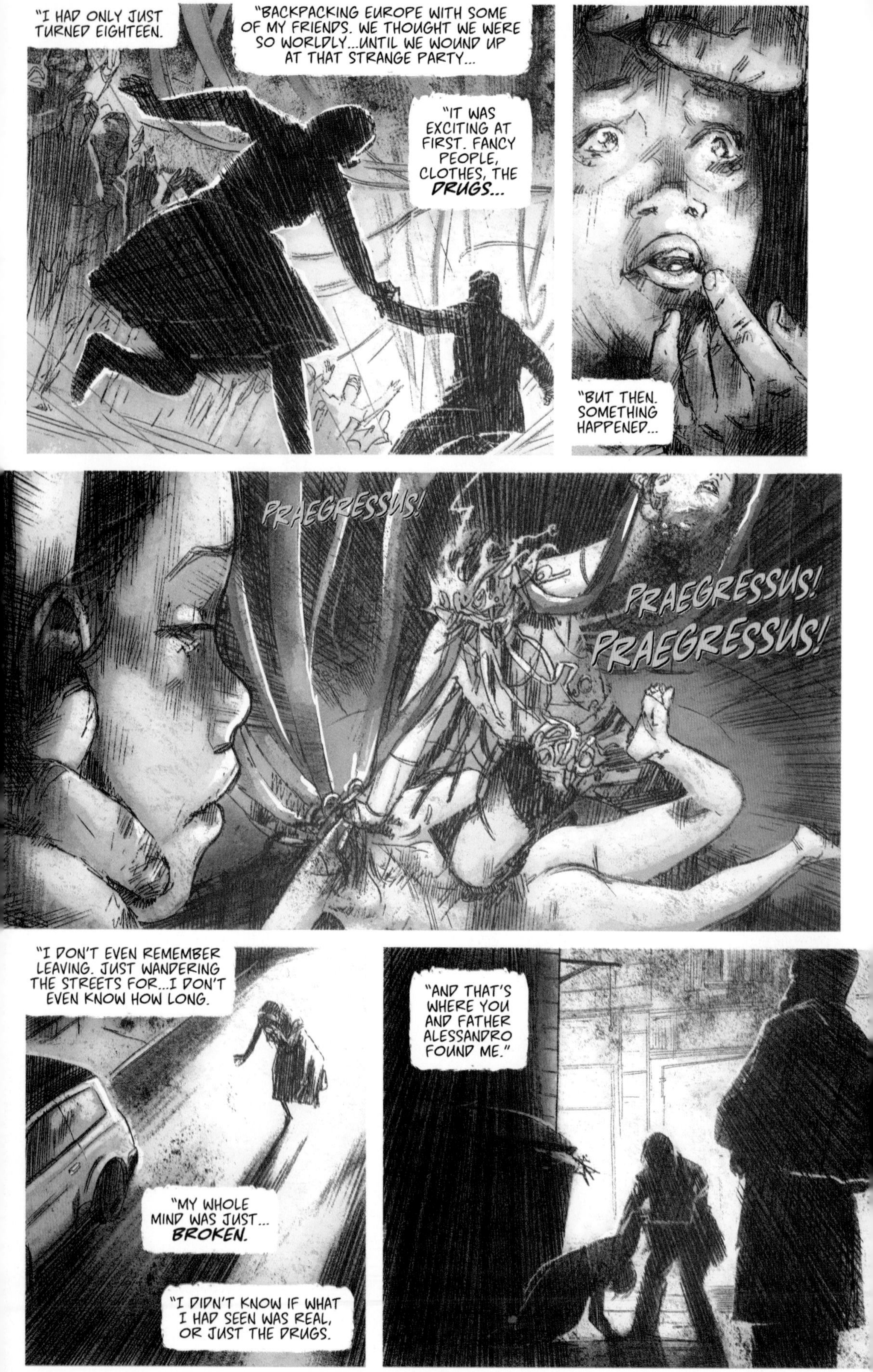
"I HAD ONLY JUST TURNED EIGHTEEN.
"BACKPACKING EUROPE WITH SOME OF MY FRIENDS. WE THOUGHT WE WERE SO WORLDLY...UNTIL WE WOUND UP AT THAT STRANGE PARTY...
"IT WAS EXCITING AT FIRST. FANCY PEOPLE, CLOTHES, THE DRUGS...
"BUT THEN. SOMETHING HAPPENED...
PRAEGRESSUS!
PRAEGRESSUS!
PRAEGRESSUS!
"I DON'T EVEN REMEMBER LEAVING. JUST WANDERING THE STREETS FOR...I DON'T EVEN KNOW HOW LONG.
"MY WHOLE MIND WAS JUST... BROKEN.
"I DIDN'T KNOW IF WHAT I HAD SEEN WAS REAL, OR JUST THE DRUGS.
"AND THAT'S WHERE YOU AND FATHER ALESSANDRO FOUND ME."

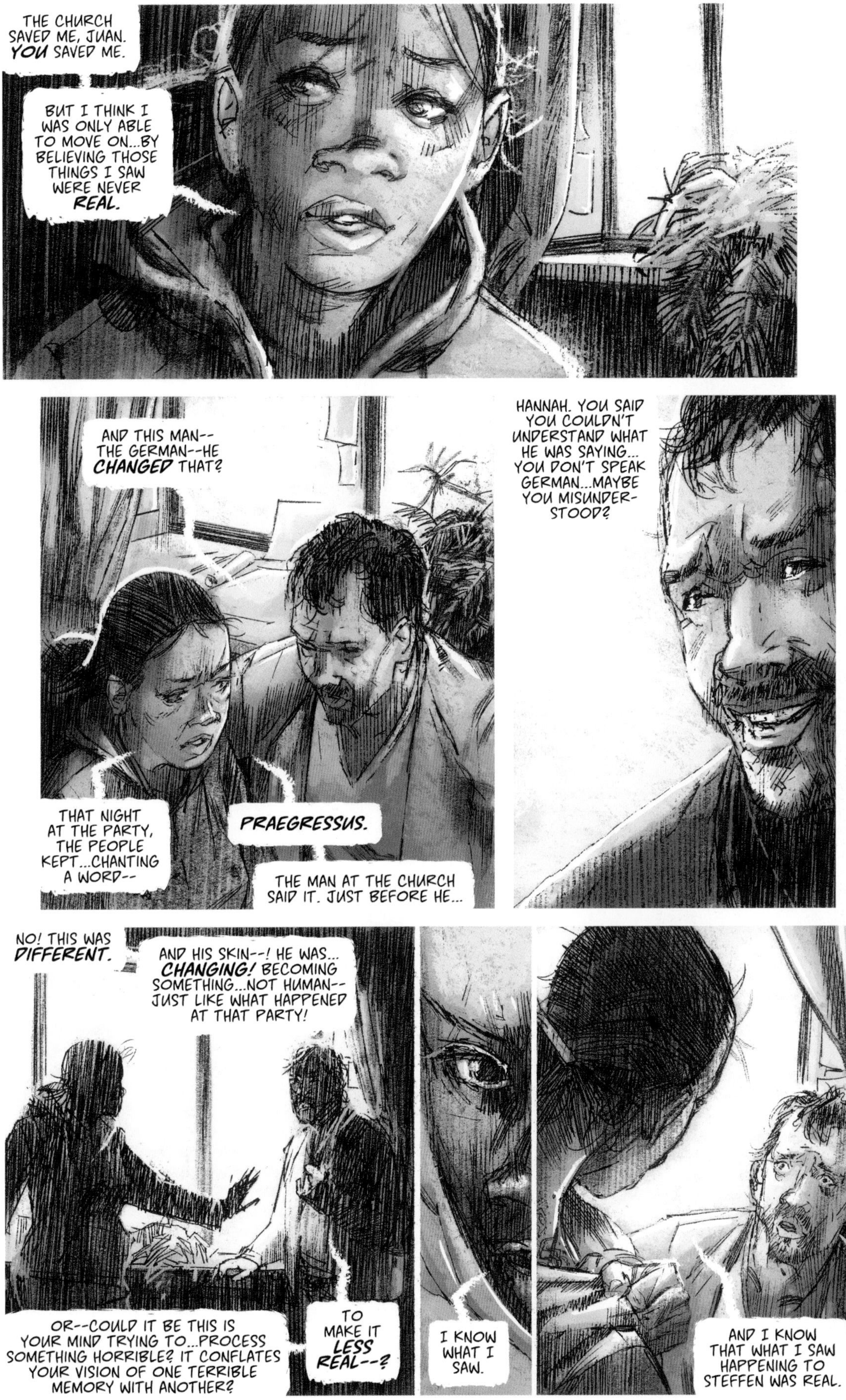
THE CHURCH SAVED ME, JUAN. YOU SAVED ME.
BUT I THINK I WAS ONLY ABLE TO MOVE ON...BY BELIEVING THOSE THINGS I SAW WERE NEVER REAL.
AND THIS MAN--THE GERMAN--HE CHANGED THAT?
THAT NIGHT AT THE PARTY, THE PEOPLE KEPT...CHANTING A WORD--
PRAEGRESSUS.
THE MAN AT THE CHURCH SAID IT. JUST BEFORE HE...
HANNAH. YOU SAID YOU COULDN'T UNDERSTAND WHAT HE WAS SAYING... YOU DON'T SPEAK GERMAN...MAYBE YOU MISUNDER-STOOD?
NO! THIS WAS DIFFERENT.
AND HIS SKIN--! HE WAS... CHANGING! BECOMING SOMETHING...NOT HUMAN--JUST LIKE WHAT HAPPENED AT THAT PARTY!
OR--COULD IT BE THIS IS YOUR MIND TRYING TO...PROCESS SOMETHING HORRIBLE? IT CONFLATES YOUR VISION OF ONE TERRIBLE MEMORY WITH ANOTHER?
TO MAKE IT LESS REAL--?
I KNOW WHAT I SAW.
AND I KNOW THAT WHAT I SAW HAPPENING TO STEFFEN WAS REAL.

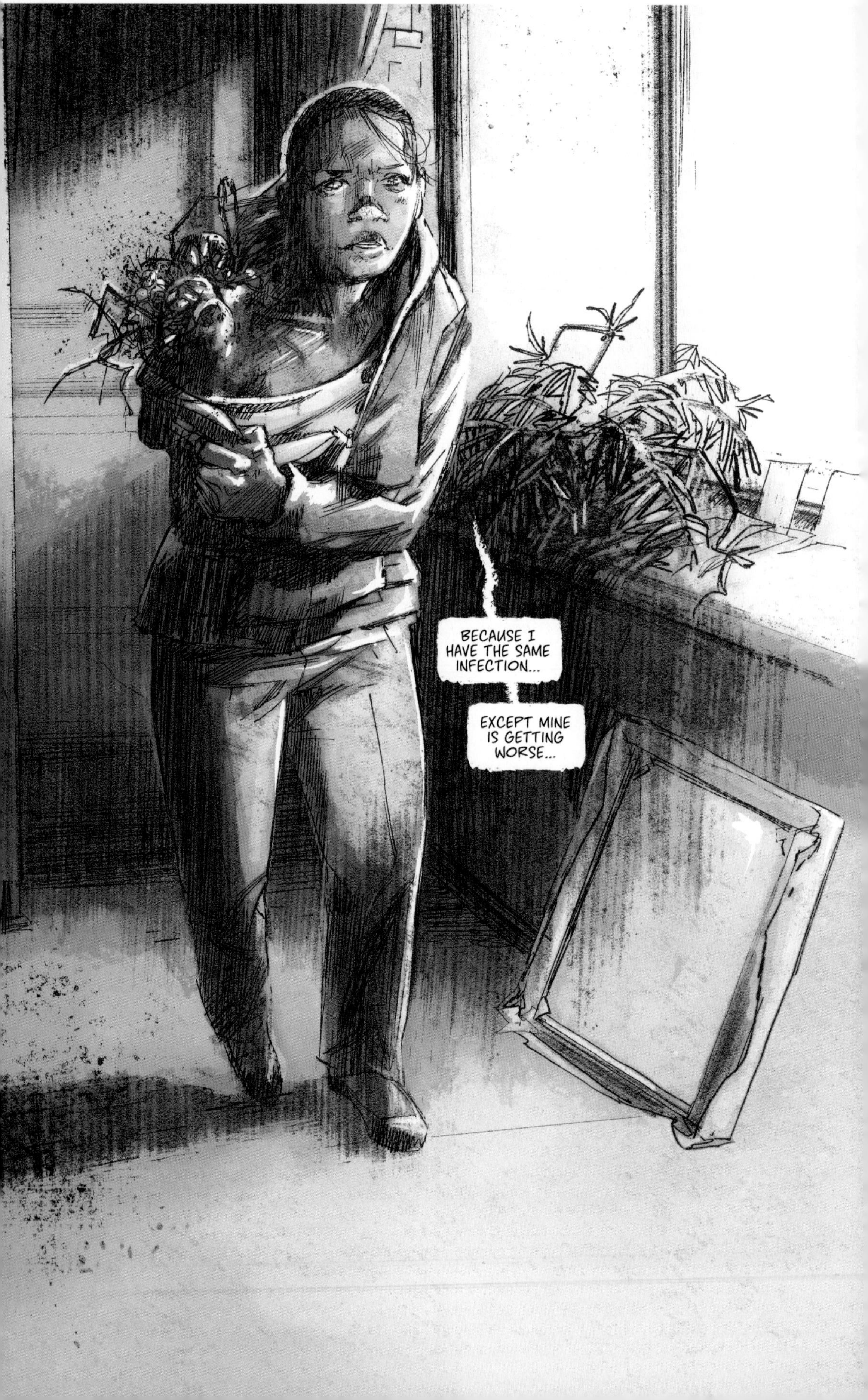
BECAUSE I HAVE THE SAME INFECTION...
EXCEPT MINE IS GETTING WORSE...

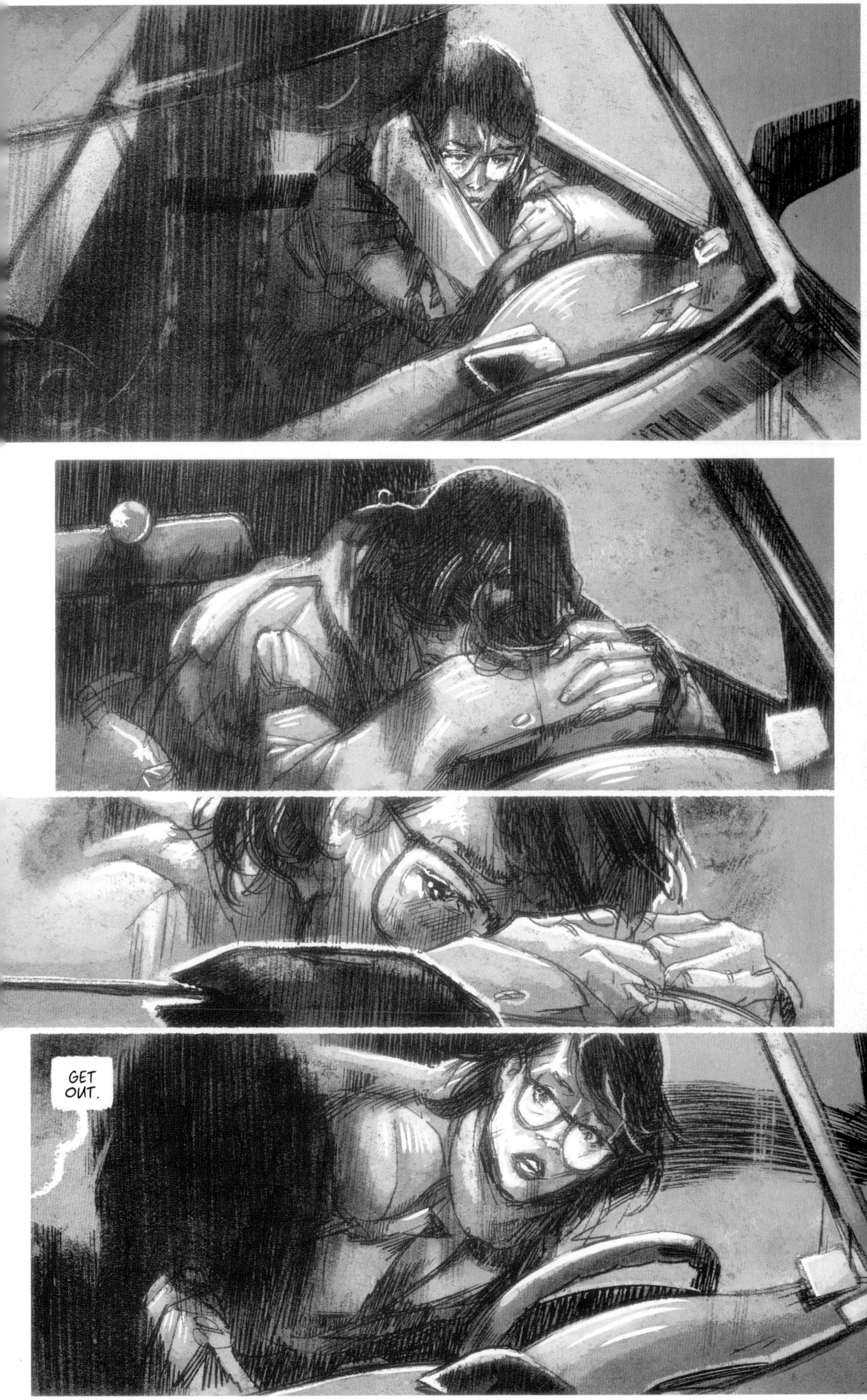
GET OUT.

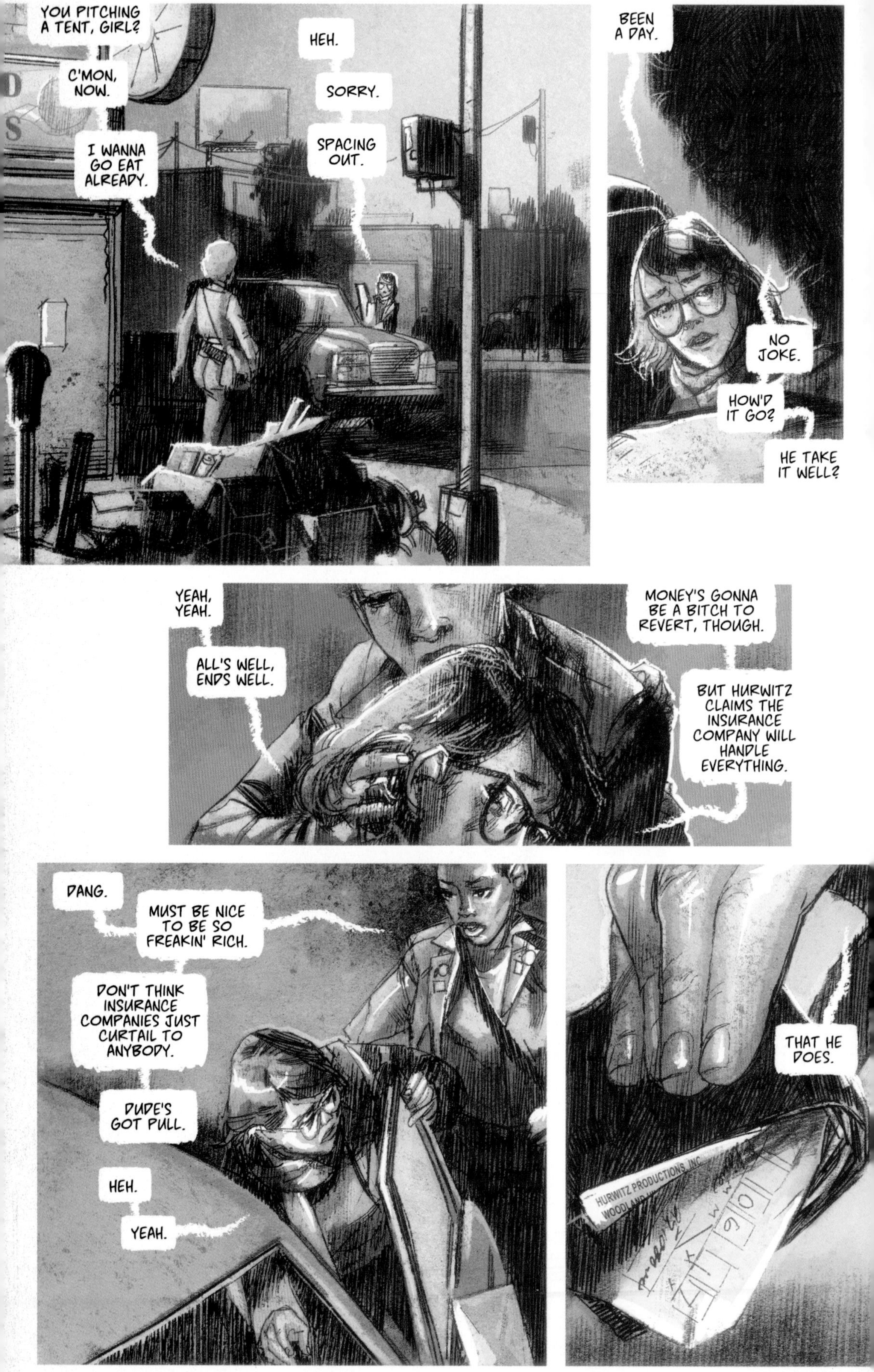

YOU PITCHING A TENT, GIRL?
C'MON, NOW.
I WANNA GO EAT ALREADY.
HEH.
SORRY.
SPACING OUT.
BEEN A DAY.
NO JOKE.
HOW'D IT GO?
HE TAKE IT WELL?
YEAH, YEAH.
ALL'S WELL, ENDS WELL.
MONEY'S GONNA BE A BITCH TO REVERT, THOUGH.
BUT HURWITZ CLAIMS THE INSURANCE COMPANY WILL HANDLE EVERYTHING.
DANG.
MUST BE NICE TO BE SO FREAKIN' RICH.
DON'T THINK INSURANCE COMPANIES JUST CURTAIL TO ANYBODY.
DUDE'S GOT PULL.
HEH.
YEAH.
THAT HE DOES.
HURWITZ PRODUCTIONS, INC.

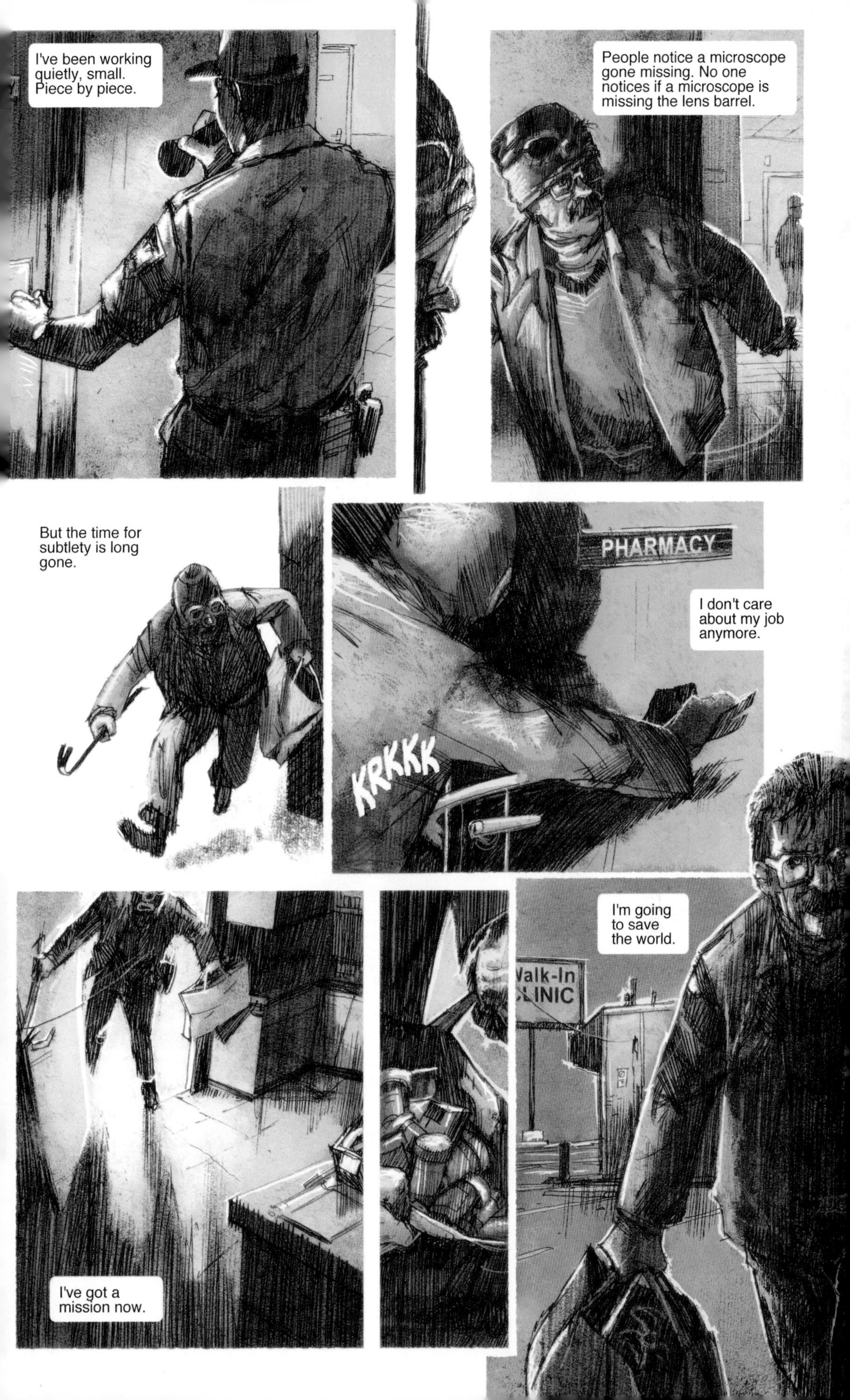

I've been working quietly, small. Piece by piece.
People notice a microscope gone missing. No one notices if a microscope is missing the lens barrel.
But the time for subtlety is long gone.
PHARMACY
I don't care about my job anymore.
KRKKK
I've got a mission now.
I'm going to save the world.
Walk-In CLINIC

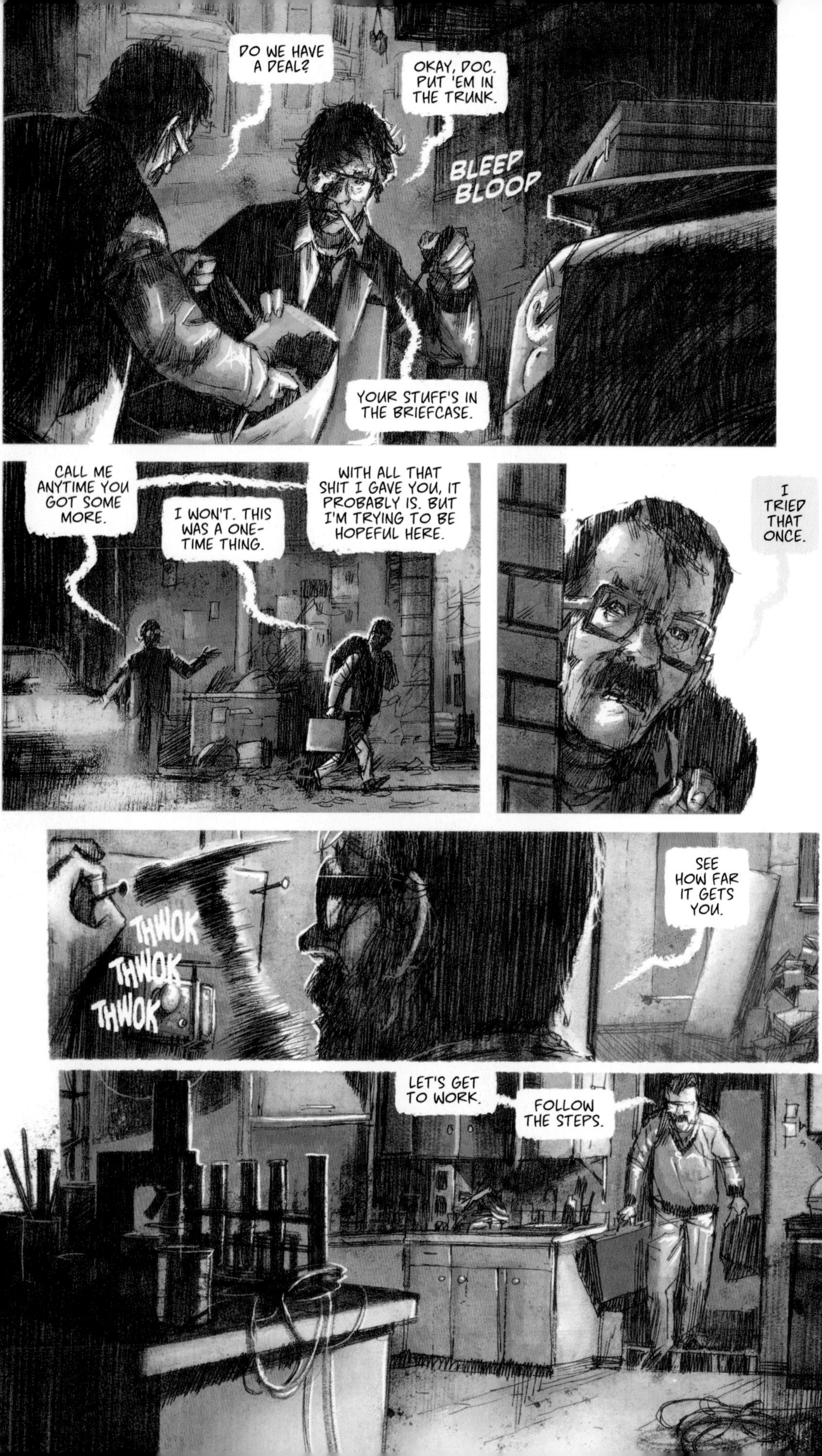
DO WE HAVE A DEAL?
OKAY, DOC. PUT 'EM IN THE TRUNK.
BLEEP BLOOP
YOUR STUFF'S IN THE BRIEFCASE.
CALL ME ANYTIME YOU GOT SOME MORE.
I WON'T. THIS WAS A ONE-TIME THING.
WITH ALL THAT SHIT I GAVE YOU, IT PROBABLY IS. BUT I'M TRYING TO BE HOPEFUL HERE.
I TRIED THAT ONCE.
THWOK THWOK THWOK
SEE HOW FAR IT GETS YOU.
LET'S GET TO WORK.
FOLLOW THE STEPS.

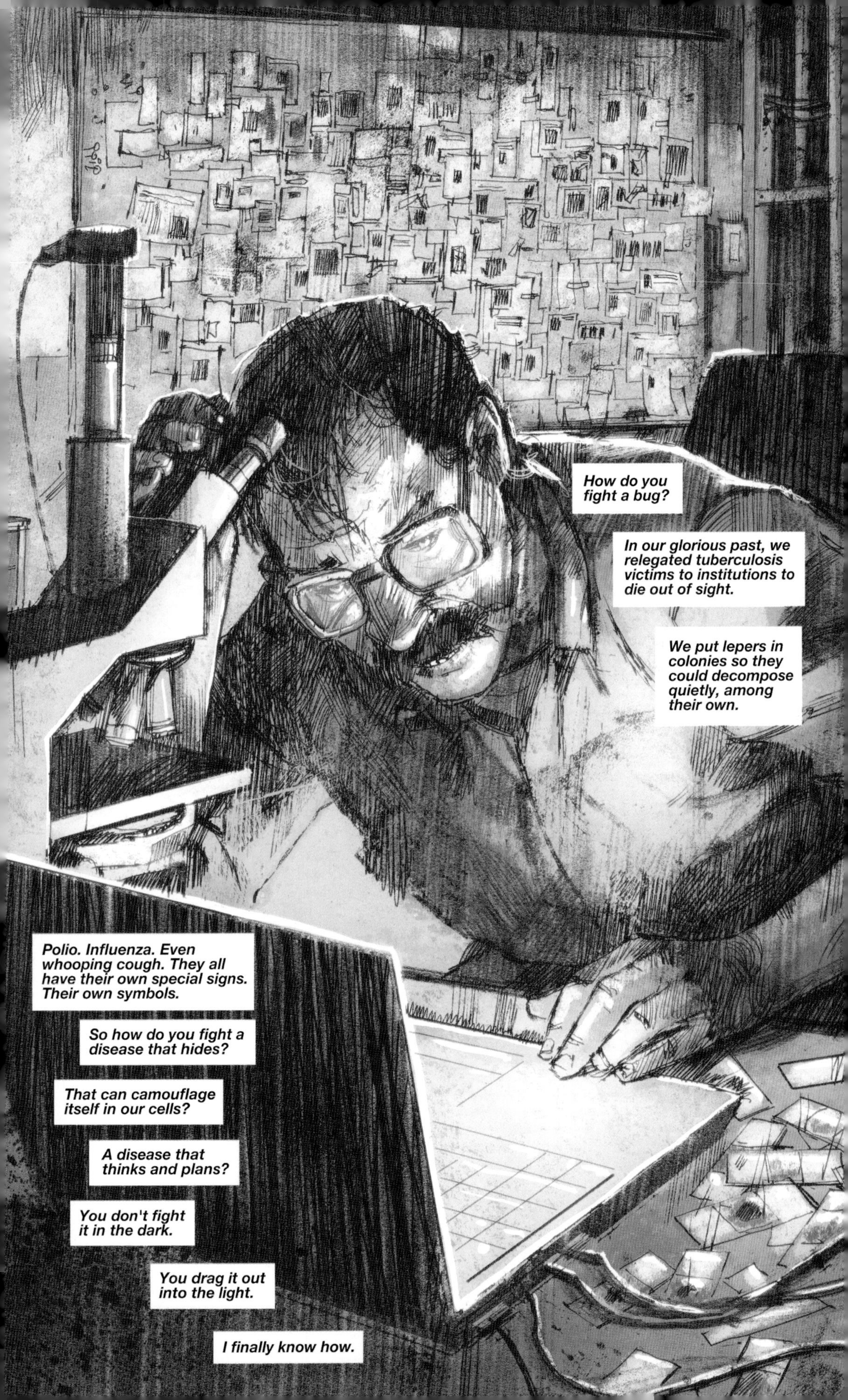
How do you fight a bug?
In our glorious past, we relegated tuberculosis victims to institutions to die out of sight.
We put lepers in colonies so they could decompose quietly, among their own.
Polio. Influenza. Even whooping cough. They all have their own special signs. Their own symbols.
So how do you fight a disease that hides?
That can camouflage itself in our cells?
A disease that thinks and plans?
You don't fight it in the dark.
You drag it out into the light.
I finally know how.

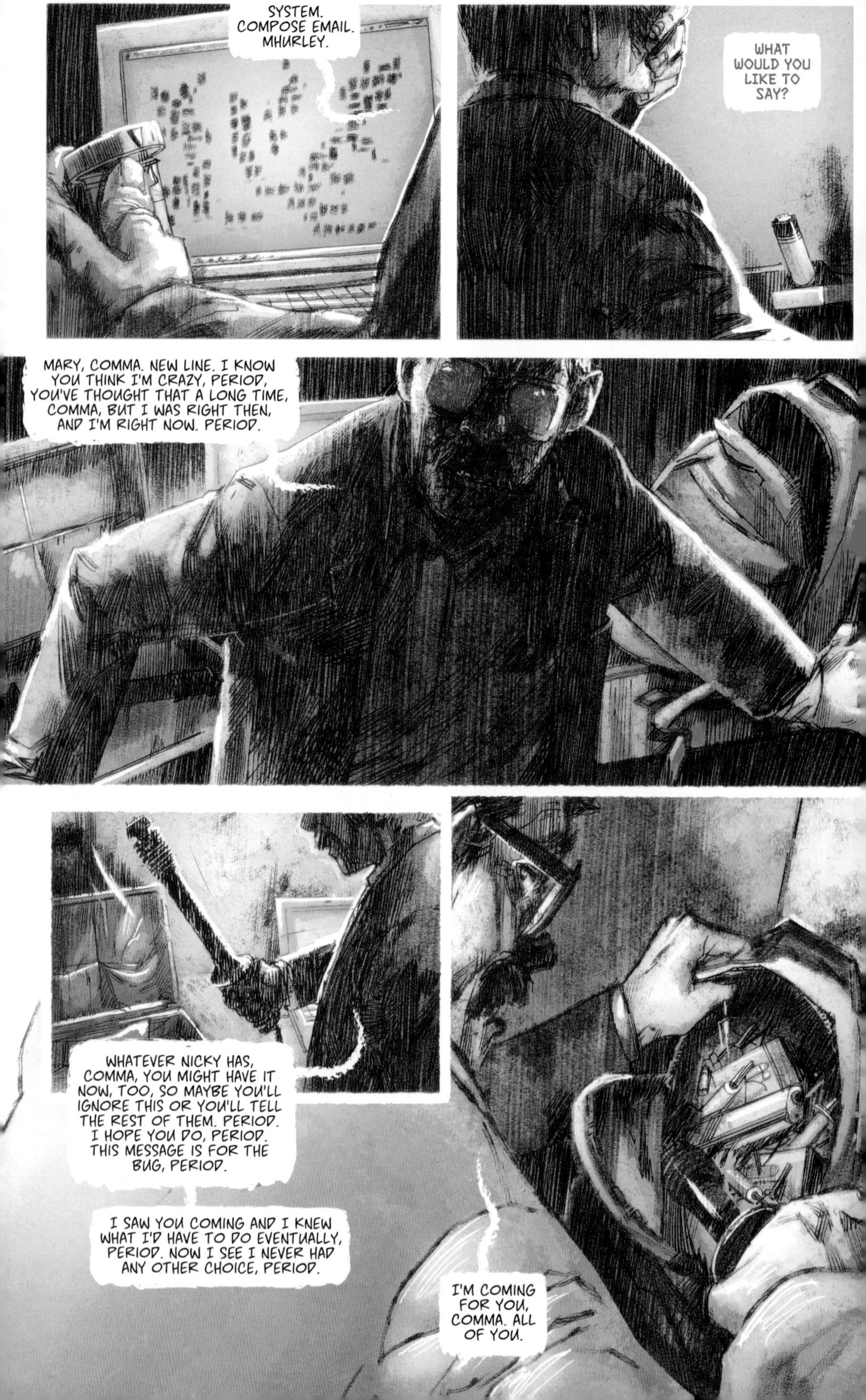
SYSTEM. COMPOSE EMAIL. MHURLEY.
WHAT WOULD YOU LIKE TO SAY?
MARY, COMMA. NEW LINE. I KNOW YOU THINK I'M CRAZY, PERIOD, YOU'VE THOUGHT THAT A LONG TIME, COMMA, BUT I WAS RIGHT THEN, AND I'M RIGHT NOW. PERIOD.
WHATEVER NICKY HAS, COMMA, YOU MIGHT HAVE IT NOW, TOO, SO MAYBE YOU'LL IGNORE THIS OR YOU'LL TELL THE REST OF THEM. PERIOD. I HOPE YOU DO, PERIOD. THIS MESSAGE IS FOR THE BUG, PERIOD.
I SAW YOU COMING AND I KNEW WHAT I'D HAVE TO DO EVENTUALLY, PERIOD. NOW I SEE I NEVER HAD ANY OTHER CHOICE, PERIOD.
I'M COMING FOR YOU, COMMA. ALL OF YOU.

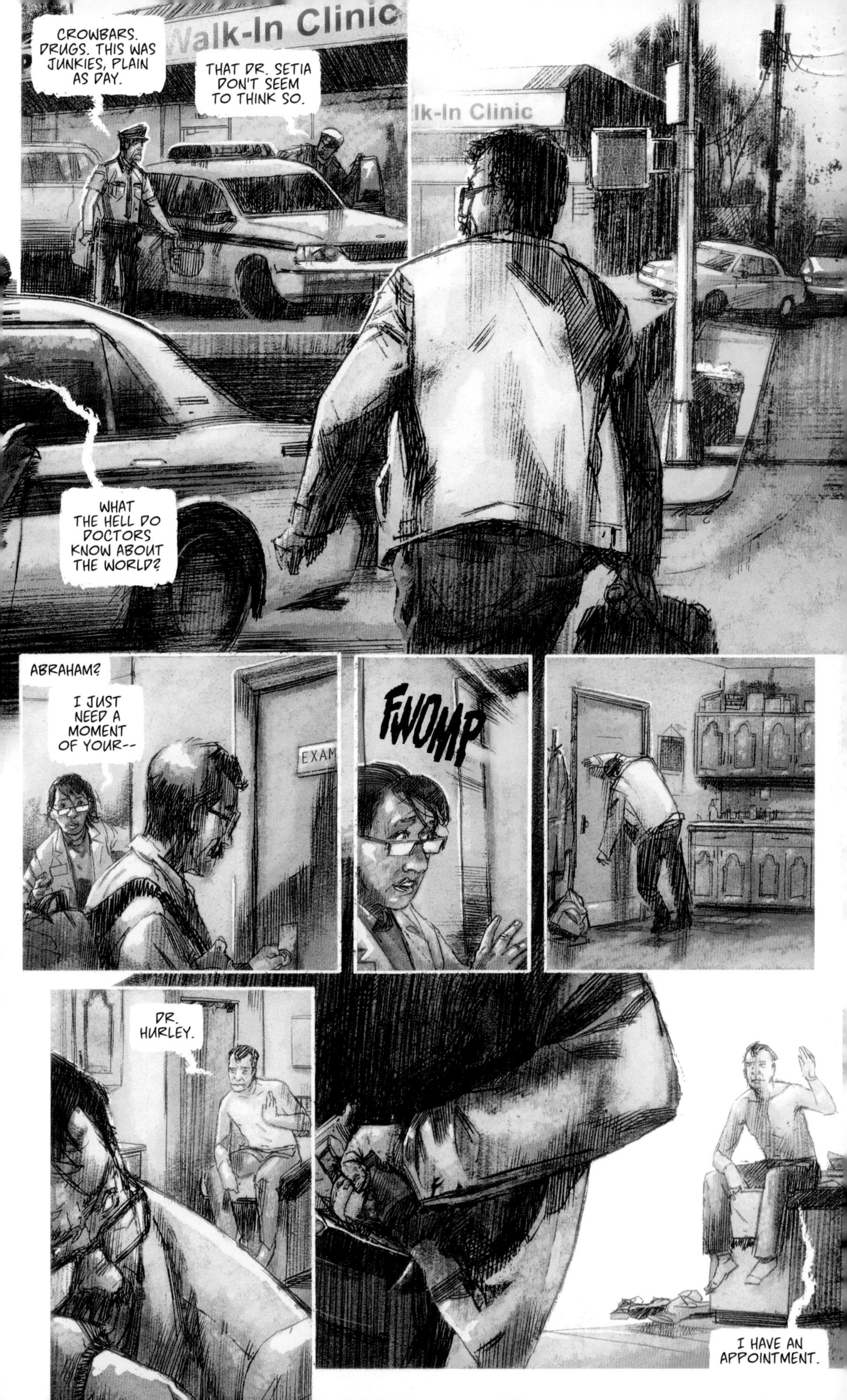
Walk-In Clinic
CROWBARS. DRUGS. THIS WAS JUNKIES, PLAIN AS DAY.
THAT DR. SETIA DON'T SEEM TO THINK SO.
lk-In Clinic
WHAT THE HELL DO DOCTORS KNOW ABOUT THE WORLD?
ABRAHAM?
I JUST NEED A MOMENT OF YOUR--
EXAM
FWOMP
DR. HURLEY.
I HAVE AN APPOINTMENT.

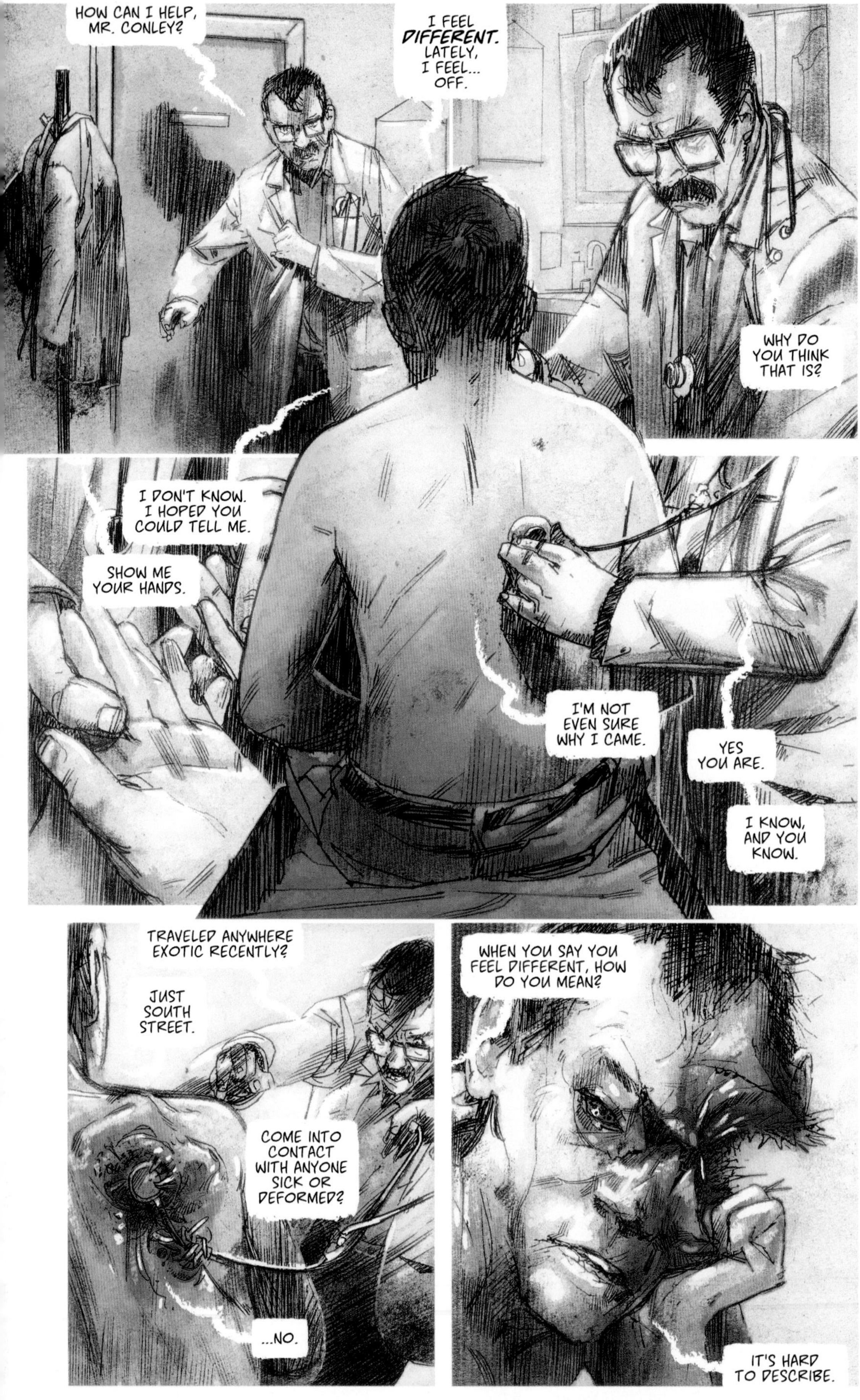
HOW CAN I HELP, MR. CONLEY?
I FEEL *DIFFERENT.* LATELY, I FEEL... OFF.
WHY DO YOU THINK THAT IS?
I DON'T KNOW. I HOPED YOU COULD TELL ME.
SHOW ME YOUR HANDS.
I'M NOT EVEN SURE WHY I CAME.
YES YOU ARE.
I KNOW, AND YOU KNOW.
TRAVELED ANYWHERE EXOTIC RECENTLY?
JUST SOUTH STREET.
COME INTO CONTACT WITH ANYONE SICK OR DEFORMED?
...NO.
WHEN YOU SAY YOU FEEL DIFFERENT, HOW DO YOU MEAN?
IT'S HARD TO DESCRIBE.

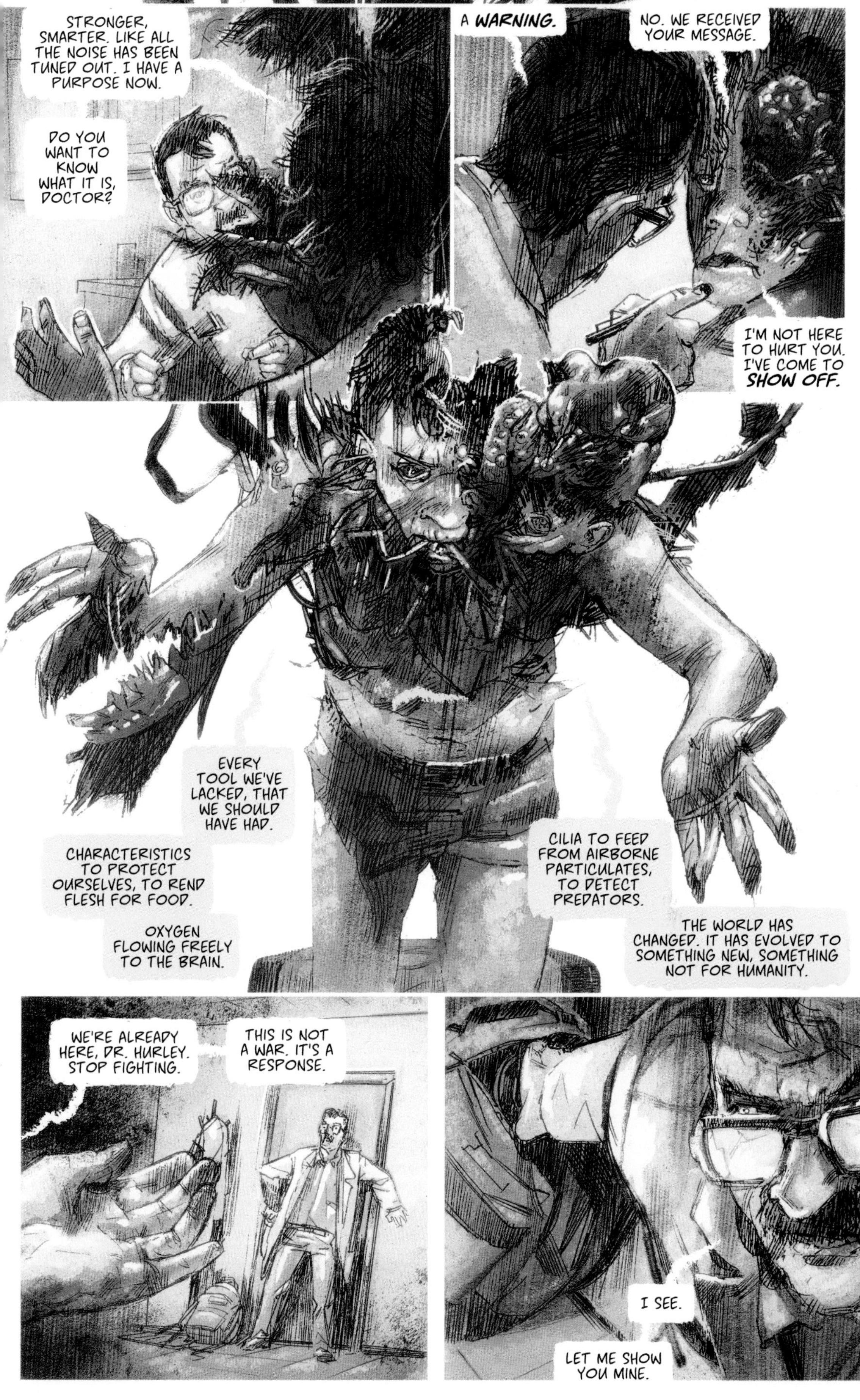
STRONGER, SMARTER. LIKE ALL THE NOISE HAS BEEN TUNED OUT. I HAVE A PURPOSE NOW.
DO YOU WANT TO KNOW WHAT IT IS, DOCTOR?
A WARNING.
NO. WE RECEIVED YOUR MESSAGE.
I'M NOT HERE TO HURT YOU. I'VE COME TO SHOW OFF.
EVERY TOOL WE'VE LACKED, THAT WE SHOULD HAVE HAD.
CHARACTERISTICS TO PROTECT OURSELVES, TO REND FLESH FOR FOOD.
OXYGEN FLOWING FREELY TO THE BRAIN.
CILIA TO FEED FROM AIRBORNE PARTICULATES, TO DETECT PREDATORS.
THE WORLD HAS CHANGED. IT HAS EVOLVED TO SOMETHING NEW, SOMETHING NOT FOR HUMANITY.
WE'RE ALREADY HERE, DR. HURLEY. STOP FIGHTING.
THIS IS NOT A WAR. IT'S A RESPONSE.
I SEE.
LET ME SHOW YOU MINE.

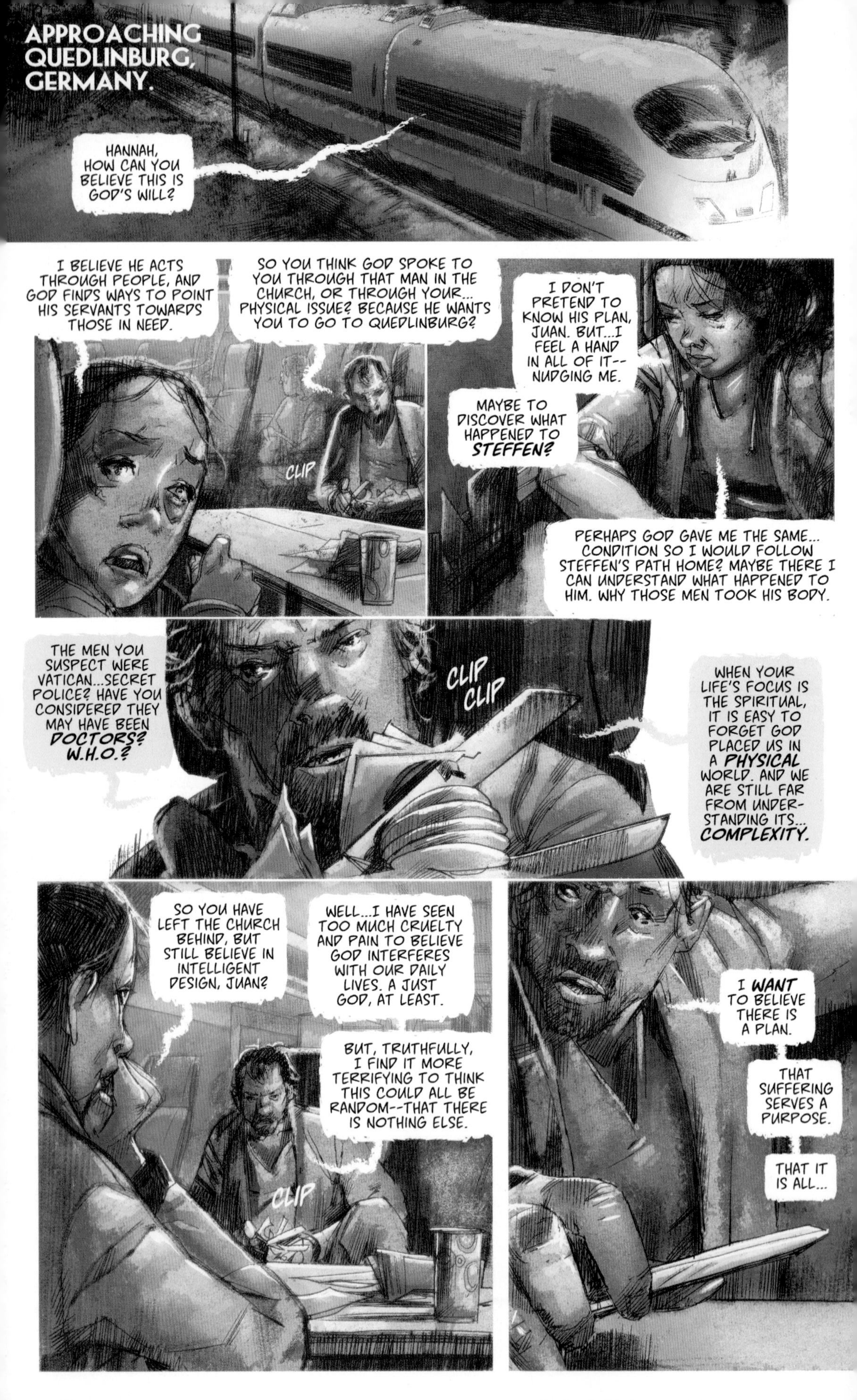
APPROACHING QUEDLINBURG, GERMANY.
HANNAH, HOW CAN YOU BELIEVE THIS IS GOD'S WILL?
I BELIEVE HE ACTS THROUGH PEOPLE, AND GOD FINDS WAYS TO POINT HIS SERVANTS TOWARDS THOSE IN NEED.
SO YOU THINK GOD SPOKE TO YOU THROUGH THAT MAN IN THE CHURCH, OR THROUGH YOUR... PHYSICAL ISSUE? BECAUSE HE WANTS YOU TO GO TO QUEDLINBURG?
CLIP
I DON'T PRETEND TO KNOW HIS PLAN, JUAN. BUT...I FEEL A HAND IN ALL OF IT--NUDGING ME.
MAYBE TO DISCOVER WHAT HAPPENED TO STEFFEN?
PERHAPS GOD GAVE ME THE SAME... CONDITION SO I WOULD FOLLOW STEFFEN'S PATH HOME? MAYBE THERE I CAN UNDERSTAND WHAT HAPPENED TO HIM. WHY THOSE MEN TOOK HIS BODY.
THE MEN YOU SUSPECT WERE VATICAN...SECRET POLICE? HAVE YOU CONSIDERED THEY MAY HAVE BEEN DOCTORS? W.H.O.?
CLIP CLIP
WHEN YOUR LIFE'S FOCUS IS THE SPIRITUAL, IT IS EASY TO FORGET GOD PLACED US IN A PHYSICAL WORLD. AND WE ARE STILL FAR FROM UNDERSTANDING ITS... COMPLEXITY.
SO YOU HAVE LEFT THE CHURCH BEHIND, BUT STILL BELIEVE IN INTELLIGENT DESIGN, JUAN?
WELL...I HAVE SEEN TOO MUCH CRUELTY AND PAIN TO BELIEVE GOD INTERFERES WITH OUR DAILY LIVES. A JUST GOD, AT LEAST.
BUT, TRUTHFULLY, I FIND IT MORE TERRIFYING TO THINK THIS COULD ALL BE RANDOM--THAT THERE IS NOTHING ELSE.
CLIP
I WANT TO BELIEVE THERE IS A PLAN.
THAT SUFFERING SERVES A PURPOSE.
THAT IT IS ALL...

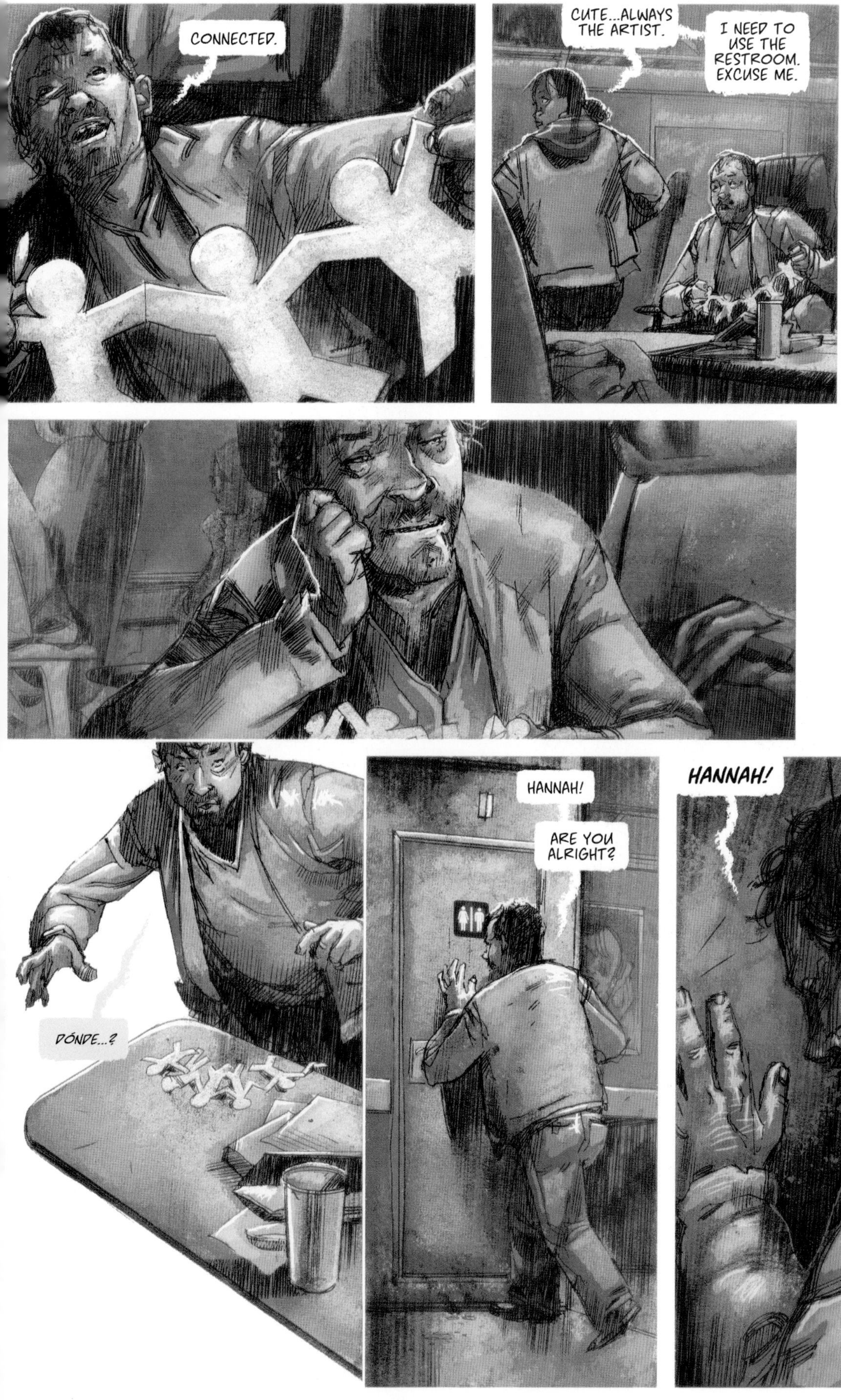
CONNECTED.
CUTE...ALWAYS THE ARTIST.
I NEED TO USE THE RESTROOM. EXCUSE ME.
DÓNDE...?
HANNAH!
ARE YOU ALRIGHT?
HANNAH!

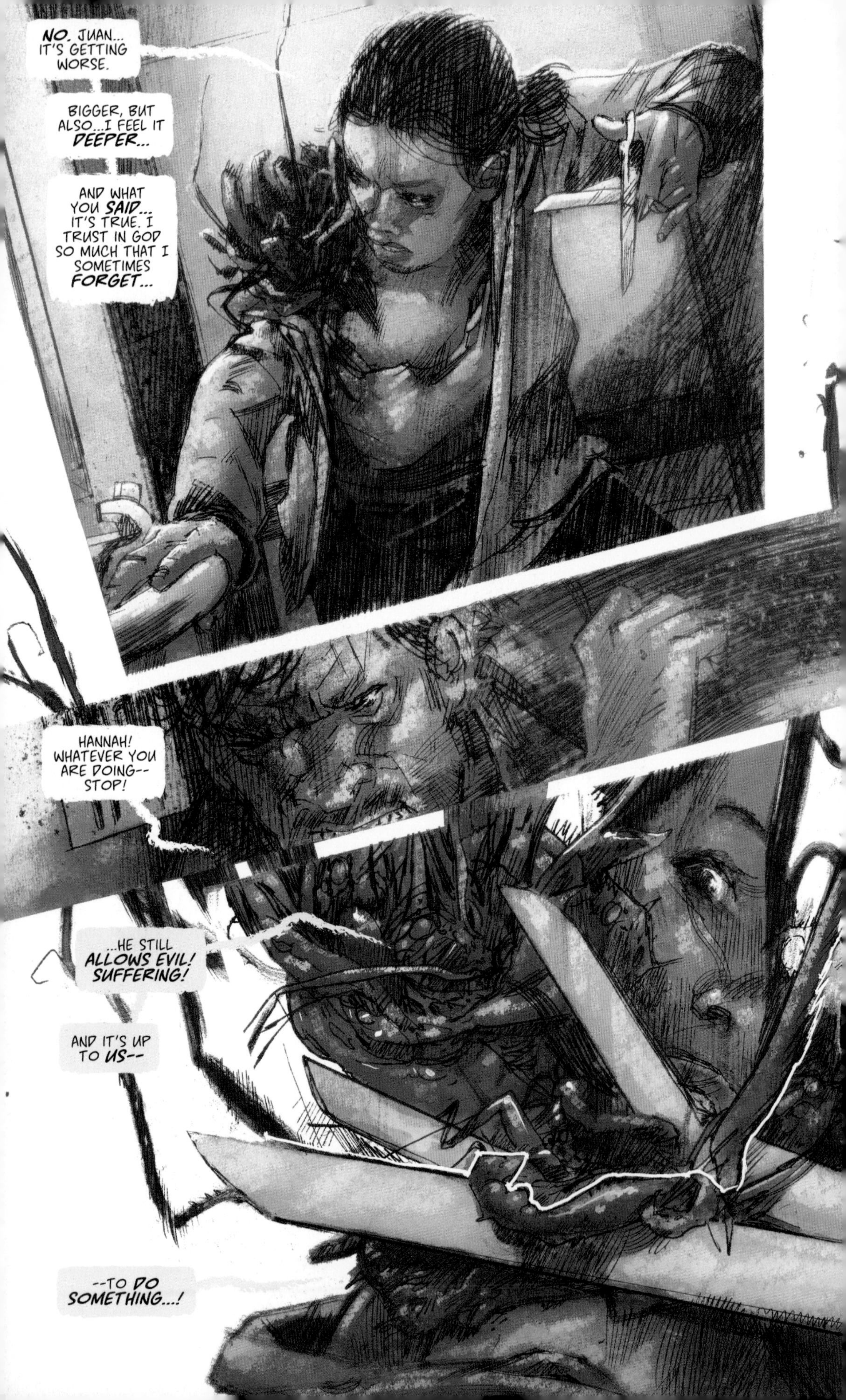
NO. JUAN... IT'S GETTING WORSE.
BIGGER, BUT ALSO...I FEEL IT DEEPER...
AND WHAT YOU SAID... IT'S TRUE. I TRUST IN GOD SO MUCH THAT I SOMETIMES FORGET...
HANNAH! WHATEVER YOU ARE DOING-- STOP!
...HE STILL ALLOWS EVIL! SUFFERING!
AND IT'S UP TO US--
--TO DO SOMETHING...!

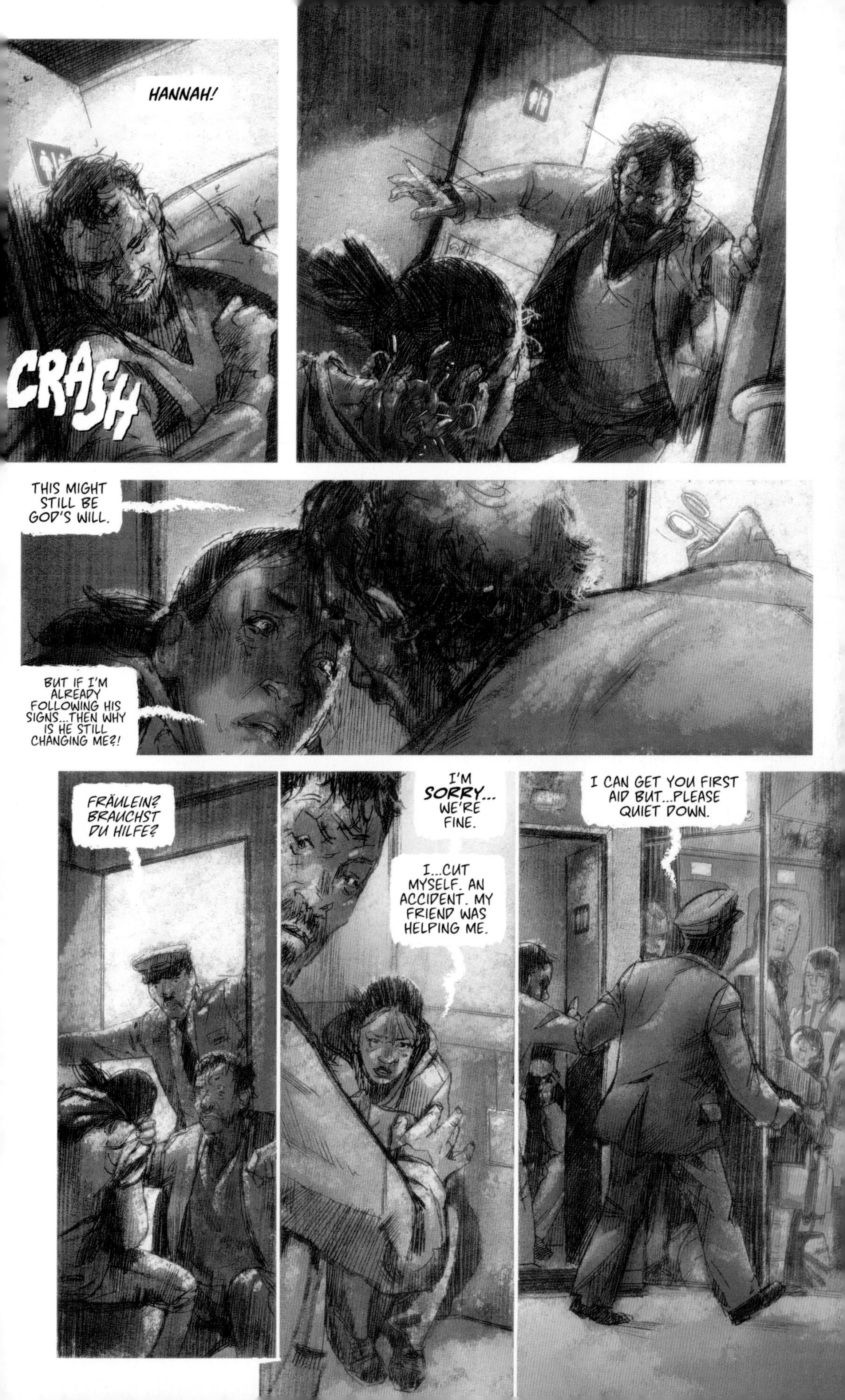
HANNAH!
CRASH
THIS MIGHT STILL BE GOD'S WILL.
BUT IF I'M ALREADY FOLLOWING HIS SIGNS...THEN WHY IS HE STILL CHANGING ME?!
FRÄULEIN? BRAUCHST DU HILFE?
I'M SORRY... WE'RE FINE.
I...CUT MYSELF. AN ACCIDENT. MY FRIEND WAS HELPING ME.
I CAN GET YOU FIRST AID BUT...PLEASE QUIET DOWN.

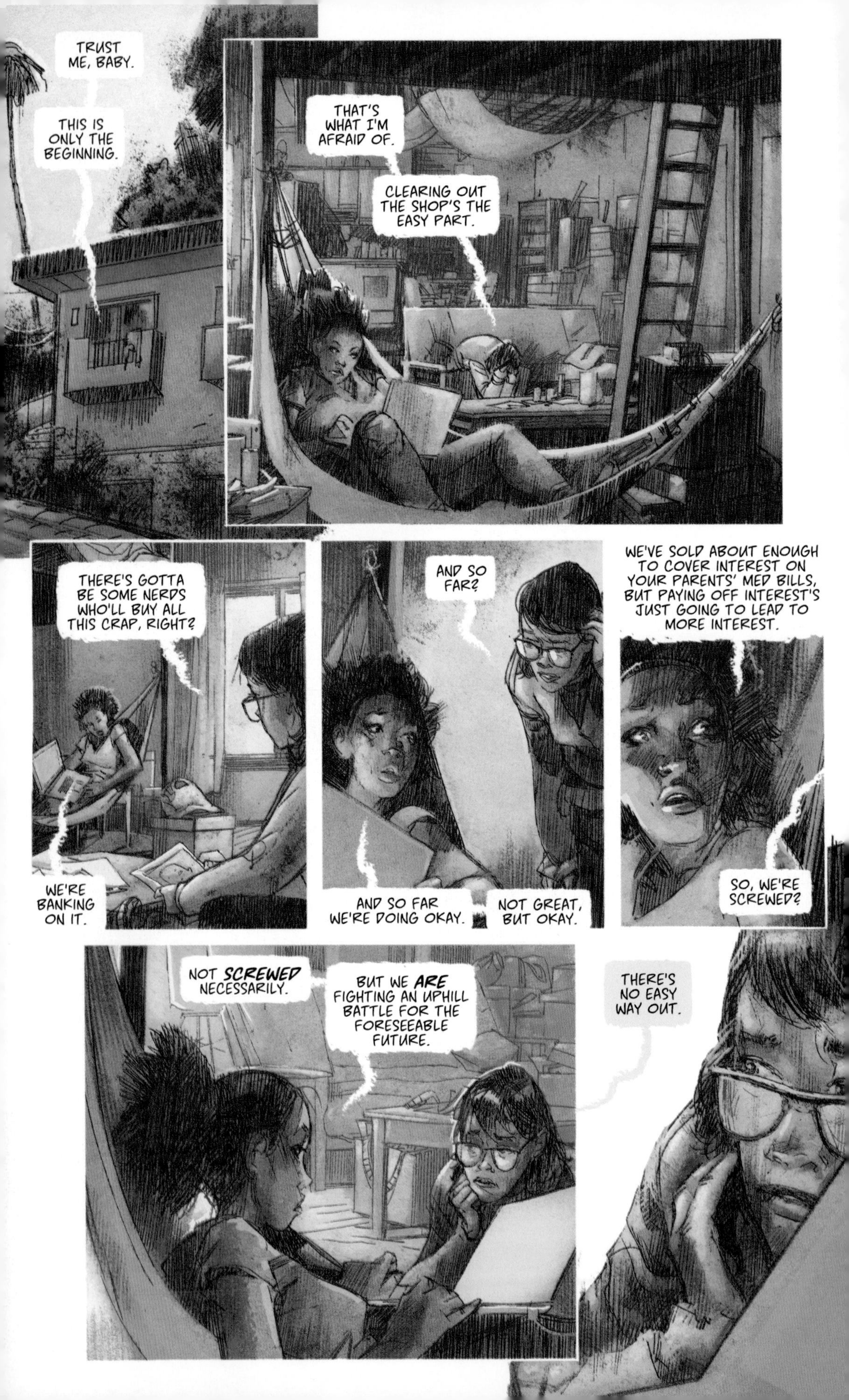
TRUST ME, BABY.
THIS IS ONLY THE BEGINNING.
THAT'S WHAT I'M AFRAID OF.
CLEARING OUT THE SHOP'S THE EASY PART.
THERE'S GOTTA BE SOME NERDS WHO'LL BUY ALL THIS CRAP, RIGHT?
WE'RE BANKING ON IT.
AND SO FAR?
AND SO FAR WE'RE DOING OKAY.
NOT GREAT, BUT OKAY.
WE'VE SOLD ABOUT ENOUGH TO COVER INTEREST ON YOUR PARENTS' MED BILLS, BUT PAYING OFF INTEREST'S JUST GOING TO LEAD TO MORE INTEREST.
SO, WE'RE SCREWED?
NOT SCREWED NECESSARILY.
BUT WE ARE FIGHTING AN UPHILL BATTLE FOR THE FORESEEABLE FUTURE.
THERE'S NO EASY WAY OUT.

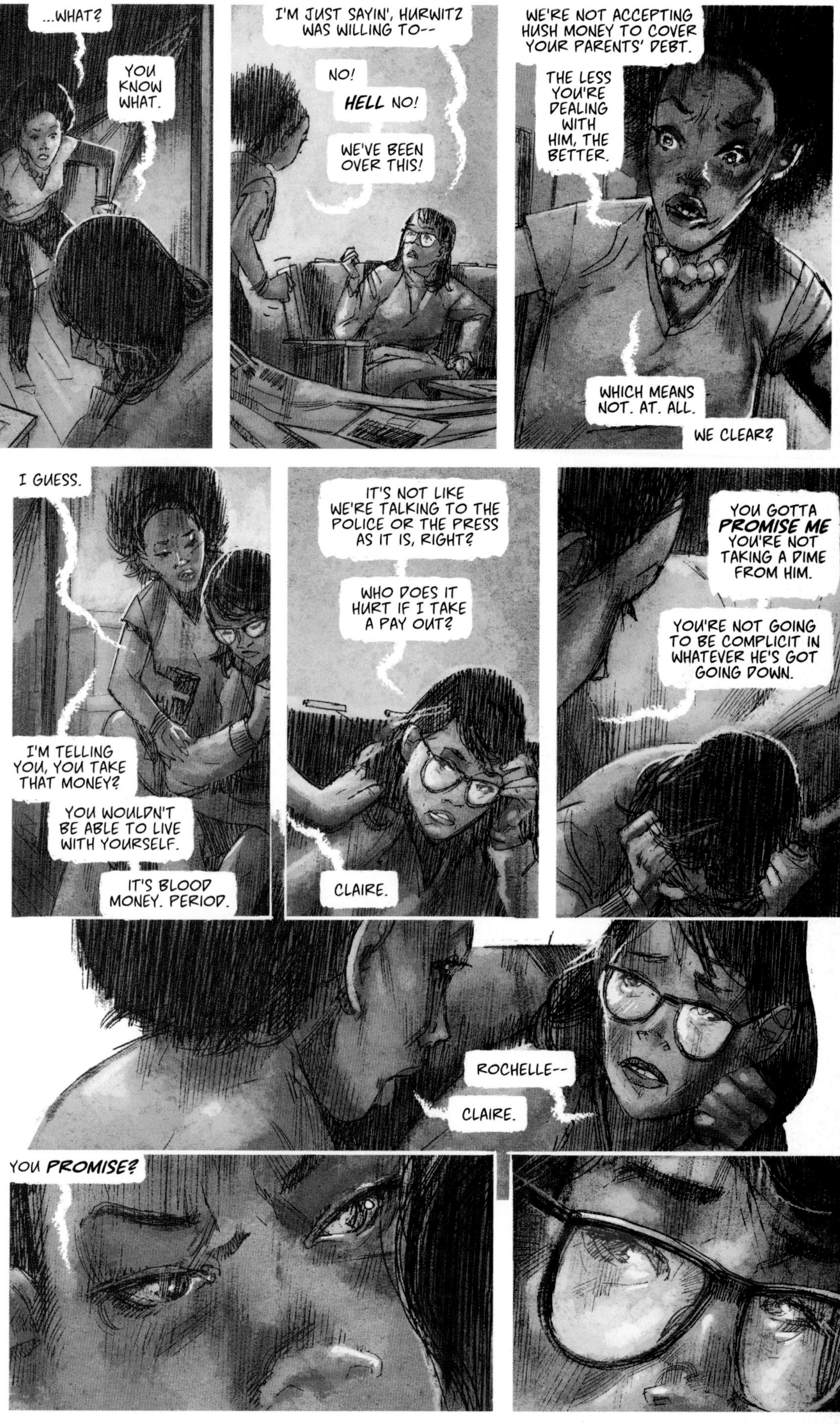
...WHAT?
YOU KNOW WHAT.
I'M JUST SAYIN', HURWITZ WAS WILLING TO--
NO!
HELL NO!
WE'VE BEEN OVER THIS!
WE'RE NOT ACCEPTING HUSH MONEY TO COVER YOUR PARENTS' DEBT.
THE LESS YOU'RE DEALING WITH HIM, THE BETTER.
WHICH MEANS NOT. AT. ALL.
WE CLEAR?
I GUESS.
IT'S NOT LIKE WE'RE TALKING TO THE POLICE OR THE PRESS AS IT IS, RIGHT?
WHO DOES IT HURT IF I TAKE A PAY OUT?
I'M TELLING YOU, YOU TAKE THAT MONEY?
YOU WOULDN'T BE ABLE TO LIVE WITH YOURSELF.
IT'S BLOOD MONEY. PERIOD.
CLAIRE.
YOU GOTTA **PROMISE ME** YOU'RE NOT TAKING A DIME FROM HIM.
YOU'RE NOT GOING TO BE COMPLICIT IN WHATEVER HE'S GOT GOING DOWN.
ROCHELLE--
CLAIRE.
YOU **PROMISE?**

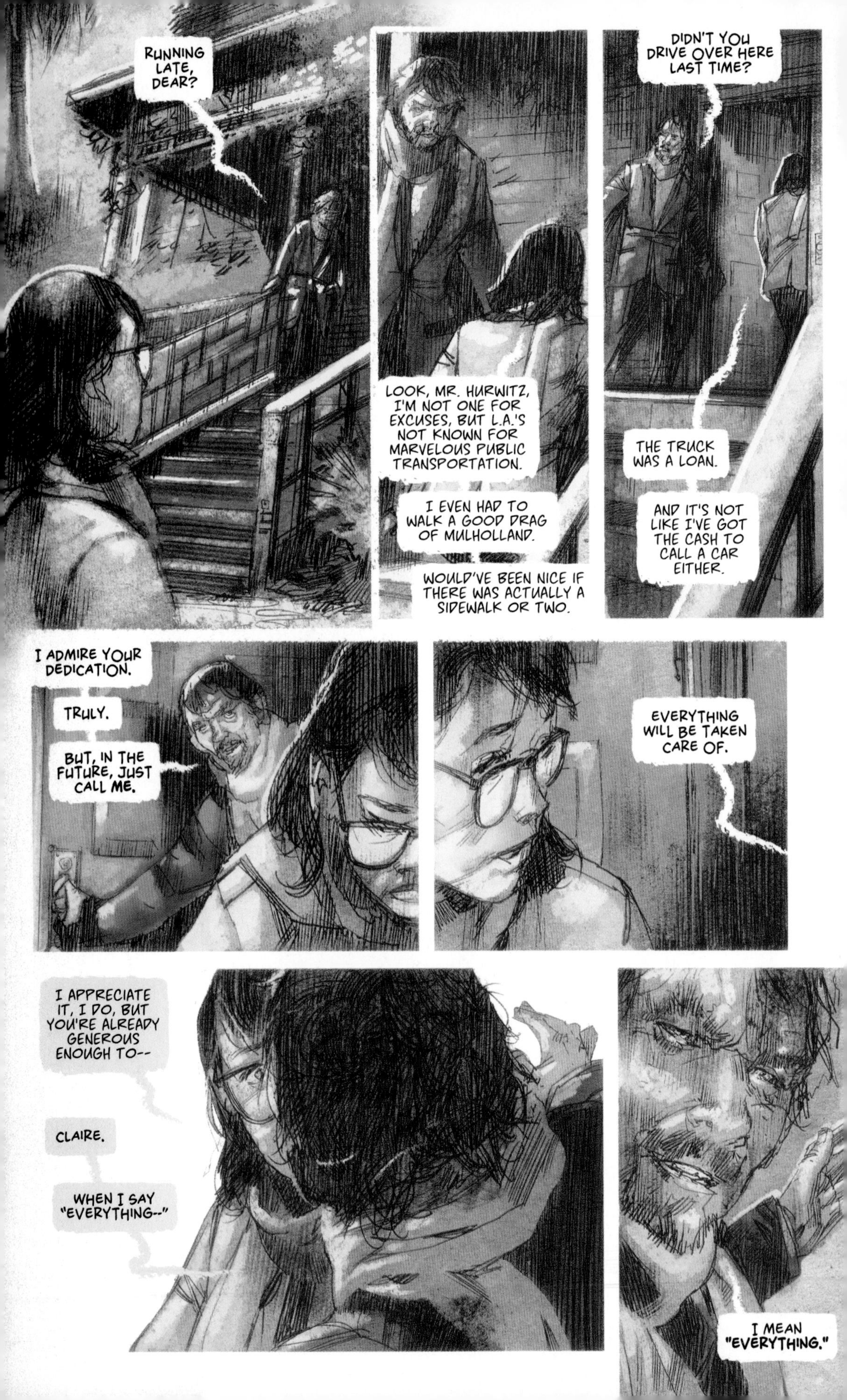
RUNNING LATE, DEAR?
LOOK, MR. HURWITZ, I'M NOT ONE FOR EXCUSES, BUT L.A.'S NOT KNOWN FOR MARVELOUS PUBLIC TRANSPORTATION.
I EVEN HAD TO WALK A GOOD DRAG OF MULHOLLAND.
WOULD'VE BEEN NICE IF THERE WAS ACTUALLY A SIDEWALK OR TWO.
DIDN'T YOU DRIVE OVER HERE LAST TIME?
THE TRUCK WAS A LOAN.
AND IT'S NOT LIKE I'VE GOT THE CASH TO CALL A CAR EITHER.
I ADMIRE YOUR DEDICATION.
TRULY.
BUT, IN THE FUTURE, JUST CALL ME.
EVERYTHING WILL BE TAKEN CARE OF.
I APPRECIATE IT, I DO, BUT YOU'RE ALREADY GENEROUS ENOUGH TO--
CLAIRE.
WHEN I SAY "EVERYTHING--"
I MEAN "EVERYTHING."

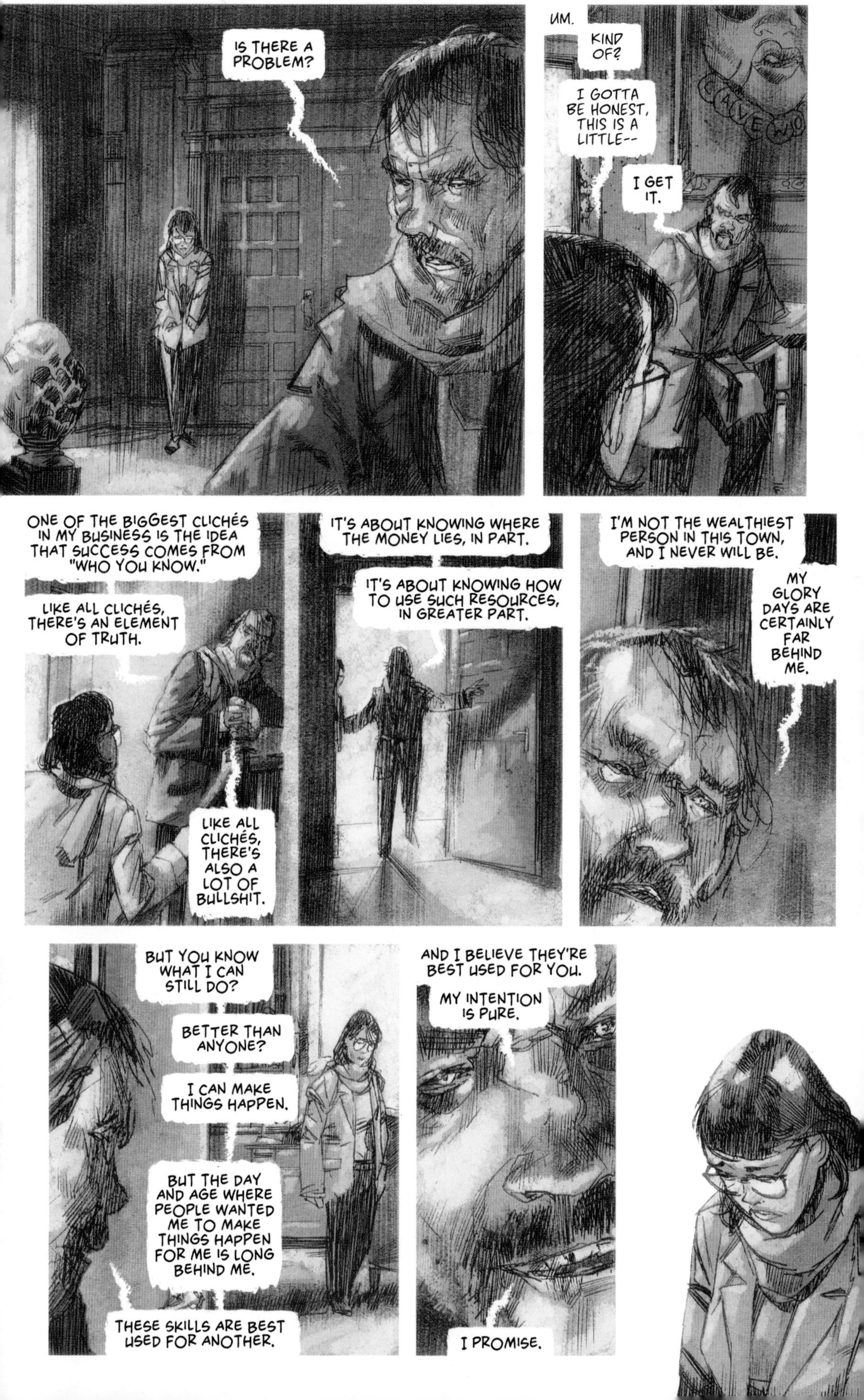
IS THERE A PROBLEM?
UM.
KIND OF?
I GOTTA BE HONEST, THIS IS A LITTLE--
I GET IT.
ONE OF THE BIGGEST CLICHÉS IN MY BUSINESS IS THE IDEA THAT SUCCESS COMES FROM "WHO YOU KNOW."
LIKE ALL CLICHÉS, THERE'S AN ELEMENT OF TRUTH.
LIKE ALL CLICHÉS, THERE'S ALSO A LOT OF BULLSHIT.
IT'S ABOUT KNOWING WHERE THE MONEY LIES, IN PART.
IT'S ABOUT KNOWING HOW TO USE SUCH RESOURCES, IN GREATER PART.
I'M NOT THE WEALTHIEST PERSON IN THIS TOWN, AND I NEVER WILL BE.
MY GLORY DAYS ARE CERTAINLY FAR BEHIND ME.
BUT YOU KNOW WHAT I CAN STILL DO?
BETTER THAN ANYONE?
I CAN MAKE THINGS HAPPEN.
BUT THE DAY AND AGE WHERE PEOPLE WANTED ME TO MAKE THINGS HAPPEN FOR ME IS LONG BEHIND ME.
THESE SKILLS ARE BEST USED FOR ANOTHER.
AND I BELIEVE THEY'RE BEST USED FOR YOU.
MY INTENTION IS PURE.
I PROMISE.

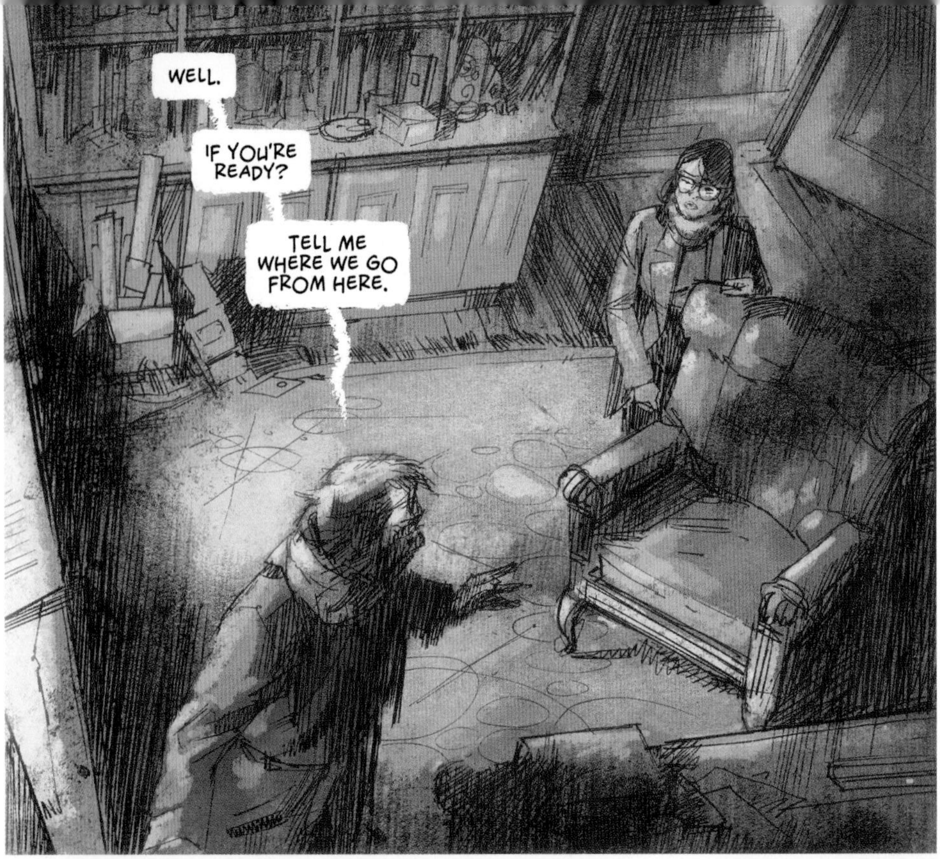
WELL.
IF YOU'RE READY?
TELL ME WHERE WE GO FROM HERE.

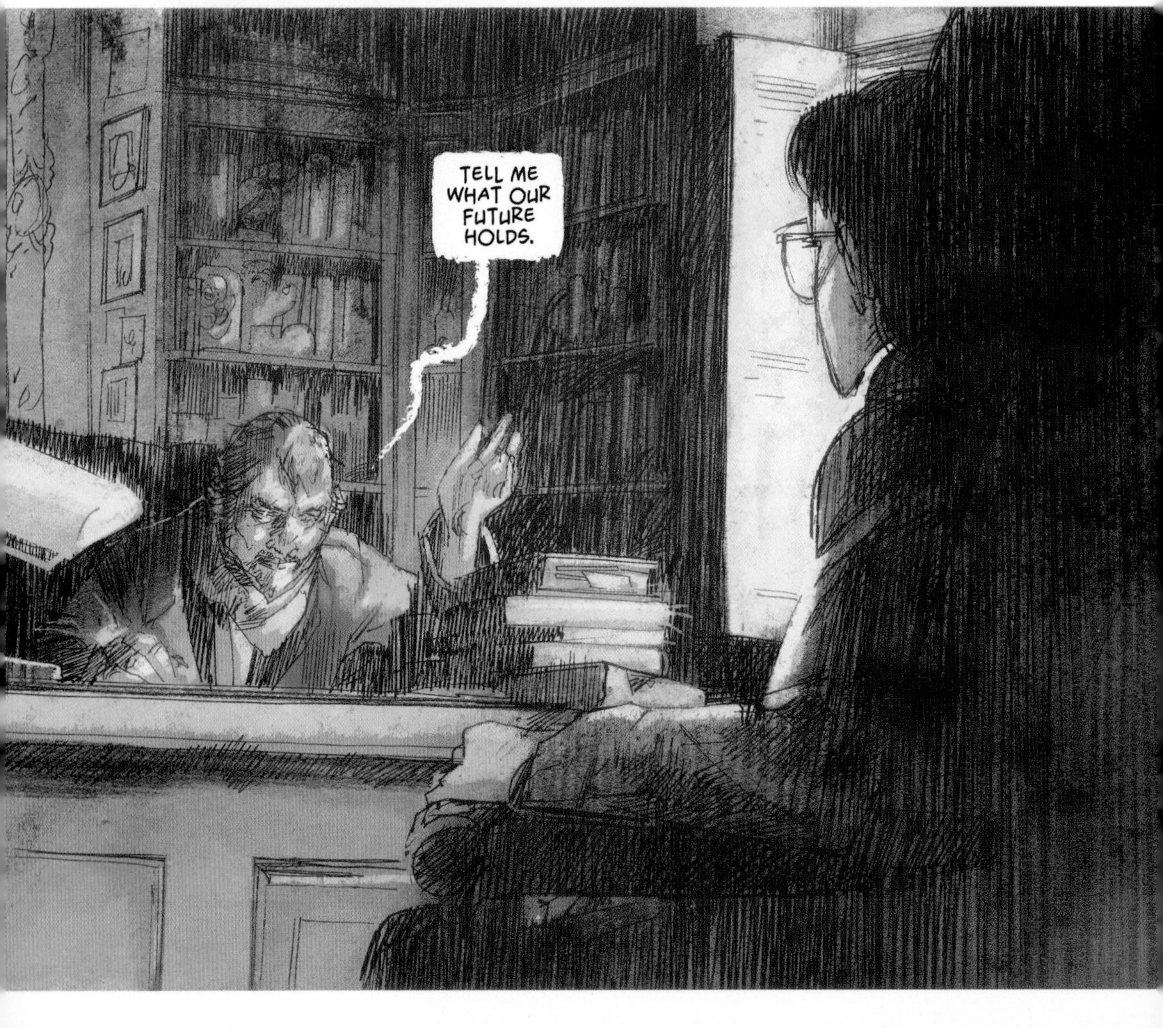
TELL ME WHAT OUR FUTURE HOLDS.

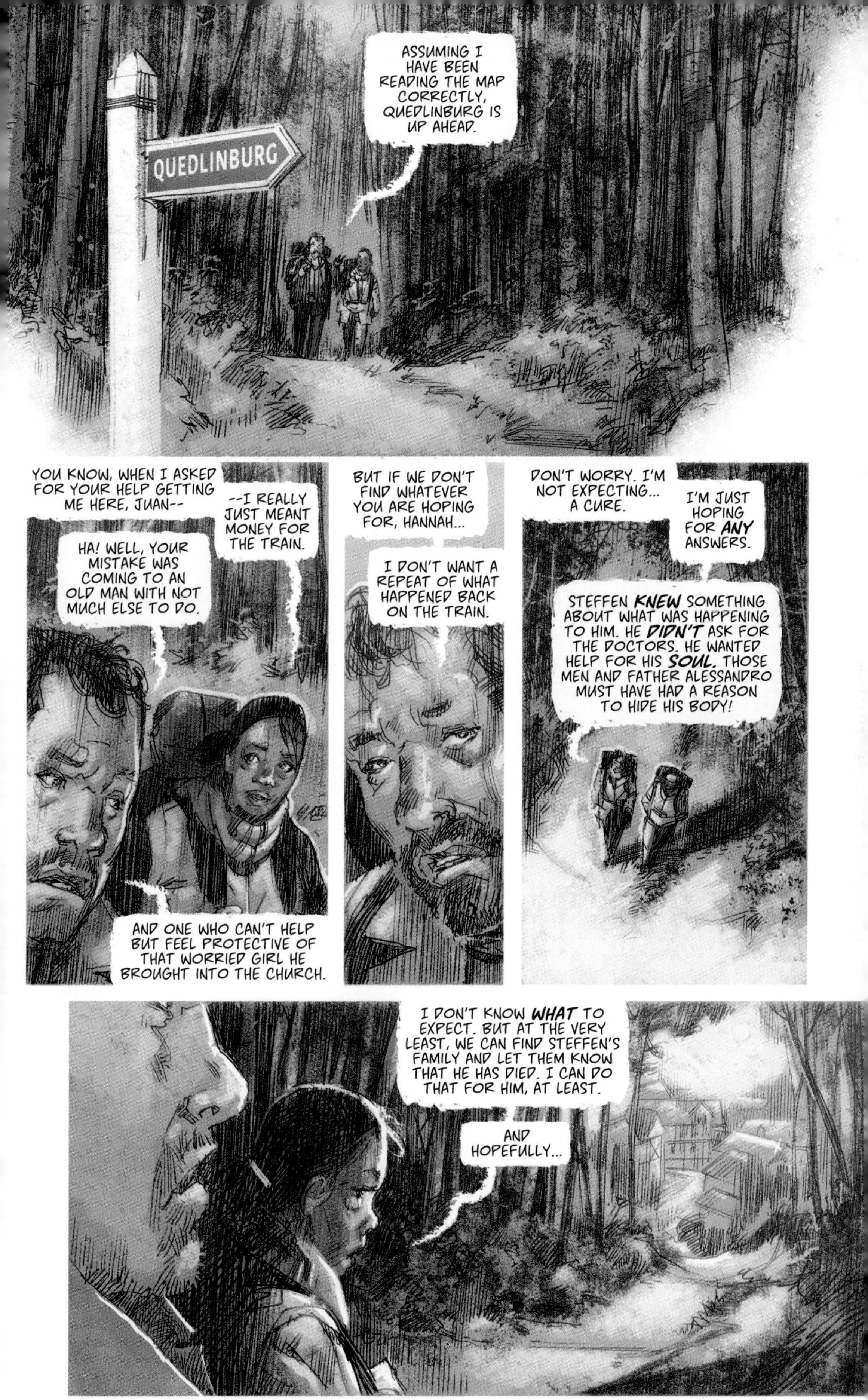

QUEDLINBURG
ASSUMING I HAVE BEEN READING THE MAP CORRECTLY, QUEDLINBURG IS UP AHEAD.
YOU KNOW, WHEN I ASKED FOR YOUR HELP GETTING ME HERE, JUAN--
--I REALLY JUST MEANT MONEY FOR THE TRAIN.
HA! WELL, YOUR MISTAKE WAS COMING TO AN OLD MAN WITH NOT MUCH ELSE TO DO.
AND ONE WHO CAN'T HELP BUT FEEL PROTECTIVE OF THAT WORRIED GIRL HE BROUGHT INTO THE CHURCH.
BUT IF WE DON'T FIND WHATEVER YOU ARE HOPING FOR, HANNAH...
I DON'T WANT A REPEAT OF WHAT HAPPENED BACK ON THE TRAIN.
DON'T WORRY. I'M NOT EXPECTING... A CURE.
I'M JUST HOPING FOR ANY ANSWERS.
STEFFEN KNEW SOMETHING ABOUT WHAT WAS HAPPENING TO HIM. HE DIDN'T ASK FOR THE DOCTORS. HE WANTED HELP FOR HIS SOUL. THOSE MEN AND FATHER ALESSANDRO MUST HAVE HAD A REASON TO HIDE HIS BODY!
I DON'T KNOW WHAT TO EXPECT. BUT AT THE VERY LEAST, WE CAN FIND STEFFEN'S FAMILY AND LET THEM KNOW THAT HE HAS DIED. I CAN DO THAT FOR HIM, AT LEAST.
AND HOPEFULLY...

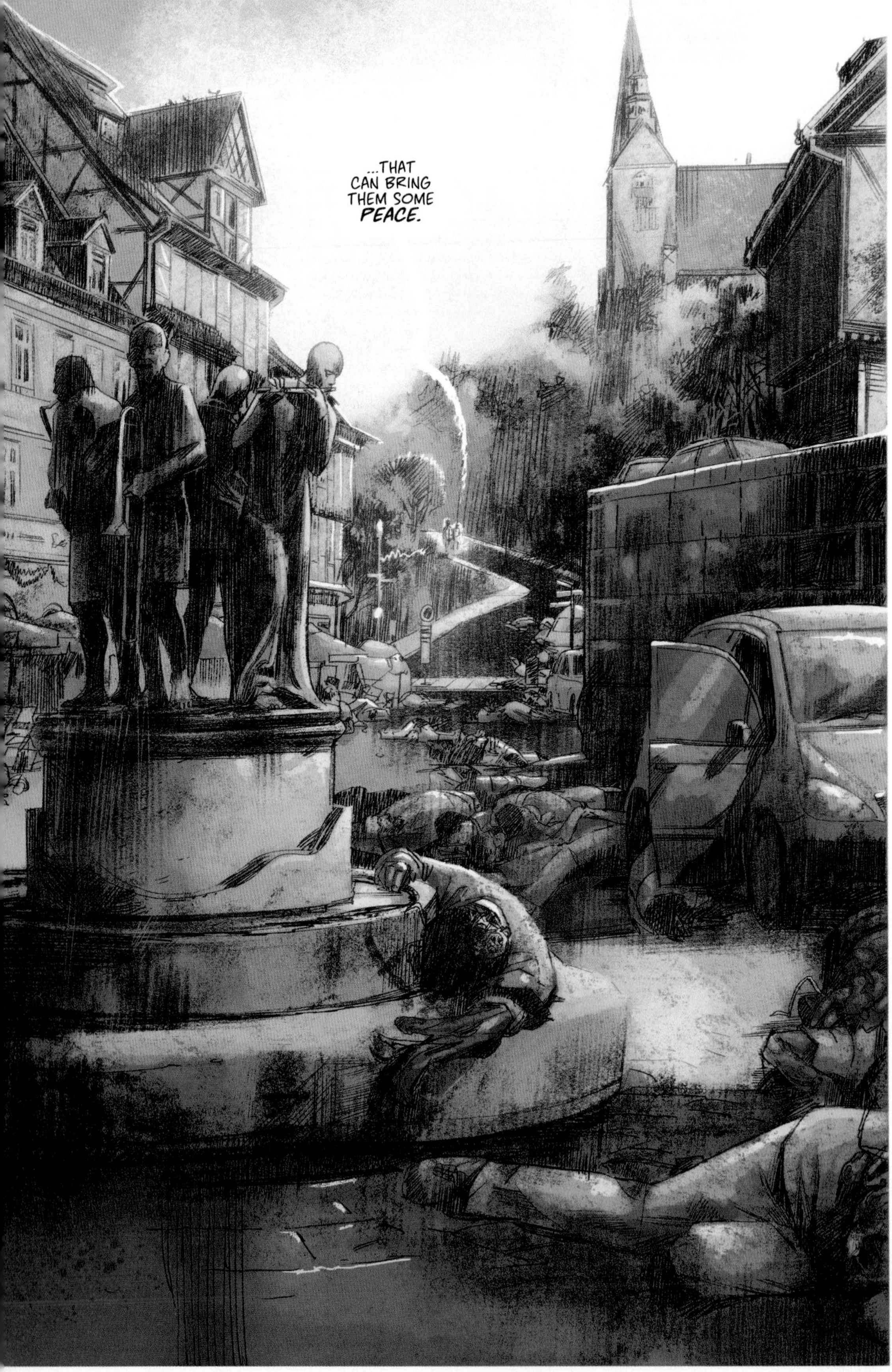
...THAT CAN BRING THEM SOME PEACE.

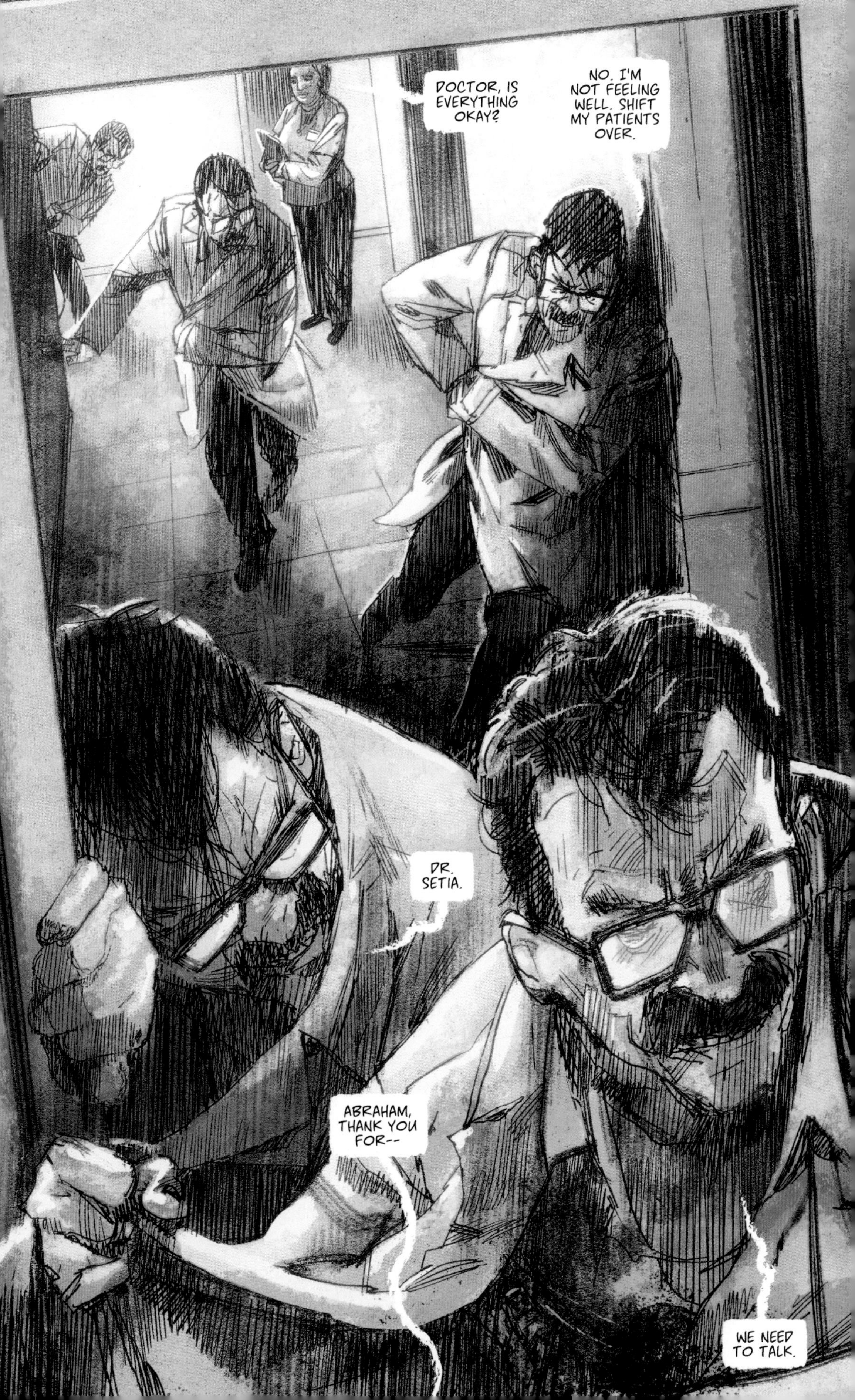
DOCTOR, IS EVERYTHING OKAY?
NO. I'M NOT FEELING WELL. SHIFT MY PATIENTS OVER.
DR. SETIA.
ABRAHAM, THANK YOU FOR--
WE NEED TO TALK.

WHAT IN GOD'S NAME...?

HAVE YOU NOTICED ANYTHING WEIRD GOING ON LATELY?

LET ME--

DON'T. ANSWER MY QUESTION.

DO THE PATIENTS SEEM DIFFERENT?

YOU'RE SCARING ME, ABRAHAM.

GOOD. THAT MEANS YOU'RE NOT INFECTED YET.

INFECTED? STOP AND TELL ME WHAT HAPPENED. WHERE IS YOUR PATIENT?

THEY'RE CHANGING. BECOMING PART OF SOMETHING ELSE. IN SECRET.

EVERYONE OUT THERE. THE WAITING ROOM IS FULL OF THEM, WHISPERING TO EACH OTHER.

THE PATIENTS ARE NORMAL, ABRAHAM. IF ANYTHING, THEY'RE HEALTHIER ACROSS THE BOARD!

YOU'RE CONFUSED. THERE'S NO CONSPIRACY OR--

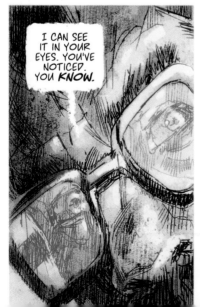

I CAN SEE IT IN YOUR EYES. YOU'VE NOTICED. YOU KNOW.

WHY ARE YOU DENYING WHAT'S HAPPENING?

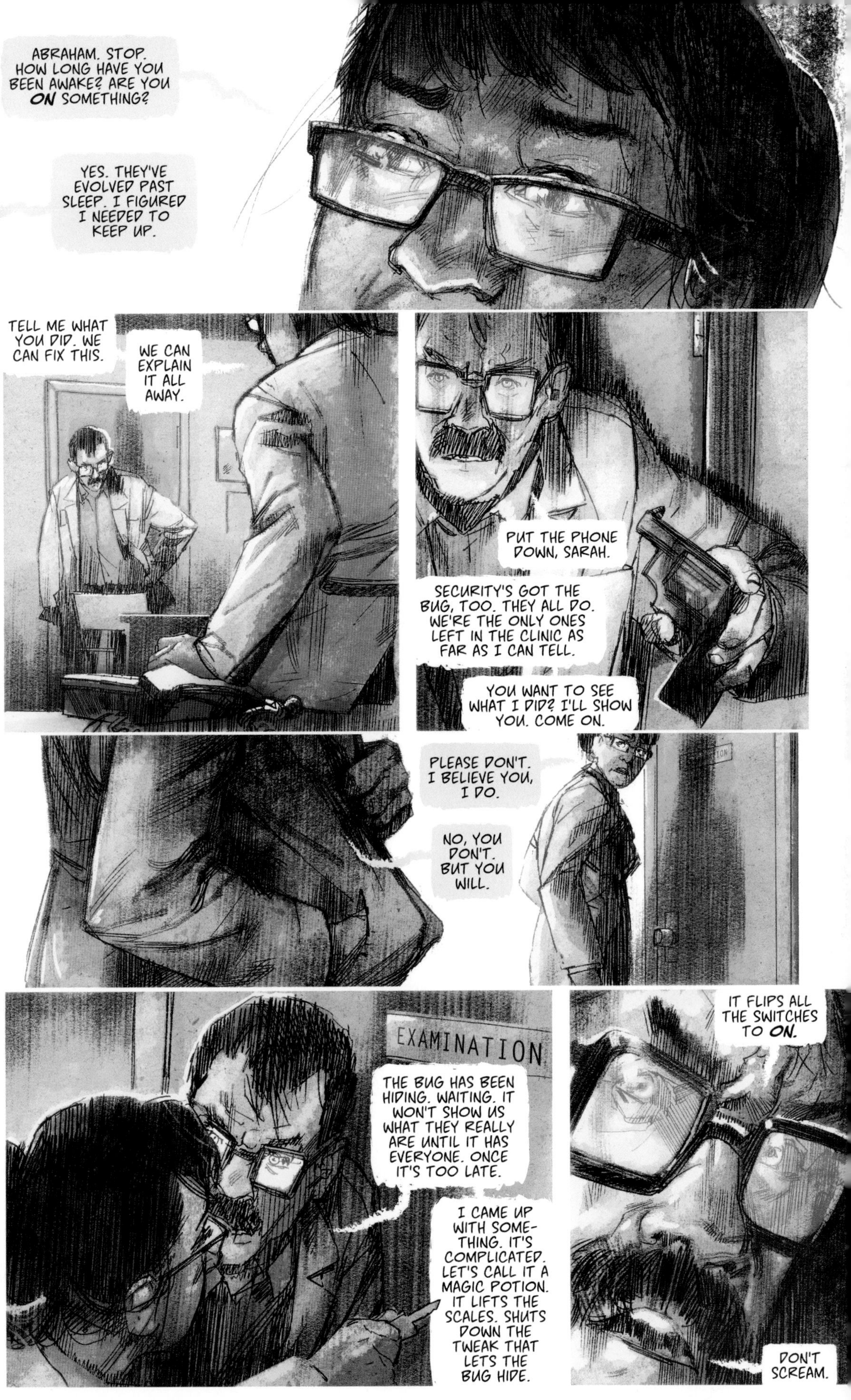
ABRAHAM. STOP. HOW LONG HAVE YOU BEEN AWAKE? ARE YOU ON SOMETHING?
YES. THEY'VE EVOLVED PAST SLEEP. I FIGURED I NEEDED TO KEEP UP.
TELL ME WHAT YOU DID. WE CAN FIX THIS.
WE CAN EXPLAIN IT ALL AWAY.
PUT THE PHONE DOWN, SARAH.
SECURITY'S GOT THE BUG, TOO. THEY ALL DO. WE'RE THE ONLY ONES LEFT IN THE CLINIC AS FAR AS I CAN TELL.
YOU WANT TO SEE WHAT I DID? I'LL SHOW YOU. COME ON.
PLEASE DON'T. I BELIEVE YOU, I DO.
NO, YOU DON'T. BUT YOU WILL.
EXAMINATION
THE BUG HAS BEEN HIDING. WAITING. IT WON'T SHOW US WHAT THEY REALLY ARE UNTIL IT HAS EVERYONE. ONCE IT'S TOO LATE.
I CAME UP WITH SOME-THING. IT'S COMPLICATED. LET'S CALL IT A MAGIC POTION. IT LIFTS THE SCALES. SHUTS DOWN THE TWEAK THAT LETS THE BUG HIDE.
IT FLIPS ALL THE SWITCHES TO ON.
DON'T SCREAM.

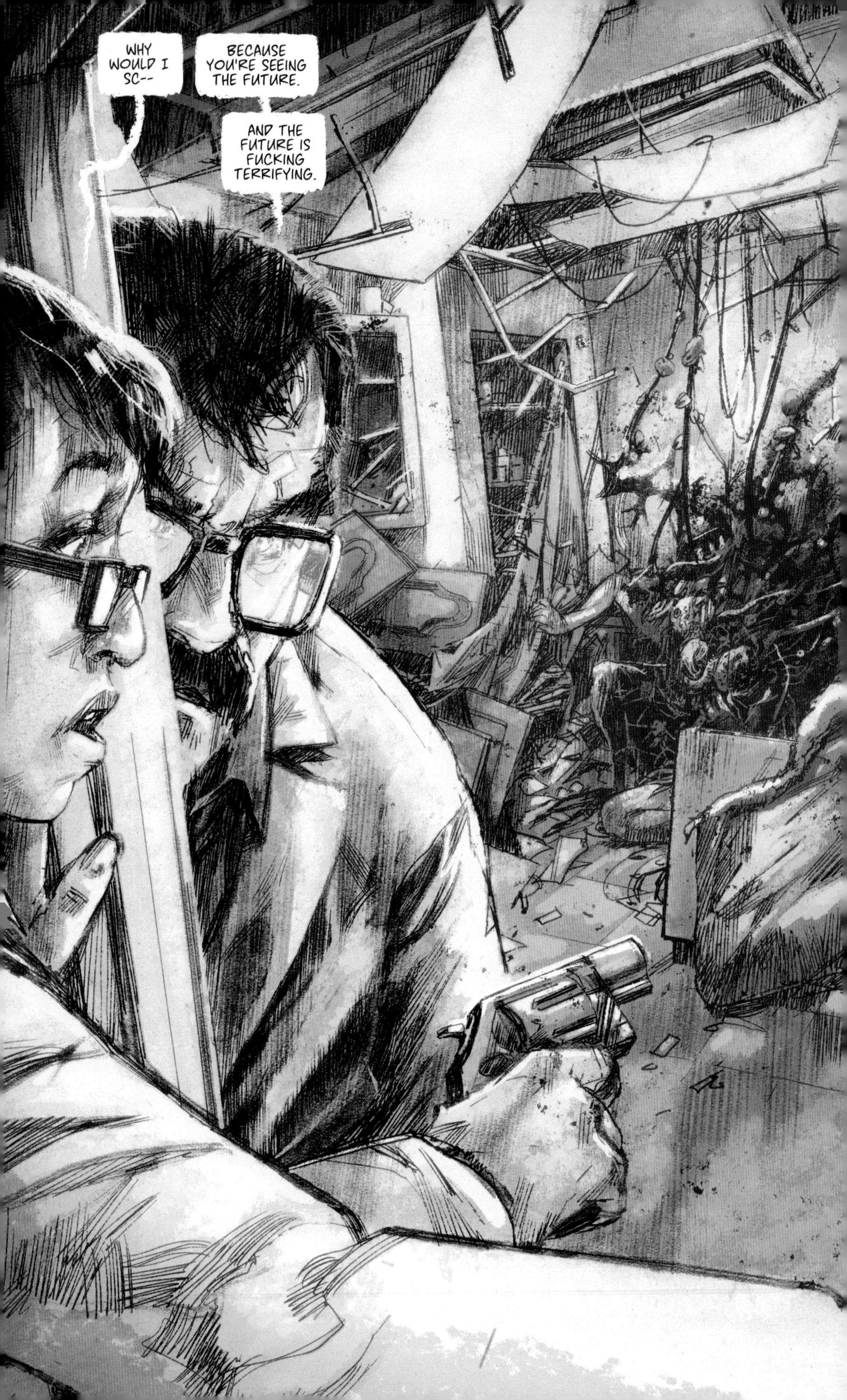
WHY WOULD I SC--
BECAUSE YOU'RE SEEING THE FUTURE.
AND THE FUTURE IS FUCKING TERRIFYING.

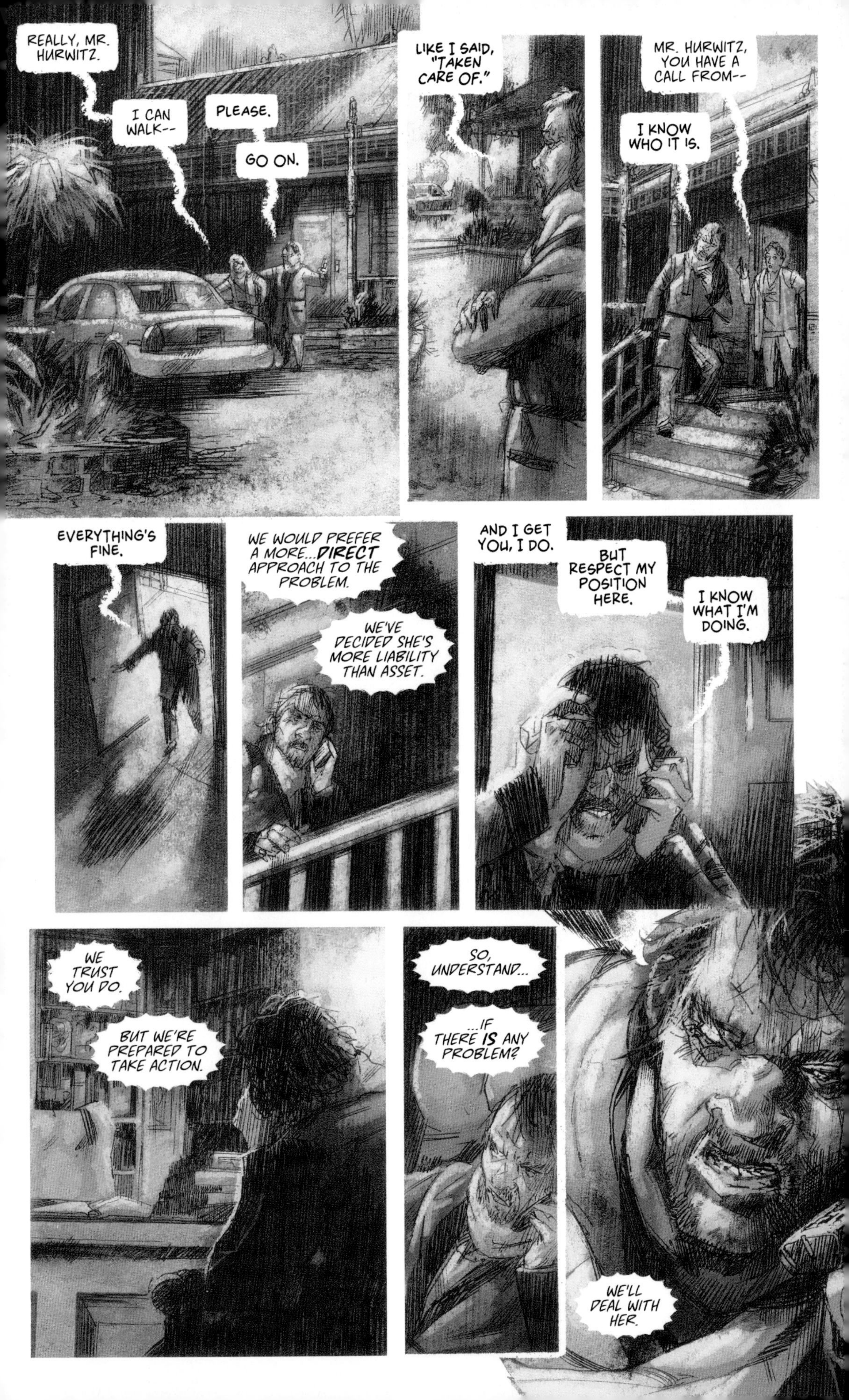
REALLY, MR. HURWITZ.
I CAN WALK--
PLEASE.
GO ON.
LIKE I SAID, "TAKEN CARE OF."
MR. HURWITZ, YOU HAVE A CALL FROM--
I KNOW WHO IT IS.
EVERYTHING'S FINE.
WE WOULD PREFER A MORE...DIRECT APPROACH TO THE PROBLEM.
WE'VE DECIDED SHE'S MORE LIABILITY THAN ASSET.
AND I GET YOU, I DO.
BUT RESPECT MY POSITION HERE.
I KNOW WHAT I'M DOING.
WE TRUST YOU DO.
BUT WE'RE PREPARED TO TAKE ACTION.
SO, UNDERSTAND...
...IF THERE IS ANY PROBLEM?
WE'LL DEAL WITH HER.

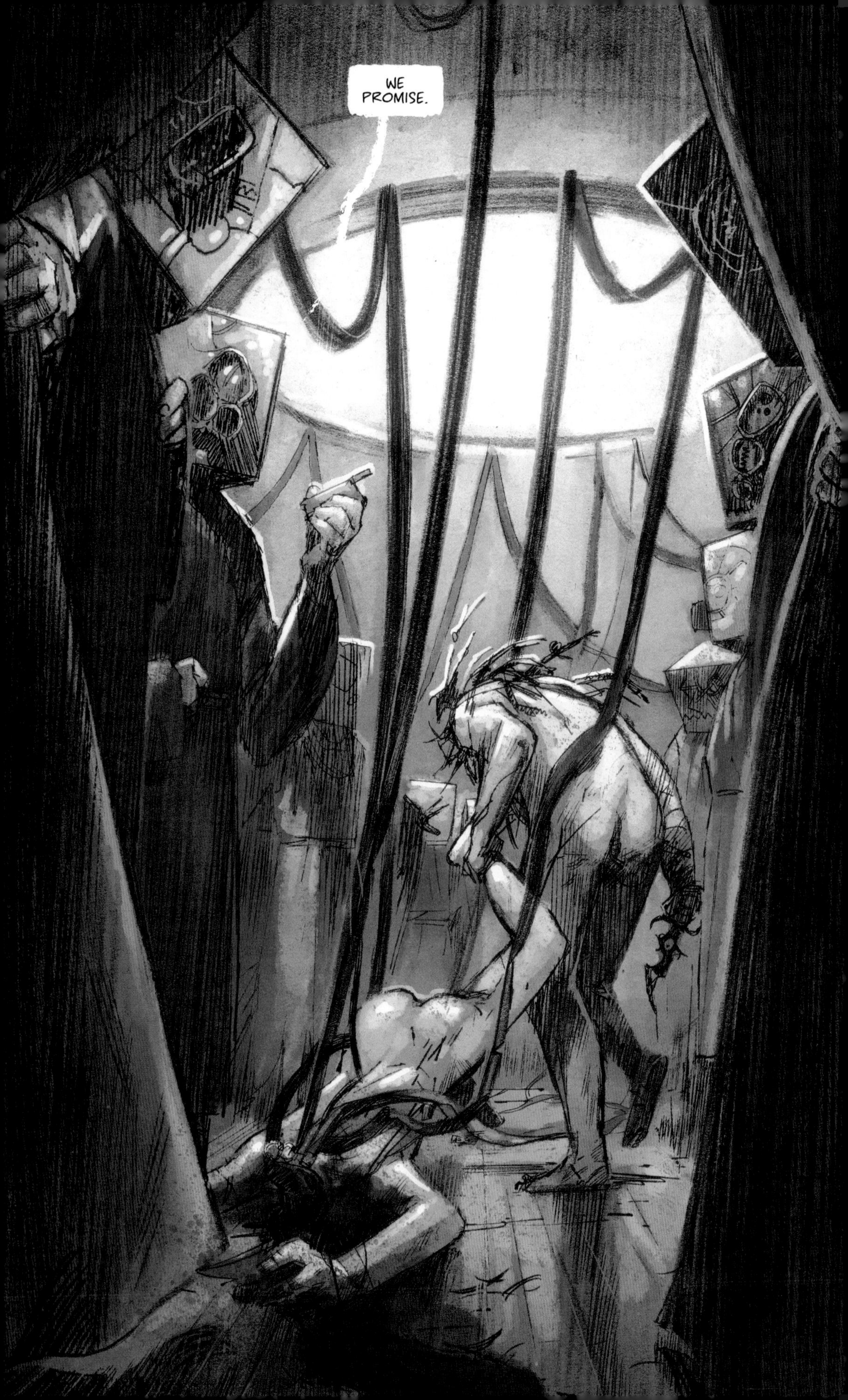
WE PROMISE.

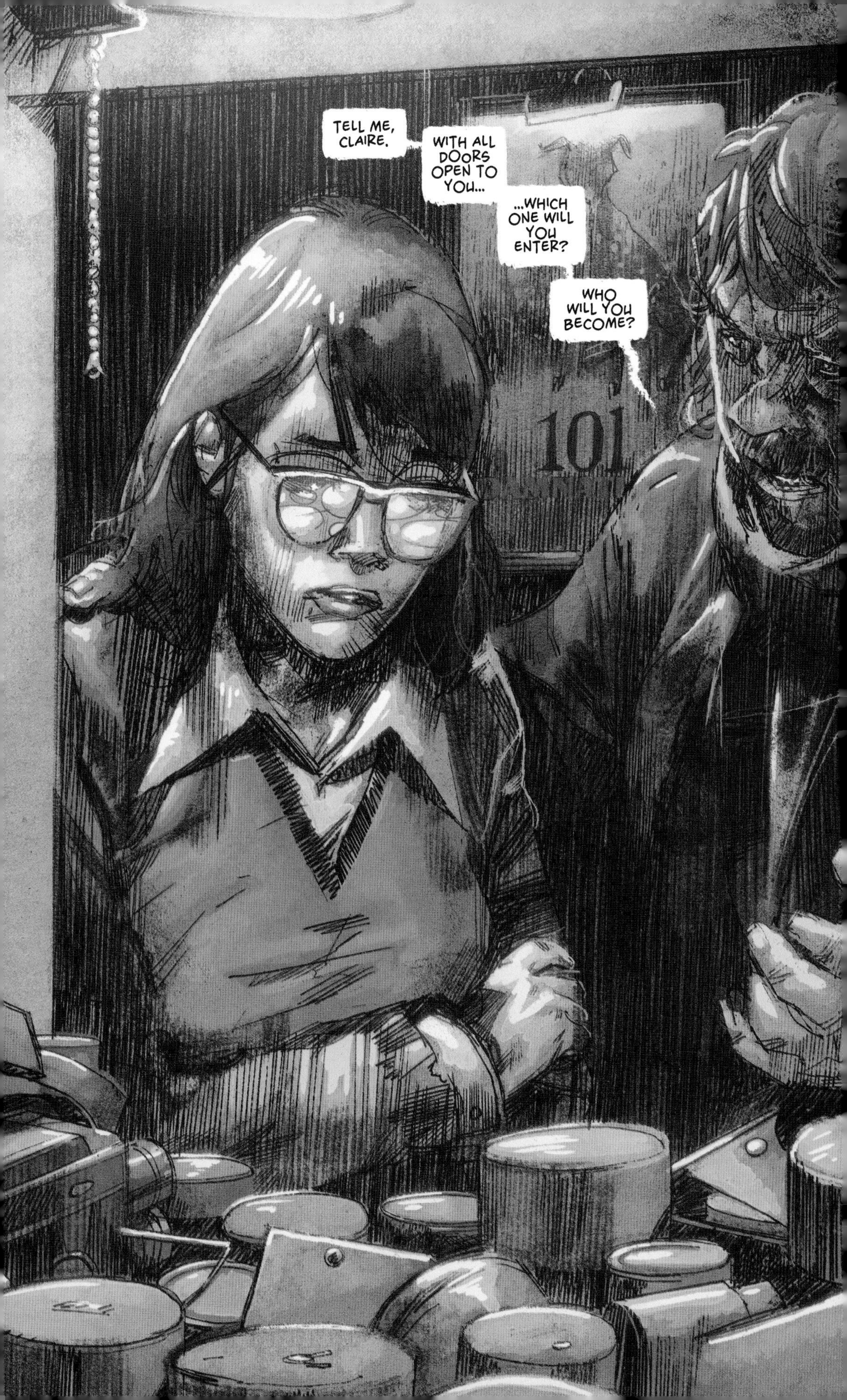
TELL ME, CLAIRE.
WITH ALL DOORS OPEN TO YOU...
...WHICH ONE WILL YOU ENTER?
WHO WILL YOU BECOME?
101

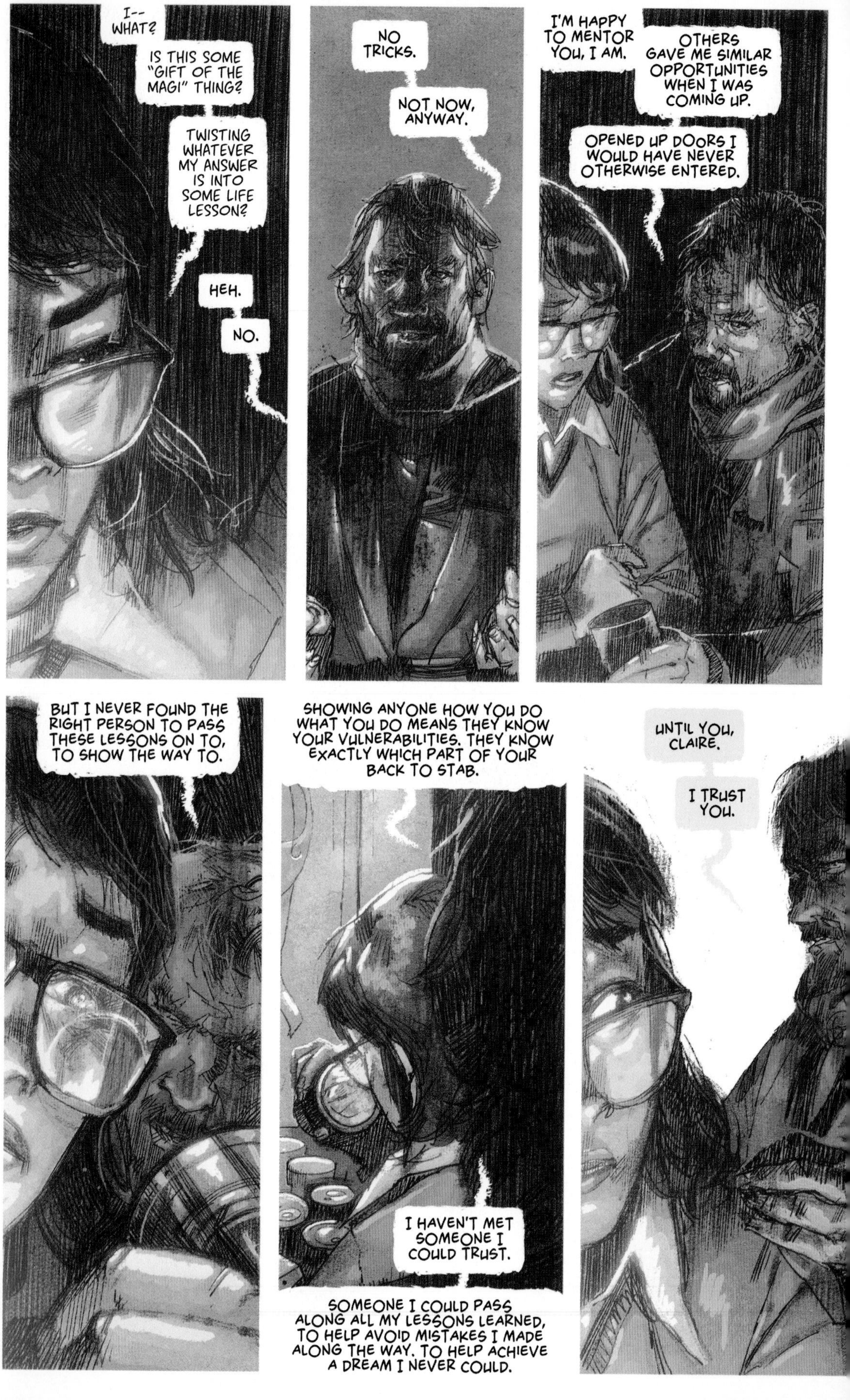
I-- WHAT?
IS THIS SOME "GIFT OF THE MAGI" THING?
TWISTING WHATEVER MY ANSWER IS INTO SOME LIFE LESSON?
HEH.
NO.
NO TRICKS.
NOT NOW, ANYWAY.
I'M HAPPY TO MENTOR YOU, I AM.
OTHERS GAVE ME SIMILAR OPPORTUNITIES WHEN I WAS COMING UP.
OPENED UP DOORS I WOULD HAVE NEVER OTHERWISE ENTERED.
BUT I NEVER FOUND THE RIGHT PERSON TO PASS THESE LESSONS ON TO, TO SHOW THE WAY TO.
SHOWING ANYONE HOW YOU DO WHAT YOU DO MEANS THEY KNOW YOUR VULNERABILITIES. THEY KNOW EXACTLY WHICH PART OF YOUR BACK TO STAB.
I HAVEN'T MET SOMEONE I COULD TRUST.
SOMEONE I COULD PASS ALONG ALL MY LESSONS LEARNED, TO HELP AVOID MISTAKES I MADE ALONG THE WAY. TO HELP ACHIEVE A DREAM I NEVER COULD.
UNTIL YOU, CLAIRE.
I TRUST YOU.

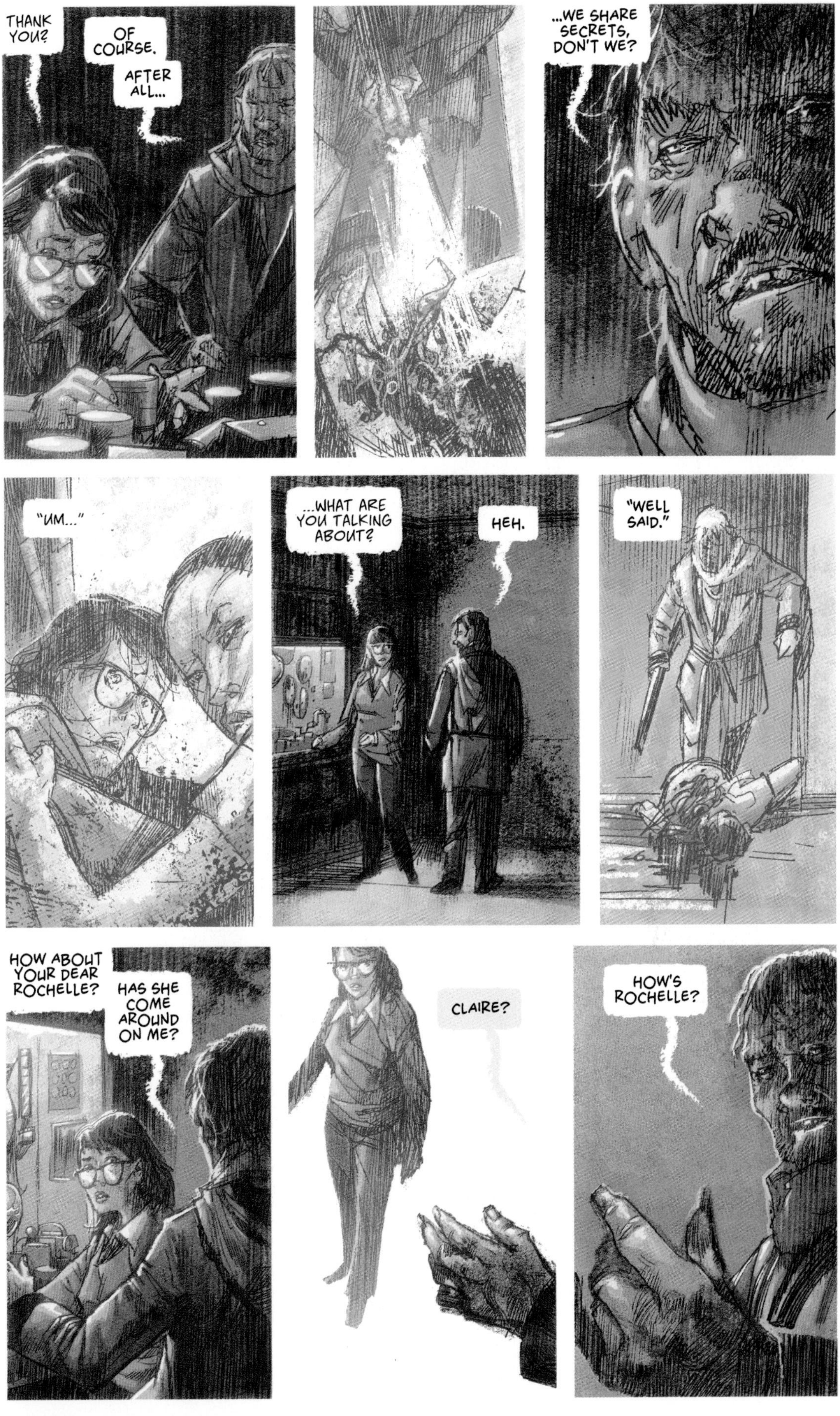
THANK YOU?
OF COURSE.
AFTER ALL...
...WE SHARE SECRETS, DON'T WE?
"UM..."
...WHAT ARE YOU TALKING ABOUT?
HEH.
"WELL SAID."
HOW ABOUT YOUR DEAR ROCHELLE?
HAS SHE COME AROUND ON ME?
CLAIRE?
HOW'S ROCHELLE?

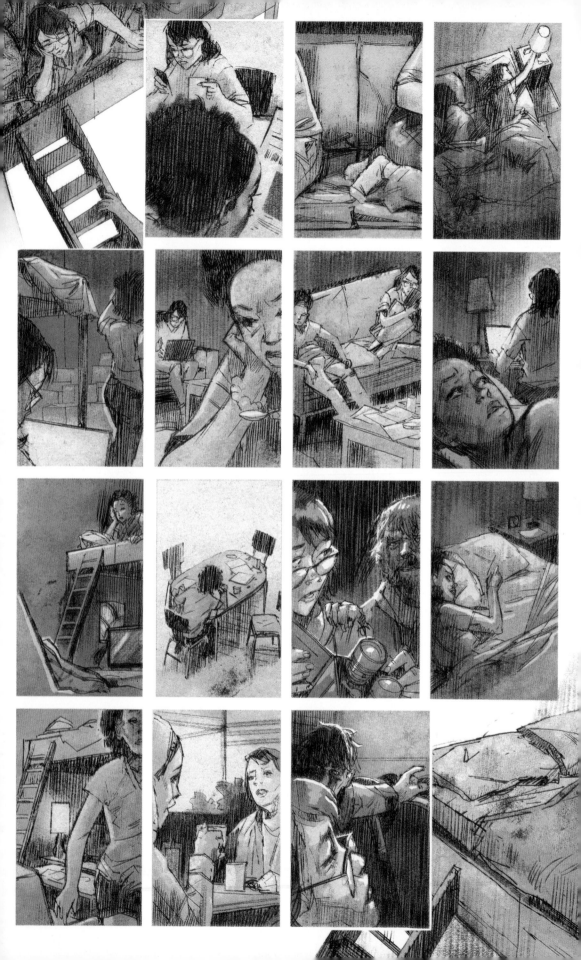

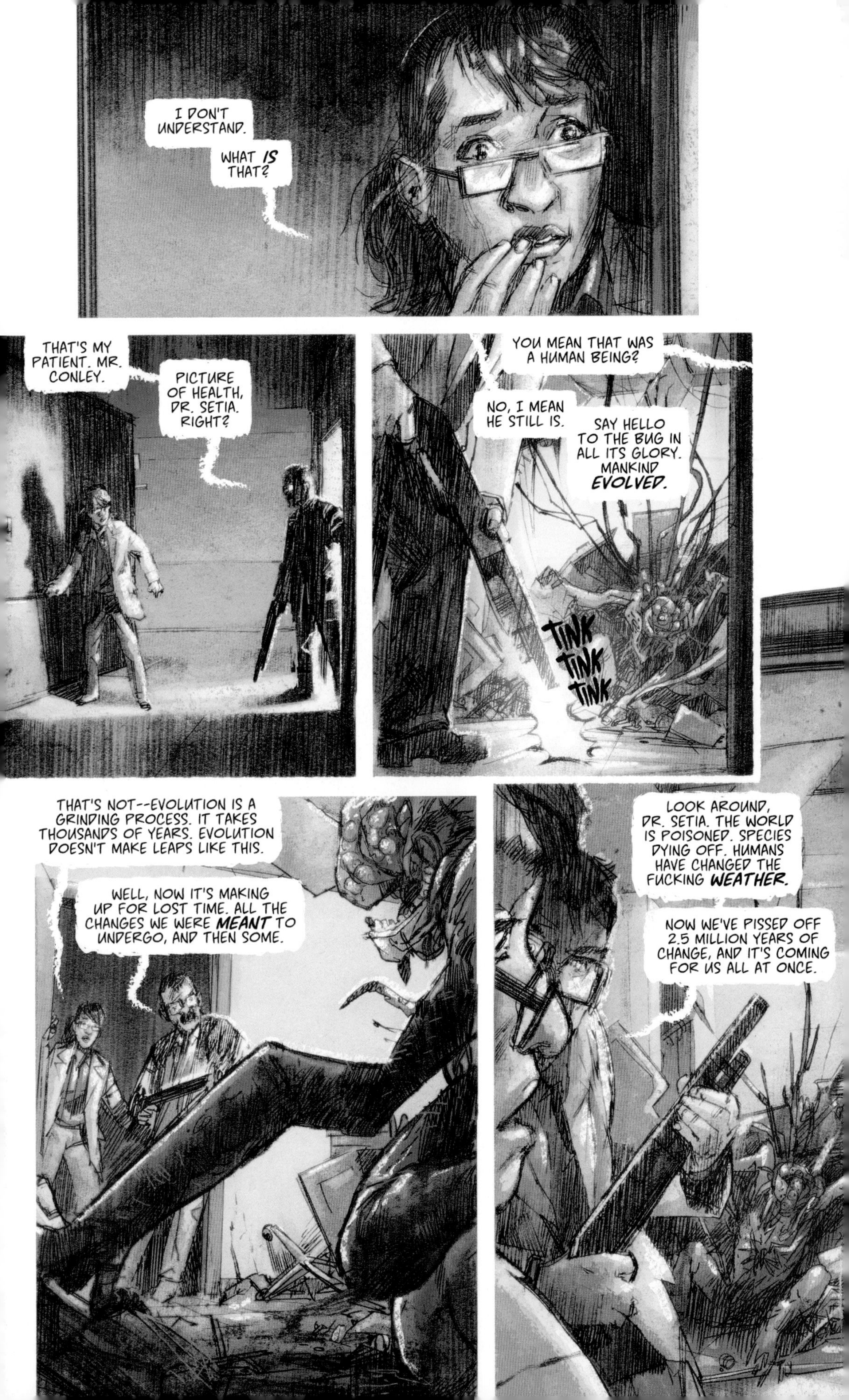
I DON'T UNDERSTAND.
WHAT IS THAT?
THAT'S MY PATIENT. MR. CONLEY.
PICTURE OF HEALTH, DR. SETIA. RIGHT?
YOU MEAN THAT WAS A HUMAN BEING?
NO, I MEAN HE STILL IS.
SAY HELLO TO THE BUG IN ALL ITS GLORY. MANKIND EVOLVED.
TINK TINK TINK
THAT'S NOT--EVOLUTION IS A GRINDING PROCESS. IT TAKES THOUSANDS OF YEARS. EVOLUTION DOESN'T MAKE LEAPS LIKE THIS.
WELL, NOW IT'S MAKING UP FOR LOST TIME. ALL THE CHANGES WE WERE MEANT TO UNDERGO, AND THEN SOME.
LOOK AROUND, DR. SETIA. THE WORLD IS POISONED. SPECIES DYING OFF. HUMANS HAVE CHANGED THE FUCKING WEATHER.
NOW WE'VE PISSED OFF 2.5 MILLION YEARS OF CHANGE, AND IT'S COMING FOR US ALL AT ONCE.

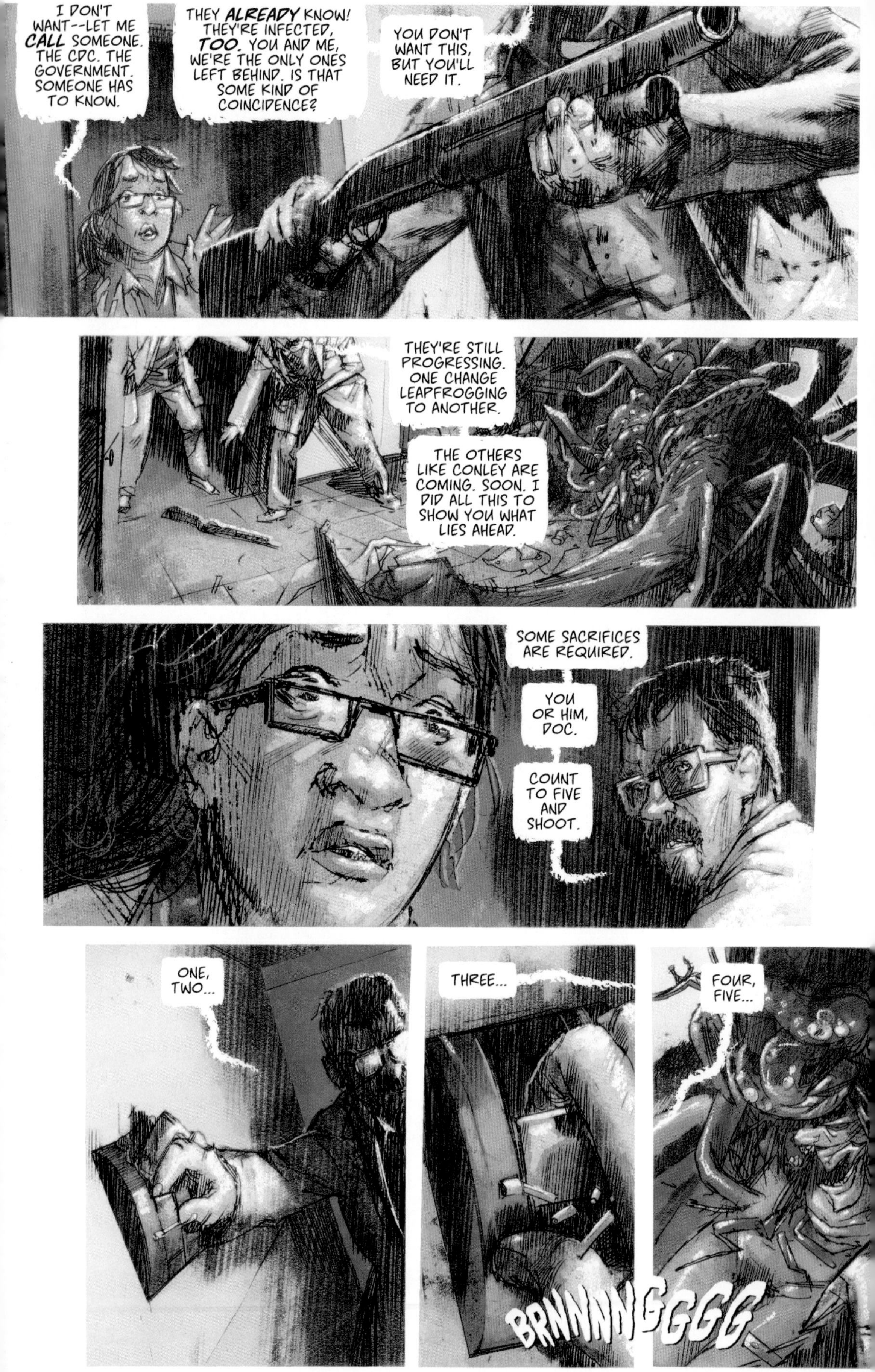
I DON'T WANT--LET ME CALL SOMEONE. THE CDC. THE GOVERNMENT. SOMEONE HAS TO KNOW.
THEY ALREADY KNOW! THEY'RE INFECTED, TOO. YOU AND ME, WE'RE THE ONLY ONES LEFT BEHIND. IS THAT SOME KIND OF COINCIDENCE?
YOU DON'T WANT THIS, BUT YOU'LL NEED IT.
THEY'RE STILL PROGRESSING. ONE CHANGE LEAPFROGGING TO ANOTHER.
THE OTHERS LIKE CONLEY ARE COMING. SOON. I DID ALL THIS TO SHOW YOU WHAT LIES AHEAD.
SOME SACRIFICES ARE REQUIRED.
YOU OR HIM, DOC.
COUNT TO FIVE AND SHOOT.
ONE, TWO...
THREE...
FOUR, FIVE...
BRNNNNGGGG

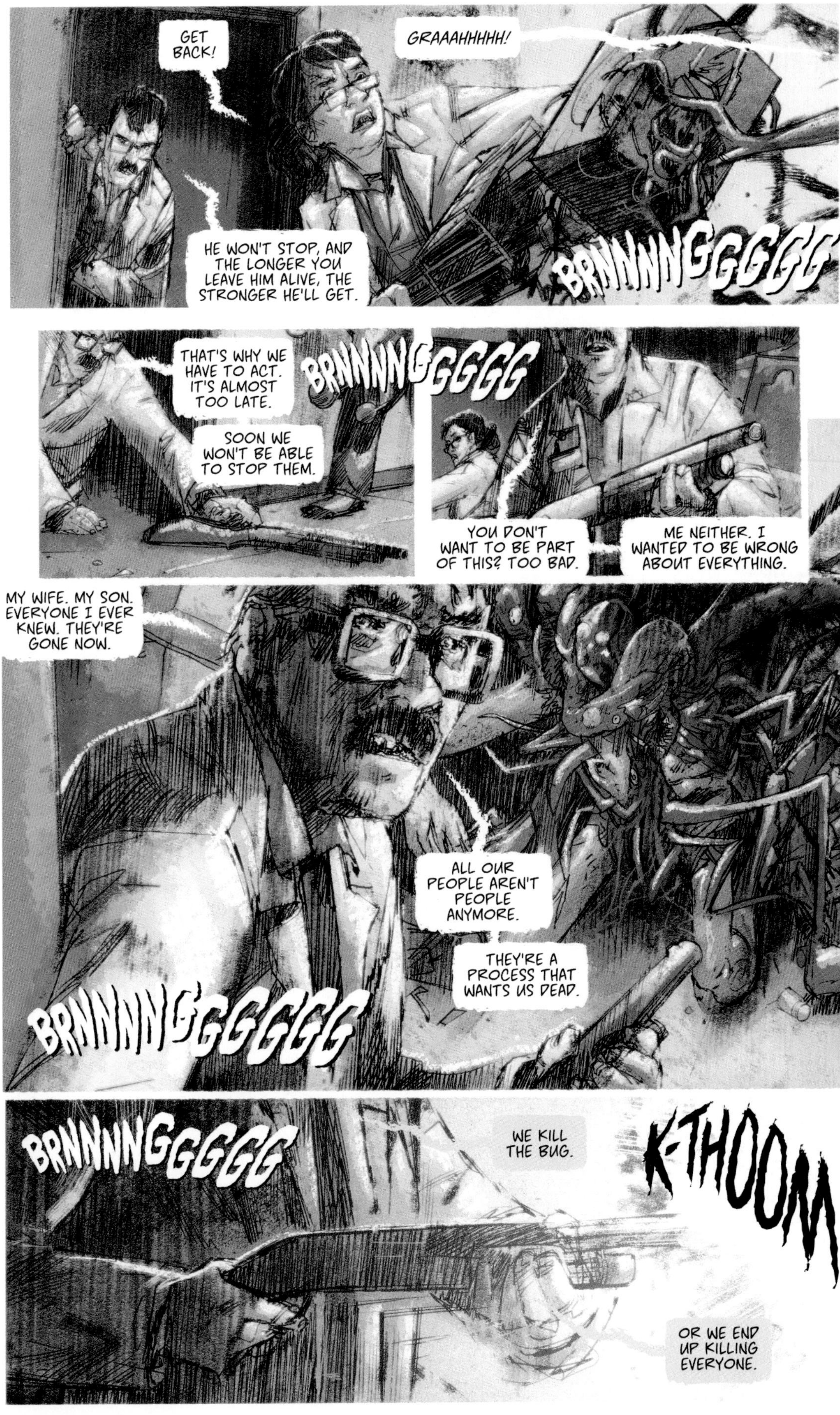
GET BACK!
GRAAAHHHHH!
HE WON'T STOP, AND THE LONGER YOU LEAVE HIM ALIVE, THE STRONGER HE'LL GET.
BRNNNNGGGGG
THAT'S WHY WE HAVE TO ACT. IT'S ALMOST TOO LATE.
SOON WE WON'T BE ABLE TO STOP THEM.
BRNNNNGGGGG
YOU DON'T WANT TO BE PART OF THIS? TOO BAD.
ME NEITHER. I WANTED TO BE WRONG ABOUT EVERYTHING.
MY WIFE. MY SON. EVERYONE I EVER KNEW. THEY'RE GONE NOW.
ALL OUR PEOPLE AREN'T PEOPLE ANYMORE.
THEY'RE A PROCESS THAT WANTS US DEAD.
BRNNNNGGGGGG
BRNNNNGGGGG
WE KILL THE BUG.
K-THOOM
OR WE END UP KILLING EVERYONE.

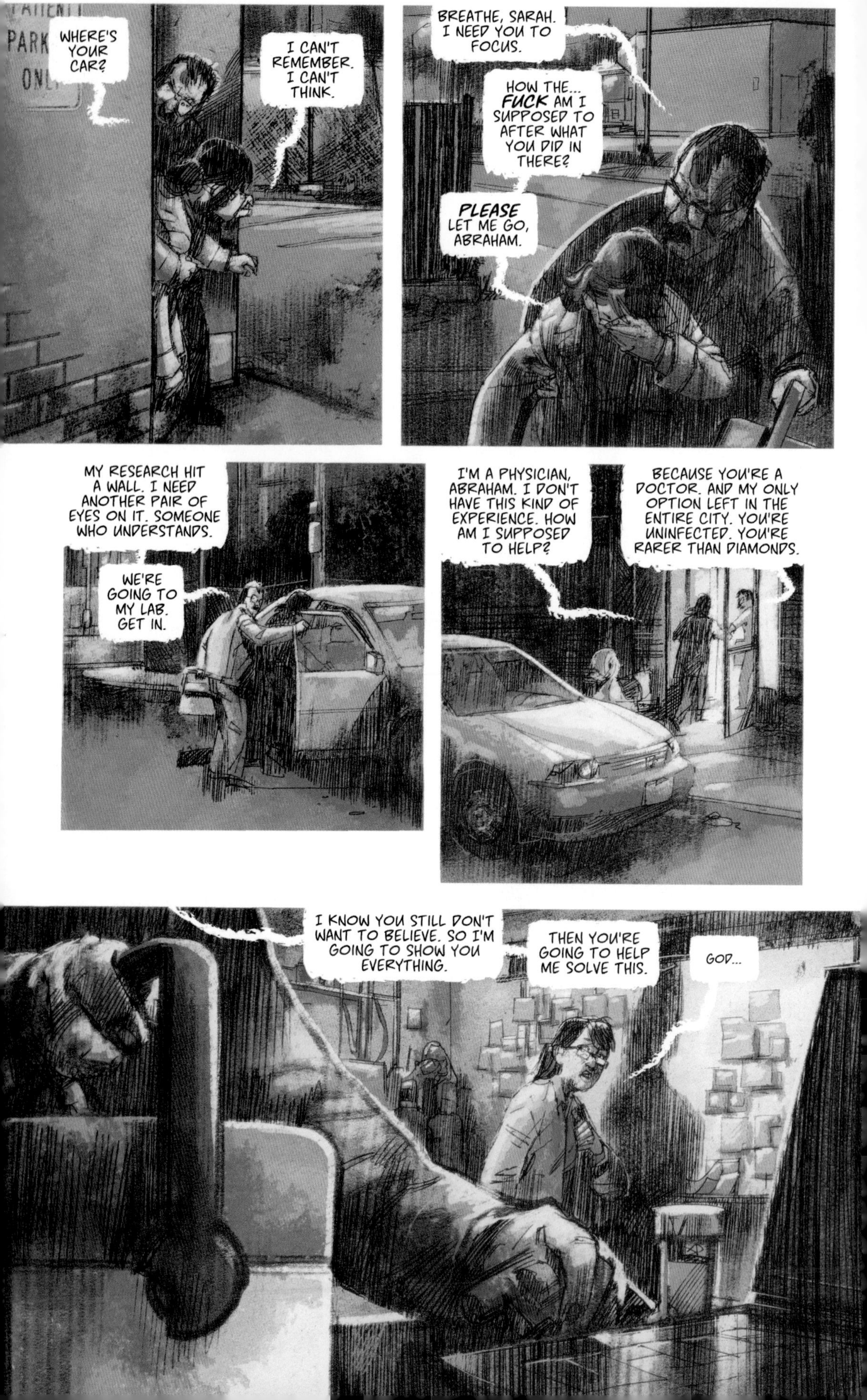

PATIENT PARKING ONLY
WHERE'S YOUR CAR?
I CAN'T REMEMBER. I CAN'T THINK.
BREATHE, SARAH. I NEED YOU TO FOCUS.
HOW THE... **FUCK** AM I SUPPOSED TO AFTER WHAT YOU DID IN THERE?
PLEASE LET ME GO, ABRAHAM.
MY RESEARCH HIT A WALL. I NEED ANOTHER PAIR OF EYES ON IT. SOMEONE WHO UNDERSTANDS.
WE'RE GOING TO MY LAB. GET IN.
I'M A PHYSICIAN, ABRAHAM. I DON'T HAVE THIS KIND OF EXPERIENCE. HOW AM I SUPPOSED TO HELP?
BECAUSE YOU'RE A DOCTOR. AND MY ONLY OPTION LEFT IN THE ENTIRE CITY. YOU'RE UNINFECTED. YOU'RE RARER THAN DIAMONDS.
I KNOW YOU STILL DON'T WANT TO BELIEVE. SO I'M GOING TO SHOW YOU EVERYTHING.
THEN YOU'RE GOING TO HELP ME SOLVE THIS.
GOD...

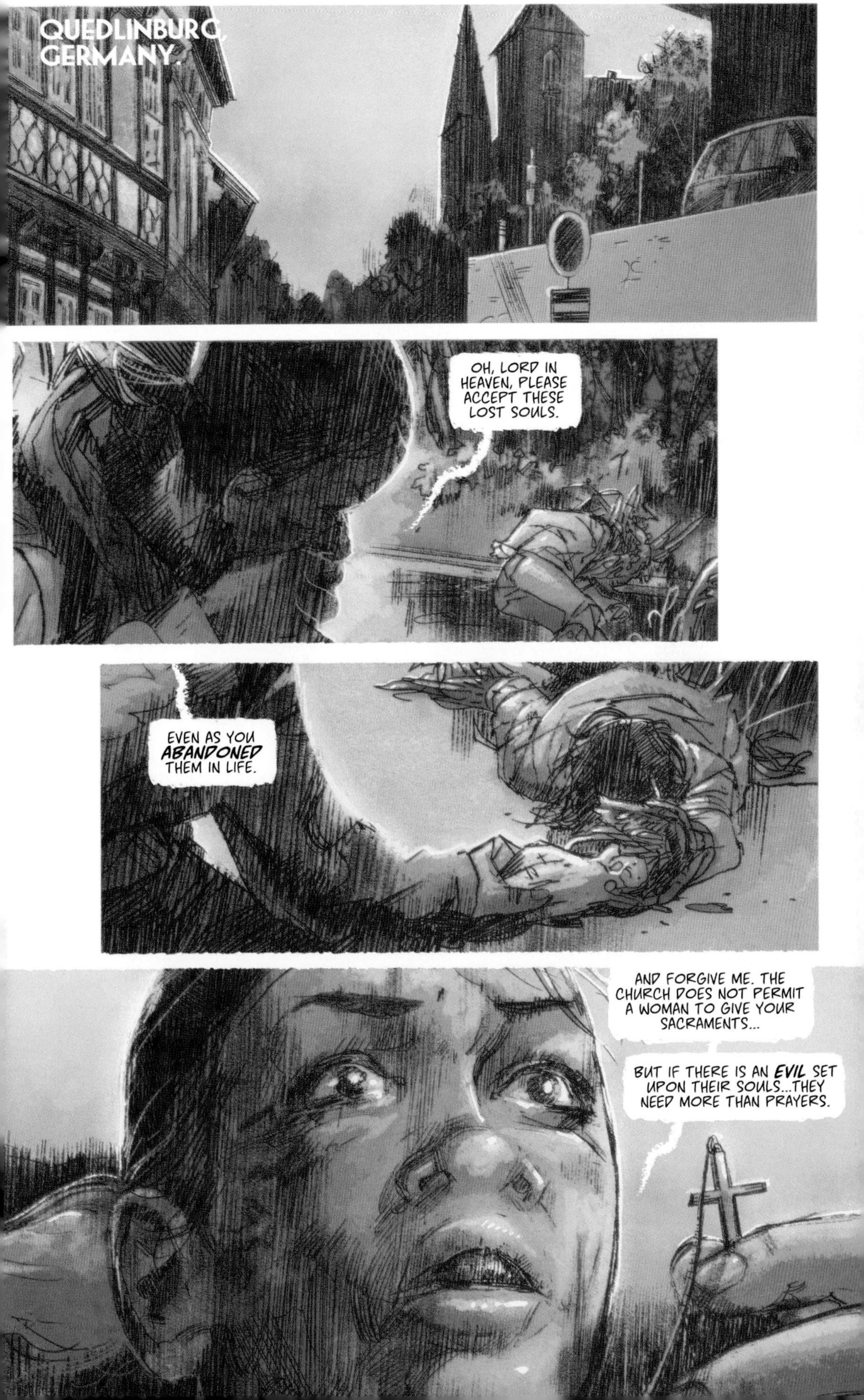
QUEDLINBURG, GERMANY.
OH, LORD IN HEAVEN, PLEASE ACCEPT THESE LOST SOULS.
EVEN AS YOU ABANDONED THEM IN LIFE.
AND FORGIVE ME. THE CHURCH DOES NOT PERMIT A WOMAN TO GIVE YOUR SACRAMENTS...
BUT IF THERE IS AN EVIL SET UPON THEIR SOULS...THEY NEED MORE THAN PRAYERS.

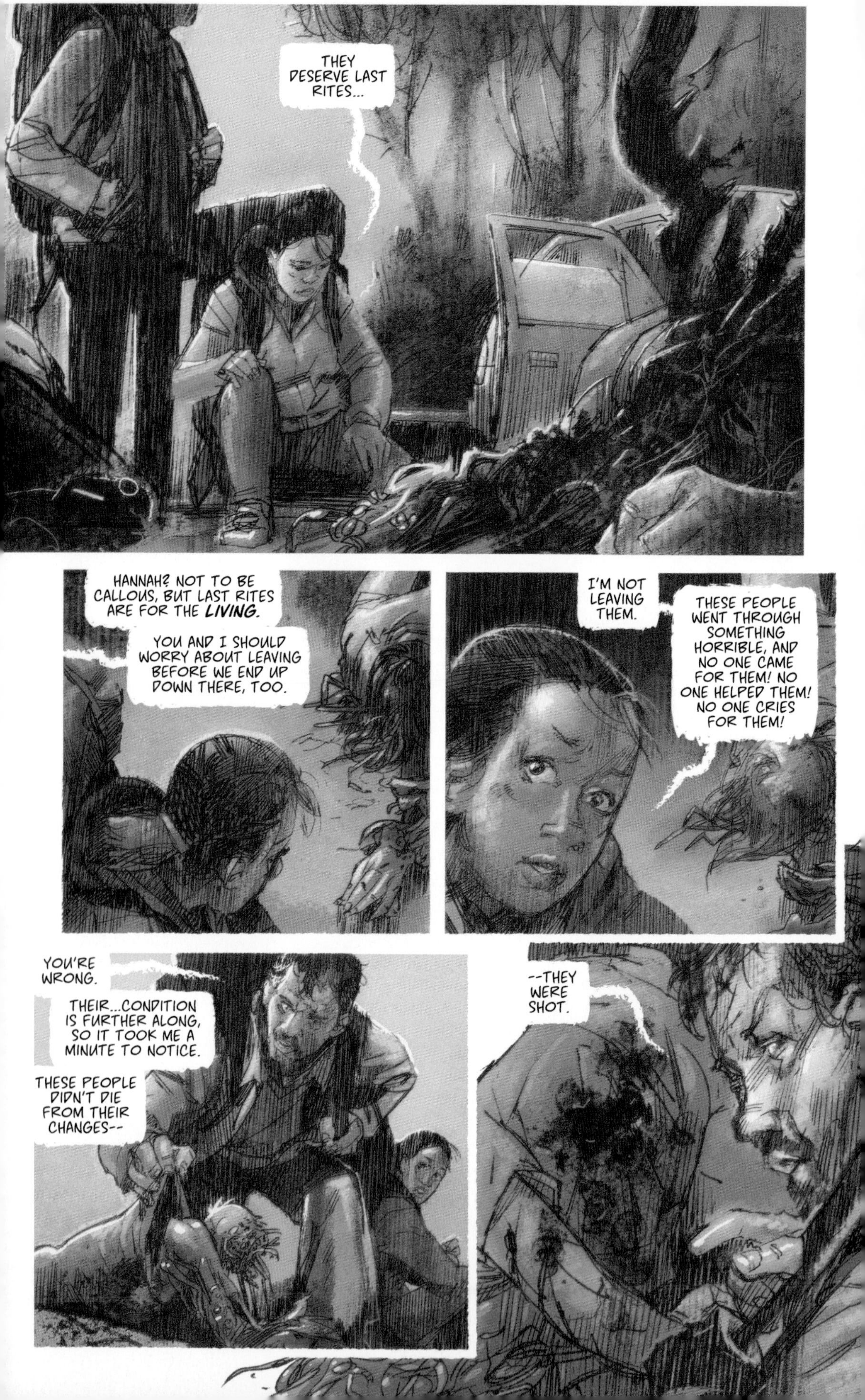
THEY DESERVE LAST RITES...
HANNAH? NOT TO BE CALLOUS, BUT LAST RITES ARE FOR THE *LIVING.*
YOU AND I SHOULD WORRY ABOUT LEAVING BEFORE WE END UP DOWN THERE, TOO.
I'M NOT LEAVING THEM.
THESE PEOPLE WENT THROUGH SOMETHING HORRIBLE, AND NO ONE CAME FOR THEM! NO ONE HELPED THEM! NO ONE CRIES FOR THEM!
YOU'RE WRONG.
THEIR...CONDITION IS FURTHER ALONG, SO IT TOOK ME A MINUTE TO NOTICE.
THESE PEOPLE DIDN'T DIE FROM THEIR CHANGES--
--THEY WERE SHOT.

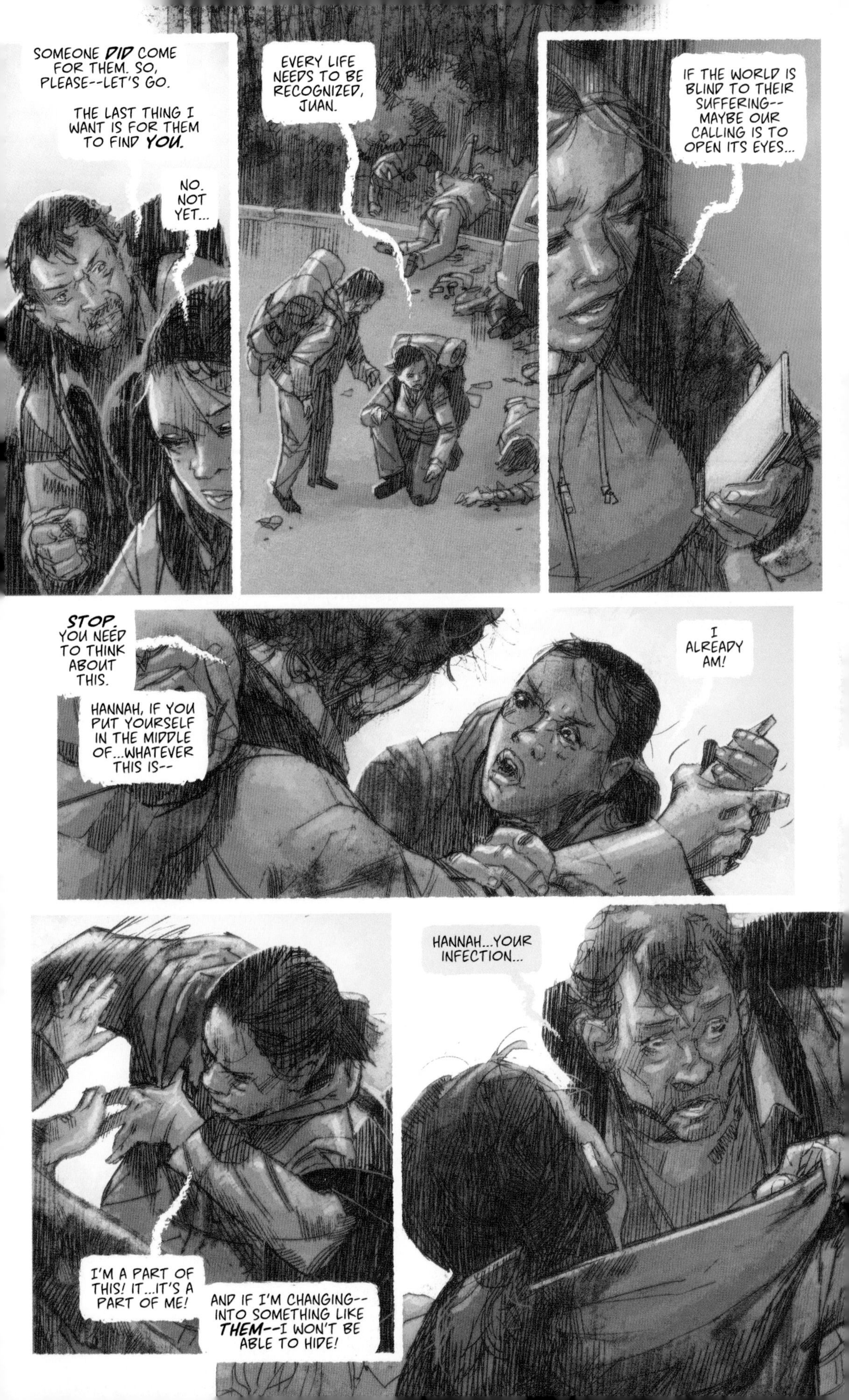
SOMEONE DID COME FOR THEM. SO, PLEASE--LET'S GO.
THE LAST THING I WANT IS FOR THEM TO FIND YOU.
NO. NOT YET...
EVERY LIFE NEEDS TO BE RECOGNIZED, JUAN.
IF THE WORLD IS BLIND TO THEIR SUFFERING-- MAYBE OUR CALLING IS TO OPEN ITS EYES...
STOP. YOU NEED TO THINK ABOUT THIS.
HANNAH, IF YOU PUT YOURSELF IN THE MIDDLE OF...WHATEVER THIS IS--
I ALREADY AM!
I'M A PART OF THIS! IT...IT'S A PART OF ME!
AND IF I'M CHANGING-- INTO SOMETHING LIKE THEM--I WON'T BE ABLE TO HIDE!
HANNAH...YOUR INFECTION...

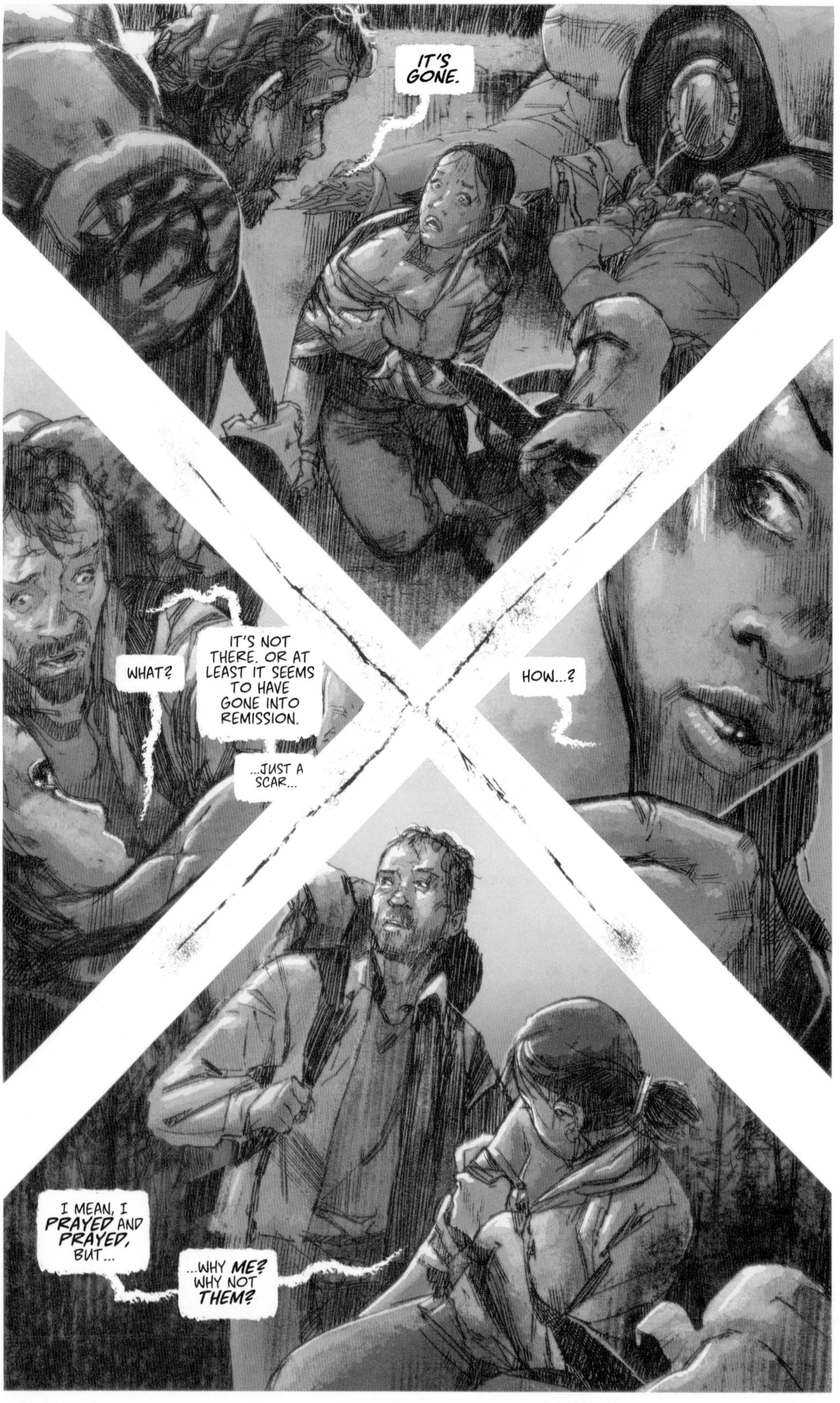
IT'S GONE.
WHAT?
IT'S NOT THERE. OR AT LEAST IT SEEMS TO HAVE GONE INTO REMISSION.
...JUST A SCAR...
HOW...?
I MEAN, I PRAYED AND PRAYED, BUT...
...WHY ME? WHY NOT THEM?

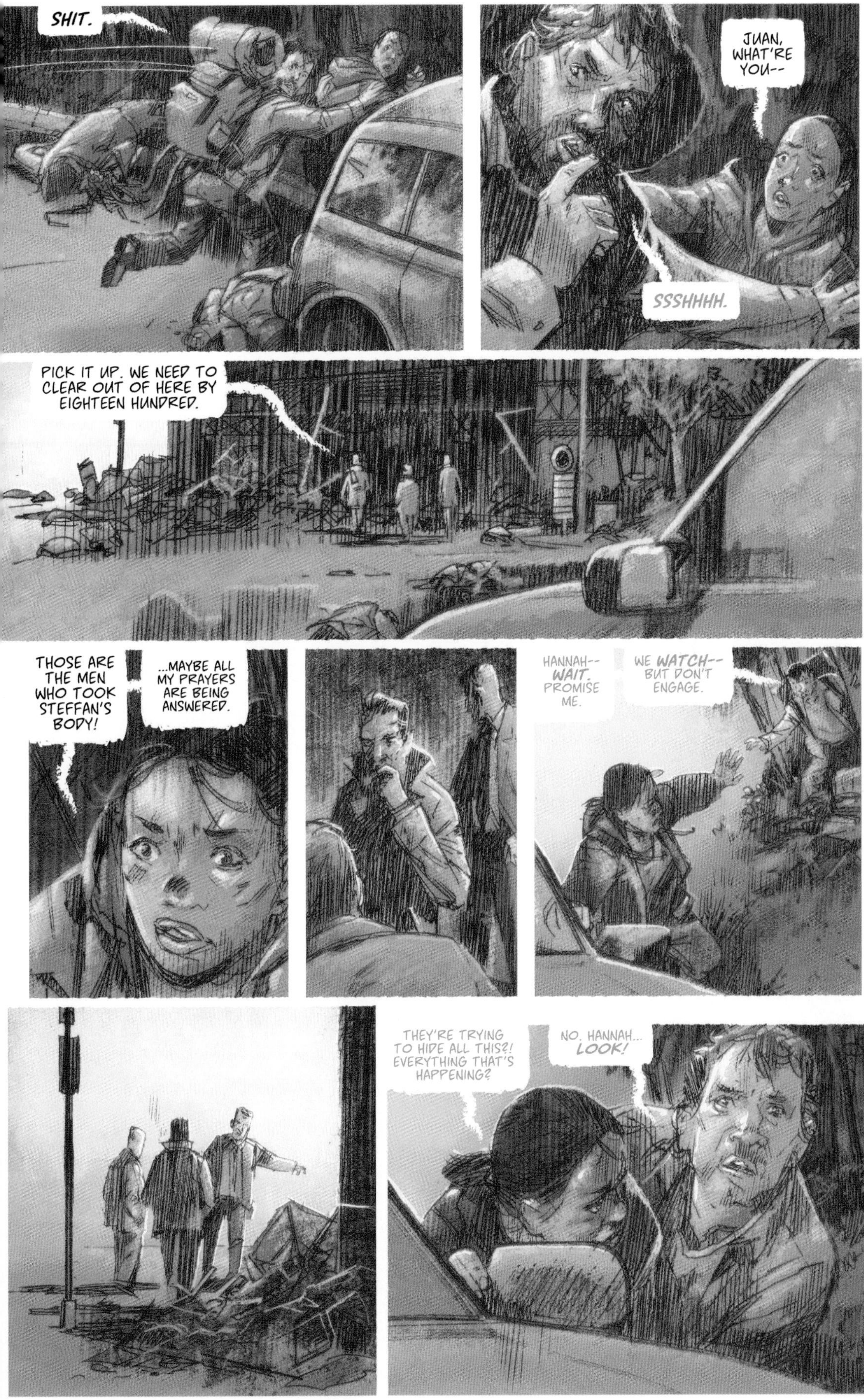

SHIT.
JUAN, WHAT'RE YOU--
SSSHHHH.
PICK IT UP. WE NEED TO CLEAR OUT OF HERE BY EIGHTEEN HUNDRED.
THOSE ARE THE MEN WHO TOOK STEFFAN'S BODY!
...MAYBE ALL MY PRAYERS ARE BEING ANSWERED.
HANNAH-- WAIT. PROMISE ME.
WE WATCH-- BUT DON'T ENGAGE.
THEY'RE TRYING TO HIDE ALL THIS?! EVERYTHING THAT'S HAPPENING?
NO. HANNAH... LOOK!

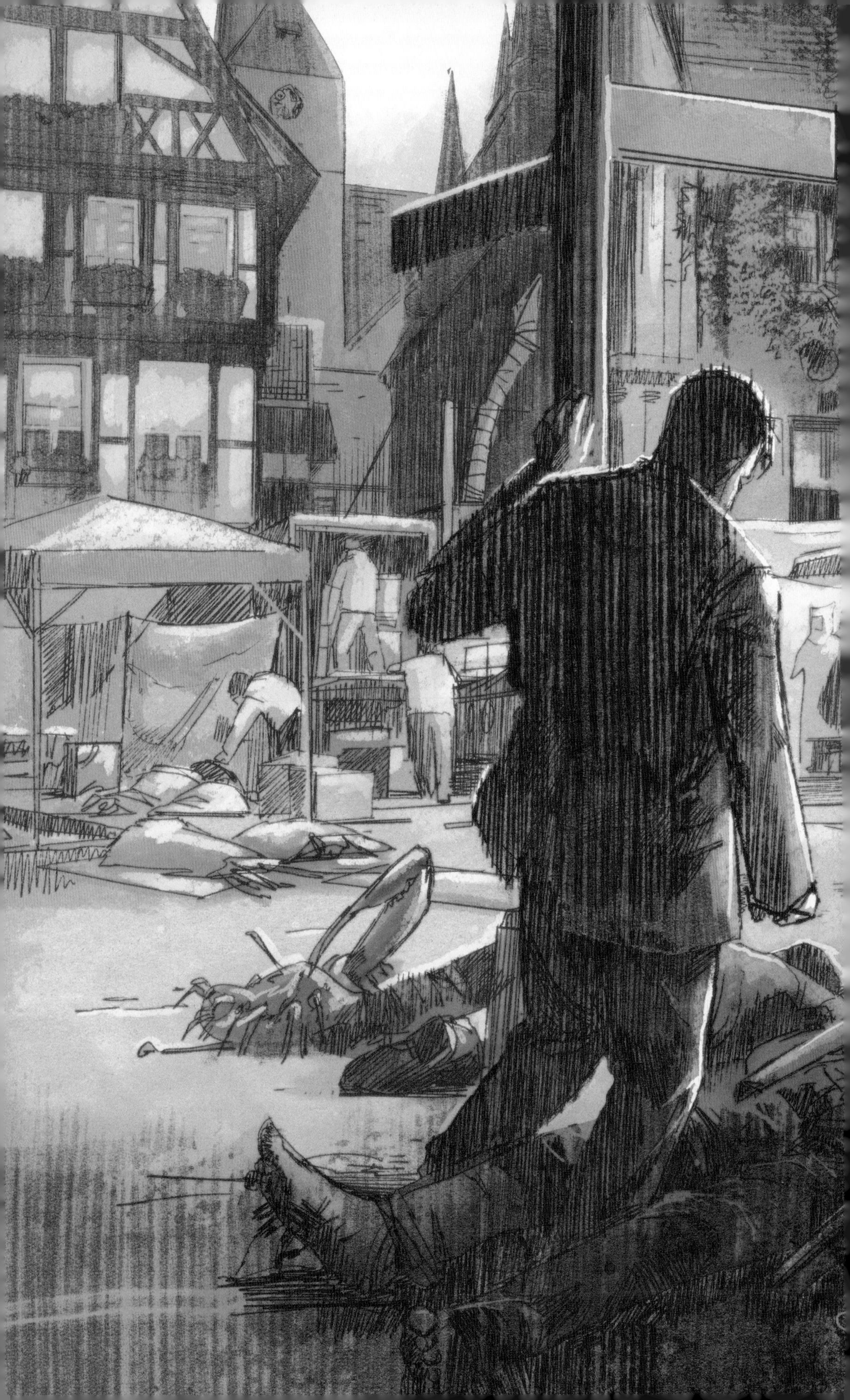

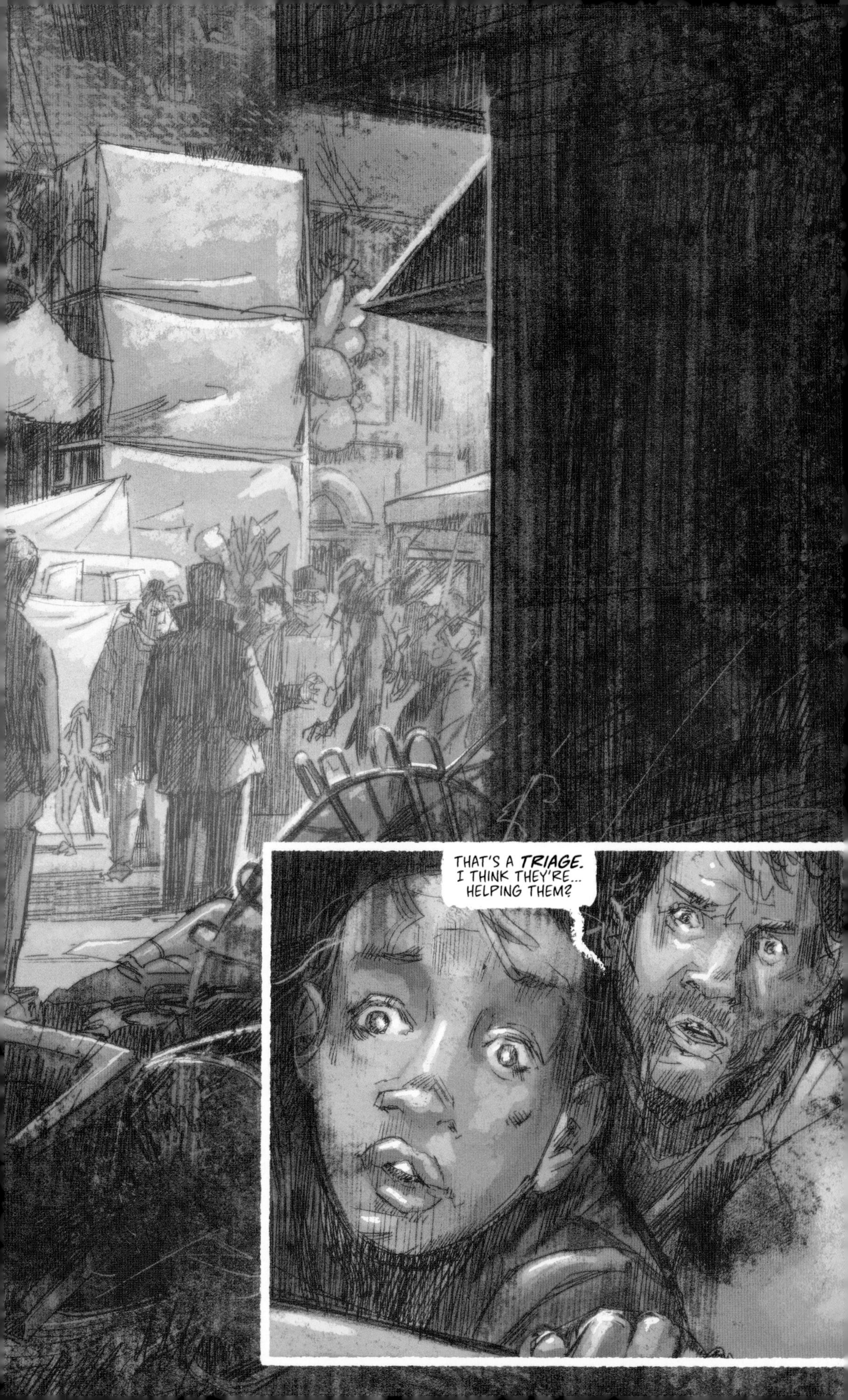

THAT'S A **TRIAGE.** I THINK THEY'RE... HELPING THEM?

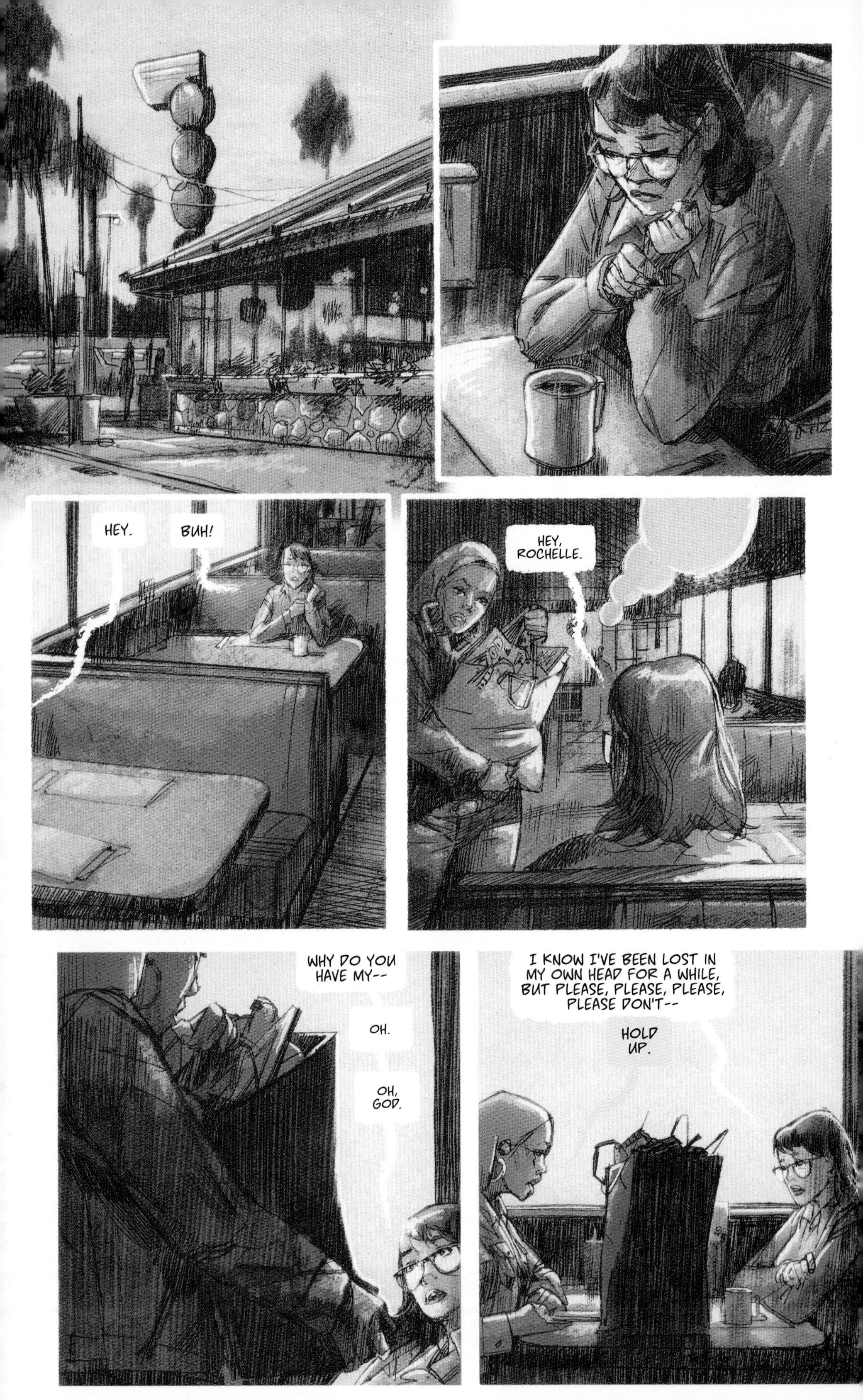
HEY.
BUH!
HEY, ROCHELLE.
WHY DO YOU HAVE MY--
OH.
OH, GOD.
I KNOW I'VE BEEN LOST IN MY OWN HEAD FOR A WHILE, BUT PLEASE, PLEASE, PLEASE, PLEASE DON'T--
HOLD UP.

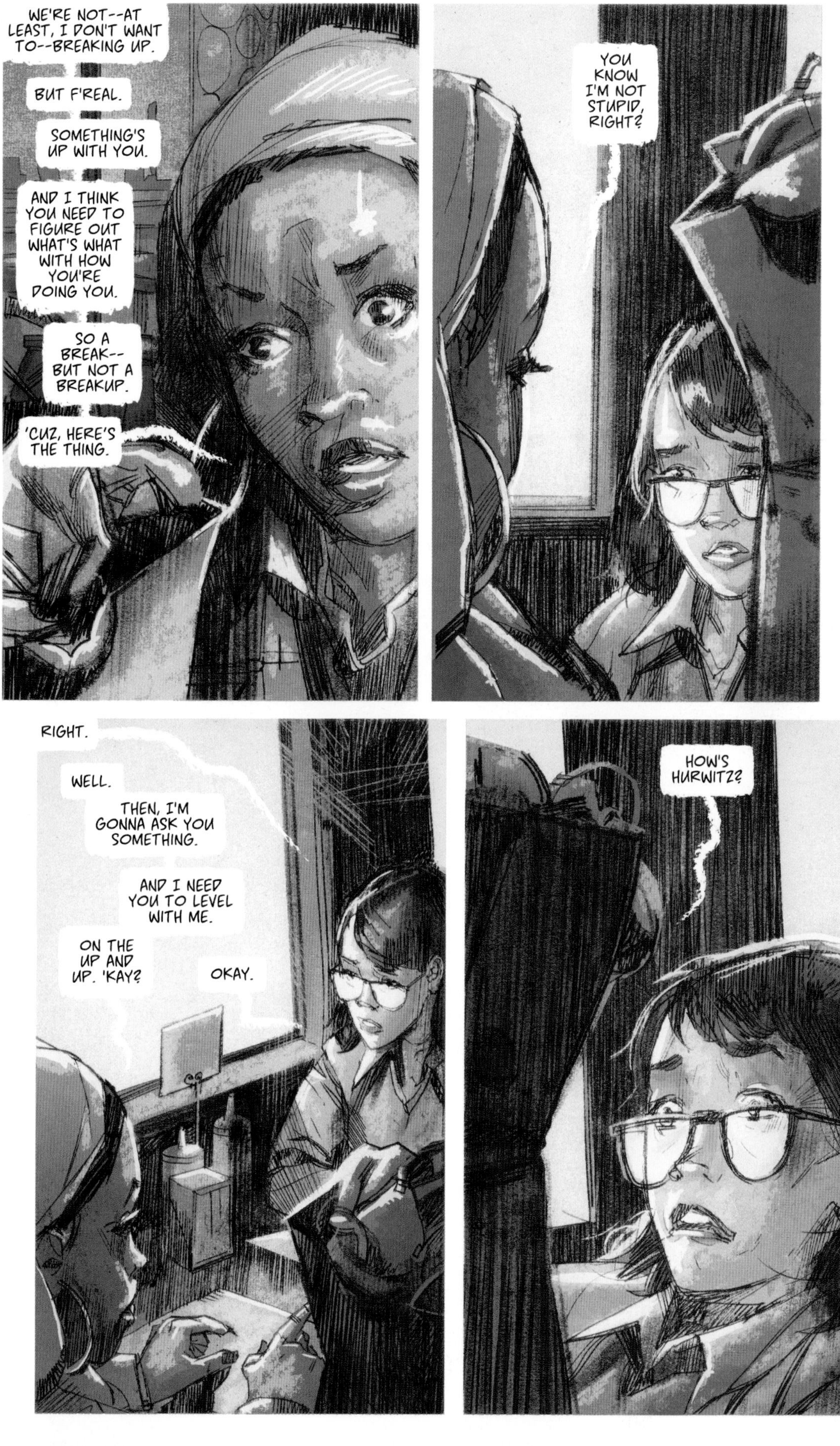
WE'RE NOT--AT LEAST, I DON'T WANT TO--BREAKING UP.
BUT F'REAL.
SOMETHING'S UP WITH YOU.
AND I THINK YOU NEED TO FIGURE OUT WHAT'S WHAT WITH HOW YOU'RE DOING YOU.
SO A BREAK--BUT NOT A BREAKUP.
'CUZ, HERE'S THE THING.
YOU KNOW I'M NOT STUPID, RIGHT?
RIGHT.
WELL.
THEN, I'M GONNA ASK YOU SOMETHING.
AND I NEED YOU TO LEVEL WITH ME.
ON THE UP AND UP. 'KAY?
OKAY.
HOW'S HURWITZ?

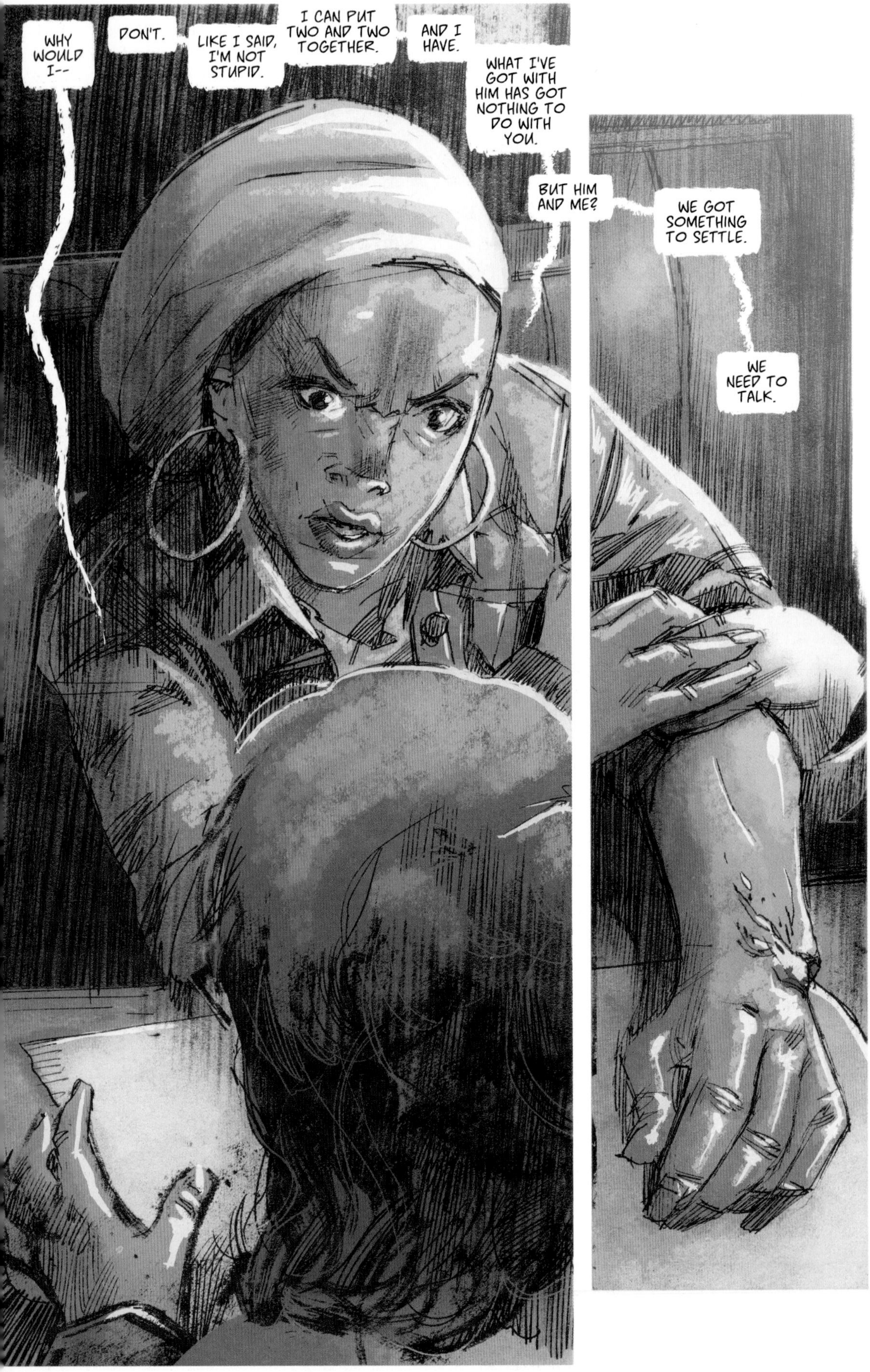
WHY WOULD I--
DON'T.
LIKE I SAID, I'M NOT STUPID.
I CAN PUT TWO AND TWO TOGETHER.
AND I HAVE.
WHAT I'VE GOT WITH HIM HAS GOT NOTHING TO DO WITH YOU.
BUT HIM AND ME?
WE GOT SOMETHING TO SETTLE.
WE NEED TO TALK.

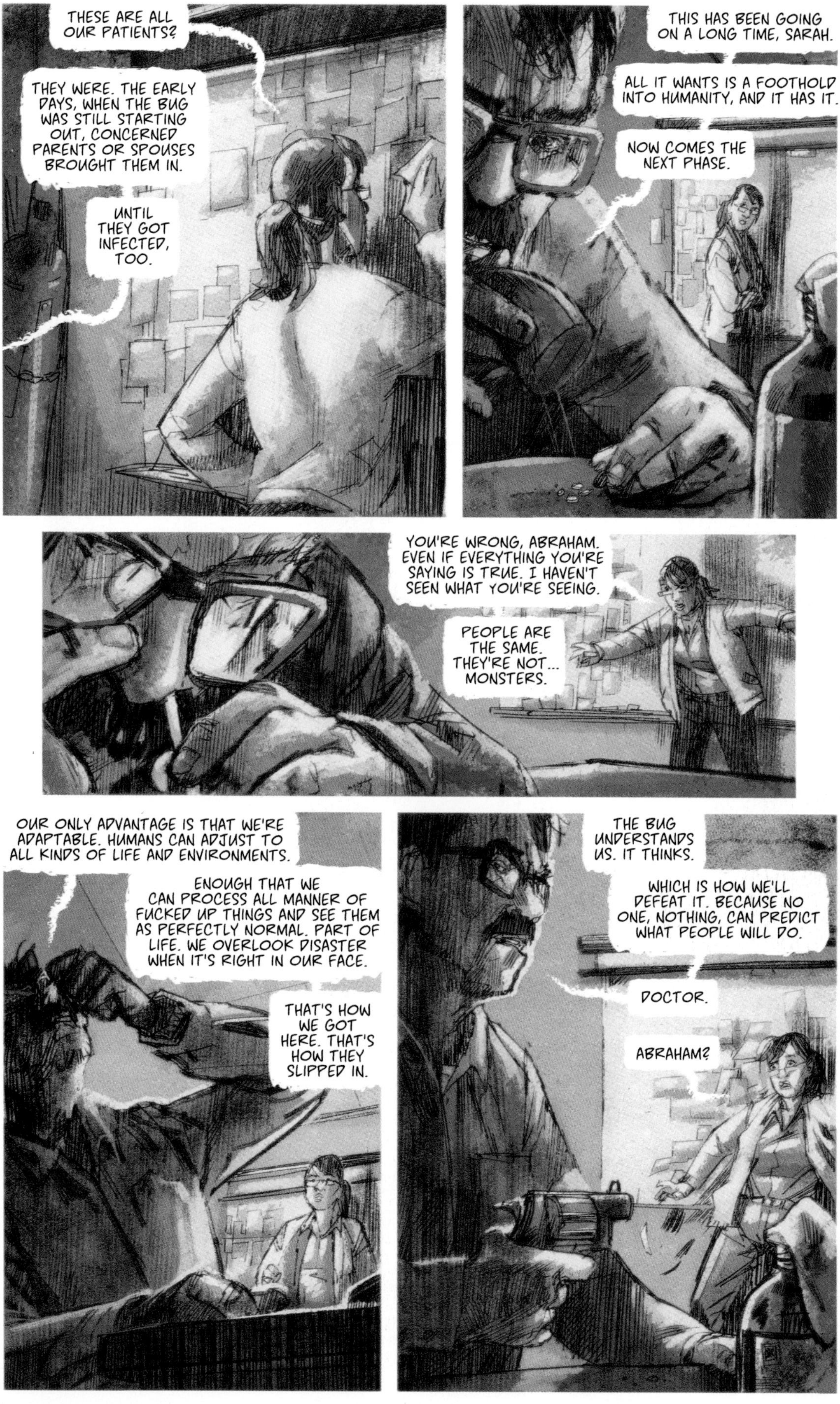
THESE ARE ALL OUR PATIENTS?
THEY WERE. THE EARLY DAYS, WHEN THE BUG WAS STILL STARTING OUT, CONCERNED PARENTS OR SPOUSES BROUGHT THEM IN.
UNTIL THEY GOT INFECTED, TOO.
THIS HAS BEEN GOING ON A LONG TIME, SARAH.
ALL IT WANTS IS A FOOTHOLD INTO HUMANITY, AND IT HAS IT.
NOW COMES THE NEXT PHASE.
YOU'RE WRONG, ABRAHAM. EVEN IF EVERYTHING YOU'RE SAYING IS TRUE. I HAVEN'T SEEN WHAT YOU'RE SEEING.
PEOPLE ARE THE SAME. THEY'RE NOT... MONSTERS.
OUR ONLY ADVANTAGE IS THAT WE'RE ADAPTABLE. HUMANS CAN ADJUST TO ALL KINDS OF LIFE AND ENVIRONMENTS.
ENOUGH THAT WE CAN PROCESS ALL MANNER OF FUCKED UP THINGS AND SEE THEM AS PERFECTLY NORMAL. PART OF LIFE. WE OVERLOOK DISASTER WHEN IT'S RIGHT IN OUR FACE.
THAT'S HOW WE GOT HERE. THAT'S HOW THEY SLIPPED IN.
THE BUG UNDERSTANDS US. IT THINKS.
WHICH IS HOW WE'LL DEFEAT IT. BECAUSE NO ONE, NOTHING, CAN PREDICT WHAT PEOPLE WILL DO.
DOCTOR.
ABRAHAM?

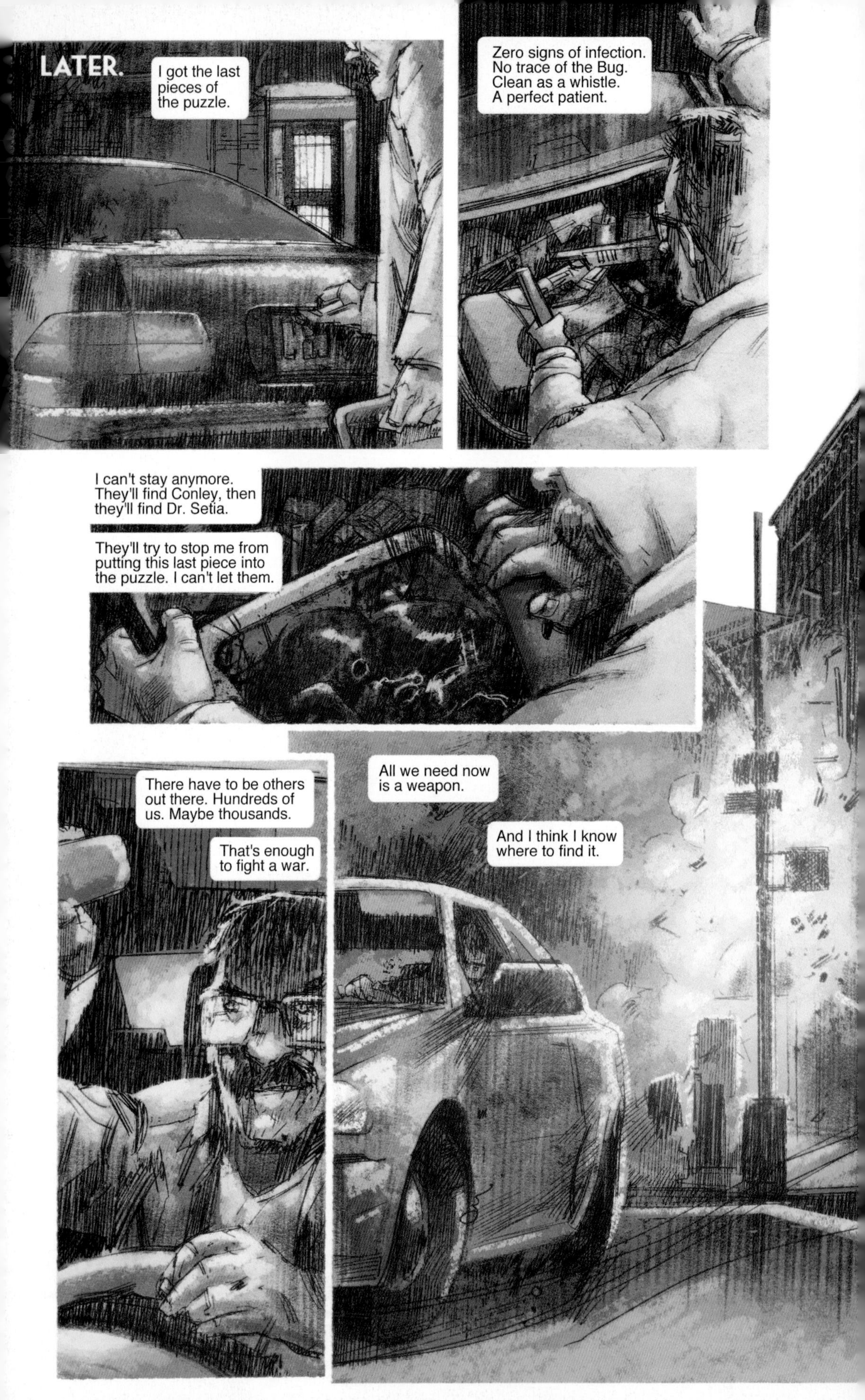
LATER.
I got the last pieces of the puzzle.
Zero signs of infection. No trace of the Bug. Clean as a whistle. A perfect patient.
I can't stay anymore. They'll find Conley, then they'll find Dr. Setia.
They'll try to stop me from putting this last piece into the puzzle. I can't let them.
There have to be others out there. Hundreds of us. Maybe thousands.
That's enough to fight a war.
All we need now is a weapon.
And I think I know where to find it.

To Be Continued...

For more tales from ROBERT KIRKMAN and SKYBOUND

Daniel Warren Johnson Mike Spicer
Extremity
VOLUME TWO WARRIOR

REDNECK
Donny CATES Lisandro ESTHERREN Dee CUNNIFFE
VOLUME ONE
Deep In The Heart

VOL. 1: ARTIST TP
ISBN: 978-1-5343-0242-6
$16.99

VOL. 2: WARRIOR TP
ISBN: 978-1-5343-0506-9
$16.99

VOL. 1: DEEP IN THE HEART TP
ISBN: 978-1-5343-0331-7
$16.99

BIRTHRIGHT

Gasolina
VOLUME 1: BIENVENIDO

CHRIS DINGESS • MATTHEW ROBERTS • OWEN GIENI
MANIFEST DESTINY
VOLUME 5 • MNEMOPHOBIA & CHRONOPHOBIA

VOLUME 5 THE NEW PATH
BY KIRKMAN & AZACETA
OUTCAST

VOL. 1: HOMECOMING TP
ISBN: 978-1-63215-231-2
$9.99

VOL. 2: CALL TO ADVENTURE TP
ISBN: 978-1-63215-446-0
$12.99

VOL. 3: ALLIES AND ENEMIES TP
ISBN: 978-1-63215-683-9
$12.99

VOL. 4: FAMILY HISTORY TP
ISBN: 978-1-63215-871-0
$12.99

VOL. 5: BELLY OF THE BEAST TP
ISBN: 978-1-53430-218-1
$12.99

VOL. 6: FATHERHOOD TP
ISBN: 978-1-53430-498-7
$14.99

VOL. 1: BIENVENIDO TP
ISBN: 978-1-5343-0506-9
$16.99

VOL. 1: FLORA & FAUNA TP
ISBN: 978-1-60706-982-9
$9.99

VOL. 2: AMPHIBIA & INSECTA TP
ISBN: 978-1-63215-052-3
$14.99

VOL. 3: CHIROPTERA & CARNIFORMAVES TP
ISBN: 978-1-63215-397-5
$14.99

VOL. 4: SASQUATCH TP
ISBN: 978-1-63215-890-1
$14.99

VOL. 5: MNEMOPHOBIA & CHRONOPHOBIA TP
ISBN: 978-1-5343-0230-3
$16.99

VOL. 1: A DARKNESS SURROUNDS HIM TP
ISBN: 978-1-63215-053-0
$9.99

VOL. 2: A VAST AND UNENDING RUIN TP
ISBN: 978-1-63215-448-4
$14.99

VOL. 3: THIS LITTLE LIGHT TP
ISBN: 978-1-63215-693-8
$14.99

VOL. 4: UNDER DEVIL'S WING TP
ISBN: 978-1-5343-0050-7
$14.99

VOL. 5: THE NEW PATH TP
ISBN: 978-1-5343-0249-5
$16.99

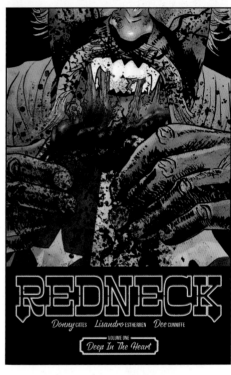